The GOLDEN TILL

A Novel

Bill Mahaney

iUniverse, Inc.
New York   Bloomington

The Golden Till
A Novel

iUniverse books may be ordered through booksellers or by contacting:

iUniverse
1663 Liberty Drive
Bloomington, IN 47403
www.iuniverse.com
1-800-Authors (1-800-288-4677)

ISBN: 978-1-4502-4595-1 (pbk)
ISBN: 978-1-4502-4597-5 (cloth)
ISBN: 978-1-4502-4596-8 (ebk)

Printed in the United States of America

iUniverse rev. date: 8/19/2010

"An exciting geological-geopolitical thriller about what might have happened if Hitler had got his hands on gold and platinum needed by the Luftwaffe to defeat the RAF in the Second World War. Intrigue, suspense and action deftly woven together in a plot that keeps the reader alert from start to finish." John Unrau, York University

Frontispiece: Lago Mucubají in the Eastern Mérida Andes is a typical glacial lake impounded by moraines dating from the last glaciation. The main transverse ridge in the middle ground is a recessional moraine deposited by stillstand of receding ice which moved up-valley and off to the left at the end of the last ice age. The cirque (glacial amphitheater) in the background once housed a small feeder glacier that fed into the main ice stream. The view is similar in size and scope to lakes and deposits in the Coromoto Valley, the main artery leading to the Humboldt Massif at ~5000 meters elevation.

Also by Bill Mahaney

Fiction

The Warmaker, iUniverse, Bloomington, Indiana,
2008, 302 pp. ISBN: 978-0-595-71611-1

Operation Black Eagle
Expected 2011

by W.C. Mahaney

Non-Fiction

The Effects of Agriculture and Urbanization on the Natural Environment
(with Frederick Ermuth)
1974, York Univ., Geographical Monographs, no. 7, 152 pp.
ISBN: 0-919604-21-8

Ice on the Equator, 1990, Wm. Caxton Ltd.,
Ellison Bay, Wisconsin, 386 pp.
ISBN: 0-940473-19-4

Atlas of Sand Grain Surface Textures and Applications
2002, Oxford University Press, Oxford, UK, 237 pp.
ISBN: 0-19-513812-0

*Hannibal's Odyssey: Environmental Background
to the Invasion of Italia, 2009*
Gorgias Press, Piscataway, N.J., 237 pp.
ISBN: 1-59333-951-7

Visit his website at www.billmahaney.com

To: Linda and Caitlin

Contents

Author's Note

Surely few natural historians have travelled as far and learned as much as Alexander von Humboldt. His explorations, together with Aimé Bonpland in the Americas in the late eighteenth and early nineteenth centuries, stand as one of the pillars of scientific achievement, breaking new ground in every field of physical and biological thought. Von Humboldt's gold-platinum find, if it did exist, would have changed the course of human history, just as his *Explorations* and *Kosmos* changed the course of exploration and scientific thought.

Foreword

The inspiration for this book came from several years of studying glaciers, especially the limits of glaciation and glacial dynamics, in the Andes of Venezuela, Bolivia, Argentina and other high mountains. During this time, I wondered what it must have taken to drive explorers *extraordinaire*, like Alexander von Humboldt and Aimé Bonpland, to seek out, describe and study the high Andean Mountains, a five-year project. Their only prospect of success would be the publication of a natural history of one of the largest and most imposing mountain chains on earth.

During the late eighteenth and early nineteenth centuries travel and communications in the northern Andes would have been slow. With a primitive road system, and movement restricted to horse and carriage or cart, movement in the countryside was restricted. Travel in the mountains meant penetrating the dense cloud forest between 1500 and 3000 meters above sea level, to reach the páramo or South American alpine, the high Andean landscape complete with raw-edged tussock grasses and *Espeletia* (*Frailejón*). In the Andes, the *Frailejón* blooms as a long-leafed tall plant with an almost iridescent green hue, very similar in form to the *Senecio* of the East African mountains. The cloud forest, one of the densest on earth, is every bit the equal of the bamboo-*Podocarpus* forests of East Africa, where, at best, one can see a distance of two or three meters. With little sunlight passing through the thick foliage, direction is only possible with a compass.

If von Humboldt and Bonpland attempted to explore the cloud forest they would have had to break off their lowland explorations and trek through the scrub semi-deciduous woodland adjacent to the giant inland Maracaibo Lake. In von Humboldt's time this lower vegetation zone was inhabited by the *Motilone*, a tribe of blowgun carrying natives known for their fierce protective and warlike nature, which they had developed from contact with Spanish invaders. As well, if they had attempted to explore the high mountains, they would have had, first to penetrate this formidable native barrier, and then make their way through the cloud forest to reach the glaciers of the high páramo. In reality, they bypassed the Venezuelan Andes to explore much of the Amazon Basin and later the high mountains of Ecuador. However, a gap in Von Humboldt's journals in 1804 provides enough time for an unrecorded expedition into the Venezuelan Andes and a time slot for the story outlined herein.

Gold in placer deposits and platinum veins in bedrock in the Mérida Andes are strictly fictional, although the mineralogy is right for both metals. Till, the sediment emplaced by glaciers, is often studied for its heavy mineral content (including gold), and much gold is dropped or emplaced as placers around the margin of glaciation. In the story, von Humboldt and Bonpland find gold and platinum, but keep the location secret to avoid a gold rush. The find remains a secret until the logs and notes made by von Humboldt turn up later on in Europe.

German agents discover von Humboldt's notes and samples in a European museum, a prime bit of military intelligence that adds momentum to the Third Reich's expanding war machine. Since the platinum contains iridium, a platinum based metal important in the manufacture of aircraft carburettors, the presence of this strategic material leads to a major raid on the Andes to recover the ore.

Iridium, a hard, lustrous silver-colored metal, stable in both air and water, and inert to all acids is the principal component of special alloys used in aircraft internal combustion engines. Its high boiling point, low thermal expansion and rare occurrence make it an extremely valuable and strategic material. In 1939, the major source of this metal was in Alaska, and the ore mined at Goodnews Bay was sold directly to Britain for use in the new Spitfire, which soon replaced the Hurricane as the operational fighter aircraft of the RAF.

Herein is the crux of the plot: the ultimate struggle of two ideologies, both believing they are on the side of right, backed by *rēx and rēgula* of their individual nations, to recover the Andean gold-platinum. Once recovered, the precious ore would provide their governments with the added financial and military might to win the forthcoming world struggle.

IN 1804, WHILE EXPLORING THE HIGH ANDES OF
VENEZUELA, ALEXANDER VON HUMBOLDT DISCOVERS
A MAJOR LODE OF GOLD AND PLATINUM. HIS LOGS
OF THE DISCOVERY LAY UNDISTURBED IN AN
ESTONIAN MUSEUM UNTIL THEY ARE REDISCOVERED
BY A VENEZUELAN GEOLOGIST IN 1939.

GOLD AND PLATINUM, SOUGHT AFTER TO SHORE UP
THE GERMAN CENTRAL BANK AND TO BUILD HIGH
PERFORMANCE CARBURETORS FOR THE MESSERSCHMITT,
BECOME AN OBSESSION OF THE GERMAN MILITARY.

IN THE SUMMER OF 1939, GERMANY SENDS A SUBMARINE
FORCE WITH PARATROOPERS TO VENEZUELA, TO
RECOVER VON HUMBOLDT'S GOLD AND PLATINUM.

ONLY JACK FORD, AN AMERICAN PROFESSOR
OF ARCHAEOLOGY, STANDS IN THE WAY
OF A SUCCESSFUL RECOVERY.

Prologue

April, 1939. Students milled around in the hall outside the lecture room at the far end of the Institute waiting for classes to start. One of the resident archaeologists in the museum, Jack Ford, stopped briefly to look at the crowd of students. Not spotting any familiar faces in the crowd, he threaded a path that would take him to his laboratory. It seemed to him that student numbers had swelled somewhat during the last few months while he had been off recovering artifacts in South America.

At the far end of the hallway, he noticed Reuben Porter, a cantankerous and windy colleague coming out of his office, fumbling with his keys. Not wanting to indulge him, Jack crossed over to the door leading to the second floor, and bounded up the stairs two at a time. At the top he turned left, hoping he had evaded Reuben, and walked quickly to his office at the end of the long corridor. He had an hour before his class started and wasting time on idle conversation with one of the *gossip artists* in the place was the very last thing he wanted to do.

Pulling on his lab coat, Jack settled onto a stool in front of his laboratory bench and searched for the keys to the lab cabinet. He unlocked the storage cabinet and took out the latest gold specimens, icons collected from a site near Machu Picchu in Peru. He placed them on the table and studied them at length. These icons had nearly cost him his life and he was lucky to have escaped in one piece, to return to the normalcy of lecturing in anthropology.

Staring at these ancient relics, he asked himself, half out loud, "What is it that makes them so sought after, so valuable?" *The earth around them, in which they were found encased, might yield valuable clues to environmental change and even age, but the relics, people would fight over or even die for. For many, they were prized beyond all value,* he thought, as he continued to study the icons.

A knock at the door interrupted Jack's reverie and brought Cedric Caine, wearing a broad grin, into the laboratory. His former professor, Cedric was also his colleague, trusted friend and advisor. An archaeologist in his own right, with an international reputation, Cedric spent most of his time trying to finance Jack's excavations in South America and elsewhere around the globe.

Jack studied his face, noting a mixture of anticipation and fear, borne of wonder that the icons had been recovered at all and anxiety over what the museum board would say about how they had been collected. Jack had no doubt Cedric would eventually get round to asking where and how he had managed to collect the icons. Above all, he knew he would have to come up with some creative answers.

Yes, he ought to smile, Jack thought. The tremendous find brought back to the museum from Peru would ratchet the museum up a notch or two in the academic world. They were the first icons of their kind in North America and supposedly unattainable despite vigorous searching by many archaeologists from all over the world. Jack had recovered the Incan gold icons from sites radiating out of the center of Inca culture at Machu Picchu, a civilization destroyed by the Spanish invasion of the Sixteenth Century.

Turning to look at Cedric once again, Jack could see he was stupefied, mouth open and clearly unable to speak, overawed by the beauty of the icons that lay before him.

Anticipating Cedric's quizzical look, Jack remarked, "Yes, Cedric, Dad will analyze the gold content. The conquistadors searched for the source of the gold, but could never find it."

"Does your father know you are back in town?"

"I talked with Dad last night. He'll be in later today to do an analysis on the samples but I have no doubt the gold content is the purest to have ever come out of South America. They are truly beautiful figures and amazing craftsmanship, a first for the museum."

As Cedric stared at the figures, Jack thought, *The Incas had not only found the placers, but exploited them by mining the gold and little silver (called platina by the Spanish, now called platinum), producing some of the most beautiful art forms ever made in South America.*

As they sat looking at the figures, Jack broke the silence, "Pizarro had searched for the source of the gold, but could never find it; he didn't understand the geology well enough to put it together. Concentrating on the vein gold, when most of the accessible sites were at lower elevations in the placers, was a big mistake."

Taking Jack's comment into account, Cedric continued to study the figures, turning them around to inspect every facet, his fingers following every suture.

Jack watched the intensity build in Cedric's face, thinking, *the people who made the figures were extraordinary craftsmen. Their descendants worshipped the icons, believing they contained supernatural powers so terrible they could be unleashed on nonbelievers.*

Just then Cedric looked at Jack and remarked, "The Indians will have put a curse on you, especially since you don't believe in the supernatural."

"We are not 'believers' exactly, Cedric, but most of us respect the religious significance of the icons. I certainly appreciate their beauty and exquisite craftsmanship."

Jack watched Cedric's reaction, thinking he might be spooked by the thought of a curse, but Cedric seemed willing to drop the subject.

The gold alpaca and llama statues, together with a wooden ceremonial vase and star-headed mace embellished with gold, formed the newest additions to the museum collection from Machu Picchu, the last Inca refuge.

Looking at Cedric, Jack pronounced, "Dad will ask about the source of the gold and this time I think I know the answer. The Incas were collecting it around the margins of the great Pleistocene glaciers in the Andes. Find the great glacial terminal moraines and you have the placers. We dug two of them and brought the samples back that should prove the theory."

Watching Cedric grow more intense, Jack waited a few precious seconds and added, "Want to finance an expedition to find the source of the gold?"

Cedric weighed the question for a minute or two, and then, stammering slightly, asserted, "Can you find it Jack, do you think, the actual source? If you could match the source to the gold figures it would be a coup for the museum."

"It can be done, Cedric, it can be done," Jack confirmed, with a wry smile.

The two scientists looked long and hard at the figures without uttering a word, and then Jack locked them away in the sample cabinet.

As Cedric went off to a committee meeting, Jack thought, *At least I am spared meetings; teaching is wearying enough and nothing like field work where discovery can come at any time. An important find might catapult one's reputation, from the dark abyss of the unknown, to the known, perhaps even the widely known.*

But, fame is not the driving force, he thought. *It's the adrenalin rush of the find, the exuberance brought about by new evidence that ultimately provides proof for a new theory. Debunking a popular theory, advanced by someone who has never dug a site, has a certain appeal. And, oh yes, there are many archaeologists with clean, unworn hands,* Jack thought.

Archaeology, the embodiment of interdisciplinary science, is the field of learning which draws upon knowledge in many disciplines, from physics to history. Thinking of the interconnectedness of several disciplines, Jack was strangely reminded *of Alexander von Humboldt, the great German explorer-scientist of the New World.*

The natural sciences had come a long way from the pioneering days of von Humboldt and Jack wondered why he had suddenly thought of the New World and von Humboldt.

It must be the icons, he told himself. Then, after thinking about the icons for a short time, he puzzled over what the great explorer would have done with them had he found them. As Jack thought more about it he decided to write up the results and publish in the mainstream science literature when the time was right. Dropping the thought from his mind, he checked to insure the gold figures were locked safely in the cabinet, and picked up his briefcase.

Jack looked at his watch and realized he had to hurry to get to class. While chuckling as he walked off, Jack thought, i*t's getting on to the end of term, and soon I'll be free to spend some months doing field work.*

Jack had offers to excavate Bronze-age sites in Britain and pre-Columbian sites in southern Canada, but the source of the Incan gold kept returning to nag him. I'll talk to Dad, he told himself, as he pushed against the classroom door with his briefcase. The sudden thought that maybe he had left his revolver in it gave him a start as he dropped the bag on the desk. No sense looking for it now. If the students saw it, they would likely be terrified and the museum did not need students more terrified than usual.

As he looked over the lectern at dozens of nondescript faces in the usual crowd — serious students, to those more pleasantly bored with the subject matter, Jack thought again about why he got into academia. "It's the field work," *he muttered half out loud.* "Teaching is just a job and a paycheck!" *The real payday comes in the field with new discoveries, and sometimes, with the right batch of students, even teaching in the field pays off!*

Just as he started to open his notes, he thought again about von Humboldt. *He would have wanted to find the source of the Incan gold, with that inquisitive mind of his, and so do I.*

PART I

Alexander von Humboldt's Expedition —
1799-1804 — and its Aftermath to 1859

One
Coastal Landing

January 10, 1804. Lake Maracaibo was shimmering with the first rays of the rising sun starting to reflect off its surface. The lake was calm, nearly motionless, in the early morning, there being almost no wind to generate waves. A low-lying mist that had smothered the lake had lifted. There was virtually no population, at least nothing visible along the coast. The trip by gunboat, on loan from the governor of Maracaibo, had taken three days and along the way Alexander von Humboldt, *scientist extraordinaire*, and his partner Aimé Bonpland had encountered few vessels, mostly fishing boats. The odd barge might pass this way, but there was little commercial traffic.

On a beach ridge covered with scrub forest, the two scientists watched their assistants unload crates of supplies and instruments noting especially that their chief porter was insuring the instruments were handled with great care. As Alexander watched the unloading process he realized that the loss of any one instrument might compromise the whole expedition and this worrisome thought kept him on edge much of the time.

Sensing his fears Bonpland remarked, "We've been lucky so far. All instruments are functional and in good repair. They've not failed us over the last four years. Not to worry, Alexander, I'm watching and always near our instruments."

It had been just over four long years since Alexander and Bonpland had arrived in South America from France. The instruments had served them well as they carried out investigations of the plant cover, soil, atmosphere and magnetic field in Venezuela, Colombia and Ecuador. But now they were nearing the end of their travels and both of them sensed that what they would

3

do here, in the Andes, would amount to the culmination, the most significant research of their entire trip.

The two men followed the final unloading of the skiff and wondered when the carts and handlers would show up to move all the gear inland. The gunboat could not unload at La Ceiba as the harbor could only take shallow-draft vessels. Alexander had been assured in Maracaibo that the carts would meet the skiff on schedule at a suitable landing place to the south where a deep channel allowed the gunboat to get close to shore. A cavalry detail had been sent south to arrange for unloading of the warship and transport to the high Andes.

The winter dry period was settling in and they had less than three months to explore the high Andes during the driest and coolest months of winter. As usual, *mañana* had set in as well and things were not going as planned. They would have to sit and wait for the locals to wake up and move. Not to be undone by it all Alexander took out his log book and started making notes and sketching the local shoreline and dunes.

Noticing that Bonpland seemed fixed in place staring at the instrument cases, Alexander remarked, "Aimé, why not take out the barometer and set it to sea level. We need accurate fixes as we move up through the coastal forest to the *páramo*. It looks like we have time on our hands."

Aimé nodded and watched as Alexander rummaged in his sack, apparently looking for something.

Finding his logbook, Alexander leaned against a tree and steadied his binoculars to take in the coastal scene unfolding before him. He had long been inquisitive about sandstone and about a kilometer away a magnificent outcrop of light-colored rock jutted out into the lake. As one of the most porous of the sedimentary rocks he had often wondered what fossils might be found in the old sandstone beds. His field studies in other parts of the world had uncovered a carbonaceous viscous material that had puzzled him, as it could be the remains of older forests, some as old as the Paleozoic and possibly related to coal. Putting this thought out of his mind he concentrated on sketching the sandstone outcrop. If the porters did not show up he would walk down the beach and investigate this site wondering what secrets might be revealed to him.

But after exploring the outcrop we must find the road up country, he thought, looking at the scrub forest and grassy dunes that extended inland. Alexander could see only a narrow rough path, one not heavily traveled but certainly not a road.

As Bonpland worked over the instruments Alexander wandered into the dune field, skirted the landing site, and moved deeper into the scrub forest to a point where a rough dirt track led deeper into the forest. As he inspected the track he realized the seldom used cart track would slow movement to at most 5-6 kilometers a day. It would take some time to gain altitude and the trek inland to the nearest habitation, Valera, would take over a week.

First we have to get to La Ceiba, another complication, he thought.

Returning to the beach and conferring with Bonpland, Alexander decided to have a look at the sandstone outcrop. Leaving Bonpland in charge he asked that a runner be sent along the coast to fetch him should the porters show up. In the meantime his curiosity was getting the best of him. Taking his boots off, he tied the laces together, flung them over his shoulder and set off, logbook and rock pick in hand, to have a look at the sandstone. The water had a soothing effect on his feet, almost the equal of the warmth he remembered from hot springs in Germany.

All of a sudden he realized he had not bathed in several days. As soon as he was out of sight of the landing party, at a place where the forest skirted the lake next to the outcrop, he took off all his clothes and dove in. Not minding the brine he basked in the therapeutic effect of the water, which proved somewhat cooler than the air despite its high temperature.

Emerging from the lake, he dried himself with his shirt, put on his clothes and boots and soon realized he was sweating profusely. The air, warmer than the water, was saturated with humidity making sweat build up at a rapid rate.

Bathing is hardly worth the effort in this cursed heat, he thought. *Once out of the water you sweat inside of ten minutes.*

The outcrop carried light colored sandstone, which he quickly deduced had come from the weathering of much older crustal material derived from the highlands. The sands were similar in content to the sandstone he had worked on in Germany and in the Alps but curiously no evidence of carbon compounds of any kind. Looking at the rock and sketching in the orientation of strata he realized its horizontality might not lend itself to the collection of carbon-rich fluids. But working down section into older rock he noticed a slight tilt in strata and deduced from this that he was working the upper part of what had once been a delta, debouching water and sediment into the ancient lake. By his estimate, based on fossil content, these younger sediments up-section dated to the Mesozoic, possibly only a few million years in age. The older lower rocks belonged to the Paleozoic Period of time.

Considering the age of the outcrop before him the controversy over age assessments of soft rock cover and its relationship to the crystalline cores of all continents took form in his mind. Hutton's famous statement about geologic time welled up in his mind — *No vestige of a beginning, no prospect of an end.*

He smiled, thinking of his many colleagues who thought the Earth was only some thousands or tens of thousands of years old. Others thought it ran into a few million years. *But could a few million years produce the proliferation of all life entombed in the rock record? The uniformity of process, a tenet of Hutton's teaching, meaning all process moved forward slowly had to be correct. The Earth is much older, perhaps tens to hundreds of millions of years older.*

After spending some time making notes he realized the rate at which the sun was moving along it would soon be mid-afternoon.

Taking out his compass he took note of north and added direction to his sketch of the outcrop. While putting his compass back in its case he wondered what the magnetic declination might be as true north and magnetic north were considered to vary from one place to another. Just how far off magnetic north might be from true north could not be determined, only conjectured. In earlier times, European navigators believed compass needles were attracted either to a magnetic mountain, or island somewhere in the far north of Canada.

The hypothesis that the Earth might act as a giant magnet, first proposed in 1600 by the English physicist William Gilbert, defined the North Magnetic Pole as the point where the Earth's magnetic field points vertically downwards. He theorized that if his compass needle pointed to a 'magnetic sink' in the far north it must deviate from true north. Hence, a magnetic declination that might be small or large depended upon one's location. The thought had captivated him for some time, and captivated him still, as he stood on the sandstone outcrop peering out across the shimmering lake, its surface devoid of waves, almost glass-like reflecting light from a sun some 30 degrees off the horizon.

As he made his way back to the landing zone a runner came to tell him the porters had arrived and the carts were being loaded. They would be in La Ceiba by nightfall.

A propitious start to the journey into the highlands, he thought.

Taking a last look at the lake, Alexander could only wonder what travail awaited him on his journey into the mountains. The temperature at sea level, even in 'winter' was a staggering 50°C, with excessive evaporation driving humidity to the highest he had ever experienced. What might the temperature be high up in the Andes at the foot of one of the mountain glaciers or even higher on the continental divide, the source of the ice? It must be below freezing.

Surely, the temperature decline could be measured in tenths of a degree Celsius per 100 m of altitude to measure the lapse rate, he thought.

Moreover, the decline in atmospheric pressure would be interesting to determine. Would one atmosphere at sea level drop to half at near 5000 m? We shall soon see.

Wandering off toward the carts, still lost in thought, he ruminated on the fortunate recent development of the Celsius Temperature Scale. The Celsius thermometer did away with the old Thermoscale instruments, and while debate ensued on use of the old Fahrenheit Temperature Scale, the new Celsius scale, based on the freezing and boiling points of water at zero and 100 degrees, was catching on in science. Anders Celsius had developed a system of weights and measures that offered to overshadow the old English system. The rank and file might still use "feet" but science was gravitating toward the meter.

"And none too soon," Alexander muttered half out loud while congratulating himself on bringing the best thermometers and barometers money could buy.

Reaching the carts Bonpland signaled the lead carts were ready to leave. Alexander fell in line with the vanguard and several soldiers who would guide them to Laceiba.

Alexander could not wait to experience the páramo and the high páramo. What curiosities might he find there?

Two

Alexander von Humboldt and the Andean Highlands

The Andes, March, 1804. A cold wind blew through the bamboo, with a light rain streaming from low, dense clouds. As he peered into the mist, Alexander von Humboldt, scientist *extraordinaire*, moved slowly and purposely. With his machete he parted the last of the foliage, crossed into an alpine meadow, with its tall grasses and strange long-leafed plants forming a rosette of indescribably beautiful iridescent flowers. *This must be the páramo*, he thought, as the Spanish called the alpine tundra, and the colorful plant the *frailejón* or *Espeletia*.

Since leaving home in 1799, he had marveled at the unparalleled beauty of New World flowers and now before him lay the jewel of South America — the Andean highlands of Venezuela, which looked so much like the mountains of his native Germany, but with such different flora.

What might the distant peaks look like?

What about snow and ice?

Could glaciers exist at equatorial latitudes as Hutton had concluded?

Amid much ridicule, he had left his native Germany to explore the equinoctial regions and pursue his thesis that decreasing temperature with altitude could maintain ice, on or near the equator. As with his friend James Hutton, he believed not only that glaciers could exist at altitude in the tropics, but also that they had expanded and contracted with past changes in climate.

And he had come far to find the answer...could he have been wrong about this? Could he have spent his inheritance proving an impossible thesis? He might have to climb higher than anticipated when he left his native Germany on the equinoctial expedition. He had climbed Chimborazo in Ecuador to prove his theory, but his explorations in 1804, going better than planned, offered the opportunity to climb the highest massif in the Mérida Andes. He had to sail from Cuba to Lake Maracaibo and then travel overland to the eastern cordillera of the Mérida Andes, but it had been worth the expense just to see the high mountains.

Von Humboldt's scientific explorations had become an obsession, and everywhere he turned nature exploded with new marvels, but the flowers were the most marvelous of all, and here there were many new species. It was almost enough to distract him from the glacier that would prove his meteorological theory, namely, that with decreasing temperature at higher altitudes, a river of ice might be maintained at or near the equator.

He estimated that now his party was eight degrees north of the equator and 3000 meters above the level of the sea, but still well south of the Tropic of Cancer. He sketched the vegetation into his logbook, noting the change from bamboo forest to alpine tundra, and although similar to the Alps, the vegetation was very different.

Temperature must control this phenomenon, he thought.

Aimé Bonpland and the load bearers came up behind him at last and started to pitch camp near a small lake dammed by blocks of gneiss and granite. Walking over to Bonpland, von Humboldt asked, "Do you recognize the telltale signs of glaciation?"

"Yes, the dam looks to be formed by a mass of large boulders, shaped in the form of an arc, all deposited presumably by ice during the last of the great ice ages."

Von Humboldt signaled his partner to follow him upstream to where a second great arc of boulders might mark a pause in the retreat of the ice.

"Surely, if the glacier had been here and retreated up-valley, there might be some remnant of it still on the water divide that forms the high crest of the Andes," he remarked.

Standing on the higher deposit, von Humboldt summed up what they had found.

"The northeastern spur of the Andes, separating the llanos to the east from the rivers that flow into Maracaibo, the great lake connected by a narrow isthmus to the Caribbean Sea, is the right place to explore. Remember, as we traveled to the west from the grasslands of the llanos, we heard of the great lake close to the Caribbean Sea. Now we have seen it for ourselves and the high mountains that feed it."

Bonpland nodded, but said nothing, simply content to take in the great beauty of the scene before them.

The blowing wind, even with a light rain, was a welcome relief from the searing and almost unbearable heat of the grasslands and drylands of the llanos and the even hotter Maracaibo Lake. He sensed his partner, and perhaps the load bearers, did not share in his exultation, but never mind. Bonpland would understand soon enough and von Humboldt was sure they would find the glacier or some small remnant of it at least. Didn't the *llaneros* of the *llanos* tell of a history of the mountain horseman who had seen at least patches of white above Los Nevados, the highest of the Andean settlements?

Of course, they had to be right and so his theory had to be correct, he thought.

They moved higher up the mountain with von Humboldt out in front. Bonpland caught up to him, and after catching his breath, which Alexander noted got heavier and heavier, he motioned to stop. He would have to make a note that heavy breathing must be due to lack of oxygen and oxygen must be rare at high altitude. It seemed strange to Bonpland, the bigger of the two men, that von Humboldt never lost his breath and always seemed ready to tackle the next slope.

Bonpland spoke first. Concerned about the large, nearly vertical, rock wall looming out of the clouds to the left, he warned, "We must go slower. The porters are beginning to grumble over the weight of their loads."

Pausing for a few seconds, he added, "The instruments are too delicate to risk a rapid ascent over this rough ground."

To the right, they could barely make out the outline of the valley floor, but it seemed to soar ever upwards and disappear into the clouds. As nightfall closed, the valley appeared desolate with shadows appearing and disappearing. Alexander removed his hat and wiping sweat from his brow noticed he was perspiring profusely.

"Take it slow," Bonpland remarked in halting French... "*lentement*, remember the problems getting here."

Alexander remembered his log book and the map he had painstakingly drawn all the way upcountry from Mérida. He reached into his pocket and pulled out the leather case complete with all notations that eventually would go into his *Travels*.

Bonpland pointed at the second ridge about 400 meters up valley. "It must have been formed like the lower one, from a pause in the retreat of the ice."

Alexander smiled that engaging smile of his, thinking, w*hat a brilliant partner I have here and what an able assistant. What he learned in the Alps he employs here and recognizing the geology and all the rest of nature is no easy task.*

Interpreting nature is harder than training for the medical profession, which is what Bonpland did before meeting Alexander.

Von Humboldt stopped and propped himself against a large boulder about the size of a small room, noticing that its composition was different from the bedrock and hence had been moved by a powerful force, presumably ice.

Von Humboldt thought, *enough for today.*

Turning, he recommended to Bonpland, "Sleep is dearer than food, my friend."

They both walked down to where the camp was already becoming a reality.

When Alexander entered the camp the load bearers motioned to him to take some tea and bread. Feeling weary, he waved them off, and after taking some water, both he and Bonpland crawled into their tent. Within minutes Alexander felt himself drift off. He dreamt of horses in his native Germany, wondering when he might make it home to recount his *Travels,* and then the details faded away into his subconscious.

*   *   *   *

The next morning, Alexander, Aimé and their workers woke to find more rain and denser clouds than the day before and still they couldn't see the crest of the range. The weather forced them to eat more than the usual biscuit and tea and what dominated was a raging thirst. Altitude had a way of doing that to climbers.

Aimé called Alexander over to check the barometer and calculate the altitude once more. Alexander stopped to lace up his boots while Aimé took the long thermometers out of their cases as the load bearers looked on in amazement at the strange instruments. What the two strangers could learn from this wild, cold place none of them could possibly imagine. After a short time, Alexander put the instruments away, and made some notations in his book.

Looking at Bonpland, he said, "Let's pack up and move up the mountain. The weather is bound to change."

With Bonpland in the lead, they started up from the lake, which they named *Coromoto*, after the drainage they had followed from Mérida, the only large settlement in these high Andean valleys. Lake *Coromoto* would be fixed forever on maps at an altitude of 3000 meters, directly on the timberline separating bamboo forest from the alpine grasslands or *páramo.*

Alexander yelled to Bonpland, "We have to try to make it to the top of the valley today or at least by tomorrow and hope the weather improves."

Bonpland agreed and muttered something about the impossibility of the weather improving.

"On upwards," Bonpland asserted, thinking, *we* *need more than hope.*

He picked up his pack and motioned to the load bearers to move along behind him.

Alexander thought, a *group on edge like this one, coupled with bad weather, will deplete morale faster than anything else. We can only wish for blue sky and sun.*

And so it went for the next few hours as they toiled up rock walls and onto lush

green meadows and then up once again. The trail led to the left of the main valley. As the clouds parted, both men noted large flutings in the bedrock, channels unlike any they had ever seen imparting a spectacular washboard appearance to the valley floor. Measuring fifteen to twenty meters deep on average, with widths of five and six meters, they stretched across the whole length of the valley from a high ridge in the distance to the second ridge of boulders below.

Bonpland pronounced, "What a monstrous flow of water or ice it must have taken to produce them."

Thinking for a few seconds, Alexander added, "Perhaps Professor Werner had been at least partially right with his *Neptunist Theory* that everything on the earth's surface formed under water."

Alexander had learned of the *Neptunist Theory* at Freiberg, where he dissected the Wernerian system of mineralogy, which worked so well in Germany in the hills of Saxony, but failed so miserably in other parts of Europe.

With Bonpland listening, Alexander related, "Nicholas Desmarest deduced the true nature of basalt in the Auvergne, noticing in particular that what Werner thought floated in the ocean, what he called *flotz,* was actually lava that issued from volcanic vents. Observing that basalt graded downward into scorched soil and upward into frothy rock filled with gas bubbles called vesicles, he considered the scoria formed as bubbles of steam rose toward the top of the flow, all trapped by the congealing lava. The rock was volcanic, not something precipitated in a universal ocean. Werner dispatched two able disciples — von Buch and D'Aubuisson — to apply the *Universal Theory* to Desmarest's outcrops but after inspecting his sites they agreed with him and this was the beginning of the end of the Neptunists."

"But surely, these flutings were caused by melting ice — tropical ice — -with water and cobble-laden water rushing out from beneath the glacier, eroding and polishing the fluting walls with a jeweler's precision," Alexander surmised.

Von Humboldt had to be right about this and here was partial proof of his glacial theory.

He motioned to Bonpland to come closer and exclaimed "What majestic forms these flutings are. What do you make of them?"

Bonpland replied, "I think water had to form them, but there is not enough to do it at present, so maybe your glacier theory is correct."

Alexander smiled, concurring with his assistant in every detail.

Soon they were negotiating some narrow rock ledges near the top of the valley, a precipice from which they could look down at the majesty of the landscape below. They felt pure exhilaration with the clouds parting and the cloud forest steaming after a rainstorm. Looking at the dense impenetrable cloud forest, it began to sink into both men that they were fortunate to have survived it. Close encounters with snakes, especially the *Mapanare*, that the load bearers said could kill you in one minute provided poignant reminders of just how lucky they had been. Fortunately the snakes were in the lower reaches of the forest below Mucuy. And they had a scene before them no one had seen, let alone studied, or tried to understand.

Alexander summarized, "I know I'm right about this place and we'll find the glacier, and when we do, we'll have proved that ice can exist in the tropics at high elevation and that it has waxed and waned with changes of climate."

Of course, Alexander couldn't know that several decades later Venezuelan cartographers would formally name the glacier Humboldt; Bonpland would have the western lobe named after him.

"But we have to find and study the glacier," Bonpland replied trying to hide his sarcasm. *Theorizing about something and proving it are two entirely different things,* he thought.

"It's here," Alexander said, "I can feel it and soon we'll see it."

The clouds moved in quickly and once again they were lost in a milky mist feeling the rush of cold rain on their skin. To Alexander cold rain simply reinforced in his mind the notion that temperature in the tropics could drop with altitude to below the freezing point producing snowpack and glaciers. But for two intrepid mountaineers such as Alexander and Aimé, this was old and familiar, the sudden shift in weather, which comes without warning. Soon the clouds lifted almost as quickly as they had appeared.

Bonpland uttered, "The 'noon rain' came early this day," toning his sarcasm for maximum effect.

Looking up at the dense cloud shrouding the high peaks, while paying scant attention to Bonpland, Alexander remarked, "From all my calculations, the glacier has to be here in the highest part of the Venezuelan Andes."

Bonpland, sweating profusely and looking haggard, nodded, but said nothing.

Alexander, looking at Bonpland, advised, "Don't forget the salt in the soup tonight, *mon ami*; you are losing too much salt and so are the load bearers. If any of the porters come down with heat exhaustion, they'll want to go down."

Hauling themselves over the flutings, and finding a trail to a distant ridge, they finally came in sight of a beautiful green lake with lush grass meadows off to the west. They unpacked and Alexander took out the instruments to measure the altitude and temperature.

Alexander remarked to Bonpland, "We must be near the 4000-meter level."

Bonpland agreed, saying, "It's now considerably cooler. Also, our breathing is somewhat more difficult."

Alexander hadn't noticed this, but then thought, *Bonpland, as usual, was right on the 'taler'* as they say in the old country. The elevation measured close to 4000 meters, scaled down to about 3950 meters approximate, after recalibration of the barometer. He called the lake *Verde* after its deep, lush green color and he wondered if the green color was caused by refraction of light striking suspended sediment in the water.

Noting its position in his log, Alexander placed it on his map as *Lago Verde* and predicted to Bonpland, "As soon as the clouds lift my friend we'll see the glacier. It has to be nearby."

For the moment, the lush meadows provided a place to camp with running water and soft grass to sleep on. Bonpland took to setting up the tents, while Alexander walked a short distance up valley trying to see through the clouds that blanketed everything. Slowly the wind picked up and the cloud or fog started to lift exposing a majestic wall of rock that rose nearly 800 meters. On top of the massif sat the glacier, with tongues of ice that flowed down into three immense valleys.

Alexander sat in the meadow and noticed Bonpland running to join him. They couldn't see the top of the glacier, but they could see the moraines, ridges of rock surrounding lobes of ice just as in the Alps and they knew now that glacier ice existed at altitude near the equator.

Alexander pulled out his logbook and started making notes, outlining the observations that would need to be taken to prove to skeptics that temperature near the equator could lapse sufficiently at high altitude to maintain ice year round. Latitude and longitude had to be precisely determined, the areal extent of the glacier measured, and thickness of the ice estimated. In addition, the rock material transported by ice had to be sampled. And above all he had to measure the moraines below the lobes of ice to see if their ages could be determined.

Age and ages of glaciation had to be conjectured with caution as many believed glaciers to be fixed features in the landscape, not fluctuating at all despite evidence exhibited by moraines and other relics of climatic change in the lower valleys. Hutton had dispatched many of these antiquated ideas but doubts lingered and fluctuating glaciers disturbed religious zealots who considered the world view fixed by god.

Were these moraines the result of an ice advance or were they emplaced when the glacier paused in its retreat cycle? In the Alps he was sure some of the moraines were the result of ice advances that started in the fifteenth century, but here he was not so sure, and it would take some time and many measurements to find out.

And what lay on the opposite side of the drainage divide? More ice? Or rock with telltale striations, or grooves, indicating ice flow to lower elevations just like on the western side?

Time would tell, but with limited supplies and near mutinous load bearers, they would have to work with speed to complete all exploration and measurements and then make their way to Maracaibo. As in the Alps, when on the highest peaks, it is one thing to get to the top and quite another to get out to the lowlands and safety.

While his mind flooded with difficult questions, Alexander turned to Bonpland, said, "Let's prepare for tomorrow. We've much to discuss."

Bonpland replied, "We'll need precise barometer readings around the irregular outline of the glacier and we'll need temperature measurements as well. Do you have the sample sacks?"

"Yes, I have several," Alexander replied.

Alexander, his mind fixed on the glacier, knew Bonpland was right. Without accurate measurements, no one would believe the existence of ice here in the Venezuelan Andes. After a meal of soup and maize bread, Alexander crawled into his tent and was soon fast asleep. Bonpland stayed up long after dark tending the fire that constantly tried to die from the wet wood and frequent gusts of wind. He knew tomorrow and the next few days would be busy and that Alexander would not leave without the requisite number of measurements and the usual load of samples.

*   *   *   *

The morning of the following day opened with a tremendous rainstorm. Alexander and Bonpland fixed breakfast but the load bearers would not leave their tents. The head porter voiced concern with the weather, and threatened to leave the two explorers at once, if they had to stay much longer in this inhospitable place. He made it plain that the entire group would follow him and so they entered into a standoff. Alexander offered a bonus to them if they would stay and see the expedition to the end. Negotiations took maximum diplomacy, the utmost cajolery, something Alexander was particularly good at.

Bonpland watched as Alexander simplified his arguments so the porters could understand what the expedition was all about. He smiled slyly, as he realized the load bearers were coming round to thinking that Alexander could actually control the weather, and that conditions would improve.

Reluctantly the porters agreed to Alexander's conditions but it took a considerable amount of flattery to get them to work in the rain.

Alexander needed them to carry the instrument cases and sample sacks, as he knew there would be measurements to make, and samples to be collected.

Bonpland suggested, "Shall we wait for better weather before attempting to climb the massif?"

He knew the answer even as he spoke.

"No," Alexander ordered, "We start from here today and climb up the middle valley to the summit."

He thought for a moment and then added, "If ice exists here what about the other high Andean summits? Ice must exist there as well."

"If the weather breaks we'll see what lies on the other nearby summits," retorted Bonpland. "They are nearly as high as peaks in the *Coromoto*."

The small group started off and once again Bonpland noticed heavy breathing and found himself having to control or shorten his steps to keep pace with his breathing. Maybe Alexander was right about the lack of oxygen at higher elevations. His professors never mentioned this in medical college, he remembered.

Sensing his friend's concern, Alexander counseled, "See what the lack of oxygen can do, Bonpland? Never fear, we shall be on top soon."

They left the lush green meadows and started across a slope of pebbles and cobbles, eventually gaining so much steepness that each forward step seemed to slip back downhill, and then they were scrambling to stand upright without slipping. Soon they were breathing heavily and Alexander motioned to stop.

Looking at Bonpland, Alexander challenged, "Let's try for the moraine as surely we will need to collect rocks and plants there, and just above the moraine we can move off the rock and onto the ice which will make climbing a bit easier."

Bonpland motioned to the load bearers to place the instrument cases on the moraine as he knew Alexander would start with the usual observations.

Alexander already had his notebook out and the beautiful drawings in it were being compared with the different flora spread out before them. For one thing, the magnificent *Rhizocarpon* lichens were laced across the rock surfaces, just as at lower elevations in the *Coromoto* and in the Alps.

What magnificent life forms these rock lichens are, thought Bonpland, *they grow well everywhere in the mountains of the New and Old Worlds. Just as other species grow on trees, here the Rhizocarpon fix themselves with hair-like tentacles directly to rock.*

Speaking to Alexander, he noted, "But here next to the ice the lichens are much smaller in diameter and there are fewer of them. Below this moraine and near base camp they are much larger and more numerous."

He thought for a minute and then added, "This could have something to do with age, don't you think? Lichen growth might be a measure of time."

"Possibly," Alexander remarked, but he was lost in his interpretations, and data he hastily recorded in his notebook. With an intense look on his face, Alexander opened his logbook and sketched in the surface features up to the glacier. Bonpland assumed they might spend the rest of the day here, lodged on this one moraine, collecting no end of samples. One never knew what to expect with Alexander, but he remembered back at Freiberg, when students thought the observations had been completed, Alexander had just begun, and he sensed the same situation here. Indeed, it was mid afternoon before Alexander was ready to move on to the glacier and make a bid for the summit.

Oddly enough the clouds lifted somewhat and the weather started to clear, an obvious effect of Alexander's 'weather control.' Wondering why Alexander did not rub it in, Bonpland could see the porters were happy enough.

Best to leave it alone, he thought.

Once on the ice, both Bonpland and Alexander remarked about the slushy character of the snow. It seemed to be melting but there was relatively little water on the surface.

Alexander thought out loud, "Could it be sublimating, going directly to vapor?" Bonpland remembered that ice could go directly to vapor if heat was intense enough, and here you have heat release from the rocks nearly all the time.

Heat cycles must be different in the tropics compared with higher latitude, he thought.

Alexander was the *professeur extraordinaire* and it seemed he could sense or see through all natural mystery. One had only to marvel at his genius and his ability to conceptualize and measure all that went on in nature. And there was so much to take in and so many questions to ask. How could ice grow up in the soil surface, without rain, following a night of frost? What caused flowers to close up at night, apparently to avoid the light frost that frequently occurred? What caused cracks to appear in the land surface, features that apparently had nothing to do with freeze-thaw but were probably related to wetting and drying? The cracks were restricted to areas with fine grained sediment. Alexander wondered if the mineralogy could play a role in this.

And so it continued, as Alexander and his *bon vivant,* Bonpland, wandered around the massif that would later carry their names on maps of the high Andes. Elevations precise to within a meter or two, and temperatures precise to within a degree Celsius were recorded and logged into a diagram showing temperature decline with altitude.

As Alexander explained, "Physical work in the atmosphere can be explained by decline in temperature and pressure."

After reaching the summit of the massif and fixing the highest peak on the massif at just under 5000 meters above the sea, they took note of other high mountains that supported snow and ice cover in the same general area. There were a few, and they were all apparently lower, except one about six kilometers to the southwest that they left unnamed. Later, following the rebellion against Spain, it would become known as *Pico Bolivar,* named after Simon Bolivar the Liberator. But on this day it was of little significance.

They had found the high summit, and most importantly, the largest glacier — quite possibly the largest ice mass in the northern Andes. Using a plane table to fix the elevations of major topographical features, they mapped the summit, as well as the lobes of ice draped over the western flank of the massif. They showed that no ice existed on the eastern flank, the rock wall there being too steep to maintain a glacier.

Their observations indicated that the trade winds seemed to blow constantly from the east and northeast, just as they did at sea. Alexander wondered if the trade winds might be part of a column of air that extended to great height in the atmosphere, perhaps much higher than the Andes itself. If so, high pressure astride the equator might send warm air equatorward and into the middle latitudes as Hadley had predicted.

Our measurements might support his theory, he thought, *at least the equatorial part of it.*

He pondered the thought and surmised Hadley was right. The extension of this made it all the more imperative to collect enough data to test it.

He wondered also about the effect of changes in land and sea on the trades. The scientific questions and hypotheses seemed endless, and Bonpland was content to listen, as Alexander spilled out the curiosity that seemed to always dominate his thinking. He simply had to know how nature worked and he continually strove to understand the *Kosmos.*

While they stood on this imposing summit, Alexander mentioned his intent to not only produce the *Travels,* but also to print as a manual of the day-to-day working of nature, both of the living and inanimate kind–The *Kosmos*.

Bonpland had seen the smile thicken before, but never with the depth that came with this revelation. It would be written and it would contain much of what they had learned in the New World.

Alexander thought briefly about what he had written in his log in the Spanish port of *La Coruña* aboard the corvette *Pizarro*.

"I shall try to find out how the forces of nature interact upon one another and how the geographic environment influences plant and animal life. In other words, I must find out about the unity of nature."

Yes, the unity of nature is the main objective.

"What remains to be done, Alexander?" asked Bonpland.

"We need a few barometric readings off the northern lobe and we need water samples from *Lago Verde*, don't forget that. The water may have suspended sediment in it and I'll want to establish the size of the grains and possibly their composition so far as possible."

As Bonpland walked away he heard the usual, "See to it Bonpland," and he realized that Alexander was already mentally running through all they had accomplished in the last few days, trying not to miss anything.

While Alexander's commands sometimes grated on Bonpland, he realized once they started trekking out there was no possibility of return. There would be only the seemingly endless expanse of cloud forest, with its poor visibility, near darkness even in the day, tarantulas, and lower down numerous snakes. They must traverse all this to reach Lake Maracaibo.

No, Bonpland thought, *I must not take Alexander's comments so personally.*

It was the small snakes Bonpland detested the most, more on the basis of what he had heard about them than anything else. To Alexander they were creatures making up the fauna of the place, and deserving of description in his notes for later incorporation into the *Travels*. To Bonpland, they looked like serpents he had seen in the Bible, and certainly all of them should be banished to the infernal regions.

The thought of tarantulas he had seen on the way in gave him a shudder as the furry little spiders could make you very sick, although none were known to kill humans. In some places there were so many that they had to be brushed off one's clothes. He thought they were the ugliest creatures he had ever seen.

Suddenly the magnitude of the slope before him in his descent brought him back to the reality of the summit. He focused on placing his feet in the right place so as not to fall. Looking behind him, he was fearful that one of the porters in his descending party might turn out a boulder, and send it cascading down on top of him. Sensing this, he decided to follow a zigzag pattern, which sent him scrambling from side to side in an attempt to avoid any falling rock.

All looked secure, as the party descended to *Lago Verde*, and began packing all the samples that would have to be carried to Mérida and eventually to Maracaibo.

The last night at *Lago Verde* was a happy event for the load bearers as they were finally on the way out. Alexander and Bonpland, on the other hand, worried that something might have been overlooked, but Bonpland was certain that Alexander with his mechanical memory and mental checklist would not forget a thing. This did not stop Alexander from checking his logbook and retiring into the tent with a candle to continue the long process into the night. Night and day in the tropics come with great regularity every twenty-four hours; thirteen hours of daylight followed by eleven hours of darkness hardly varying throughout the year.

Three

Gold-Platinum Deposits and Escape to Maracaibo

The next day, the expedition rose to find a brilliant blue sky and radiant landscape. After breakfast, with spirits soaring, the group quickly shouldered their packs, and started off on the long trek around Lago Verde to the flutings they had admired on the way in.

Alexander halted the group with a wave of his arm, motioned for Bonpland to come forward, instructing, "I want to take more measurements, but this time I want to crisscross the valley, and come down the western slope. Send the men down the eastern side as they have the heavier packs. Tell them to make camp at *Lago Coromoto* and to wait for us there."

Bonpland nodded, remarking, "They'll not like this, Alexander."

"I know but the flutings are too important to pass over without some investigation."

Bonpland walked over to the load bearers, but when he told them about the plan they became restless, as they wanted only to leave the place with haste. However, they were told to wait and wait they would until the work was complete. They argued for an additional bonus on top of the previous one but mention of von Humboldt's knowledge of anti-snake venom and treatment helped convince the workers to relax and wait even as their headman argued for an increase. They would enter the cloud forest soon as they exited the mountain and there resided the *Mapanare*, most lethal of all snakes. After all, Alexander had promised a change in the weather and he had produced it. They had witnessed Alexander's knowledge of snakes and assumed he could work wonders in the event someone got bit.

These arguments swayed the porters somewhat but Bonpland could see they were bracing themselves to carry more samples and for this they wanted more pay. It simply amounted to how much Alexander would have to shell out to satisfy them.

Bonpland watched the head porter with interest as he negotiated a final price with him, noting his bargaining posture and wishing he could emulate it. He chided himself at his inability to push a negotiation like this to the ultimate level, usually coming in second.

Bonpland had to admit the work was tiring in the extreme, the only reward being to get to a campsite and drop the packs. The headman was good at summing up the negative side of their work. After all, Alexander was paying the porters three to four times what they would make from any other employer. But it was always the same arrangement with the other porters standing back letting the head porter wind his way along an uphill grade ending with a demand for more pay. The only question was whether or not one pay bonus would suffice. Finally, with an increased amount agreed upon, the porters moved on promising to set up camp, start a fire and prepare some food.

Bonpland returned to where Alexander was standing. He wondered how Alexander would find a way across the immense flutings on the other side of the valley and he knew one wrong slip might mean disaster. They were in the middle of the valley, trying to jump from one ridge to the other, when Bonpland noticed a yellow lustrous surface shining in the bright sunlight, a long band quite different from the normal light and dark banded rock.

Bonpland hesitated, and then called, "Alexander, come here and have a look at this."

Alexander scrambled over and lowered himself to find an immense vein of yellow rock partly covered with silt dust.

Looking over the outcrop, Alexander offered, "It must extend for several meters upstream, and I think it penetrates the rock to a considerable degree,"

Bonpland, who by now was busy fixing a rope, preparing to lower himself another ten meters from where Alexander was inspecting the rock, nodded in assent but did not answer.

The outcrop most certainly was not pyrite. Alexander took out his hammer and chiseled out a piece to take for analysis, but he had seen enough gold in Europe to know this was a major find. However, in contrast to all the scientific discoveries he had made here, finding the gold was rather minor. For anyone interested in mining the gold accessibility would prove problematic. It would take an immense amount of black powder to blow the rock and recover the gold. Then there would be the problem of removing the gold to the lowlands.

Lacking red color, the gold was copper-free, and without appreciable silver it had to be high grade. The sunlight reflecting off the gold made Alexander wish he had some mercury, cyanide or *aqua regia* to test the gold, but from the color and luster it was, or seemed to be, very pure material. Yet, he lacked the chemicals and there was no way to get them. If he had brought some mercury he could use it to consolidate the gold, and after the mercury burned off, he would have melted clusters of the precious metal.

Studying the veins, he wondered *if the crazed look on miners' faces had anything to do with mercury, for mercury fumes seemed to cause nausea.*

Then with a start he realized there were more important things to attend.

Bonpland and Alexander spent the rest of the afternoon fixing the location of the gold lode, describing the occurrence in great detail, as to thickness and character of exposed veins. It was the softest gold he had ever seen and almost 100 percent pure, he was sure. In addition to the gold vein, they discovered a grey metal that most certainly was platinum, or what pre-Columbian Indians had called 'little silver.' The Conquistadors had described major finds of *platina* (platinum) in Colombia, but none were known in Venezuela despite a long history of looking for it. Alexander knew he had made a major discovery.

After sketching the deposit in his logbook, Alexander made a few notes and concluded that later analysis would likely indicate the gold-platinum find to be one of the major deposits in South America, if not the entire world.

When a dozen samples had been collected they tried to locate the load bearers at *Lago Coromoto.* They could see small black dots moving about near the lower moraine and concluded the rest of the group was safely encamped near the lake. The estimated altitude of the gold find was between 3500 and 3800 meters above the sea, and they started their descent after deciding to keep the find secret, at least for the time being.

At *Lago Coromoto* they joined the load bearers who had prepared supper. After a brief meal with little conversation they dropped off to sleep. Alexander dozed off but his subconscious kept working on the gold and platinum veins to such an extent that he awakened with a start realizing that vein gold, stripped by ice and transported by meltwater, would leave gold grains and even nuggets in pockets around the margin of the ice. He smiled, thinking, *we will find placers near the terminus of the former glacier.*

Perhaps platinum placers could be found here? That would be a rare scientific find.

Alexander and Bonpland talked about their discovery. Alexander summed up their situation saying, "We can't leave this place without first looking for pockets of gold or platinum around the former ice margin."

Watching Bonpland's reaction, he continued, "Gold dust and gold leaves washed downstream from vein outcrops might have tumbled along in glacial streams, just as in the Alps. These could be welded into larger flakes, eventually becoming nuggets of considerable size."

Bonpland sat cross-legged, staring at the wall of the tent, looking rather at a loss for words.

Watching his partner intently, Alexander summarized the situation, "I never expected this although the rock relationships are right for gold. As in Mexico, with the silver lode, we are just lucky to have found this one. If we hadn't stopped to study the flutings we'd never have found the gold..." his voice trailing off as he thought about what he had just said.

Alexander knew there was trouble in this, for if the load bearers found out about the gold, the situation might turn ugly. He might have to drive them off. But the load bearers were a necessity to move the samples and instruments, which were worth an inestimable amount of money.

"Somehow we'll have to invent *a problem* to tie up the load bearers," Alexander proposed. "If you occupy the porters I can search for pockets of gold, and other heavy minerals. I know they have to be present around the moraine. It's simply a question of finding the gold pockets, or placers, establish their frequency and size, and of course, collect samples for later analysis."

"Can you pan the samples?"

That was the question turning over and over in Alexander's mind. He would need a pan in which to wash samples, and separate the heavy minerals including the gold, from the lighter ones. And several samples would be needed to assess the extent of the gold and platinum reserve. The moraine in which the pockets were likely to be found was a bouldery mass, with much of the fine material washed away by meltwater at the end of the last glaciation.

Bonpland came up with the idea of using the load bearers to carry out a detailed analysis of the moraine. "I'll occupy the load bearers, with the task of helping to move the instrument crates about, and take several measurements, all of which will take time."

"Meanwhile," Alexander outlined, "working alone it should be possible to concentrate on panning the deposits around the moraine and in the down valley reach, to see if gold placers can be found. While you work on the moraine with the porters sketch out a map of the valley. I will put in the vein gold and placer sites later."

Both Bonpland and Alexander knew they had stumbled onto a major find, one that offered not only new scientific information but the prospect of wealth that might be used to further their scientific endeavors. The major problem at the moment was to leave with a quantity of precious metal and avoid alerting the local people to its presence, the latter reality most certainly would result in a panic rush to extract the gold. The Mexican fiasco would start all over again and some would make a profit most would acquire nothing at all.

*   *   *   *

The next day, soon after daybreak, they split up. Bonpland moved slightly upstream, and Alexander, using a frying pan as a crude gold pan, worked the placer deposits in the bamboo just below the 3000-meter level. He worked with devilish speed as the porters had little to do in camp and were becoming restless. It was only a matter of time before the head porter might manage to stir up emotions and argue for more pay or a very quick exit off the mountain. He could understand their point of view but he knew he could not leave until he had satisfied himself about the extent of the precious metals. He had to finish the work or mutiny would break out amongst the porters and it might get totally out of hand.

Soon he discovered that almost all the deposits had some gold and platinum in them, and quite a few had considerable quantities. Some grains were of nugget size and many had been folded around quartz grains, most probably as a result of transport in the ice or in meltwater streams. Kneeling on the terrace gravels of a small stream issuing out from under the moraine, Alexander worked with great purpose, separating large quantities of gold and platinum, stashing the metal in sample bags. He kept on digging at new locations and was astounded by the amount of gold he found. This would take a lot less time than he had anticipated and he hurriedly made notes of where and how much he collected in his crude pan.

Alexander had finished with approximately forty sites across the valley, working up into the front of the moraine where the amount of gold increased manyfold. Unlike the vein gold, the placers could be dug out, for the most part by hand, and with a crude water sorting box, the gold could be easily extracted. Here, it was mixed with till or glacial sediment in proportions much greater than what he had seen in Europe. Even the size of the nuggets was beyond his expectations, and he began to realize that distance to the source controlled the size of the nuggets, the source being no more than two or three kilometers up valley.

The scientist in him came to the fore, as he realized he would have to test this hypothesis in the Alps where some of the vein gold was at a much greater distance up valley from the placers. The realization that glaciers had existed here, and had played a part in emplacing the gold, was more exciting to von

Humboldt than the existence of the gold itself. He began to consider how he could use the gold to finance his explorations and he remembered that his royal permit from the Spanish Foreign Minister included a specific clause indicating any mineral wealth he might find would become the property of the Spanish Government.

That he might be required to leave this wealth to a foreign power, especially one in decline, with such a deplorable record in the treatment of different ethnic groups, disturbed him greatly. He had all his life championed freedom of expression and civility toward diverse people regardless of religion or race, and while he appreciated the permit allowed him to carry out his field research he had nothing but aversion to the official policies of the Spanish Government.

"After my experience with silver finds in Mexico, I'll have to think twice about alerting the Spanish authorities to our gold-platinum find," he blurted out loud even though no one could hear him.

While a tiny gold flake would start the American gold rush in 1849, a find of this magnitude would create frenzy in South America. The Spanish had scoured the continent looking for gold, silver and platinum and they had found none in the Mérida Andes.

Hurriedly, he collected samples from several of the sites noted in his logbook, and once he was satisfied the collection was sufficient to study the specimens at a later time, he loaded all the samples, well camouflaged to hide the gold and platinum, into his own pack and decided to carry them off closer to camp. He returned to pick up second and third loads, which he cached close to camp. Later, he and Bonpland would sort and distribute the samples amongst the porters. He would have to keep the porters in a 'tight column' to guard against any one of them stopping to inspect the cargo they were carrying.

Bonpland was a master of sorting the loads and reminded Alexander about their resolution to keep the find secret. In any case there was as much new science in the gold discovery as financial reward. Perhaps the German crown would be interested since they were already financing various economic enterprises in South America; with the growing world market extending from Europe to South America, perhaps this would become a *fait accompli*. But first they had to break camp, slip unimpeded through the cloud forest to Mérida, avoid any notice of the gold they carried and then move their cargo to Maracaibo.

After the cloud forest, the travel route extended through the *Timotocuica* Indian country to the lower scrub lands and the coast. Alexander remembered their previous encounters with the *Motilone* along the coast who had killed foreigners who refused to pay tolls and they likely would refuse to recognize a royal permit from the Spanish Government. Only time would tell what might happen on the way out. On the way in escorting troops had kept the *Motilone* at bay.

Thinking again of the gold and platinum, Alexander focused on the samples he had in hand and realized that even now he had the equivalent of a considerable quantity of funds. Just how much he wasn't sure but most probably something in the range of several thousand pounds sterling, perhaps more.

*　*　*　*

Once back at camp, Alexander walked up valley to meet Bonpland. Leaving the load bearers to pack the equipment down valley, they went over their plan to move into and through the cloud forest in the next few days. Bonpland brought up the problem with the load bearers indicating that they had to move fast lest the handlers decide to cut and run. The head porter had discussed their anxieties with him and it was clear they were near the end of their patience. They could not understand why anyone would want to spend time studying rocks and plants.

Bonpland remarked, "Dealing with that brigand of a head porter nearly makes me retch. He picks his nose when talking with you. It's disgusting dealing with him."

Alexander replied, "We'll buy them off again if we have to. Find something for them to do; anything will suffice. Have them dig a few holes. Disgusting or not we need these people to get us out of here with our samples."

Bonpland nodded but offered nothing, knowing Alexander would not break camp until he was satisfied all data had been logged and samples collected. Bonpland left early to keep the porters busy while Alexander stayed to work the upper valley. Upon returning to camp Alexander was gratified to see the porters at work putting in two deep pits. He would have to do some analysis on the sediment succession but that would only take a short time, although it would add to the sample load.

Who knows what we might find with two random sections, he thought, breaking out into a wide grin. His grin evaporated as it suddenly dawned on him that the sections might contain gold and platinum.

If the metals are present in the pits the porters will suspect the content of their loads, the thought making him wish he had directed the porters to some other inane activity.

But, as he lowered himself into each pit, he realized the deposits were related to a lateral drainage devoid of any precious metal. With the porters watching he collected very small samples for analysis and then ordered the pits closed.

As the pits were being closed up, Bonpland considered, *hopefully, the porters will sleep well tonight and forget about mutiny.*

Sending the porters back to camp he finished a sketch of the valley (Plate One) placing the vein gold and platinum sites in their order of importance. Finally, he added the location of the placers and decided to have Alexander do a final check against his logs.

After a long night in their tent, Alexander and Bonpland woke the load bearers early, and set off through the bamboo, wishing their eyes were better adjusted to near-night conditions. The smell of the forest was very different from the *páramo* because of the greater peat accumulations and range of flowering species there.

The flowers distracted Bonpland and Alexander, who stopped frequently to take notes on new species and to make drawings of them. Alexander noted the increased thickness of soil at lower altitudes, with greater accumulations of iron, judging from the increased red and yellow colors below the surface.

Perhaps this is the material my friend and colleague Johann Goethe is keen on studying, he thought. Goethe related the colors to the broad family of iron oxides and hydroxides, formed from the weathering of fresh rock, which led eventually to the genesis of iron ore.

Alexander had seen such deposits in Brazil. Stopping at one exposure in a stream cut where the reddish soil was prominently displayed, he wondered how the oxides could form at high altitude where temperature was lower.

Perhaps rainfall is more important, the key to its genesis, he thought. *Or maybe there is more native iron in these rocks than I thought.*

But for now the important thing, he considered, *is to get through the cloud forest to Mucuy, and reach Mérida without incident. If we are caught with the gold and platina we might languish in a Spanish jail.*

They had gone only a few hundred meters when Luis, one of the load bearers, lost his footing, and badly sprained his ankle. After bandaging his ankle Alexander worried about how the load would be split up. Luis could walk but carrying a pack was another matter entirely.

After shifting several packs, Bonpland remarked, "Each load bearer will have to carry over fifty kilos each and the going will be much slower. If we lose the path we forged on the way in we'll have to cut a new one, and this will take longer, much longer by the look of it."

Alexander absorbed his remarks without comment.

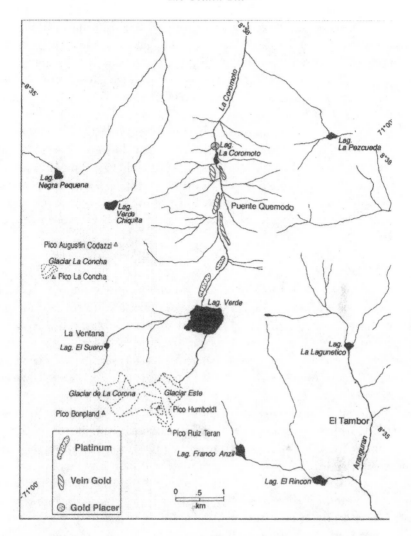

Plate One. The area of the *Coromoto* Valley from the high
eastern Andes to *Lago Coromoto*. The approach to the Humboldt
Massif is from Mucuy and the interior Rio Chama Valley.

On the way in they had covered barely two kilometers per day or less,
sometimes only 300-400 meters, and often they had gone in circles when on
flat land between drainages. Hopefully, they could avoid this by following the
Coromoto River all the way to the Río Chama. But there were innumerable
obstacles to be overcome, and part of the way down they would have to cross
over to the north, as the chasm was too precipitous and deep for them to
move along the river.

They moved on slowly and finally Luis could walk no farther, and so they fixed up a stretcher on strong *Polylepis* branches, taking turns pulling him on an improvised stretcher through the thick undergrowth. It was slow going, but they were making progress, and at the end of the fourth day, Alexander took out his barometer and estimated the elevation at approximately 2350 meters above the sea. They had to be close to the trailhead, as Mucuy at 2100 meters, was quite possibly only about four or five kilometers away.

As he put the barometer back in its case Alexander realized his shirt was saturated with sweat almost as if he had been out in the rain. Looking around at the others he noted they too were in the same state. If they were up in the páramo and the wind were to come up some would most certainly get sick.

As it is now, he thought, *we need to get out of the forest and deeper in the valley.*

The next morning the expedition got underway early after a close call with another snake. This time a saddle snake sitting on a pack had nearly caught Bonpland off guard, but luckily he jumped quickly out of the way, and the snake scurried off into the undergrowth. Alexander smiled as once again, his partner had proved to be quick, a survivor, and he would need a survivor to help him escape to Germany with the samples and the gold.

The look on Bonpland's face, one of sheer terror, said it all, Alexander thought. *Aimé really hates these creatures, yet they are part of nature, an important interconnected part.*

Thinking about the snake for a moment, he realized they might be closer to the 2000-meter level, as snakes were generally found at lower elevations.

"Take care, Bonpland, keep your eyes on the ground, as there are likely cousins of that beast lurking in the bush," he said sporting a wry smile.

They moved off, the stocky figure of Bonpland disappearing into the trees, no more than three meters away. It was impossible to see him clearly, but Alexander could hear his machete working its way through the wall of vegetation. They had lost the trail once again, and it would be awhile before they found it, and could reorient themselves.

We might hack on into the forest, or return the way we've come, and look for the place where we strayed from the original track, he thought.

In this case it seemed best to continue on until they picked up the original trail.

Later, Julio, one of the load bearers, sitting on a log, was bitten by a *Mapanare*, one of the most dangerous snakes in the Andes. Alexander reached Julio in an instant and after pinning him to the ground, took out his knife, put a deep incision in his leg over the bite, and with great speed sucked and spit out several mouthfuls of blood. The wound bled profusely and each time Alexander came up for air the sight of Julio, wide-eyed with fear, made him gulp faster, hold him tighter and close the gap between suckings. The knife wound must have hurt more than the bite, but Alexander knew he had to move with speed to vacate venom from the wound else Julio would be dead inside of a minute.

After several suckings, Alexander tore off his shirt and bound up the wound.

Staring at his wounded porter, Alexander knew it was all a matter of venom concentration, the ratio of venom to blood. If reduced to a low level, Julio would live; if not Julio would die. It was simple chemistry and Julio was still alive, although with racing heart and looking the worse for wear.

Alexander, legs spread out, leaned against a *Podocarpus* tree and realized he was exhausted after two to three minutes of heart pounding, adrenalin-pumping exercise to vacate Julio's wound of the deadly venom. He felt his pulse slow and satisfied himself that his quick action had saved the porter's life.

Julio would be lucky to walk out, but at least he was alive, although his white countenance underscored his terror at encountering the snake. He'd walk but carrying a pack would be difficult if not impossible. Redistributing his load, once again, would strain relations with the other porters, their packs already overloaded.

If we have another encounter with a snake we'll have to discard some of the samples, the worst possible outcome, thought Alexander.

It was late on the fifth day when Alexander in the lead spotted sunlight through the trees ahead and realized he must be approaching a clearing, apparently the Mucuy trailhead. He worked hard with his machete. Behind him he could hear Bonpland and the load bearers cutting through the underbrush, widening the trail, making a path for the group to follow. Slowly the light increased and in a few minutes he was standing in a clearing.

In the distance a *Podocarpus*, probably two centuries old, spread an enormous canopy over the grass. He headed for it, dropping his pack at its base, thankful for the opportunity to rest.

Using his pack as a pillow, Alexander unlaced his boots and looked at his feet, gnarled, callused and red from the long trek off the mountain. He was truly glad to have escaped out of the cloud forest! And he could see from the look on Bonpland's face, as he emerged from the thick foliage, that 'civilization' such as this, was welcome indeed. Bonpland emerged with the rest of the expedition and soon every man was on the ground relishing the chance to rest in an open space. In the distance they could see a few agricultural plots and some rangeland with cattle grazing near the river.

Now they could move to Mérida, along the dirt track, on the far side of the Río Chama. Soon they would be in the Governor's headquarters, where hopefully they could report on their scientific work without mentioning the gold and platinum, and leave quietly for the coast.

The governor might insist on a military escort, as the *Motilone* Indians were likely to interfere with two relatively unguarded travelers trying to make it to the coast. In Maracaibo City, ships frequently left for ports in the Caribbean, or for Spain itself, so passage on them with the royal permit in hand was not likely to be a problem. The only problem would be keeping the gold and platinum a secret.

*   *   *   *

The short trek to Mérida proved even shorter when two provincial wagons came along the Río Chama road. After producing his royal permit, Alexander, Bonpland and the load bearers were taken to the *Alcaldia,* or mayor's building, where they met the provincial governor.

In Mérida, Alexander thanked his load bearers for their help, and paying them off in pesos, added two generous bonuses as agreed upon, as well as a third for carting all the samples to provincial headquarters. After helping to store all the samples in the *Alcaldia,* the load bearers departed up country to their homes, while Alexander and Bonpland looked forward to a warm bath and dinner with the governor.

Colonel Bivard, a French officer in the service of Spain, had been Governor of Mérida Province for several years. He was tall, bearded, and appeared to know his business judging by the questions he asked. With a face modeled on a bird of prey, initially he gave Alexander the impression he might be suspicious of his cargo. However, Alexander soon realized the Governor, intrigued by von Humboldt's mission to study the geology, flora and fauna of the Andes and surrounding lowlands, inquired of his research results. He never asked about the samples they carried out, much to Alexander's surprise. Having heard of von Humboldt and Bonpland's explorations in other parts of South America, the Governor was clearly impressed with the countries they had visited. As anticipated, with their proposed trip to Maracaibo City, he warned of a possible encounter with the *Motilone* Indians, which might prove deadly.

"Normally the *Motilone* leave a few dead as carrion for the crows and they are often in conflict with my troops," he said.

Not as fierce as the headhunters in Ecuador or the Guajoros (Wayu Etnia) along the Colombian border, they were still much feared by regular troops who would shoot it out with them rather than risk capture.

"They are masters of ambush," the governor remarked. "One can never tell when they might strike with their blowguns. They have even penetrated inland to Timotes where they have attacked provincial troops and caused considerable havoc."

The governor feigned an interest in the Andean glaciers, but clearly he was not interested in any finds the expedition might have made. Alexander quickly deflected any interest in the possibility of gold and silver and concentrated on till, the major product of glaciation, as being his main interest along with the flora and fauna.

The governor insisted on supplying a military escort to protect Alexander and Bonpland on their trek to the coast. Lieutenant Chavez of the dragoons was detailed to escort them to Maracaibo City where they would take ship for Cuba. Alexander agreed, and after a short stay of three days, he and Bonpland left for the highland village of Apartaderos, a two-day ride on horseback.

At Apartaderos, they stayed only long enough to visit the glacial lagoon at Mucubaji, where they fixed the elevation, took some temperature readings, and made a sketch of the giant moraines similar to the ones they had seen in the *Coromoto*. While Bonpland stayed with the troopers, Alexander slipped off to investigate the possibility of heavy minerals and gold in deposits adjacent to the terminal moraine near the lagoon. Finding lots of black minerals, some pyrite but no gold, he concluded the *Coromoto* had to be a special drainage with plentiful gold up stream, and quite different from Mucubaji. There might be other rivers with gold deposits, but there was little time to hunt for them, and it was best to proceed with haste to the lowlands.

Leaving Apartaderos, the column ascended the long grade toward *Aguila* Peak, one of the highest in the western cordillera. Once over the top they traveled down the Motatán River toward Timotes where they billeted themselves for the night. The road ahead would become perilous and the dreaded *Motilone* might try to hold them up. The following day they rode for several hours and then encamped in a clearing that could be defended in case of attack.

Next day, they left early and traversed a track through scrub forest without incident, but as they came out onto the coastal plain, a force of *Motilone* attacked the column without notice and two soldiers were wounded. Lt. Chavez, at the head of his cavalry, drove off the attackers and returned to guide the group toward the Maracaibo ferry, some sixty kilometers away. Late the following day, after a short ferry trip across the isthmus, they could see a Spanish *Man-of-War* anchored in the harbor. Provided it would take passengers, the Man-of-War was a quick ticket to one of the islands.

*　　*　　*　　*

The Captain of the *Man-of-War*, one Domingo Rodriguez, looked over the royal permit and pronounced, "I want to see some of the specimens collected in the Andes," Announcing that he was an expert on rocks and minerals, Alexander wondered just how much he really did know but he tried not to show any concern.

Bonpland led him to the packs and carefully pulled out samples of the flora, rocks and sediment collected near the Humboldt Glacier. The Captain, impressed by the number of samples, nearly stumbled onto the gold by opening Alexander's sack, but the sample he took out came from Mucubaji and contained only dull looking stones, samples of gneiss and granite.

Nothing to get excited about, Bonpland thought.

Bonpland, not normally given to any emotion, emitted a sigh of relief to Alexander's obvious chagrin, and then resumed taking out samples of rock and pressed flowers.

Captain Rodriguez soon tired of this, bid the two explorers to join him in his cabin for dinner, and ordered the deck officer to see to their quarters with the other officers.

Bonpland and Alexander closed up the sacks and supervised their storage in their cabins, taking care to insure the gold sacks were safely stowed under their bunks.

As he left, the Captain advised they would weigh anchor and sail with the tide.

Four

Paris: Writing the Travels

August, 1804. The voyage to Cuba took six days even with favorable winds and a stop over in Jamaica. Both Alexander and Bonpland were weary when they departed ship, but they immediately reported to the Spanish Governor in the city. After, they were provided with transport to Philadelphia where they met with Thomas Jefferson, President of the United States. From the U.S. they sailed to Bordeaux where they were spirited on to Paris by a French cavalry detail. In the great city, Alexander and Aimé had many friends who would put them up. Once there, they had time to sort out their samples, and think about writing up the results of their explorations. The equinoctial expedition to the New World had taken five years out of their lives. Both men had matured and aged in the process, but they were exuberant at their good fortune and their incredible luck at escaping with the Andean gold and platinum.

Finding the ore was a favorable omen and one that might provide a catalyst to propel them into some similar endeavor in the future. So much waited to be discovered and explained, and with luck the French and German crowns might reward them handsomely. Bonpland elected to stay in Paris, and pursue his interests at the French Court, while von Humboldt started off overland to Berlin. He had been away from home since 1799, a new century had dawned, and no doubt new possibilities awaited him. He was already nearly five years into the new century. His brother, Wilhelm, would fill him in on family matters when he got home, and he had many friends and contacts in Berlin who would undoubtedly help him reestablish himself.

When the need arose, Alexander could mingle in the upper class of society, both in the Spanish dominions of South America and in Europe. Like his brother, Wilhelm, he inherited some of the family's fluidity with language, and in addition to natural science, he had a keen interest in verbal communication as a means of cultural expression. He had studied many natural and cultural phenomena, whilst his brother concentrated on, and became, one of the leading linguists of the European enlightenment.

Along the familiar route to Berlin, von Humboldt marveled at some of the changes. The roads had been improved, no doubt as a by-product of frequent wars, and German attempts to finally put an end to Napoléon. Money seemed to be used to a greater degree than when he was last in the area, and farms appeared to be more productive as evidenced by a larger supply of food in the markets. The population, although still small, was more active and travel seemed easier judging by the number of people on the road. Maybe he had been in South America too long, but the forests here seemed to have been replaced to a greater extent by farmland. In any case he longed to see Berlin, his home since childhood, and the family house now occupied by his aunt and brother. Now, with his personal knowledge of and experience with many primitive Andean and Amazonian languages, he wondered how far his brother had come in his pursuit of proving that culture emanated from language.

While Wilhelm could outperform him in every civilized tongue, he had little experience with languages of the New World, and Alexander couldn't wait to spill all this on him. His aunt would force him to go to church, but this was minor payment for the comfort of the family estate, and the chance to write his *Travels*. Berlin could not appear on the horizon fast enough.

Situated in the wide valley of the Spree River, the landscape of Berlin was glaciated just like the *Coromoto* in Venezuela. As the capital of the Kingdom of Prussia, the city was also the capital of Germany, and one of the major literary centers of Europe. With its various lakes along the western perimeter, Berlin had been a center of intellectual pursuits since the end of the Fifteenth Century. Yes, for Alexander this could be the setting in which to write the *Travels* and the *Kosmos*. Truly the future beckoned and he would pursue his lifelong dream of writing about the New World and its natural history. It was his destiny and he had learned so much.

After meeting his brother, Wilhelm, and spending a few weeks at the family estate he found relatively little interest among academics about his explorations and botanical discoveries in the New World. Mercantile interests seemed to have replaced scientific endeavors in the time that he had been away. Even his brother tired of hearing about the importance of Andean dialects and other 'scientific' information he had collected. As he added up the cost of producing his reports, Alexander soon realized that with the dwindling family fortune, he would need some of the gold-platinum to pay assistants to help with the analysis and report preparation. Although he missed his long time partner and associate Aimé Bonpland, he realized he missed Paris even more.

Since there seemed to be little interest in his explorations, he decided to return to Paris, for there his major collaborators François Arago and Aimé Bonpland would be close by, and they were *non pareil* with their knowledge of science and interests similar to his. In addition, an invitation from the French Government and the French Academy to act as scientific advisor had arrived in Berlin. It seemed he might do better in Paris after all and weighing all his options a change in venue seemed inescapable. Despite protestations from Wilhelm, Alexander packed and left for Paris.

After all, he had left most of his personal belongings with François and his sudden longing for the intellectual stimulation of life in the Latin Quarter had overwhelmed him. His fortune, left to him by his mother, was seriously depleted and he would now have to watch his expenditures and live frugally. He would need to sell some of the gold to pay assistants and he would need this help for many years to sort through all his samples.

Prior to his expedition, Alexander had been generous with students who lacked the means to continue studying. He would find it difficult to limit support, but he would have to watch his finances, and balance his time at the Academy of Sciences while writing the report of his explorations. Even magnanimity had its limits, but with the publication of the *Travels* foremost in his mind, he was anxious to proceed with writing it. While *The Travels* had proved a first choice for a title, he began to think of his book as a personal narrative of the natural history of the New World.

Slowly *The Personal Narrative of a Journey to the Equinoctial Regions of the New Continent* welled up in his mind. Yes, this would be the title and *Travels* or *Personal Narrative* would form the last two volumes.

Alexander had an immense amount of new information, a large collection of plants and minerals, and of course the placer gold and platinum samples.

Should he include the *Coromoto* gold-platinum lode in his *Travels?* He thought long and hard about this. He had also collected a great amount of information on temperature variations, geodetic information on the elevation of prominent physical features across Central and South America, geomagnetic fluctuations, as well as latitude and longitude.

Surely it would take time to collate all this information, secure a publisher, and above all it would also take a prodigious amount of money to hire assistants. Of course, the gold and platinum samples were with Bonpland and the fastest route to Paris was overland by coach. Three days later he bid goodbye to Wilhelm and left for France.

*　　*　　*　　*

After a long and arduous trip through Strasbourg, Alexander arrived in Paris and went immediately to see Bonpland and start unpacking the samples. The two friends spent many weeks recounting the route they had traveled and the major discoveries they had made.

Finally, one day, Bonpland shocked Alexander saying, "I have several business ventures in mind and I'll not have much time to devote to writing up and publishing our results."

Alexander seemed frozen in space, totally electrified. After what seemed a long, almost interminable time, he replied, "I know you are losing interest in the gold samples. It seems impossible to return to South America to lay claim to the find."

Alexander wondered if he could change his friend's mind but waited anxiously to hear what he would propose.

Being a man of great personal integrity, Bonpland pronounced, "I found the gold Alexander, but without you, I would never have stumbled across it. In any case you may need the samples you have to finance the publication of your book. I wish you the best of luck with it."

Alexander understood, but it disturbed him that Bonpland would give up the great enterprise after their arduous journey, with all the hardships they had endured. With great reluctance, Alexander established new lodgings in the Latin Quarter and made plans to move the samples and notebooks.

While in the field in the Americas, Alexander had routinely posted notes and information to his brother in Berlin. But the continental blockade, in force at the time, had prevented delivery and most of his records were lost. Luckily he had copies and his eighty-odd notebooks had survived along with all the samples collected en route. Still more important, no one suspected that the samples contained gold and till from the Andes of Venezuela. It might be a good idea to keep it this way.

Upon his return to Cuba, and while visiting the local governor, he had inquired about the possibility of organizing mining ventures in Venezuela, feigning an interest in the vast gold and silver reserves in the Orinoco River area. He was told the royal permit from the Spanish Crown did not include mining enterprises of any kind. So, it would seem for the time being he would have to keep the *Coromoto* gold and platinum find a secret, and see what developed. There was a lingering distrust of Spain in Venezuela and in a short time the political situation might change...for the better? If Spain were to lose its hold on its colony it might prove possible to recover the gold in the *Coromoto* and have another chance to explore the Andean highlands.

Alexander folded his original notes and maps, excepting the log of his gold-platinum find, and placed them with the original draft of the *Travels*.

Being eager to get to work he thought about several associates he could contact. In the meantime there was interesting conversation to be had and to give in the salons of Paris, stimulating discussions with Arago, and most importantly the cataloging and collation of the samples returned from South America. The first task would challenge his prodigious memory. He would have to read the entire log of the trip, to insure that all was in correct chronological order, and then he would need to systematically catalog all his samples.

The gold and platinum he separated from his other scientific samples. His notes regarding the exact location of the gold-platinum ore he drew up on separate maps and folded them into his personal diary along with the samples.

If his financial situation worsened, he would need the gold and platinum to stave off creditors; the maps and description of the vein gold and placer deposits would stay with his diary for the time being. Alexander made a mental note to closely monitor reports of the political climate in Venezuela. There were already rumors of a young Venezuelan bureaucrat named Simon Bolivar, who espoused a new national identity for Venezuela, but little was known about his political base and degree of popular support. This might be worth something in the end, but first there was the expedition account, the *Travels,* to concentrate on, and he knew the importance of completing it.

If only Bonpland had stayed on to help, but oh well *'c'est la vie'.* He would see to it himself and with speed. He was as quick with the printed page as with the impenetrable mountain wall and the implacable bureaucrat. He had a great feeling about it. All would transpire as he willed it.

Alexander began to plan the writing of the *Travels* by considering the collaborators who would be only too glad to help out. There was Arago of course, other French scientists he knew from the Royal Society, and he could count on them for inspiration at least. While Bonpland faded from the scene, Professor von Baer from Estonia would no doubt assist with the biological samples on his frequent visits to Paris. French engravers were the best in the world at this time and he would need them to put his maps and illustrations into publishable form.

Alexander calculated his book would consume some twenty to twenty-five, and maybe even thirty volumes of new scientific data. Most importantly the meteorological data of daily and nightly temperatures, the first of their kind in the tropics, had already aroused keen interest among physical geographers. His new idea of connecting places on the ground with lines of equal temperature — called isotherms on maps — was already being discussed at the University of Paris. He even envisaged a weather map, showing temperature and barometric pressure distributions, that he thought he could use to predict weather trends. Certainly he would need to hire two or three student assistants to help with the daunting task of assembling all this information.

While many places and events flooded through his mind, Alexander thought of the great glacier in the Mérida Andes, his new information on glaciation, and especially the presence of ice and snow in the equatorial latitudes. He had found it with Bonpland and also he had found the till, carried by a glacier and emplaced underneath, around the sides of, and at the end of the ice just as in the Alps.

So, Hutton had been right after all, and glaciation seemed to be a worldwide phenomenon. How would members of the Academy respond to this, and more importantly what would professors at the Sorbonne, and his friend Arago, say about it?

*   *   *   *

A few days later at the Academy of Sciences Alexander was introduced to a young Swiss student from the Bernese Oberland, Louis Agassiz, who listened intently to von Humboldt's description of glaciers in Colombia, Ecuador and Venezuela.

At the end of his discussion, Agassiz barely twenty years old, addressed the assembly, saying, "I have seen similar situations in the Alps just as Monsieur von Humboldt describes in South America. I consider it quite likely that glacial sediment, material emplaced by ice, is widespread in the world and quite possibly, it is the result of a former large and great extent of ice."

There was a general stirring amongst the members who thought that most of the sediment Alexander and Louis described had been emplaced by ocean water. Afterwards Louis confided to Alexander, "Much greater evidence is needed to prove the new *Glacial Theory*. I will have to return to Switzerland and continue mapping the Bernese Oberland."

Alexander offered, "I'll be happy to assist in any way possible, including the prospect of funding, if you need it."

Of course, he reminded himself, *this hinges on getting my reports into publication, which will bring in revenue.*

One long day of writing followed another and there were numerous problems with the sample descriptions that stumped his student assistants. Only Alexander could sort out the answers to these questions, and this of course, meant an interruption in writing. However, slowly the *Travels* began to take shape, and Alexander realized that working as hard as he had, he would have to take time off, as his nerves were frayed to the breaking point.

Perhaps it's time to visit Wilhelm in Berlin, he thought.

It was now 1828. Only part of the expedition report was in print, and producing enough income to insure eventual success with the entire record, once he managed to complete it, was still a long way off. Nevertheless he was receiving generous royalties.

Then he remembered that Professor von Baer would arrive in Paris and he had requested a visit with Alexander. Perhaps he would return to Berlin with von Baer, visit his brother in Berlin, and maybe travel overland to visit von Baer's Museum of Natural History in Tartu, Estonia. Time would tell, but he hoped von Baer would arrive soon, as he was nearing the limit of endurance, and he needed a change of pace for a while. Von Baer, a respected biologist, and man with a worldwide reputation, was interested in the New World flora and no doubt he would have some interesting insight into what Alexander would tell him.

In the meantime, despite his royalties, finances were continually running on the low side. Alexander would have to sell some of the gold to finance his writing. As soon as his assistants left for the day he collected some of the gold and took it to the goldsmiths who were most eager to purchase it. He had already sold a portion of the entire sample and the goldsmiths paid a high price for his samples. And no wonder, for after testing it with *aqua regia* and mercury, they knew it was very pure and very rare. The absence of copper and low silver content of his gold samples fetched a high price amongst Parisian goldsmiths.

He had enough gold to support his writing and sample analysis for another five or six years, but by then he should have enough in print to bring in a reasonable income. No need to worry!

Five

Sojurn to Tartu

1829. When von Baer arrived in Paris he was entertained by members of the French Academy and at one of their meetings he finally met Alexander. The two men had much to discuss regarding the flora and fauna of South America and Alexander showed von Baer the immense collection he had brought back. Alexander outlined the *Travels* he was working on and also his plans for the *Kosmos* that he hoped to begin writing in the next year or two. Von Baer had never met anyone like von Humboldt. His knowledge of biology was astounding considering that he was first and foremost essentially an engineer, expert on mining, geology and mineralogy.

Alexander had a keen grasp not only of biology and engineering, but also astronomy, human cultures and language. Moreover, his knowledge of history and politics made him a much sought after authority in the salons of Paris. And since his appointment to the French Government, as scientific authority, paid some of the bills, von Humboldt found he spent more time in audience with government ministers than he did writing the *Travels*. His nerves were frayed and he preferred to spend more time with his book.

Sensing that von Humboldt was stressed to the limit, von Baer asked if he might consider visiting Estonia to give a few lectures at Tartu University. After a short time he replied, "I can't afford the time away from the book and most of all I cannot afford to not attend the academy."

To this von Baer proposed, "All could be arranged for a paid leave and he personally could pay von Humboldt's travels to Estonia and return to Paris."

Alexander could hardly believe his good fortune and he agreed at once to visit Estonia. Von Baer mentioned that they could go via Berlin and Alexander offered to introduce him to his famous brother while they were in the capital city.

After stopping in Berlin for a short time, where a reunion with his brother took several days, the two men continued on their way. The trip to Tartu, a university city founded by the Swedes in the sixteenth century, proved a pleasant diversion for Alexander. Once in Tartu, von Humboldt was impressed with the library at the Tartu Museum, and his quarters at von Baer's estate in the oldest part of the city. By this time Alexander and his host had established a firm friendship, one that strengthened after he gave several lectures to the science faculty at the university, talks that drew extensively on his South American travels.

Alexander's notion of the relationship between a biotic region and its physical geography proved especially interesting to biologists, physical geographers and other scientists. But it was his conclusions on the effect of volcanism, as an eruptive force in the molding of the earth's surface, and his engaging lecture using examples from Colombia and Ecuador, that impressed a large audience of faculty and students. This was all the more important because it outlined the flaws of the *Neptunist Theory,* namely, that all surface features were formed from the action of water.

In one lecture, Alexander quoted from his *Political Essay on the Kingdom of New Spain,* a work which contained a synthesis of the geography and geology of Mexico including commentary on the political, social and economic conditions there. From this, his passionate attack on the evils of slavery, and his view of the depravity of forcible confinement and imprisonment of other humans, impressed his listeners.

Later, von Baer would hear of the effect it had on English investment, and the terrible loss of life in Mexican silver mines. Of course, he also lectured on ocean currents, as the cold current off the western coast of South America had been named for him — *Humboldt Current.*

Glaciation, one of his favorite topics, he discussed at length and his ideas on the origin of till, the material deposited by ice, proved of special interest in a country like Estonia that had been completely covered by the last great ice sheet. As he summed up his ideas on glaciation, he thought, *I won't mention the enormous gold reserves in the Coromoto but if the audience only knew what lay there, buried in glacial rubble, they would bolt to South America and start a new gold rush.*

An incredulous audience asked questions regarding the nature of the black man in society, necessity of slavery, mining of precious metals, *etc.* While some argued against ice on the equator as a physical impossibility, Alexander took great pains to frame up his data to test hypotheses and arrive at rational conclusions. His logical arguments and clear examples impressed many of the students and faculty who listened to his enthusiastic lectures.

While in Tartu, von Humboldt showed himself to be generous with his time. He held many discussions with students, some lasting hours. As the epitome of the 19th century scientist, who had a vision of the immense achievements that were possible with a scientific career, he could explain, even to the common man, what science could do for the citizenry. His gregarious nature and friendly attitude brought respect and admiration and he clearly enjoyed his time with von Baer.

Because Estonia carried on extensive trade with Russia in precious metals Alexander wished he had brought some gold samples with him. It would be more lucrative for him to sell off some of the gold here, and above all there would be less gossip around about where the gold came from. He realized there was little hope of recovering the main lode of Andean gold-platinum, but he considered that his maps and descriptions of the gold deposits should be stored in a safe place. For now, he would leave his gold platinum notes in his Andean logbooks.

Alexander was so impressed with von Baer after his sojourn in Estonia, so much so that upon returning to France, he inquired of his friend Arago as to the name of a competent solicitor. He wished to write up his last will and testament to insure his library, logbooks, and samples would be protected after his death. It came as a complete surprise to Arago when von Humboldt mentioned he planned to will his personal estate to von Baer, and provide the funds to transfer all his prized possessions to the Museum of Natural History in Tartu.

Alexander von Humboldt was now sixty and more than half way through his life. Little did Alexander realize that in scarcely thirty years his notebooks and samples would find their way to the Tartu Museum where they would rest undisturbed for nearly eight decades. He would die just after Charles Darwin published the Origin of Species, in 1859, and eighty years before Heinrich Jahn would 'rediscover' his logbooks in the Tartu museum.

PART II

1939

Eighty years is a long time for manuscripts and samples to lie undisturbed in a museum or institute. Sooner or later a curator would likely tend to sort and analyze samples, or an inquisitive researcher could match the samples with geological sections and come to realize the truly stupendous find that von Humboldt had stumbled upon.

It seems that, while Tartu Museum was the famous resting place of von Humboldt's library and sample collection, the samples were left undisturbed in the original sample bags and in the crate von Humboldt had brought back to France from South America. The geological documentation of his samples, contained in his original logbooks, had been overlooked by researchers, the bulk of whom were more interested in his Orinoco and Apure explorations, first ascent of Chimborazo, and meteorological and geomagnetic research. A failing amongst many researchers, including professional historians, is the desire to use the most recent publication on a subject, bypassing or overlooking original material which might prove more beneficial in pursuing a topic or testing a hypothesis.

Thus, it seems the location of von Humboldt's original logs important, as they no doubt were to the reputation of the Tartu Museum, were largely forgotten or ignored for many years. Like many works that sink into oblivion, or are lost for a time, these would assume almost unparalleled importance just prior to the start of World War II.

Six

Professor Jahn and *the Travels*

Caracas, January, 1939 — Professor Heinrich Jahn rose early as he liked to lecture in the early hours before the heat settled in over the city. The afternoon got to be unbearably hot and humid and this he couldn't stand even though he was a native Venezuelan.

Growing up in the German colony, Colonia Tovar, outside Caracas he relished the cool mountain air even during the day. His grandparents had been with the advance colonists, under the Italian geographer and army colonel Agostino Codazzi, who ventured to Venezuela in 1848. Settling on the Caribbean coast, they soon realized it was impossible for Europeans to live there, what with the mosquitoes, snakes and extreme heat. Moving up country, they settled in the mountains south of Caracas where the heat wasn't so overpowering, the humidity more conducive to human health.

After moving upcountry the colonists built a thriving farm community, so much so that Heinrich's parents had sufficient income to send him to university in Caracas. An excellent student, Heinrich excelled in science and eventually earned certificates in geology and chemistry. He first joined the Venezuelan Government mining ministry, but later decided to follow a career as university lecturer. For the last ten years he had carried out research in the Andes and had taken part in geological surveys intending to look at mining possibilities between Maracaibo and the vast expanse of the llanos.

Now that Germany had become one of the great centers of mining and engineering in Europe, he hoped his application to study there for a year would be favorably received. This morning he stopped for coffee on his way into the university. He felt particularly weary, and thinking the coffee would wake him up for class, he spent an unusually long time watching traffic in the nearby boulevard as he thought over his forthcoming lecture. Somehow the speeding cars seemed to stimulate his thoughts as he organized the major concepts he would discuss in class. He needed something to keep his spirits up, as the latest crop of students were not particularly keen, and their disinterest and lack of enthusiasm troubled him. He had heard of new ideas floating about Germany — new concepts about drifting continents — and he longed for the opportunity to hear about and discuss them.

The long and impressive Boconó Fault, reaching from Ecuador to Venezuela, extended right through Caracas. Might it help explain the drifting continent theory? He had long wondered about the fault — a 2000 km long split in the earth's surface which divided the interior of South America from the coast. Could the massive continental slabs be slipping past one another moving in transverse directions?

As he sipped his coffee, Heinrich realized that he needed to meet with geologists in Berlin and at Humboldt University, and he desperately hoped his application to study abroad would be successful.

He finished his coffee, paid the waiter, and slipped out into the morning air. It was already hot and humid and it promised to be an unpleasant day in class despite newly installed ceiling fans in the faculty lecture rooms. If the weather could be used to foretell the future, this was not a particularly good omen in which to predict the way events of the day might unfold.

Striding along *Avenue el Paraiso* toward the geology faculty, he passed by the German Club, nodding to the chef who was on his way to work. He crossed the street and entered the geology department through the rear doors and went directly to his laboratory. On the way his secretary stopped him and told him there was a message in his mailbox.

Forgetting about his application for the moment, Heinrich took the stairs two at a time, and nearly ran into Professor Ramon Gonzales, his mentor and Professor of Geochemistry. Ramon was usually at his best cajoling the female members of staff, but this morning he had a strange look on his face as he studied his former student.

Finally Ramon smiled, letting it all out in one burst, "Your application is in and you are appointed to the next group of faculty to study abroad. You have the *Grand Marachel* fellowship you lucky devil, you. They turned me down again, but you have it and you can leave before the summer term."

Heinrich wondered how Ramon knew all this, but he had learned not to ask. Ramon always knew! Hurriedly he opened the envelope to find the certificate indicating he would be paid while on leave, and in addition, he would receive a handsome stipend for travel. One stipulation was that he would have to visit other European countries, especially those with mining expertise. He wondered where he might go. Perhaps his German colleagues would have some ideas. France was a possibility, but the French had not made great advances in mining geology. He would have to give this some thought.

For the moment the main thing would be to alert colleagues in Germany that he would be coming and to prepare a schedule of places to visit and people to see. He would start with *Herr* Rolsch at the Germany Embassy in Caracas and ask his advice as he seemed to have unlimited knowledge of German universities, their faculties, and programs.

Also he would write to Professor Born in Helsinki and ask about the prospect of visiting his laboratory there. Surely this would be an important year and a milestone in his life. And above all he would pack von Humboldt's *Travels* and take it with him. He hadn't read it in ten years, and where better to read about South America than in Germany, the home of the famous author. He had learned so much from his first reading that he thought a second might lead him to find other areas in the Andes with important mining potential. It was surely worth a try.

And tonight he would dine at the German Club, his favorite café, as they always had a supply of German beer. After a good night's sleep he would book passage to Germany and maybe read the *Travels* on board ship. He remembered how depressed he had been in the morning. Now with the good news his depression evaporated and everything seemed clear to him. Hot humid weather was certainly not a bad omen or foreboding of the future as he had thought earlier.

Claro, he thought.

Heinrich had not paid much attention to politics but the present worsening worldwide political situation did not bode well for the future. Later, as he drifted off to sleep he wondered what might happen next. He considered Hitler's move to annex Austria was a step in the right direction but there were other countries outraged at the *Anschluss* and the buildup of the German Army. If war broke out he would fight for the homeland. He was a German first, Venezuelan second. Strangely, his last flickering thought involved geology and war. Would geology prove important in the coming conflict?

*   *   *   *

The next day he rose early and hoped to get to the German Embassy when it opened at 9 AM. With any kind of luck he would be able to get a visa within a week as the Germans were always fast once the paperwork was in order.

He was greeted immediately by *Herr* Rolsch, a rather rotund man with an equally round and unsmiling face, who uttered, "We know about your appointment, Professor. Your papers will be ready in three days."

Somewhat taken aback, Heinrich asked, "How do you know about it?"

Rolsch answered, "We have our sources and there is little that goes on in government here that we do not know about. You'll have a wonderful year in Germany."

Yes, Heinrich thought, *the rest of 1939 would be wonderful in Germany.*

"Ah, *Herr* Rolsch, I'll be traveling to some other countries as well."

He realized, from the startled look on *Herr* Rolsch's face, he did not know all that went on in the Venezuelan government. But it would not do to rub it in. Like most other people, the Germans did not like to appear slow in the intelligence area and it was often best to keep information like this to oneself.

Heinrich left the embassy and walked briskly back to the university. *It's wise,* he thought, *to send a wire to the Mining Institute in Berlin, and then to arrange passage on the next ship.*

He had much to do and to plan, but first he had to select those books and papers in his office that he would need to take with him. Professor Ramon would help him but he would need to hurry. And he would need to find von Humboldt's *Travels* and make sure it was with him on ship. For some reason he thought it was important to reread the entire book.

Once in the department, he looked for Professor Ramon. If there were any recent developments, Ramon would know about them. He found Ramon talking with one of the secretaries. While motioning for him to follow to his office he wondered when or if Ramon actually did any work. He was usually flirting with female staff and rumors were everywhere about how many children he actually had fathered.

When he reached the office, Heinrich requested, "Check with the telephone operator about passage and tickets to Germany while I start organizing papers to take with me to Germany."

Ramon obliged, and wearing a wicked smile, departed out the door and literally bounded down the staircase.

Heinrich busied himself with various boxes of papers and started selecting those he considered important enough to take with him.

First and foremost Heinrich would have to concentrate on mining as this was his *forte* and if he was lucky enough to find a major ore deposit — say one of gold or silver — he might be able to retire early and forget teaching. Or maybe he could even win a post in the newly formed Geological Survey of Venezuela. He would have to work hard at this, but then he remembered von Humboldt's tome once again, and the thought kept nagging at him that somehow the book would play a major role in his forthcoming trip to Europe.

But just how this was to come about he wasn't sure...then once again, he considered von Humboldt's keen observations regarding base metals and precious metals. He remembered his knowledge of silver and gold in Mexico and Venezuela and how this led to so much foreign capital being expended after the publication of the *Travels*. A lot of this capital had come from England and America after the *Travels* had been translated into English and financiers realized the immense profits to be made from mining in Middle and South America. With this, his mind drifted off to the forthcoming ocean voyage and he realized he was very tired.

*   *   *   *

On April thirty, Heinrich took ship for Germany. He spent the next two weeks holed up in his cabin reading the *Travels* and several mining bulletins he had brought with him. Occasionally he spent time in the ship's bar drinking one or more of the fine lagers the ship had brought from Germany. She was a fast ship of the German overseas line, making nearly twenty knots even in heavy seas, which seemed to dominate this crossing. She would dock in Wilhelmshaven on May fifteen.

Several members of the German Embassy in Caracas were aboard ship apparently returning to the homeland along with members of the Venezuelan consular staff. As rumors of a coming war were everywhere now, the ship's bar was buzzing with talk of the impending conflict between Germany and the French-English alliance. Poland was making belligerent statements that seemed to enrage Hitler, and England continued to take a moderate stand, even after the *Anschluss* or annexation of Austria by Germany.

Heinrich felt very lucky to be going back to his homeland for the first time and at a time when Germany seemed to be at the very center of world events. Everyone was watching Hitler to see what he would do next and he seemed to catch all the world's leaders off guard. At last the victims of the Versailles Treaty were aggressively righting the wrongs of the last twenty years and the Allies for once seemed uncertain of what to do and where to turn.

After the First War, the Big Four — Britain, U.S., Italy, and France — forged the treaty and placed the responsibility for the war on Germany. With revenge in mind, the Versailles Treaty was the culmination of their collective effort to subjugate Germany, and along with it came enormous reparation payments. Now that their former unity of purpose had evaporated, Hitler was keeping them busy hopping about Europe, restoring Germany's hegemony over neighboring countries. And German science was rising to unprecedented heights in every field. Yes, Berlin was the right place to be for the next little while.

Heinrich read largely through the day, taking in the latest news at night, and it seemed time was on his side. In the late afternoon he took tea in the lounge and followed up with a beer or two in the bar listening to seemingly endless political discussions. The topic of conversation was always about European politics.

What will the Americans do if Hitler continues with various political annexations? This question seemed to dominate discussion night after night.

There was not a single other scientific person on board, and no way to talk geology with anyone. He couldn't wait much longer for the ship to dock and see what the institute had to offer. He wished the fatherland well, but then he didn't come here to fight. He came to do science!

The ship docked at Wilhelmshaven two hours ahead of time and Heinrich was happy to disembark. On the wharf he looked for someone from the institute who would pick him up and escort him to Berlin. Scanning the crowd he noticed a tall man with a beard carrying a sign with his name on it.

After a short introduction his escort, *Herr* Zimmerman, inquired, "I hope you had a pleasant voyage Professor."

"Yes, although I could do without rough seas and storms. They seem to have followed us all across the Atlantic."

Zimmerman told they would take the train to Berlin immediately. Passing many soldiers in the streets, Heinrich became acutely aware of military vehicles that seemed to stretch out forever. They eventually made their way through the busy train station and boarded a train bound for the capital.

As the train pulled out of the station, Heinrich was astounded at the military presence in the city. Army trucks and equipment were everywhere and men in uniform seemed to exist in never ending streams moving with great purpose and in large numbers. Surely the entire 100,000-man army of Germany, as dictated by the 1918-Armistice, was parked right here in Wilhelmshaven. A general reorganization and buildup of the army had to have begun, if the activity he witnessed here was going on everywhere in Germany.

*   *   *   *

Berlin, May, 1939. After a long train ride, *Herr* Zimmerman and Heinrich arrived in Berlin. There was considerable activity in the capital, much of it involving the military. Aircraft were continually taking off and landing and the streets were filled with army, air force and navy personnel. Everyone seemed intent on getting somewhere and the average person had the look of seriousness of purpose, as if life itself depended upon it. The streets and cafes were full and bands played in the parks.

Yet, while everyone seemed serious about getting somewhere, or doing something, and while people talked, they didn't laugh to a great extent. This seemed perplexing to Heinrich for, if the Germans were really on the rise economically and politically, they ought to be happy about it. Then he remembered the terrible stories he had heard about the First World War, the starvation and terrible slaughter of the nation's manhood, and he understood the somber attitude of the populace. Could they be headed in the same direction once again? If so, a rising economy and aggressive political strategy might not bring the kind of victory Hitler envisaged.

Heinrich mentioned to *Herr* Zimmerman, "There seems to be a great deal of military traffic."

Looking somewhat perplexed his guide answered *"Ja*, of course, Professor. We're faced with the Allied Alliance and we will have to fight sooner or later."

Heinrich didn't answer but realized the 'fight' might be close indeed.

Heinrich's office in the Mining Institute was larger and better equipped than his office in Caracas. He was given an enormous desk and access to technical works far superior to anything he had had in Venezuela. Down the hall, the map library, with its massive worldwide holdings, was far better than anything he had ever seen. The main library had every major international geological journal, and with over a million books cataloged, it surpassed any geology library in the world.

I am lucky to have a year here, he told himself. He remembered Jung's notion of 'synchronicity,' where events that place a person in the right place, at the right time, happen only infrequently in a lifetime.

Thinking all this through he knew he was very lucky indeed. And here he was in exactly the right place, at exactly the right time...and then strangely he thought of von Humboldt's *Travels*.

What was it? What connection could there be between the *Travels* and Berlin, other than von Humboldt's connection with his birthplace. There was something of far greater importance here, but he couldn't put his finger on it, and it nagged him.

Oh well, it'll come to me, he told himself.

He had finished reading the *Travels* on board ship and he had made many notes of von Humboldt's observations and interpretations of Venezuelan geology. He would have to go over them again and see if there was something he had missed.

*   *   *   *

The first three weeks in Berlin passed quickly and Heinrich had many visitors from the institute as he familiarized himself with the organization of the place and the people in it. A message had come from Professor Born in Helsinki advising him that he could come to Finland at his leisure. He was also invited to stop in Tallinn to see Professor Mahamae, who specialized in the chemistry of ore deposits and was an expert on gold and silver mining in Russia and Finland. It would be well worth his while also to see the Museum in Tartu, which had considerable holdings of European geology.

While he mulled this over, *Herr Direktor* of the institute called Heinrich into his office. Eyeing his visitor inquisitively, he asked, "Now that you've settled in, what about your research plans?"

Pausing to gauge his reaction, he continued, "The institute has just organized an exchange program with Finland and it might be a good idea if you were to leave for Finland in the next couple of weeks. The political situation might change at any moment, and this is an ideal time to leave for three or four weeks."

Heinrich offered, "I am agreeable to leaving as soon as possible."

Herr Direktor answered, "I'll send one of the institute scientists along to finalize the exchange agreement; thereafter, you will be free to meet with Finnish geologists and to visit Tallinn and Tartu."

Herr Direktor realized it would be useful to have firsthand knowledge of Estonian mining and the extent of mapping in the northern Baltic states. Just two days before, German Army Intelligence officers had paid a visit to *Herr Direktor* with that very thought in mind. No doubt German authorities knew all about his visitor to the institute and planned to put him to some use.

So many men had been pressed into military service that *Herr Direktor* had a hard time finding geology graduates to fill vacancies in the institute. Even female graduates were hard to come by as they were directed into semi-military service with the Commissary, Intelligence and Quartermaster Corps.

The military was only now coming around to realizing that the mining institute was of some military importance. Indeed, Heinrich Himmler would pay him a visit in a week. And *Reichsführer* Himmler was nearly at the top of the political ladder in Germany these days, a man of power and influence. If only he could persuade Himmler to assign military personnel to the mining institute. In the meantime, let Heinrich Jahn take his leave, visit Finland and the Baltic countries, and report back. Some information would no doubt be better than the scanty reports they had at present.

*   *   *   *

Heinrich sent off a cable to Professor Born and received a reply within a day to come as soon as possible. So, once again he packed his bags, tossed his copy of the *Travels* in with a bottle of cognac, and placed the bag by the door. It would be good to leave early, he thought. And he would check his mailbox at the institute before leaving.

His assigned companion, *Herr* Schmidt, a graduate of Humboldt University, had been left in the Mining Institute because he had a physical disability making him unfit for military service. A powerfully-built short man, he seemed to have a considerable amount of field training for such a young fellow, and he also seemed to know a lot about base metals. Even though he spoke with a lisp, Heinrich enjoyed listening to his Swabian dialect, which was quite distinct and different from his own 'foreign German.'

Learning German at home in Venezuela, Heinrich grew up with an older version of Bavarian German, which had changed somewhat over the time his parents had spent in Venezuela. He and *Herr* Schmidt got on quite well, and this promised to be a splendid trip, to a part of the world he had never expected to see.

Arriving in Helsinki harbor, Heinrich and *Herr* Schmidt took a taxi to the Mining Institute, part of the Geological Survey of Finland, in the main government district. There they met Professor Born who was eager to talk to Heinrich about South America. Several Finns had worked on geological projects in South America, mainly in Argentina, and there was much interest in the New World. Heinrich provided some general details of the research he had been engaged in and mentioned his interest in continental drift. Professor Born articulated, "Ah, exactly nine years ago, Alfred Wegener delivered a series of lectures on continental drift to the geologists at Helsinki, and a copy of his lectures is in the library here."

Heinrich replied, "I'd have liked to meet him. It's tragic he froze to death in Greenland."

Professor Born agreed, "Yes, very tragic. He was putting together a newer version of his continental drift theory when he died," and then rising, he added, "I'll show you the library and grant you exclusive access to it and to the archives."

For several days Heinrich and *Herr* Schmidt took exhaustive notes on the holdings of the geological survey where they were given catalogs of available maps of the Baltic area and Finland including the relative scales of each series. It seems the Finns had been hard at work mapping the entire area, not only for topography, but also for surface and subsurface geological features. Their magnetic anomaly and gravimetric maps proved the equal of, or better, than those in Germany.

After nearly two weeks in the library and government archives, the two scientists sailed for Tallinn aboard the Gulf of Finland ferry *Polarstar*.

Landing in Tallinn they were met by Professor Mahamae's assistant who took them directly to the Museum of Natural History at Tartu. An imposing structure built in 1632, the Museum formed part of the impressive Tartu University, with a strong faculty in the natural sciences. Settlement at Tartu dated to the fifth century, with Yaroslav the Wise of Kiev, establishing the fort that gave the city its Russian name, Yurev. Tartu University, suppressed in 1656, was reopened in 1802, following a destructive fire in 1775. The Tartu Museum, a major part of the science faculty, had been enlarged just prior to von Humboldt's visit in 1821, and again in the 1920's.

Professor Volli Mahamae, a former alpine geologist, was now Dean of the Faculty of Sciences at Tartu. Considered the resident authority on precious metals in Eurasia, he was eager to meet with Heinrich and discuss the mining potential of South America. The two men hit it off from the start, and along with *Herr* Schmidt they had many fruitful discussions, not only of South America, but also of Germany where mine engineering was considered the best in the world. Professor Mahamae took his visitors on a tour of Tartu and eventually they wound up in the Museum.

Arrangements were made for both visitors to have unrestricted access to the museum and to its collections.

"Incidentally," remarked Dean Mahamae, "did you know that the original manuscript of von Humboldt's *Travels* is in the Museum here in Tartu?"

Heinrich replied, "I am thoroughly familiar with von Humboldt's work, and yes, I would like very much to see it."

Incredulously, Heinrich thought, *could this be the connection between von Humboldt and Venezuela?*

He could scarcely believe his good fortune. If the original was here, he surely wanted to look through it. But first there were the samples to look at and it appeared some of von Humboldt's collection was housed here at Tartu.

Dean Mahamae invited Heinrich and *Herr* Schmidt to his house where they continued their discussion into the wee hours of the morning along with a few bottles of fine wine. Heinrich told Mahamae of his interest in von Humboldt and the Dean offered to make the *Travels* available for him to study at his leisure. Heinrich thanked him for that, mentioning that even though he had a copy of the famous work with him, he would welcome the chance to study von Humboldt's draft manuscript that presumably would have his original notes.

Dean Mahamae admitted he had looked at it but had never studied it in detail.

"After all," he cautioned, "it consists of thirty volumes plus some additional notes that were never incorporated into the original."

After a short pause, he continued, "von Humboldt visited Estonia while writing the *Travels*, as a guest of Professor von Baer, the resident authority on natural history. The two scientists became fast friends."

Dean Mahamae added, "When von Humboldt died in 1859, von Baer went to Berlin as his literary executor, and discovered that von Humboldt had willed the original draft and notes of the *Travels* and the *Kosmos* to him for the Museum at Tartu University. Von Baer brought the volumes to the Museum where they've been kept for eighty years. The volumes are in the rare books section, while the appended notes are filed in the biological archives." Dean Mahamae had both the notes and the original volumes placed in a reading room at Heinrich's disposal.

Eventually their conversation drifted to the topic of the day — international tensions in the area. German influence in the area could only be described as substantial, even paramount, since the defeat of the Red Army by the Estonians in the 1920's. Despite military reversals, the Russians were becoming increasingly belligerent and interested in enlarging their sphere of influence to include political control of the Baltic States. Just as Jahn and Mahamae met in Tartu, the German and Russian governments were drafting the secret Nazi-Soviet Non-Aggression Treaty.

* * * *

The next five days were taken up with discussions of one kind or another and with time spent looking over the vast map and geological bulletin holdings of the university. Finally Heinrich had a chance to spend two days on von Humboldt's *Travels*.

There might be something in von Humboldt's original notes about precious metals that he had missed in the *Travels* and he would go over them with the finest of fine-toothed combs. He confided to *Herr* Schmidt, "I have a deep interest in von Humboldt and his explorations in my native land. And for the first time I will have the chance to look at von Humboldt's samples."

As Schmidt looked at him, a half smile crossing his face, Heinrich thought, *what might that hold in store for me?*

He briefly looked over the thirty volumes of the original draft of the *Travels*. The original was essentially the same as his personal, abbreviated copy published in 1889. However, the notes were considerably different, there being a wealth of new information on the geology of Mexico, especially noting the grade of silver reported in the official government documents had been fraudulently reported, possibly to drive up investment.

Also, curiously there were comments about Venezuela, especially the Andes, and then he found the maps showing the glacial limit in the *Coromoto*, and the position of *auriferous veins and la platina*. Only a chemist or mineralogist would recognize this as gold and platinum and the auriferous placers — "gold placers", Heinrich muttered out loud.

"A platinum placer," he continued out loud as if he was exclaiming to someone.

"*Grus Gott* (Greet God), what a find," he added, staring at the manuscript, talking to himself.

"So, von Humboldt managed to explore the Mérida Andes," he continued out loud. He stared at the notes and maps for what seemed like a long time.

At first Heinrich couldn't believe his eyes. There was the *Coromoto* drainage, just as he knew it, and here it was on von Humboldt's map with several 'x's' marking what he considered to be placer gold and vein gold deposits. Upstream, arrows pointed at vein gold and platinum in the middle of the valley, and there were numerous bits and pieces of data about tills, meltwater deposits, and rock flutings complete with measurements of thickness and areal extent. It was a very complete and accurate geological description, quite authentic, and presumably in von Humboldt's own hand. There were numerous remarks from Bonpland and some of the handwriting was apparently from him.

Von Humboldt had kept all reference to the Venezuelan Andes secret. He mentioned only his explorations of the Orinoco, the llanos and the Apure River in his *Travels*.

Heinrich sat staring at the logs for a long time not believing von Humboldt's description and analysis at first. Carefully rereading the logs, he began piecing it together, and realized the combination of an inaccessible part of the Andes, and the intervention of synchronicity...von Humboldt, in his quest for science had stumbled on a rare find of immense proportions. A find so incredible, it would be of immense importance to the fatherland, the birthplace of von Humboldt himself.

Considering his options, Heinrich thought of his future, of the extreme wealth that was his for the taking and what it would mean if he kept the information secret. He could return to Venezuela, mine the site himself and retire.

Heinrich decided not to send a wire to Germany as it would not be wise to alert other interested parties to the news of his find. He carefully hid the *Coromoto* maps and surveys in the middle of papers that Professor Born had given him. Even if he was searched, he doubted that anyone would see anything special and important about maps of the Andes and most probably the section descriptions would appear to be nothing more than the work of someone looking at rocks. He was careful to separate the maps from the sections, so that an inquiring mind would not connect them. Small samples of gold and platinum were hidden along with the documents, samples with enough mass so that they could be analyzed in Germany.

Herr Schmidt had looked at some of the reprints and passed over the maps without a second notice. However, he did mention that the sections looked to be very old, which made him somewhat inquisitive about their origin and what information they contained. Heinrich's mention of base metal deposits in the llanos seemed to contain him.

After bidding Dean Mahamae goodbye, Professor Jahn and *Herr* Schmidt boarded a train for Riga, transferring there to a German ship bound for Sassnitz. Once in Germany, they took a train to Berlin. Watching his partner settle down in the train compartment, with a bulletin on Russian gold from the Finnish Mining Institute, Professor Jahn thought long and hard about his discovery. He was well aware of the military importance of platinum-based metals, not to mention the gold. He was also well aware of what the find might mean for him, personally, especially if he were to keep it secret.

The historical significance of von Humboldt's discovery by itself was important enough to publish. The first description of a platinum placer by a pre-eminent scientist of the 19th Century, along with the analysis of precious metals collected by him in a major mountain range, would amount to a major addition to the scientific literature. Considering all that was in von Humboldt's logs and all that could be gained from the analysis of the samples he had collected at Tartu, Heinrich could make quite a name for himself. He was well aware of the importance of the samples to his discipline and for Germany. He hadn't made up his mind about whether to divulge what he had found to the mining institute director or simply stay mum and let sleeping dogs lie. Soon he would have to go one way or the other.

*　　*　　*　　*

After arriving in Berlin, Heinrich went directly to the Mining Institute straight away intending to meet *Herr Direktor* but discovered he had left for a late afternoon meeting. Heinrich sorted through his mail and decided to wait until tomorrow to see *Herr Direktor* and tell him what he had found in Estonia. He had made up his mind to turn the discovery of the gold-platinum ore over to the fatherland, and if handled properly, he was sure it would provide funds to help support Germany's rise to new independence in world affairs. Now it would be up to him to prove to *Herr Direktor* and possibly to

German intelligence the importance of von Humboldt's gold — *-the golden till* — -to the Reich.

The question was whether or not the gold and platinum could be recovered. He was sure it was still intact and unexplored by anyone else. He knew the area and also he knew the difficulties the Germans would face in trying to recover it. The *Coromoto* lay 150 km inland from the coast at Maracaibo and the only way in was by road, a long torturous and narrow track surfaced mainly with gravel. Depending on the insertion path, the dreaded *Motilone* might prove to be valuable allies, or terrible adversaries. If they knew about the gold they would most certainly try to take it themselves. The Venezuelan Army might go either way, as some were sympathetic to the Germans, and others favored the Americans.

And then there was the forest — the cloud forest — with its impenetrable wall of trees, snakes, tarantulas and darkness. It was as formidable as the *Motilone* might be, if provoked. It would take a determined force to penetrate the area, find the gold and platinum, and recover it, most probably with considerable blasting. His thoughts trailed off.

First, he would have to convince *Herr Direktor* of the Mining Institute, of his credibility and intentions. Second, he would have to demonstrate the authenticity of von Humboldt's notes that the maps were genuine beyond any doubt. This might be quite a task, but then he had read all of von Humboldt's material, and he was sure it was genuine. Beyond that he had some of von Humboldt's samples.

*   *   *   *

The next day Heinrich arrived at the institute at eight AM. His appointment with the *Direktor* was at nine and he had much to organize before then. For one thing he had to find his maps of the *Coromoto* that he was sure he had packed with him when he left Venezuela. He needed the maps of the entire Río Chama but that would take some time and he would have to request them through channels. A thought ran through his mind that maybe the institute had them in their files but he would have to check on this later on. In the meantime he ruffled through his maps, and not finding the *Coromoto* maps he started once more, only more slowly.

The second time around he found the maps. The scale was not large, only 1:50,000, approximately one inch to the mile, but it was sufficient to show the area and he knew now his credibility was on the rise, and he could show exactly what von Humboldt had mapped over a century ago. It was uncanny how accurate von Humboldt's maps were when compared with the plane table maps drawn up by Venezuelan cartographers. Von Humboldt was truly an amazing man, a genius in his own right.

Herr Direktor was exactly on time. He greeted Heinrich with considerable inquisitiveness wondering why he had not slept in after his long trip. But being eager to find out what Heinrich had brought with him from Finland and Estonia, he reminded himself of what Reichsführer Himmler had said nearly a month ago.

By direct order of the Führer, he recounted what Himmler had told him, "Your Mining Institute is to consider itself an arm of German Intelligence and you are to report directly to my aide. If there are any problems you are to report directly to me. Any recruits in the German military with geological backgrounds will be seconded to the Mining Institute and given an appropriate position. All information collected by the institute is to be considered secret, and Army Intelligence officers will decide what could be published and what is to remain the property of the state, and hence the property of the military."

Herr Direktor would never forget the order, let alone the stench of bad breath and cigarette smoke that emanated from Himmler. The Reichsführer had a tendency to closely approach anyone he talked to, adjusting his stance nearer the receiver of his messages, if one tried to shift away.

But no matter, he thought.

He would have to dissect the information Heinrich was about to give him and he would have to do it quickly. It was not impossible that Himmler's agents already knew what Heinrich had found in Estonia.

Heinrich recounted in great detail von Humboldt's expedition of 1799-1804 and the map he had drawn of the eastern cordillera in the upper *Coromoto* Valley, now named the Humboldt Massif. Using his own personal knowledge of the area, drawing upon all of his expertise as a geologist, Heinrich set out what he believed to be a significant find. After viewing the samples and precious metal reports written by von Humboldt, *Herr Direktor* fell into his chair.

Gathering a certain amount of decorum, he asked, "Where did you find the map again?"

"In von Humboldt's original notes of the *Travels* in the Tartu Museum. It's unpublished," *Herr Direktor*.

"There is the problem of authenticity," concluded the *Direktor*. "Are you sure they are authentic?"

"Beyond a reasonable doubt, *Herr Direktor*. As you will see, I am very familiar not only with von Humboldt's writings, but also with his field area. I know the region very well, and if you'll permit me, I have the maps of the area with me and I can show you von Humboldt's unpublished maps as well as official Venezuelan maps."

Herr Direktor rose and motioned for Heinrich to lead the way.

The two men walked to Heinrich's office. Heinrich closed the door and locked it. He carefully took out the maps and sections, unfurling and flattening them on the table. *Herr Direktor* stood looking at von Humboldt's maps, and then at the official topographic maps, noting the similarity. Not being a field geologist, he was slow to recognize the subtleties in the landscape, but he did note they were approximately the same. The descriptions of the gold veins interested him a great deal, and knowing more about precious ores in metamorphic terrain, he marveled at von Humboldt's precise sketches, apparently made very quickly, but engaging to the eye nonetheless. If von Humboldt didn't draw the sections, they had to be drawn by someone with a superb knowledge of geology and precious metals.

Herr Direktor sank into a chair, the Coromoto map in hand, as Heinrich reached into his desk drawer retrieving samples of Humboldt's gold and platinum. Opening the two sample bags he passed them to the *Direktor* who clearly evoked a mask of total astonishment. The samples were not only the purest he had ever seen, they were his ticket to rapid advancement in the government, perhaps even to the mining ministry.

It crossed his mind that Heinrich could have drawn the maps and sections, but he dismissed this, as the maps were old and faded. He said nothing but knew he should report this to German Intelligence as soon as possible. He would see *Oberst* Koenen tomorrow, or given the gravity of the situation, perhaps he should see him today. It would not do to hesitate, especially with the Reichsführer looking over shoulders and having spies everywhere. He would call as soon as Heinrich finished showing him the information. He would also tell *Herr* Schmidt to keep an eye on Heinrich, a close eye but he wouldn't tell him why. So far, only the two of them knew about the gold and platinum, and it would be a good idea to keep it that way until *Oberst* Koenen was apprized of the situation.

*   *   *   *

Oberst Koenen, monocle in place, looked every bit the intelligence officer. In another time he could have been a university professor or an accountant. He sat erect behind a huge wooden desk, large even by German standards, with every paper clip and pen neatly organized. When his secretary advised him that *Herr Direktor* requested to see him immediately, his first thought was to let it wait since he was totally engrossed in another matter. But his secretary suggested the matter was urgent, so he reluctantly agreed to see *Herr Direktor* at once. Heinrich accompanied *Herr Direktor* and the two men entered *Oberst*

Koenen's office where they presented the information to him, sketching out key points, leaving the details out.

Eyeing the *Direktor* and Heinrich, *Oberst* Koenen pronounced, "I suppose authenticity is the question here. We'll authenticate the maps and accompanying documents with our handwriting section and our own archivists. Also, the samples will have to be analyzed. Until then, and we will be swift I assure you, I think Professor Jahn will be required to stay in Berlin. We'll be in touch."

As they walked back to the Institute, Heinrich mentioned, "*Oberst* Koenen seemed skeptical of the information we presented and he was anything but friendly."

Herr Direktor predicted, "He'll check the information and find it to be absolutely genuine. It'll just take some time."

He looked at Heinrich who nodded but said nothing.

It'll just take some time, Heinrich thought. The two men walked slowly, purposefully and silent, all the way to the Institute.

For all my work, the Oberst will probably get a medal for this, he thought.

Seven

Hitler and *Aguila Negra*

June, 1939. Adolf Hitler rose earlier than usual, thinking about intelligence reports he had been briefed on the previous evening. The financial burden of resetting German industry on a war footing was looming large in the minds of some of his ministers and they continued to squabble amongst themselves over how to divide available funds.

Reichsminister Albert Speer, for example, argued that, "It could be done, but somehow they needed more capital than was available now, or likely to become available in the near future."

Speer's statement kept playing over and over again in his mind, but he dismissed his minister's lack of optimism, thinking he would find a way to do it.

One simply couldn't build the tanks, ships and airplanes that Hitler demanded of his ministers without funds and the funds were not in the banks, or among annexed/allied states like Austria and Italy. Hitler thought of alternative sources such as the Jewish population but even if they were fleeced of every *pfennig*, the Reich would need more, much more. The Swiss could be counted on to a point, but they loaned money at exorbitantly high interest rates, and the Central German Bank had warned against borrowing heavily to finance military expansion.

German merchantmen were hard at work along the Atlantic Coast, raising wrecks from the Spanish Main, and these had provided much needed additions to the coffers in Berlin, but still the Reich needed more capital, either in the form of gold and silver, or as loaned cash.

But then, Hitler remembered the French gold reserve, which was said to number billions of francs. He had written a memo advising his general staff to prepare a force to seize the French gold once the invasion had begun. The problem was timing, and he was sure the French treasury could not move fast enough to escape the juggernaut that would be headed their way, once he decided on an invasion date. He started to think about the French gold and then was wakened from his semi-somnambulant state by his aide, *Oberst* Stradl, who informed him that General Nagel wanted to see him as soon as possible. In fact, he waited outside and Hitler motioned to send him in.

Nagel, chief of the military financial section, had access to Hitler almost on a minute's notice. Since money loomed as the largest and most important problem in the Third Reich, Nagel was seen in the Chancellory almost daily. He had one of the largest staffs in a nearby office and ultimate power over the Central German Bank.

Hitler started, "What is it Nagel? We just met yesterday. Is there something of great importance bringing you here so early?"

"*Jawohl mein Führer*, of the gravest importance," replied Nagel. He then quickly recounted what Heinrich Jahn and *Herr Direktor* had told *Oberst* Koenen.

Hitler stood transfixed upon hearing the news.

After a moment, Hitler asked, "And the information is absolutely correct; there is no doubt as to its authenticity?"

"Absolutely no doubt *mein Führer*," Nagel concurred. "The staff in the archives and handwriting sections believes the documents to be in the hand and authorship of von Humboldt. The maps in the *Travels* are accurate and have been compared with maps supplied by Professor Jahn and from our own map section. They match perfectly and Professor Jahn is sure the gold and platinum are still in place in the Andes."

Letting this sink in, Nagel continued after a few seconds, "Our analytical section confirms the gold and platinum are of the highest quality; the gold is 99.9 % pure with virtually no silver. More than that, Professor Jahn is sure there is likely enough gold and platinum to make this one of the largest finds in South America. He's a true patriot, mein Führer, and should be well rewarded for bringing the gold and platinum to our attention."

Almost immediately, Nagel continued, "Analysis being conducted on the platinum samples Jahn provided confirm they contain iridium which we need for our fighter aircraft. The only problem is how to get it out and back to Germany. With iridium, we could build carburetor parts as technically efficient, and possibly superior, to those in the Spitfire. There is zero expansion and contraction with iridium fuel jets and our Messerschmitt fighter would have higher velocity and greater climbing speed."

As if struck by lightning, Hitler was swaying with the report in one hand, looking intensely at the floor. Falling into his chair, he folded the report into its 'eyes only' cover and closed it.

With Hitler staring at the report folder for what seemed like the longest time, Nagel became somewhat uneasy and started to shift in his chair. He thought about asking permission to smoke but decided against it. For a good two minutes, Hitler stared at the neatly folded report, and then rising slowly, uttered, "Leave this to me, Nagel."

"Bring Professor Jahn and the Mining Institute Direktor, what's his name, here tomorrow. I want to speak with them directly. Keep all this in strict confidence Nagel. And send in *Oberst* Stradl on your way out."

Sinking back into his chair, Hitler remembered a platinum briefing from the *Luftwaffe,* a singular plan to shadow a British merchantman sailing from Alaska with a load of the precious metal. *Reichmarshall* Goering wanted a U-boat for the mission but Admiral Donitz could not spare a boat with the war looming. As he thought it over, Venezuela seemed a more opportune target.

*   *   *   *

General Nagel left for his office and used a secure line to contact *Herr Direktor* at the Mining Institute. He informed *Herr Direktor* to report to the financial office at nine AM the following morning and to bring all relevant documents. Nothing was to be said or written of this project until so authorized.

Heinrich was stunned that on short notice he and *Herr Direktor* were summoned to the Chancellory to see Hitler, but he thought it was a sign that his information was believed and would be acted upon. The next morning he rose early and was in his office at seven AM. *Herr Direktor* came in soon after and together the two men left by taxi for the Chancellory and their meeting with General Nagel.

After seeing reports from the archival and analytical sections, the general had become a firm believer in the gold-platinum lode. He greeted Heinrich enthusiastically, congratulating him on his find, saying it might prove instrumental in financing important programs being planned at the highest levels.

Germans everywhere would be thankful for Heinrich's diligence and perseverance in tracking down the gold-platinum find. Almost as an afterthought he asked what the word 'till' meant and how glaciation entered into the gold deposit. Heinrich was in the middle of explaining how glaciation could concentrate the gold, when they were summoned to Hitler's office in the Chancellory.

Hitler was staring wide-eyed at the gold-platinum report when they entered. He immediately bounded to Heinrich and enthusiastically shook his hand, looking it seemed right through him. Bidding all to sit, Hitler went into a minor tirade that his intelligence section could not precisely determine how much gold and platinum might be in the *Coromoto* Valley in Venezuela. But then, he smiled, pointing out that it was too far away for his intelligence section to know about it, closing his remark with an expressionless, almost glassy stare.

He added, though, "Out intelligence people are very knowledgeable about South America in general and Venezuela in particular."

Hitler looked at the ceiling as he asked Heinrich pointed questions about the gold and platinum. He actually went from an irrational stance, to sober logical questioning, starting with von Humboldt and ending with Professor Jahn's final appraisal of all documents that he had taken to *Herr Direktor's* office.

Professor Jahn described the gold, platinum and iridium he had analyzed in von Humboldt's collection. Platinum, a steel gray-colored, ductile, malleable metal was considered strategic to the war effort. Highly resistant to corrosion, it was used as a chemical catalyst, for the manufacture of acid-proof containers, ignition fuses for bombs, and various micro-implements including dental equipment, not to mention airplane carburetors.

As Heinrich described the process of making a black powder of metallic platinum by reduction of platinum salts he could see from the faces of his audience that he had lost most of them, including Hitler.

This is rather little different from teaching a university class, he thought.

Reichsführer Himmler interjected, "About the iridium, *Herr* Professor, how is it related to platinum?"

Professor Jahn continued with a brief description of iridium, "As named from the iris of the eye, which has a membrane giving colors like the rainbow, it's famous for the changing color of some of its salts. As a white colored chemical element, with considerable heft, found in platinum ores, it's important in the manufacture of many scientific instruments and especially airplane parts. It's extremely stable, especially to air and water, and occurs along with osmium and rhodium in platinum. Associated with iron, iridium is magnetic. At this time less than two tons per year are mined worldwide and most of this goes to Britain"

Thinking it best to keep his summary short, *Herr* Jahn stopped to gauge the effect of his summary on Hitler and his aides. No, it would not do to add more technical details. *Better to leave it like this,* he thought.

Hitler summarized the main points of what Nagel and Heinrich had offered, and then suddenly broke off the discussion telling Heinrich and

Herr Direktor, "You'll be contacted soon and you are not to reveal any of this conversation, to members of the Institute, or anyone else."

They nodded their assent and started to leave. Hitler asked them to wait outside and motioned to General Nagel and Reichsführer Himmler to stay.

Once they had left, Hitler turned to Nagel, "I want your report and assessment of this on my desk tomorrow. From now on this matter will be handled by C section of Army Intelligence."

"Jawohl mein Führer," replied the General. As he turned to leave he knew that with C section involved the military wheels would turn very fast indeed. Hitler was thinking about taking action to recover the gold and platinum.

Looking at Himmler, Hitler directed, "Review the report and assessment and report to me as soon as possible." *Reichsführer* Himmler saluted and left behind Nagel.

*   *   *   *

General Fritz Bayer, chief of C section in Army Intelligence, was working late when he was summoned to the Chancellory to meet with Reichsführer Himmler the following day. He wondered what could be so pressing as to require his presence on short notice.

To his astonishment Hitler was present, along with General Nagel, and the *Direktor* of the Mining Institute.

Herr Direktor outlined the find of Humboldt's gold and platinum in the Andes, along with measures taken to authenticate the maps and documents that had been retrieved from Tartu, and additional information supplied by Professor Jahn.

Hitler interrupted near the end that the gold and platinum had been found by Alexander von Humboldt, a great German natural scientist, and rightfully belonged to the Third Reich. It was Germany's destiny to recover the gold and platinum; and the question of ownership was a *non sequitur,* as it did not follow from any previous agreement.

To Bayer it seemed everyone in the room except *Herr Direktor* was transfixed on the gold and platinum and not on the problem of getting to it and getting it out. Nevertheless, Hitler ordered Bayer to prepare a feasibility study to recover the precious metals and to maintain top secret status. The project, code named *Black Eagle–'Aguila Negra,'* was to be given top priority.

Only Bayer, and a handful of others, knew the platinum also contained iridium, a metal of strategic military importance. Finding traces of this metal in the von Humboldt samples was a prime motivator in giving the mission 'black status' which meant top secret. The Germans knew that the Americans had discovered platinum near Goodnews Bay in Alaska and that they were secretly selling it to the British.

A U-boat had monitored ships hauling cargo out of Goodnews Bay through the Beaufort Sea but with war on the horizon the U-boat had been recalled to the Atlantic. German intelligence had prepared a feasibility study to capture a UK merchant vessel with platinum or torpedo shipping from Goodnews Bay if and when war started. And, of course, to attack a US vessel the Americans would have to declare war on Germany for the plan to go operational. At the moment the Americans were centered on a non-interventionist policy. Everything depended on the flag carried by merchant vessels leaving the Beaufort seaport. UK flag vessels would be fair game once war was declared.

Mulling this over in his mind General Bayer concluded, *the operational situation could change and fast.*

German intelligence also knew the Americans had found platinum metals somewhere in Montana, but Army Intelligence had not yet fixed the exact location of the mine. In fact, naval and army intelligence were competing with one another to solve the platinum problem. The Venezuelan platinum find had come completely out of thin air, but both intelligence services had wasted no time bringing Professor Jahn's information through the system, to the attention of the Führer.

For the moment not even Professor Jahn was to know of the project and only members of C section could plan it.

"Time is of the essence," Bayer was told by Hitler and he was to report directly to Reichsführer Himmler. With a salute of *Heil Hitler*, the meeting broke up.

*   *   *   *

General Bayer went directly to his office and summoned two of his top aides—Major Mueller and *Oberst* Rommel (no relation to the famous general). Both were experienced line officers and Mueller had knowledge of demolitions having served with an engineer battalion in the Spanish Civil War. They would work out the details of recovering the vein gold and platinum. Mueller also had experience in South America, spoke Spanish, and had worked with submariners. And this project needed ingress and egress by submarine, as there was no other way in and out. But as Germany had one of the finest submarine fleets in the world, with well-trained officers and men, there should be no problem with overseas transport. They had U-boats poised to enter Caribbean waters once war broke out and that was only a matter of time. It would be best, however, if the gold and platinum could be recovered before the outbreak of hostilities.

Soon both Mueller and Rommel appeared and Bayer briefed them on the feasibility study, cautioning them to keep everything 'eyes only' for the moment. Then he remarked that his American intelligence contacts had recently reported the "eyes only" form of briefing employed by the American intelligence services. He thought the phrase useful and had started using it in Berlin. If it got back to the Americans, he would soon find out about it from Wehrmacht agents in Washington, and he would know there was a spy in his department. No one else in Berlin was authorized to use the "eyes only" direction. Time would tell.

Mueller and Rommel were directed to plan the project, find a man to lead it, preferably someone who spoke fluent Spanish, and an agent or agents to assist in Venezuela. The submarine service would need to lend a boat, possibly two boats, and the commander would have to be knowledgeable about the Caribbean. They were to give this the highest priority and to avoid alerting the usual diplomatic contacts. If the ore could be smuggled out of Venezuela, they were to consider using surface vessels, which would remove the risk of losing a U-boat.

All planning was to be executed in house and a report prepared for Reichsführer Himmler in the shortest possible time. *Black Eagle* would be a deceptive mission, designed to operate in hostile territory, with maximum assistance from Army and Naval Intelligence.

The force was to be kept as small as possible to give it a reasonable chance of success. The possibility that the force could go in under cover of a geological or agricultural mission was to be considered. Out of uniform, the force would be considered spies, and if captured, they would likely be jailed or executed. Since Venezuela and Germany did not have an extradition treaty the force would have no hope of returning to Germany if discovered. The planners had to consider taking Professor Jahn with them, as he was fluent in the native language, and also knowledgeable about the field area and the cargo.

Both Mueller and Rommel, impressed by the hurdles confronting them in planning this operation, as well as the problems a force would face in the field, started by enumerating all the assets they would need to successfully mine and remove a sizable portion of the gold-platinum lode. For one thing, access to the coast was fairly straightforward through Lake Maracaibo and isolated sections of beach could be found to land on. The landing force insertion had to come with no, or little moon, and at a sufficient distance from local towns to insure they landed undetected. The force would have to move upcountry through the towns of Valera, and Timotes to Apartaderos and down the Río Chama to Mucuy. There was no way to do it without detection by local farmers and possible contact with Venezuelan police or troops.

The land distance of approximately 150 kilometers was just too great for an invading force to penetrate and retreat with a heavy cargo of gold and platinum. Very soon both officers realized they would need subterfuge to make this work and the invading force would have to go as 'foreign experts' on loan to the Venezuelan government. This could be arranged and with forged papers and internal agents they stood a much better chance of success. Professor Jahn was the likely contact here, and since he was knowledgeable about Venezuelan Government policies and foreign-assisted projects, he would be the key person upon which the whole project hinged. Without him it would not succeed, but with him it could be pulled off provided there were no unforeseen local problems. They would have to ascertain Jahn's allegiance to the Third Reich. After all, he was also a citizen of Venezuela.

The report *Black Eagle — Aguila Negra* was on General Bayer's desk within two weeks. Reading it over quickly, he decided to leave it for the following day when he could devote several hours to it. If there was a flaw in it, he had to find it before Himmler did, as Himmler put up with C section, but always wanted to embarrass other officers whenever possible. And then there was Bormann, one of Hitler's ablest *leutnants*. An automaton really, but always watching, never speaking, and insanely jealous of C section and the secret files they worked on.

Admiral Canaris, head of German Military Intelligence, had warned Bayer of possible flaws and their consequences. No, a flaw was the last thing he wanted now and he would take at least two days to look over *Black Eagle*. Rommel and Mueller were good planners, very skilled and reliable, but one had to be careful. As he thumbed through the report, he noticed they had come to the conclusion that Jahn had to be included in the mission. He, too, had reached the same conclusion over a week ago. Perhaps the greatest concern would be the top secret status of the mission as Hitler was concerned about expressing German ambitions in Latin America to any great degree. If *Aguila Negra* were to be discovered, especially by the Americans, there could be a great deal of 'heavy weather' ahead. American concern about German control over some of the resources of South America, especially after the defeat of Republican forces in the Spanish Civil War, might reach a new pitch, if a German mission to recover strategic metals were exposed in Venezuela.

General Bayer thought about the British for a moment. If their agents got onto this, they would use it to fuel American anxiety about the strengthened role of Germany in the Caribbean, the southern gateway to the United States. Even though neutral, President Roosevelt, and indeed the whole of the U.S. Government, was friendly to Britain, so much so that they were not above selling strategic metals to their friends. Yes, *Aguila Negra* was important to the Reich and Hitler wanted it to go ahead, but there could be grave consequences if British or American intelligence found out about it. Hitler had a way of deflecting blame on to subordinates, and if this mission failed, Bayer would be remembered as the planner.

Yes, undoubtedly, I will be the first to go, he thought.

*   *   *   *

The next day General Bayer read the project report over several times and concluded that Mueller and Rommel had looked at every aspect of it. Insertion would require U-boats, as well as an experienced force and dedicated commander. The biggest problem would be to carry out rock blasting without alerting the local population, and this could be achieved by timing the blasts to coincide with late afternoon thunderstorms, or with low yield sticks of dynamite that did not make too much noise. Everything seemed to hinge on Professor Jahn. Would he do it? And did he have contacts in Venezuela who could be relied on for help? These were the major questions.

Both Mueller and Rommel argued for three boats but only two could be spared from the U-boat flotillas now operational. Given the time constraints there was no way to avoid using submarines. Smuggling out several thousand kilograms of gold and platinum was considered too risky. As General Bayer reviewed the report his two planners poured over army and navy files searching for the right units to carry out the mission.

Looking over the naval engineering schedules, Rommel turned to Mueller asserting, "Look at this Mueller. Two prototype U-boats — 501 and 231, both built to larger standards than usual and commanded by officers with extensive field training."

Coming over to Rommel's desk, Mueller was pleased to see that both boats had completed 'sea trials' and were judged operational.

"Just what we need," he pronounced, "but Admiral Donitz will not want to release them."

"Now we need to look at the personnel files on both commanding officers."

After scanning all the personnel files on available officers to lead the mission, two in particular caught their attention: *Kapitän* Walter Hahn, recently promoted to command of U-501 following trials in the Baltic and the North Sea, was also a nautical engineer. Along with *Kapitänleutnant* Adolph Langsdorff he had successfully penetrated the harbor nets at Scapa Flow in a secret exercise to test the defenses of the United Kingdom's Home Fleet.

Lying undetected within the great natural harbor, both boats could have sunk the *Ark Royal* and the *King George V*, two of the most prized possessions in the Royal Navy. Slipping out without notice, the two subs returned to Germany where Adolf Hitler had personally presented the Iron Cross with oak leaves and sword to *Kapitänleutnant* Hahn, promoting him to *Kapitän*. They had found the leader of the naval portion of *Aguila Negra*, code named *Humpback*.

The obvious choice for commander of the second boat was Adolph Langsdorff. Both men worked well together and had been shipmates since their days in the Naval Academy.

To round out the mission, Mueller and Rommel discovered an armed merchantman, actually a submarine tender, under the command of *Kapitän* Dirk Pirien, a navy veteran, on maneuvers in the Atlantic. Pirien, an experienced officer and veteran of the First War, had a long history of combined operations with U-boats. His record showed experience in the Caribbean and he was familiar with Venezuelan coastal waters. His ship, the *Sonne*, was perfect for the mission.

Upon recommending Hahn and Langsdorff to General Bayer, Mueller was stunned when the General asked Mueller if he would command the land segment of *Aguila Negra*–code named *Raven*.

General Bayer summed up his qualifications, "You speak the language fluently and you have the experience necessary to successfully complete the mission. You'll have the pick of the paratroopers who volunteer for the mission. To maintain absolute secrecy, the mission objective will be outlined to the force just prior to leaving Germany. All last minute leaves for volunteers will be canceled."

Major Mueller would have the chance to meet Hahn and Langsdorff before making a decision. Both naval officers were in Bremen, and Bayer was leaving immediately by plane for the U-boat base, to put the proposal to them.

Major Mueller saluted and replied "*Herr* General, I am prepared to do whatever is necessary to carry out the mission."

*   *   *   *

Later that evening, a Luftwaffe Heinkel landed at Bremen Naval Air Station and General Bayer and Major Mueller left by car for the U-boat base. Arriving at the naval base, both officers could see U-501 tied up in the sub pens. As they approached the massive boat, they were challenged by naval security, and asked for their identity papers. General Bayer and Major Mueller saluted and showed their identity cards from C section which indicated the highest security clearance. Security around the U-boats was tight as usual.

Across the river, Major Mueller could see two U-boats casting off their lines and making way with the current toward the boom which guarded the entrance to the sub pens. He folded his pass into his wallet and followed

General Bayer past the guard to the jetty where U-501 was tied up. He wondered what *Kapitän* Hahn looked like and knew he would find out soon enough.

Once through the outer perimeter they were again challenged by the night watch for U-501. They produced their identification and started up the gangway where *Kapitän* Hahn waited with *Kapitänleutnant* Langsdorff. Hahn was moderate in size, no more than 175 or 180 cm (~5 ft., 10 in.), with straight black hair and pale face that seemed scarred from wind and weather. The Major wondered how someone in the U-boat service could have a weather-beaten face.

Hahn's eyes were dark and intense well fitted to a stern face that seemed indifferent to smiling. His white-topped cap was slightly soiled indicating he had seen service, and while the rest of his garb including leather trousers and sea boots hardly singled him out for attention, his Knight's Cross with Oak Leaves and Sword caused Mueller to stiffen to attention.

After sizing up Hahn, the Major noted Langsdorff provided a near mirror image of Hahn in stature but with the demeanor of a salesman or accountant with no outward nautical appearance. His record, though, indicated he had graduated at the top of his class in the naval academy and achieved top scores with fleet operations. His narrow set eyes and stern face gave the impression of someone who acted on facts, emotion a foreign concept.

Had he been an accountant he would have gone over the books with the finest of combs, the Major thought.

After greeting and saluting the two visitors, *Kapitän* Hahn led the way below to the officer's wardroom. They passed a seaman at the bottom of the rail, part of the night watch, and Mueller noted he carried a sidearm.

As Hahn entered he called his second-in-command and told him, "Post a guard. We're not to be disturbed for any reason."

His second-in-command answered *"Jawohl, Herr Kapitän"* and shut the door behind him. The room was dark with a red glow, much darker than Mueller imagined it could be to see anything, much less read.

Maybe you adjust to it, he thought.

As this thought embedded itself in his mind his eyes slowly dilated taking in more light, the red images around him taking shape.

Once seated, *Kapitän* Hahn offered, "Would you like something hot?"

They both nodded, saying, "We'd like some of the famous navy coffee, *Black Death*."

Major Mueller looked around the ward room noting the small spaces, very confining from what he had been told by naval officers. Along the companionway he could see bunks stacked from floor to ceiling, only a draw curtain separating bunks from passage. Like many before him, the Major wondered how he would fare traveling on a U-boat with seasickness stalking him at every turn.

Looking at *Kapitän* Hahn he mentioned as he swung his legs under the table, "Is seasickness a problem with landlubbers like me?"

Kapitän Hahn studied the Major for a minute, replied, "Seasickness is like an old friend, returning when you least expect it. I've had many unfortunate encounters with it."

Major Mueller slumped in his seat thinking he would react badly to it. At that moment the curtain parted and a seaman entered with coffee and four cups on a tray.

After tasting some hot coffee, General Bayer asserted, "We've come to brief you on a mission of the utmost importance to the Reich and to the German military. He outlined the operational plan (Plate Two) called *Aguila Negra,* indicating in the process that both Hahn and Langsdorff, and their crews, could refuse the mission, if they wished. The General explained the need for large U-boats and the special nature of both U-501 and 231, including the special training of the crews in navigation, especially in shallow water.

General Bayer paused near the end of his briefing and looked Hahn and Langsdorff over trying to judge their reaction but their faces wore a mask of neutrality giving no emotion, no hint of a reaction. Thinking he might have overstated the situation he decided the two officers would have to go with his briefing. He could tell them no more. They knew only that they would put a land force to shore, leave for a time and return when the cargo was delivered at the exfiltration point. He added only that *Kapitän* Hahn would be overall mission commander; Major Mueller would command *Raven*, the land segment.

Kapitän Hahn could outline the general nature of the mission to his men, but revealing the specific objective would be going too far. It was top secret. He would need an answer at daybreak and both he and Major Mueller would be billeted in the Naval Air Station. Both Hahn and Langsdorff were to report to him there at 0800 hours the following morning.

Finishing the excellent coffee, General Bayer and Major Mueller thanked the two naval officers for their hospitality, saying, "We look forward to seeing you in the morning."

As they parted, Langsdorff left with them to return to U-231.

Kapitän Hahn called his men to stations, outlined the mission in general and indicated they were being asked to volunteer. He directed, "I will go! Any man, who, for one reason or another, does not wish to volunteer, can transfer out."

The vote was unanimous as the entire crew volunteered for the mission.

He expected the same to happen on Langsdorff's boat, as the crew would stay with their commander. He was sure of it!

Soon a courier arrived with a sealed message for *Kapitän* Hahn. Breaking the seal, he read, "Vote unanimous. U-231 volunteers to a man for *Aguila Negra*. I await your orders," signed A. Langsdorff.

Walter smiled and thought, *once more, we sail into the 'thick of things' on an ultra-secret mission.*

Next morning, after meeting with the General and Major Mueller, there would be a lot of planning to figure out how to reduce the crew to a skeleton force, to add some thirty to forty paratroopers as passengers, and above all carry the heavy cargo they were expecting later on. They would see to it somehow.

Plate Two. Map of the landing force insertion area and tactical exercise of *Aguila Negra*. The invading force tactical plan involved penetrating the coastal forest, Western Range and Rio Chama Valley to Mucuy and on to the Humboldt Massif.

Eight

Army Intelligence and Jack Ford

Chicago. June, 1939. Professor Jack Ford finished lecturing and stopped by the director's office for a chat, as he was wont to do on the odd Friday. Cedric Caine, at sixty-two, directed the Museum of Natural History in Chicago, one of the most prestigious teaching and research institutions of its kind in North America.

Jack was looking tense, perhaps as a result of his latest escapade in Bolivia, trying to recover Incan gold in competition with the French. It was always the French, or the Germans it seemed, and their intelligence was always good, and so were their agents.

Cedric pulled out two sherry glasses and the two archaeologists sat down to discuss the latest find.

Incan gold was rumored buried all over South America, as far north as Venezuela. In fact, the *Timotocuicas* Indians were known to have hidden gold icons outside their settlements in secret shrines, and Jack was eager to have a go at finding them, and their source.

Friday at most universities was a time when faculty and students alike slipped out early. The laboratories and classrooms emptied by early afternoon as faculty and students found better things to do. This Friday was no exception, so when two gentlemen appeared at the other end of the corridor, Jack thought they must be salesmen, or maybe just curious visitors. They most certainly were not students, but as he studied their clothing, he thought, m*aybe they're government people.*

They wore the same sport jackets and wool trousers with neutral colors and of course they wore ties matching the rest of their apparel. One carried a briefcase. Cedric rose from his chair and went out to see what they wanted. After a few minutes, Jack noticed that all three were headed in his direction.

Cedric was a great friend, and an even greater museum director, but he had a habit of deflecting problems directly at Jack and this would prove to be no exception. Jack had a strange feeling about this!

The two men introduced themselves as Mr. Huston and Mr. Smith of the historical section of the Library of Congress. They were interested in Venezuelan gold and other rare metals and had found out that Professor Jack Ford was an expert on gold in South America. They wondered if they could ask some questions.

Jack answered that he would do what he could. "What is it specifically you want to know?"

Mr. Huston continued, "We've been told there are massive gold and other rare metal deposits, especially platinum, near Mérida, in the Venezuelan Andes."

Somewhat taken aback, Jack thought for a moment, remarked, "Most gold is from further south. It was imported into the area as religious articles some centuries before the Spanish conquest. As far as I know there are no vein gold or placer deposits anywhere in the Mérida Andes. Platinum might be a possibility as Mérida is close to the platinum fields of Colombia, but to my knowledge no platinum finds are documented in the Venezuelan Andes."

With this admission from Jack the two 'historians' stiffened somewhat in their chairs whilst both gave themselves quizzical looks that verbalized as, *What!*

To Jack it was almost if they disbelieved what he had just said.

A silence ensued for a few seconds as Jack tried to figure out what these two government agents were all about. Breaking the spell, he let slip, "Remember the Spanish scoured Venezuela for gold and other precious metals. They left few stones unturned if you'll pardon the pun."

Putting on that 'I told you so' kind of look, Jack leaned back in his chair putting his feet up on a shelf.

The two men questioned him about Alexander von Humboldt. Jack thought for a few seconds and summarized what he knew about the famous naturalist.

"Von Humboldt was a scientist interested in natural history, not gold exploration, although I remember he was an expert mining engineer and mineralogist."

This seemed a pertinent connection for the two historians who relaxed somewhat, and by now Jack was wondering who they really worked for, as they didn't seem to know much about history. Mr. Smith, the smaller of the two agents, had the largest head with matching teeth Jack had ever seen, and he wondered how 'the face' would key out in his *Atlas of Ethnic People*. Probably, 'extra primitive,' he considered, as he broke into a wide wry smile. He must remember to tell Cedric about this.

Cedric sat bolt upright in his chair with a quizzical look that evoked both astonishment and bewilderment. He had heard it all before, various discussions about archaeological gold, but this time it seemed to involve a lot of other precious metals.

After a while Jack asked again, "What specifically are you looking for?"

The two men looked at each other, and back at Jack, finally admitting, "We work for Army Intelligence in Washington and we've intercepted information which leads us to believe that Hitler is interested in recovering a large gold-platinum find in Venezuela. The Germans plan to use it to finance their war machine. It's is an incredible find, we believe, somewhere near Mérida, in the Andes. Our informant claims there is a map based on von Humboldt's *Travels* or *Personal Narrative*, with exact descriptions of the gold and platinum deposits found originally by von Humboldt himself."

The two agents mentioned nothing about the iridium.

Jack thought long and hard and finally summed up, "I'm sure there's no mention of gold or platinum in the Andes, but I'll check the *Travels* and let you know. As far as I remember von Humboldt skirted the Venezuelan Andes, although he did considerable research in the Andes of Colombia and Ecuador."

The more Jack thought about it, the more he wondered about the possibility of gold and other rare metals in place there. The geological setting was right for gold and possibly platinum, only no one had reported it. If there was gold and platinum, and if the Germans recovered it, they would have a massive amount to finance their war machine and iridium for their fighter aircraft.

After thinking it over for a minute or two, Jack offered, "I'll read through the *Travels* and let you know what I find."

*   *   *   *

Over the next few days Jack read over the *Travels* and consulted with his father the elder Professor Felix Ford, on a likely location for gold and platinum in the Andes. Although retired, the elder member of the Ford clan was an international authority on precious metals. Jack often relied on his expertise to locate important deposits of gold in South America and elsewhere. Comparing notes, Jack and his father arrived at the same conclusion with similar passages in the *Travels,* all neatly underlined.

Jack looked at his dad, smiled and concluded, "While it isn't documented, it's possible that von Humboldt found gold and platinum and didn't report it."

Pausing for a few seconds, he summarized what they had both read, saying "Gold is most certainly not documented in the *Travels*, although it could be mentioned in the thirty volumes originally published in the nineteenth century. Maybe the Germans stumbled on passages of interest in the main work."

Jack looked at his father and began to think this was the likely connection. He could read it in his father's face. *Dad could never hide an idea*, he thought.

Jack could talk his way out of any situation with a 'poker' face but his dad always gave his hand away.

Jack summarized what they'd read out loud and locked it into his memory.

Alexander von Humboldt had been quite upset that his comments on silver in Mexico had led to an influx of investment that made human conditions worse and a very few individuals wealthy in the extreme. Maybe he'd decided to keep the Venezuelan find a secret. But why would he do this and for what reason? Was it to avoid a repetition of the fraudulent silver reports, or for some other reason?

Jack looked intently at his dad and waited but his father just shrugged, stood up, walked over to a bookcase and filed the *Travels*. Turning to face Jack, his demeanor metamorphosed from quizzical to informative. He pursed his lips as he always did, rested his chin on his index finger, and looked at Jack, concluding, "We can't prove von Humboldt found the gold and platinum but I think the Germans either surmise he found the metals or they have proof. If they are organizing a force to mine it and take it to Germany, they must have samples — real proof."

Jack focused on his beer without looking up, "I agree. I think von Humboldt kept his find secret and the Germans have stumbled on his samples. They wouldn't try such an aggressive move without proof. The samples must exist."

*   *   *   *

About two weeks later Mr. Smith and Mr. Huston returned to the museum and asked to see Jack and Cedric. Sitting in Professor Caine's office, Mr. Smith pronounced "We have authorization to hire Jack, er Professor Ford, as a civilian contractor for Army Intelligence. We want Professor Ford to fly to Venezuela, meet up with an internal agent by the name of Señor Sanchez, and investigate the area of the Mérida Andes to see if there is any truth to the intelligence we have from Germany. Our information is that a German raiding party is preparing to leave Germany momentarily, and it will travel by merchantman and submarine to Lake Maracaibo, where a small force will be dropped for an unspecified time to carry out the mission."

Pausing for a few seconds, Mr. Huston added, "The United States cannot put a full force ashore in a foreign country, but we can send Jack on a special mission, ostensibly as an archaeologist doing work for his museum."

It's a perfect cover, the agent thought but it would not do to mention it. He hastened to add, "Will you agree to this arrangement and release Dr. Ford to do 'research' in the Andes?"

Both agents turned to look at Cedric with inexpressive faces.

Cedric and Jack looked at each other with disguised amusement for they knew they now had the backing to look for the Bolivian gold figures, as well as a gold-platinum lode belonging to the great naturalist, Alexander von Humboldt.

What a find! Either one would be a major coup for the museum, Jack thought.

As he listened to the two agents spell out restrictions, Jack's face broke into a wry smile again as he realized Cedric would be relieved of the added problem of raising funds. With any luck the French would not know of the gold and so he would not meet any competition from the French side. But there could be German agents lurking about and Jack wondered *if Mr. Huston and Mr. Smith could be double agents working for the German Reich?*

Looking intently at the two men, both wearing identical suits, he put the idea out of his mind. They were US Government agents. They had short hair. They probably drove Plymouths. No doubt about it!

"Substantial payment would be forthcoming to the museum and to Jack and expenses are not a problem," advised Mr. Smith.

Jack mentioned use of a floatplane out of Key West, with a pilot he knew and trusted.

Both men nodded and Mr. Huston remarked, "That'll be possible. All other expenses will be covered by the U.S. Government. We'll meet you at Key West with cash, lots of it."

Jack added, "One additional item concerns my father, also Professor Ford, who just happens to be a geologist and natural historian. He'll be invaluable and he has contacts in Venezuela who might help. I'll need him but I may have to persuade him to come along."

"There should be no problem," one of the two men muttered. "You'll have to move fast to be in place when the Germans land,"

Mr. Huston, the taller of the two men concluded, "If something goes wrong, and you are captured, we'll disavow any knowledge of you and your mission. Is that clear, Professor Ford?"

"Yes, as always," answered Jack.

As he looked at Mr. Huston, Jack thought, *how I dislike government agents, always self-serving with inflated egos, they have to hire someone to work for them as they can't do anything themselves.*

Almost as an afterthought, he asked, "What about contacts?"

"Our agent in Venezuela, Señor Sanchez, will serve as communication link with us. When you finalize your plans, let us know when and where you want to meet with him. He'll pass all relevant information to you as soon as you arrive in South America," replied Mr. Huston.

*   *   *   *

After the two men left, Cedric summed up, "This one will be a lot more dangerous than any of your other projects."

"I know," concluded Jack, "But then I always go prepared," and he pulled a *kukri*, two *pukka's* and revolver from his briefcase and tossed them on the desk.

Looking intently at the revolver, Cedric thought to ask if Jack had carried it into class but decided not to dwell on it. The less he knew the better it was for the museum.

One revolver and three knives. Not very good odds against the Germans, Cedric thought.

Facing Cedric, Jack queried, "I guess you and Ted Cross can cover my classes while I'm gone?"

"Oh yes, no problem with that," Cedric replied but his mind was clearly elsewhere.

"I'll have to pack tonight, and ring up Pat, to see if he's free to leave in the next few days. I'll need a good pilot, as usual, and Pat Murray is one of the best. Also I'll need more ammunition and this time I'll bring a rifle. But first I'll have to drive over to Dad's place, and see if he'll help with contacts in South America, and come along as the geological expert."

Pausing to gauge the look on Cedric's face, he added, "Dad will put up a fuss about going, but I'll be hard pressed to pull this one off without his help."

Jack remembered his father's fluency with German, spoken without an accent. This might prove a major asset at some point.

Jack looked at Cedric and affirmed, "Since the demise of U-1 in 1927, the United States Government has not had a coherent intelligence family. It is not even up to Civil War standards, so I'm surprised that Huston and Smith have any information-gathering network at all. They must be Army officers in civilian clothes and most probably they simply receive intelligence from the British."

Cedric, with his hand on his chin, simply nodded, said nothing. Looking directly at Cedric, Jack queried, "I wonder who sanctioned the mission?" Continuing, he added, "It could come directly from FDR."

Studying Jack closely, Cedric answered, "Do you think? From the President?"

*　　*　　*　　*

Little did Jack and Cedric know that the previous day FDR had signed an order to stop the German recovery mission by all possible means and at all cost. No German code name had been assigned to it by their British contacts but sources indicated the German Mission was underway. FDR had conferred with two of his highest-ranking officers—Frank Knox, Secretary of the Navy and W.J. ('Wild Bill') Donovan of the President's Strategic Intelligence Section, soon to be transformed into the Office of Strategic Services (OSS). Within the President's inner circle, authority did not go any higher than that which had sanctioned the U.S. mission to Venezuela.

President Roosevelt made it clear to Donovan and Knox that the U.S. would not allow German activity in the Caribbean Sea, despite the presence of British and French colonies there. Army Intelligence believed that Hitler would follow the path of least resistance avoiding naval operations that might bring American belligerency. Nevertheless, recent reports from British Intelligence confirmed the German mission was operational. FDR pointed out that a gold find was one thing, but iridium was quite another, and the United States would do everything to stop the Germans from acquiring it. Donovan and Knox were authorized to find a way to stop them—whatever its code name. Expense was not a problem!

President Roosevelt was taken aback when the two officers recommended sending one individual, Jack Ford, a professor at The Chicago Museum of Natural History. As an archaeologist, he had worked for Army Intelligence on various "fact-finding missions" in the past, and had a way of getting things done. He had worked in Turkey on excavations that had provided useful information about German activity there, and most importantly, he had considerable experience in South America. Moreover, he spoke Spanish. While he had trained as a reserve officer in college, and had never served in the active army, his knowledge of weapons and demolitions was equivalent to any army officer. He was considered an excellent leader. Given his past performance, Secretary Knox and 'Wild Bill' Donovan would let him pick his own team, and as the President indicated, expense was not an issue here.

They cautioned that to be on the safe side, in case Jack Ford failed, they would disavow any knowledge of him as an operative of the United States Government.

The President eyed his two intelligence officers thinking how lucky he was to have Donovan and Knox as advisors. Indeed, Roosevelt and Donovan knew each other from their law school days at Columbia University and Donovan was well respected by the President. While he did not have a Security Council, as such, he realized that when he needed foreign intelligence, Donovan was his most trusted source. Knox was an organizer and could supply intelligence officers to assist Donovan in filtering through information supplied by foreign governments and the few agents working abroad for the United States.

Donovan's job was to assess risks to the U.S. Government, and it would seem that very soon, with ever widening German covert activity, the U.S. would have to start mounting operations in foreign lands, which was presently illegal. With isolationist sentiment running at an unprecedented high in the U.S., it would be political suicide for the U.S. to get involved in altercations with the Germans. As President, he had given the German covert operation a lot of thought. Since the time of President Madison, the U.S. had considered the Caribbean an American lake, and as President he couldn't allow an unfriendly power to operate there covertly or in the open.

Roosevelt smiled slightly while reaching for his cigarette holder. He thought about lighting up and then remembered Eleanor admonishing him for smoking too much. Dropping his bone-hollowed holder into its slot, he looked directly at 'Wild Bill' and asked, "Any problems with Mr. Hoover?"

Thinking for only a second or two, Donovan replied, "None that I know of Chief, but he did inquire about our new operation in New York City and requested we keep the FBI informed about our internal U.S. operations. I agreed, but I'll check with you before we tell him anything."

President Roosevelt acknowledged this information with a smile, but said nothing. The President normally favored an operating philosophy of competitive administration, allowing competing administrators to battle for turf, a kind of 'survival of the fittest' in the burgeoning political environment of pre-World War II Washington.

J. Edgar Hoover was an excellent administrator, and as head of the national police force, considered intelligence to fall within his mandate of fighting crime across the country. Hoover even wanted permission to set up an FBI liaison position in Army Intelligence to monitor movement of aliens entering the United States. Secretary Knox, with Roosevelt's approval, had vetoed this idea knowing that Hoover would take it personally and harbor a grudge.

So, Hoover watched and waited, albeit nervously, while Donovan established his newly formed Strategic Intelligence Section (SIS) in New York early in 1939. As a top-secret installation, Donovan operated under the authority of the Joint Chiefs of Staff, and as its Director, reported directly to the President. With a handful of officers acquired from among various Army and Navy branches, Donovan knew that what started as intelligence gathering would likely end up as full scale espionage, with much more than a technical staff. Agents would have to be recruited and trained, secret facilities constructed at various localities across the country, and intricate relations established with Allies abroad. Indeed, Roosevelt had directed him to carry out a top secret feasibility study for a Central Intelligence Service, the next stage in the evolution of SIS.

Roosevelt knew Donovan's small section would likely evolve into a full department within Army or Naval Intelligence, and if war broke out, into a much larger department. It would certainly be larger and better equipped than U-1. The U.S. had had intelligence gathering services off and on since the Civil War when both sides realized the importance of planning operations based on accurate up-to-date information about the enemy. But while the Union Army botched most of the intelligence gathered by its agents, the Confederates had been quick to act and gain the initiative. What killed the Confederate side was lack of men and *materiel,* not intelligence. It seemed to Roosevelt that without adequate intelligence the U.S. might fall prey to the Germans with their superbly organized military. And the Germans must surely have spies in the U.S. reporting on everything from the Congress to disposition of U.S. troops.

Yes, the President thought, Donovan, with all his contacts worldwide is the obvious choice for Director of a new Central Intelligence Service. Nevertheless, Donovan and Hoover would compete for the position of 'supreme spymaster.' Of this he was sure!

And it would be interesting to see who would come out on top. There were rumors around about Hoover's 'secret other life' but there was no doubt he would be a formidable adversary. However, the President would have the final word, and Donovan would be the logical choice. Whatever the outcome, a new intelligence agency would fall under the command of the Joint Chiefs and General Marshall.

"Warriors of the night," he muttered half aloud as Knox and Donovan looked at the President with nearly identical, bemused expressions, wondering what Franklin had been thinking. They might have guessed, but couldn't know exactly, that in little short of a year, the SIS with a greatly enlarged staff and expanded worldwide operation would move to New York. Located next to a British import-export firm operating as a front for William Stephenson's Anti-

Espionage Unit, they would begin gathering worldwide military intelligence on a great scale.

A forerunner of MI5, British Anti-Espionage had far reaching power to plan operations and deploy agents to deal with political and military objectives as might assist the war effort. Indeed the Americans had much to learn from the British who had been playing *The Great Game* for nearly a century and a half, training agents to infiltrate other nations and gather military information. By June 1942, Roosevelt would transform Donovan's Strategic Section into the OSS, forerunner of the CIA, and they would join the British in training agents to carry out intelligence gathering and espionage against the Axis powers.

President Roosevelt leaned back in his chair, looking intently at the two men, summarizing, "Let's hope Dr. Ford is successful. Our information is that if the platinum metal reaches Germany and the Germans refine and incorporate the iridium in the Messerschmitt, Britain may not be able to stop the coming air war that may well bring defeat. This project has the highest importance to the survival of the free world."

With that Secretary Knox and 'Wild Bill' Donovan nodded and got up to leave.

"By the way, gentlemen," remarked the President, "Whether or not Professor Ford is successful, I want to meet him when this is over."

The two men smiled, nodded, and then left the Lincoln Room of the White House where FDR held all his strategy and intelligence briefings. The very fact that he allotted an hour to them indicated it was a matter of the highest priority.

*   *   *   *

As they walked out of the White House, Secretary Knox looked at 'Wild Bill,' asking, "Are you sure one man is enough. You know this fellow Ford a lot better than I, but I would feel a bit more secure if we sent in some of our marines, perhaps."

Studying his friend's face for a while, Donovan could see a greater measure of concern than had registered earlier in the day when they discussed the mission together.

"No," Wild Bill answered. "Ford is the man for the job, trust me. I knew him at Columbia when I was there. He was capable of almost anything when he was a student, and he has since proved he has the ability for the sort of mission that we have here. He's a respected academic at a top institution, and his father a renowned geologist; they often confer on matters related to gold, which is what is at the center of the mission. Dr. Ford will pull it off one way or the other."

Secretary Knox replied, "Dr. Ford has an impressive resume, to say the least, it's just that he's hopelessly outnumbered."

Wild Bill smiled, summarizing, "He's almost always outnumbered, but he usually comes out on top. You'll see."

The two men walked along the Potomac on the way to their offices in Naval Headquarters. Donovan thought it ironic that Army Intelligence was directed from Naval Headquarters with liaison to SIS in New York. If war broke out, there would have to be a massive reorganization of the little nucleus of intelligence officers in the U.S. Government. They couldn't possibly handle a worldwide conflict!

Before parting Secretary Knox advised, "Better set up a project contact in Naval Headquarters. Who do you have as an operative in Venezuela?"

Wild Bill looked at the Sec Nav, answering, Señor Sanchez and he's already in Maracaibo."

Secretary Knox looked pleased.

Donovan added, "He's our top man in South America, well connected, and his information is always the best. He'll give Dr. Ford all the assistance he needs."

*　　*　　*　　*

Dr. Felix Ford was home reading when Jack pulled up. At sixty-eight, the elder member of the Ford Clan found retirement from university teaching among the most difficult milestones in his long and illustrious career. Providing his son with advice and information on his field projects just did not fill up enough of the day to keep him busy. Oh yes, he had the odd contract to look for precious metals here and there, but the thrill of teaching young would-be geologists and natural historians had vanished when he left his post at the university. But then the younger Dr. Ford usually had some interesting project in mind, something that would take his mind off the boredom of retirement.

But normally he'd call first, he thought...

He leaned back in his chair, placed a scrap of paper to mark the page in the book he was reading, and waited to see what his son was planning.

He had learned that when the younger Dr. Ford came unannounced there was trouble in the air. He couldn't wait to see what he was up to this time, as Jack had been hiding out from a French student who wanted to marry him, and she had been following him all over the campus. It had created quite a scandal and both Cedric and the museum board were happy when the girl became disenchanted, gave up, and left the country. No one was happier than Jack's father, as Jack had been hiding in his loft for weeks, to avoid having the girl find him at his own place. So what was he up to now?

Jack strolled up on the porch, through the door and went right to the refrigerator. As usual he found a bottle of beer and settled down, studying his father briefly, thinking, *he won't like this.*

Felix, looking inquisitive, said nothing.

Finally, Jack spoke, "What do you know about Venezuela? More importantly," he added, "Who do you know in Venezuela?"

"Another mission," his father exclaimed, "or just a vacation?"

"A little of both," Jack remarked. "But I need you to come along, and above all I need a contact in Venezuela, preferably someone who knows the geological scene. Can you think of anyone?"

His father, stunned momentarily, studied his son's face intently and realized this project must be very important and more than that, it must involve something other than artifacts.

Finally he asked, "What are we looking for, or let me rephrase, what is it that you're looking for?"

"Gold and platinum," Jack replied.

"Precious metals found by Alexander von Humboldt about 135 years ago — a lot of it. And the Germans are after it."

His father stiffened in his seat, as he had never become accustomed to the dangers inherent in many of Jack's 'scientific projects,' and this one seemed to have more danger in it than usual. Yes, they had read the *Travels* together and had concluded that von Humboldt had probably found the gold and platinum the government agents had inquired about but going after the gold and the Germans was more than he bargained for.

"How many Germans?" his father asked.

"Probably a lot of them and most probably they are working with agents in Venezuela. That's why I need a contact there and you're the likely source. Can you think of anyone?"

"Do you mean you are going down there to take on the Germans?" Felix recoiled slightly on saying this but recovered realizing Jack wanted him along on this one.

Stammering slightly, Felix blurted, "You mean we, don't you? You want me to go with you? What about funds?"

"I have a contract. It gets me out of teaching and Cedric is overjoyed he won't have to pay for it. We have lots of funds."

After a short reflection and some hesitation, Felix replied, "One fellow in particular who might help is Professor Pedro y Gomez, a colleague teaching at *UPEL* in Caracas. He's knowledgeable about the Andes and mining in particular.

Also, his daughter, hmm…her name will come to me. Celine, I think her name is, just happens to be a geologist. Both of them live in Caracas. I'll cable them tomorrow."

"No cables! German agents might have them staked out."

"We'll fly to Caracas and seek them out and I'd like to leave on the weekend."

"The weekend," Felix mumbled, thinking, *why is everything so rushed with Jack?*

Thinking for nearly a full minute, Jack asked, "What does *UPEL* stand for?"

"It stands for *Universidad Pedagogica Experimental Libertador*, a major university in Venezuela."

"Do you have tickets?" asked the elder Dr. Ford.

"Only to Key West,"

"And from there?"

"We use my friend Pat and his float plane."

"To Caracas in a float plane? Astonishing!" his father remarked, shaking his head.

Jack needed sleep badly so he finished his beer and left knowing his father had already made up his mind to go. The next day he cabled Pat, getting an almost instant reply that he wasn't booked with much fishing traffic, and could leave at any time.

Jack told him, "I'm on my way with Dad, and the destination is Caracas, through the island chain. We'll need the extra fuel tanks plus the usual extra food bags. Packs and sleeping bags would likely come in handy. Also the HF radio should be refitted in the float. Hopefully, it might reach the US."

*   *   *   *

Looking over his Curtiss Model 71 *Seagull*, Pat had to admit she was one fine aircraft. Originally built as a scouting and observational aircraft by Curtiss, Douglas and Voight, the first prototype was the X03C-l, renamed the Curtiss Model 71, built in 1933, and first flown in 1934. Built as float planes, some models had twin wheels in the central float. The Curtiss 71 soon became the 71A and SOC — 1 and these were modified in several ways to hold two to four passengers. Pat thought himself very lucky to have purchased a modified four-seat plane as a decommissioned aircraft from the U.S. Navy.

Powered with a 447-kW, 600 horsepower Pratt and Whitney R-1340-18 Wasp piston engine of the new radial design, the *Seagull* had a maximum speed of 265 kph (165 mph) and a ceiling of 4500 m, although with some loss of speed and greater consumption of fuel. Her empty weight was just over 1700 kg, and her maximum take-off weight of just under 2500 kg, meant she was perfect for the mission at hand. Landing in high-altitude lakes was tricky but he had done it many times with this bird.

Jack didn't say anything about high altitude, he thought, *but then he almost always operated in the mountains.*

After Pat got Jack's message he knew he had better check the engine to make sure all was okay before they headed south. Parts would be scarce down there and maybe it would be a good thing to bring a spare fuel pump and fuel lines. On the last project with Jack he had to retune the engine while Jack was off looking for a cave full of Peruvian gold. They had barely made it out after the Indians discovered Jack in one of their sacred shrines. The danger this time might be even greater, so he would bring extra spark plugs as well.

Looking at his bloodied finger, Pat realized he had been in a hurry to change the plugs and had pinched his fingers between the plug and the engine housing. With a large fist and even larger fingers he always had trouble wedging his fingers into small spaces and there was nothing smaller than the spark plugs on aircraft engines. His finger started to throb but he knew he would have to concentrate on completing the tune up. Jack and his father would arrive soon and Jack always wanted to get a move on.

*   *   *   *

Jack and his father flew out of Chicago on Pan Am to Washington and then on to Miami. From Miami they were picked up by intelligence agents and spirited to Pat's float base in Key West. Intelligence had checked on Mr. Pat Murray, to find that whenever Jack had gone on a museum mission, Mr. Murray accompanied him. While not completely unknown to the police, he was mainly clean, and hence, cleared to go on the mission. There was the question of an illegal firearm owned by Mr. Murray but there were no convictions.

The agents looked at Jack, with his leather flying jacket, wool fedora, and half growth of whiskers, standing next to his father wearing a wool sport jacket and Irish rain hat. Pat, with his grease stained hands and unkempt hair, looked a cross between pilot and mechanic. He would likely do to fly the two to Venezuela, but could the three of them take on a German force that might have platoon strength? Only Mr. Huston and Mr. Smith knew the full details of the mission, but the other agents with them surmised it must be important to get so much attention and so fast.

Pat started packing their gear and soon they were ready to get underway.

Jack climbed in first with his pack stowed in the rear compartment. Then he climbed into the co-pilot's right-hand seat and started looking at the air charts, to plot a course south, and slightly east to Caracas, Venezuela. Looking at the float plane Jack's father wished he had decided to take a commercial airline into Caracas. They might be lucky to make it to Venezuela, much less get to the Andes in this thing. Oh well, he had faith in his son as most fathers do. They taxied out into the open sea and were soon airborne.

The next stop would be Haiti for refueling, and then on to Cayman, Margarita Island and ultimately *Macuto* near Caracas. Professor Gomez was in for a surprise and the elder Dr. Ford hoped he would be at home. He hadn't seen him in five years.

Nine
Professor Gomez

June 30, 1939. Finishing a breakfast of fruit, complete with mangoes, papaya and melon, Professor Gomez was trying to hurry. For some reason he had overslept and his daughter Celine had as well. They were both late for classes, and they had to hurry to make it to the university by 9 AM. Even though classes started late from time to time, he liked to begin on the dot. He would make it by nine one way or the other. Celine was gathering up all her papers as she was due in the laboratory at about the same time. Shortly, they left their apartment and briskly walked five blocks to the campus.

Celine, at twenty-eight, had finished her doctorate in geology following in her famous father's footsteps. She was a mineralogist studying metamorphic terrane and of course she was very interested in the genesis of precious metals. Celine went off to the lab and Professor Gomez met his 9 and 11 AM classes. Around noon, as he walked back to his office, he caught sight of Professor Ford, his old friend from America. He couldn't believe his eyes. Also, there were two younger men with him who Professor Gomez did not know. One of the two wore a flying jacket that had seen better days. The third carried a worried look on his thin face looking like a character out of Conrad, a seaman perhaps sporting a newly sprouted beard. The third man, Professor Felix Ford, wore his usual attire. The one in the flying jacket was much younger and boyish looking.

As he approached them he saw Professor Ford's face light up and then he realized that the other man had to be his son. The third man must be a friend. He wondered what in the world would bring them all the way to Caracas.

They exchanged greetings and Professor Gomez ushered them into the geology building and up the stairs to his office. Professor Ford introduced his son and Pat and they settled down to talk. After some initial preamble the elder Ford let his son take the lead.

Jack explained the information they had about von Humboldt and the gold and precious metal location. Without beating around the bush he asked if Professor Gomez would help them find the gold and platinum they thought might be in the Andes.

Professor Gomez was clearly intrigued. Just then his daughter walked in and was surprised to see the three men in her father's office. He explained to her that these American friends were following in the footsteps of the famous Alexander von Humboldt.

Celine warily eyed the three. The eldest was clearly a professor, most probably one of high distinction, as he had the look of a field person, a naturalist or geologist. He was much like her famous father, a man with curiosity written across his face. The second, younger and quite good looking, had the adventurous look about him, and could be anything from a rancher to a government agent. He dressed like hunters she had seen in the Andes. The third fellow with a square face and stocky build might be an engineer or a mechanic. His flying jacket suggested he might be a pilot.

Her father, rising from his chair, introduced her to the elder Dr. Ford, then to his son Professor Jack Ford, and to Pat.

To her utter amazement she found the younger Dr. Ford to be nearly a carbon copy of his father whom she had heard much about from her father. He was clearly the leader of the three, and after her father's introduction, the elder Professor Ford mentioned their visit and where it might be safe to discuss it. He looked at Professor Gomez with the quizzical look that suggested and what about your daughter?

Professor Gomez advised, "You know that my daughter is my chief assistant and a specialist in her own right. My daughter knows as much about Venezuela as I do."

Jack weighed the options. Professor Gomez, this small white-haired man who had the look of a plantation farmer, was the key to the whole operation. Realizing they couldn't operate without Gomez, and presumably his daughter, he decided to follow his gut instincts and brief the professor and Celine. Thinking they would find one place as safe as another for a briefing, Jack decided to chance it and outline the mission, or most of it, right here in the professor's office. He was taking a gamble, a very big gamble, but for once he had few alternatives.

Correction he told himself, *I have no alternative.*

"This is the situation, professor. Our intelligence services believe that a Venezuelan professor by the name of Jahn has located maps and other information originally drawn up by Alexander von Humboldt, all related to gold-platinum ore in the Mérida Andes. He found this information, including maps, section descriptions and samples, while visiting Estonia and apparently it has been in the archives there for the last eighty years."

Jack continued, saying, "After removing this information from the Tartu Museum, Professor Jahn brought it to Germany and turned it over to the director of the German Mining Institute who delivered it to German Intelligence. Apparently it was brought to the attention of Hitler who ordered a feasibility study. It has now turned into a secret operation with the goal to recover the gold and platinum and bring it to Germany."

Pausing briefly to restructure the information in his mind, Jack continued, "The information we have is sketchy, at best, but we believe a force of German soldiers is en route to Venezuela at this very moment. Our information is that they will be landing somewhere along the Lake Maracaibo coast by submarine. We think they may be led by Professor Jahn, and that they will be working under cover, either as agricultural advisers or advisers to the Venezuelan Geological Survey. We do not know how many are in the force but there must be sufficient manpower to bring in explosives, as they hope to extricate some, or all of the gold and platinum in one operation.

We are here to foil their mission and if possible to see that the gold-platinum ore does not get to Germany. Since you are the knowledgeable authority on Andean geology we need your help to locate the exact location of the gold and thwart the German mission."

Jack studied the professor's face and thought, *nothing perturbs this guy. He looks as though he expected this all along.*

Professor Gomez looked intrigued by what Jack had said. Thinking for a moment and lacking any emotion, added, "I know Jahn. He's a professor at *UPEL* and a very bright mining engineer. Have you thought about the authenticity of the find? Do you really think it's possible that von Humboldt actually did find the gold and platinum and then not report it? It seems rather strange to say the least."

Jack replied, "German Intelligence, according to our reports, is convinced the gold and platinum are real and still in place, so much so that they have mounted a full scale operation to find it, complete with all the hazards if they are discovered. American Intelligence wants to monitor their progress and they think there is a logical connection between von Humboldt in the Andes around 140 years ago, the association with Estonia through his friend Karl Ernst Ritter von Baer and the Tartu University Museum, and Professor Jahn."

After pausing for a few seconds, Jack continued, "Jahn has been fully researched, and although it is possible he manufactured the information, it is highly unlikely he would turn over false documentation to German

Intelligence. They have a way of making traitors pay for treasonous acts like this. No, my own assessment is that Jahn is a German patriot and he sees this as his duty to the fatherland. He's a Venezuelan second, a German first, it seems."

Professor Gomez seemed to agree, but for a moment he stared out the window into the haze that was already beginning to form off in the distance. He marveled at Jack, the young scientist, and son of his oldest and trusted friend, right in the middle of what amounted to a military mission. *I must trust this fellow*, he thought, but if Jack is wrong about the German mission to recover the gold, there might be some repercussions. Nevertheless Jack's father was part of the American group and his integrity was without question. Yes, Jack's story is a credible one.

As he thought over what Jack had just outlined, Professor Gomez slumped back in his chair, brushed his grey hair with both hands, obviously deep in thought.

Breaking the silence, Jack opened, "What can you tell us about Jahn, professor?"

"You mean about his position here and his trip to Germany."

"No, we know about his position here and where he is now. Tell me about the man. Is he clever, an opportunist perhaps?"

"He's a very bright geologist, very knowledgeable about minerals and the Andes. He's a good teacher and an excellent field geologist. If, by chance, he happened on to a mineral find connected with von Humboldt in the Andes, he would very quickly put two and two together. He's of German ancestry, as you know, and he no doubt has strong ties to the fatherland with many relatives in Germany. He's clever but no opportunist."

"Is he rash, apt to do things on first impulse?"

"No, he's anything but rash. He'll observe and study a situation and then act."

"Does he have any military experience?"

Professor Gomez looked at Celine who showed no emotion at the line of questioning coming from Jack. Looking back at Jack, Professor Gomez said, "None that I know of. He was never in the army."

"What does he look like Professor? Do you have a photograph of him?"

Professor Gomez looked first at Jack with a surprised look and then once again at Celine.

Watching Gomez, Jack began to realize that Celine might know more about Jahn than her father.

Seemingly at a loss for words, Professor Gomez waited for his daughter to answer Jack.

Celine, looked directly at her father, and with a cool, almost acidic voice, remarked, "I went out with him for a time and I can find a photograph."

Professor Gomez looked relieved that Celine had offered the photograph.

Jack, somewhat taken aback by her revelation, wasn't prepared for this and all of a sudden he realized that he was sweating. As he wiped his forehead, he asked himself, *why not? She's a good looking woman and Jahn no doubt is an average type who knows a good thing when he sees it. Her relationship with Jahn might compromise the mission.*

Jack took all this into account and tried to forget Celine's romantic attachment with Jahn. Realizing he had blushed slightly, he regained his composure and asked, "Is he a capable man in the bush, used to using firearms and explosives?"

"Firearms are forbidden for citizens here, but explosives he's very familiar with. He's probably had permission to carry a rifle on excursions but only occasionally."

Pausing for a moment, Professor Gomez asked the prime question, "Do you really think he'll come back with an armed German force?"

"It's quite possible Professor, quite possible indeed."

Jack relaxed a little, leaned back in his chair and looked at his Dad and Pat. He was about to ask another question when Pat intervened, "About float bases, Professor. Is there one in operation at Bobures? I note in my logs that there was one there two years ago."

"I believe so but we must check to be sure."

Celine, added, "I have known Heinrich since I was a child. I took courses from him. I later dated him although I eventually broke it off. Even though he's of German ancestry I don't believe he would aid the Nazis cause. He's no fascist."

Jack focused on the fact that she broke off the relationship. Whatever lay behind the split, Celine was a forceful woman. She was beautiful to be sure but a determined woman who knew her own mind. He was beginning to like her. She was in her late twenties he judged, with a face that was both strong and serene, marked by calm blue eyes, the latter most unusual in someone of Spanish descent. He found himself focusing on her clothes, tight-fitting black trousers and high-laced boots that complemented her jet-black hair tied neatly in a bun, all very Spanish in expression. Perhaps more Spanish than Venezuelan? Her engaging smile formed a parabolic curve on her lips giving her an attractive facial geometry, one he found alluring.

Celine had the steadiest eyes he had ever seen and high cheekbones that tended to accentuate her various changes in expression. In any other circumstance she would have had a paralyzing effect on Jack. He realized he must seem the antithesis of what she might find romantically attractive but then he reminded himself this was no romantic enterprise. His last romance with the French student had sent him into a tailspin, one from which he was still recovering, an escapade that had nearly cost him his job. Jack collected his thoughts trying to avoid looking directly at Celine. And he sensed she took this as a snub.

As they absorbed what she said, silence filled the room. Finally, Jack concluded, "Fascist or not, he's German and he's presumably alerted German Intelligence about the existence and location of the gold-platinum ore body in the Andes. I think he'll return with a German force to mine the ore and return it to Germany. If they're successful, God help us."

"We must first help ourselves, *amigos*" advised Professor Gomez.

After a long silence, Professor Gomez continued, "I wonder where in the world the Germans will be headed: the western or eastern cordillera? It'll be necessary to observe them as they land and follow them to find out where the gold is hidden. Could the gold and platinum have survived the onslaught of the conquistadors and all the miners who followed? It seems impossible."

But many inaccessible valleys have never been explored for precious metals, so it is possible the gold-platinum ore is located in one of them, he thought.

With his chin resting on his hands, planted firmly on his desk, Professor Gomez summarized, "A great many people have searched for gold in the Mérida Andes and none has been found. Von Humboldt did not mention the Mérida Andes in the *Travels*. Still, it is a possibility and I have always counseled Celine to think about panning the sediment at the lower limit of glaciation in the drainages between Mérida and Santo Domingo."

The more Professor Gomez thought about it, the more he realized there were gaps in the chronology of von Humboldt's explorations, periods of time when the great explorer said little about where he was and what he was doing. Some gaps occurred in 1801 when he was in Venezuela, others in 1804 when he was in Cuba.

Suddenly it hit him! "If there's gold and platinum in the Mérida Andes, I bet it's located somewhere around Apartaderos," he blurted out.

Professor Gomez fumbled through some maps on a filing cabinet, and then finding the 1:250,000 sheet, pointed to the area. Jack was off his seat first, and soon he and Celine were peering at the area, with such intensity that neither of them realized how close they were to one another.

As they studied the maps together, Celine realized Jack's obsessive character was similar to her own. They were both interested in geology, but while she was interested in the science, he was interested in the gold. She had heard about his exploits in other parts of South America, his many narrow escapes and treasures of Incan gold that he had recovered for his museum. But was it for science or for personal reward?

Celine pulled back from the maps and studied Jack for a time. Her father had told her about the elder Professor Ford who carried a remarkable facial resemblance to Jack but in build was very different. Jack, built around a lithe and taut frame, was smaller and thinner than his father who had put on some weight with age. Age was catching up to Jack judging by thin strands of grey hair that gave his brown hair a streaked appearance. His demeanor suggested he might fade into or stand out in any crowd. His long nose seemed to extend right up through the crown of his hat. *He must never take his hat off,* she thought.

Jack was reputed to change form, a metamorphosis that must just be part of the myth that had grown up around him, she thought. Everyone spoke of his skill with the knife, the curved long knife that he no doubt had in his pack. And the revolver he was known to carry must be stashed in his coat. She remembered the story of some French archaeologists who had to run to escape the knife, only to run faster when Jack planted a blade into a tree next to them. Later Jack escaped across a gorge with some Incan icons.

But her thoughts trailed off...Jack was an interesting looking fellow and much like his famous father, the inestimable elder Professor Ford. Looking at the son again she found it hard to believe he also was a professor. But what would her father do now? Join them? If he did join them she would not let him go out alone.

After a short spell, Professor Gomez concluded "There's only one logical course and that is to take leave in the Andes. Perhaps we should go fishing for a while? I hear the '*trucha*' are biting well this time of year."

"But first we need a plan," asserted Jack, who had been working up a scheme since they left Florida. But everything hinged on the cooperation of Professor Gomez and his daughter.

Looking at Professor Gomez and Celine, Jack said, "If you agree, this is what we'll do. Pat will ferry you and Dad to Bobures where you'll organize a botanical field trip along the coast, with my father as visiting botanist. Pat will fly back and pick up Celine and me and we'll join you in Bobures soon thereafter. We'll secure the float plane at the Bobures wharf and Pat will stay there until we need him."

Pat and Professor Gomez nodded their assent. "If we're lucky our intelligence contact will let us know when the Germans are to land and approximately where."

"But first let's have a few drinks and supper at the German Club," offered Professor Gomez. "The food is delicious and the beer is the best in the world."

Jack hated the Nazis but the thought of good old German lager was just too much for him, so he agreed.

After some thought, Jack added, "There could be German agents about, but with our cover as naturalists on a collecting expedition, we'd best be open about everything. Dinner at the German Club seems the best strategy."

As they walked along toward the German Club, the elder Professor Ford asked, "Is this wise?"

"Trust me Dad, this is the wisest thing we can do. The best way to hunt the enemy is to stay close to them."

Somewhat shocked, the elder Professor Ford wondered how his son could keep his nerve up like this.

*   *   *   *

The German Club, built on a large tract of land near the *Universidad* campus, was a building of colonial architectural design, often frequented by faculty and staff. The grounds were open and spacious with many trees and a large open area for dining outside. Membership in the club was required to eat there, as was formal attire. While this latter requirement was no problem for the elder Professor Ford, it was for Pat and Jack. However, Professor Gomez, being about equal in size, had graciously agreed to provide them with the requisite blazer and tie.

Showing up at the gate, the Americans did not go unnoticed by the club staff. Jack had cautioned them to be careful about what they said. After finishing full meals of *chuletta* and cabbage salad, and a few beers, they left the club and retired to Professor Gomez's apartment. Waving away Jack's protests about staying with him, the professor and Celine led the way home, being careful to notice if anyone followed. It seemed their departure from the Club went unnoticed and no one trailed them through the nearly deserted streets.

The chief waiter, however, had taken notice of Professor Pedro y Gomez, his daughter and three American *amigos*. His contacts at the German Embassy had told him to report anything that involved geology or mining professors from the university, or any strange British or Americans who might show up. He didn't know why geology could be important to them but it was good not to be too inquisitive. He lifted the phone and dialed a number. After a single ring the phone was answered by Mr. Lorsch of the German Embassy, who took down all the information and passed it upstairs to the Intelligence officer.

Ten

Flight to Bobures

Professor Gomez called a colleague he could trust. He didn't reveal any secret matters, only that he had to go along the coast on a collecting expedition on short notice. As he frequently worked for mining companies, his colleague was not surprised when he asked him to cover his classes for two weeks. The summer session was nearing the end and his graduate students would take care of his exams.

Professor Gomez smiled, and advised Jack, "All is set now and we can leave when you're ready."

"Good."

Jack would likely hear from his Intelligence contact soon and he hoped they would send information on where and when the Germans would land. That would make the whole project a lot easier.

They had given Intelligence until 0800 tomorrow to let them know if they should change their plans. Otherwise their contact was instructed to find them at the Grand Hotel in Bobures sometime after 0800, on July fifteen. By 0800, the following day no contact had been made, and Jack realized they would have to leave to stay on schedule.

Professors Gomez and Ford took a taxi to the coast, and left in the float plane, while Jack and Celine went shopping for supplies. Pat would return late that afternoon and stay with them near the float base on the coast. They would fly out to Bobures the following morning and meet their fathers at the Grand Hotel.

While shopping Celine was amazed at how calm the younger Ford was. His greatest interest appeared to center around selecting certain grades of coffee. With a great and dangerous mission in the offing he was engrossed in selecting coffees with different aromas. He seemed oblivious to the possibility of failure and utterly preoccupied with choosing just the right food.

He's unique, she thought, *highly focused and quite unlike most men I've known*. Then she remembered stories her father had told her of the elder Ford who was renowned for collecting specimens in the most inhospitable places. Perhaps Jack had inherited his calm demeanor and adventurous spirit from his father?

'*Magni nominus umbra*,' Celine voiced out loud, remembering from Latin class, and loosely translated as '*the shadow of a great name*.'

Then she realized no one was listening. Was the young Dr. Ford a mere 'shadow' of his famous father, or a towering presence in his own right?

He seemed to be quite the leader, well organized, and in control. It was too soon to assess his scientific skills, but she imagined he had learned much from his father.

Shortly after they wrapped up all their purchases and drove to the coast. Pat would be returning soon with the plane and they had to secure lodging for the night. Celine almost wished Pat wasn't coming back tonight, as it would be interesting to stay the night alone with this interesting American. She knew many men in her profession, but she didn't feel at all romantically inclined toward any of them, except Heinrich Jahn. And now they were likely to run into Jahn while they were trying to assess what the Germans were up to in the mountains.

Was Jack a different type altogether?

She had best try not to ask herself so many questions and forget getting too familiar with Jack, especially with her father so close. She had to concentrate on the mission. Would the Germans come and if so what could they do to stop them. There were only five of them, and the Germans might outnumber them ten times or more.

Too many questions, she thought. They would just have to wait and see.

As they drove along, Celine asked, "Have you worked in South America before?"

Looking over at her, Jack replied, "Many times, maybe too many times, but I like it here."

"Why?" she asked.

"I'm an archaeologist and this is one of the richest areas in terms of cultural heritage in the New World. And I love the mountains," Jack replied.

Celine studied Jack's face for a time as they drove along and she realized he meant what he said. He had a serious demeanor like his father and he appeared to have a passion for his science that would guide his every move. She was sure of it.

Jack asked several questions about Venezuela and Celine's position at the university. With a wide grin, he added, "I guess we're both, more or less, the sum total of what our fathers wanted us to be. You, a geologist; me an 'artifact hunter.' Dad wanted me to go into geology, but I got hooked on archaeology in grade school."

"When did you decide on geology?" he asked.

"Early," she said, "I guess, in high school. I began working with Papa when I was five."

Soon they were driving along the wharf looking for the float but Pat was still out somewhere over the coast. After a few minutes, they could hear the whine of the big float and then caught sight of the plane circling off in the distance.

Watching the plane, Celine remarked, "Pat seems to know his trade."

"He knows it alright. He's one of the best damn pilots I've ever flown with, anywhere."

Realizing he let a swear word slip, Jack looked for a reaction. Sensing none he let it go but reminded himself to watch it in future. *These Catholics probably do not take to swearing much,* he thought.

Pat came around low overhead, looked the float base over, saw Jack and Celine on the dock, and then flared and landed easily even with a high swell. He taxied into the slot reserved for him and cut the engine. When Jack and Celine approached the plane, he yelled across that he had some minor repairs and refueling to look after. Jack grabbed the line and tied the plane up. He motioned toward the hotel on the side of the hill, yelled, "We'll stay the night and head out early in the morning."

Pat advised, "I'll be up directly, go ahead."

The two climbed up the dirt path to avoid taking the switchback walk and Jack noticed that the long strides up the steep hill didn't bother Celine one bit. They were at sea level and he was just a little short of breath when they reached the hotel.

It's a physiological law, he thought, *and I'm getting older and slower. How much longer can I keep this up? And what will happen in the Andes at 3000 meters and higher?*

"Well, time will tell," he muttered half out loud to himself. He would just have to wait and see.

Near the top of the hill, Celine slipped after dislodging a pebble. Sliding backwards a short distance, Jack caught her and pulled her the short distance to the top of the trail.

She wound her arm through his, saying, "You'd better make sure I don't fall again."

"I'll do that Celine."

And I won't read too much into this either, he thought.

She said nothing but just let Jack pull her along the path to the hotel. She kept her arm folded with his and seemed to like it that way.

"So," he taunted her, "you're more woman than geologist."

"You'd better watch it professor. I'm a bit of both."

Once at the hotel they ordered afternoon tea and waited for Pat to join them.

*   *   *   *

Next morning, just after a breakfast of strong coffee and corn *arepas,* the three lugged their packs to the dock and loaded them into the float plane. Jack helped Celine in and then passed her duffle bag in after her. She buckled up in the rear seat, to help distribute the load. Jack took the right seat up front. Pat got into the left seat, went through his pre-flight check list, and cranked over the engine. After checking the altimeter, fuel supply, oil pressure, rudder, ailerons, and elevator controls, he radioed the marine operator he was preparing to take off. The altimeter was still acting up and he would have to watch it closely, as he would be flying around the northern Andes where peaks rose to 5000 meters elevation, much higher than the operational altitude of the aircraft.

Pat idled the engine while waiting for the signal to taxi out from the wharf.

"I hate waiting for the okay to taxi at these float bases," he uttered to Jack who was busy looking over the air chart and topographic maps.

"There's not a plane in sight, yet the office is sitting on the mike. The engine is overheating and so am I."

Just as the 'I' came out, Jack muttered something about cutting across country once they were airborne and Pat got clearance to take off. As he pushed the throttle forward, Jack who had been leaning forward, fell back into the leather seat, his aeronautical maps falling on his lap.

"You shouldn't get so impatient Pat. Impatient people never live a long life."

"I won't live any life sitting here idling my engine."

With the all clear sign, Pat taxied out into the open water, checked for other aircraft, and then gave the big beast full throttle to take off. Soon they were airborne and came up to cruising altitude at around 1500 meters, with a nice view of the ochre-colored coast, complete with its ancient red soil and woodland canopy.

*   *   *   *

The flight to Bobures took about five hours and Jack realized that the day before Pat had probably flown at least ten hours, which meant that with repairs to the plane and refueling, Pat had worked a very long day. But that was the lot of a bush pilot, long days, punctuated with periods of inactivity, and occasionally sheer terror if mechanical failure occurred in the air. And inactivity he would have, until the Germans showed up, at which time they might have to beat a hasty retreat. Jack wondered if his intelligence contact would be on schedule at Bobures, as without some idea of when the invasion would take place, they would have a hard time finding the German force. Find it they must, because once inland it would be hit and miss, if they tried to anticipate where the Germans might be headed.

For the first time Jack realized the enormity of the problems facing them. The Germans had everything going for them. They had naval support on their side as well as numerical superiority and precise information as to where they were headed. Jack had nothing like this, except surprise. But could the Germans have been alerted from someone in American intelligence, or had the Venezuelans found out about it? After all, Venezuela had its own intelligence network and they might be inclined to help the Germans like the Argentineans had been doing.

Soon Lake Maracaibo came into view, with the town of Bobures situated along its eastern shore. Pat overflew the harbor and set up a landing pattern to put down close to the float base. Shortly they were taxiing in and Jack saw his father and Professor Gomez on the dock. After tying up, they unloaded everything and carried it into a car they had rented. Then they drove off to the Grand Hotel, and as Jack hoped, to a cold *cerveza*. He had heard the *Polar* Brewing Company had set up production of one of the finest lagers in South America, and he couldn't wait to sample one.

The hotel management had been told that they were a botanical collecting expedition from *UPEL*. This suited Jack just fine. It was perfect cover for what they were really up to. After dinner they retired to their rooms. At 2000 hours, the phone rang and a Señor Sanchez asked for Dr. Ford. Jack pulled out the photograph he had of Señor Sanchez and memorized the face. He had to confirm his identity before talking with him. Opening his pack he unfurled a .44 caliber colt, opened and spun the cylinder to insure he had it fully loaded. Securing a shoulder holster over his shirt, he slipped the revolver into it, and donned his jacket.

Watching his son slip the revolver under his jacket, prompted Felix to ask, "Is the revolver absolutely necessary?"

Until I know that Sanchez is really Sanchez, yes Dad, the revolver is insurance.

"Really, you think you might start shooting in a hotel?"

"It's a possibility."

The elder Professor Ford was speechless just as Celine and Professor Gomez entered the room wondering what interchange had taken place.

Noting that all were watching, Jack winked slightly, saying, "Best to go fully dressed."

Shaking his head, Felix could only say, "In this heat?"

"Heat or not, you can bet Sanchez is armed. Tit for tat, dad."

Taking one last look at the photo Jack thought, *the revolver is probably overkill but I would look pretty strange walking into the hotel lobby wearing my knives. Best to sort Sanchez out first and insure he's really the American agent. The Germans might have sent an imposter and an imposter would have only one mission, a killing one.*

* * * *

Jack walked into the hotel lobby which was nearly deserted except for a middle-age gentleman seated beneath a large palm and an elderly woman sipping wine at a small table at the opposite end of the room. The woman approached her wine with the determination of a seasoned drinker paying no attention to Jack. Señor Sanchez matched his photograph perfectly with the exception of his black mustache which seemed thicker than when the photo was taken. The clerk at the registration desk was having difficulty staying awake. Thankful there was no crowd, Jack relaxed as he tried to 'size up' his contact and felt the holster strap on his revolver loosen somewhat.

Sitting across from his contact, and out of earshot of anyone else, Sr. Sanchez wasted little time after inquiring about his trip in from Caracas. Jack was told the German insertion would take place about thirty-five km to the north along the Maracaibo coast at midnight three days from now. The main objective was near or close to Mucuy in the Eastern Cordillera. Señor Sanchez advised that Army Intelligence was sure the disembarkation of the German raiders would be along the Maracaibo coast.

The Germans would insert and disembark by U-boat. Because the telephone system did not extend inland to any great degree, it would be impossible to communicate once they left Bobures. He would wait at the Palace Hotel in Maracaibo and gave Jack a 'safe number' to call in Caracas if need be. Jack could continue to communicate with Army Intelligence directly or through Sr. Sanchez.

Jack wondered how Army Intelligence had sourced all this information but decided not to ask. No doubt British Intelligence fed all intel to Washington.

Jack thanked Señor Sanchez, shaking his hand while taking an imprint of the room and its occupants to insure nothing had changed, and then went to his room to report to his father and the others. They had a lot of planning to undertake to be in the right position when the Germans landed. There might be no need to be on hand for the landing, if they could move up country to intercept the Germans, either near Mucuy or at Apartaderos, the two main strategic positions shown on the map.

Would it be earlier or later? Jack wondered, trying not to dwell on it too much. After thinking he talked it over with his companions, considering it would be best to lie in wait at the coast and follow the Germans once they landed.

Jack summed it up, "Following the raiders to Apartaderos, which is a larger place, will make it easier to keep our cover. We can trail them down river toward Mérida. If discovered, we can say we've finished our research and are moving down toward a major center to re-supply ourselves."

They argued the pros and cons of this, retired to their rooms and then fell asleep.

*   *   *   *

The next morning Jack was up early studying the maps and noticed the lake at Mucubaji adjacent to Apartaderos. Why not use the float plane to fly to Mucubaji, tie up there, and wait at Apartaderos for the Germans to come to them? This was risky in case the Germans had other plans and Mucuy was not included in them.

At that point, Professor Gomez mentioned that he knew some of the *Motilone* along the coast, and he thought he could persuade one or two of them to keep an eye on the Germans when they landed.

There was a risk in alerting them, but surely the *Motilone* would know about the Germans soon enough, and even if they believed they were advising agriculturalists, they would not like them crossing the coastal lands they believed rightly belonged to them. Getting inland for the Germans was one thing but getting out would be quite another. He thought the *Motilone* he knew would help out and he proposed that he and Jack stay, observe the landing, and see which way the Germans headed.

In the meantime, Pat could fly to *Mucubaji,* to see if it was suitable to land his float plane, and hide it along the shore. Later, he could ferry the elder Dr. Ford and Celine there, and they could wait in Apartaderos for Jack and Professor Gomez. Jack liked this plan, particularly because it provided cover for their apparent 'botanical' expedition. After some discussion, they decided to let Pat fly up country while they reconnoitered the coast, and tried to establish contact with the *Motilone.*

Five hours later, Jack, his father, Celine and Professor Gomez drove up a dirt track from the coastal highway to a palm forest, to find a rather dilapidated place with a rundown banana plantation at the other end. Sitting on a stool in front of a broken down building was a short man, with thick black hair matted and strung out to his neck. He squinted slightly in the sunlight and then muttered something that brought two others out of the house. The three men appeared to recognize the professor and seemed friendly.

Listening to Professor Gomez speaking in the *Motilone* tongue, Jack didn't have a clue what was being said.

Soon Professor Gomez turned to Jack, remarked, "They'll help, but first they want to see you use the knife at your side."

"Why? What do they want to me to do with it?"

"They'll test you to see if you can use the tools of your trade. They are curious about your curved knife *amigo*. They want to see you use it," cautioned Professor Gomez, who thought, *don't miss, Jack. This is an important test, perhaps beyond all measure.*

Jack reached over his shoulder, pulled the *kukri*, flipped it tip to butt and took a bottle off the railing at five meters away.

"Is that good enough," he said confidently, flashing a wicked smile as he realized the *Motilone* appeared sufficiently impressed. They had never seen a curved blade like this, the quick and precise use of it caught them off guard. Being warriors they understood the value of a weapon, particularly a blade like this, but Jack wondered if he would have to use it on them sometime. Better not to think about it. They were told the Germans were acting as advisors to the farmers in the area, but they might be gathering intelligence for an invasion. Professor Gomez mentioned nothing about the gold.

If the *Motilone* knew there was gold involved, he and the rest of his group might find it difficult to leave even now. They agreed that Jack and Professor Gomez would return in two days time and lie in wait for the raiding force scheduled to land the next night.

Later, they drove back to Bobures to see what Pat had found in the mountains. Once in the hotel they discovered Pat had returned and all was well. *Mucubaji*, although a small lake, seemed perfect for his plane and he could easily hide it along the shore. The flying distance was barely 100 kilometers and he would not need to refuel. With his extra tanks he had plenty of fuel to fly in and out.

So far, so good, thought Jack. Everything seemed to be shaping up pretty well. Their intelligence was almost as good as the Germans and now they had enlisted help from some of the *Motilone*. Although not entirely trustworthy, they could ably assist in locating the raiding party and tracking it inland at least as far as Timotes. After that it would be up to Jack and his party to take over and then there was the minor problem of either thwarting the German mission or stealing the gold from them. The major problem was that Jack had not the slightest idea where the gold-platinum ore was located.

While he thought this over, Professor Gomez remarked, "If the Germans are really going to Mucuy, they must be planning a trek into the Humboldt Glacier. While there is no documentation of von Humboldt exploring in the Mérida Andes, the gold and platinum must be in the high Andes above Mucuy. It would be difficult to get to and little is known of it. Even less is known of the trail in through the treacherous cloud forest."

Professor Gomez thought again about the long gap in von Humboldt's *Travels* in 1804. Was it possible he explored the area without reporting it? He would have had to sail from Cuba to Venezuela, explore the Andes, and return to Cuba in less than three months.

Professor Gomez is proving his worth, thought Jack. *Now we have some idea of the objective, but it is impossible to beat the Germans to it because we do not know exactly the location of the gold and platinum. Without von Humboldt's maps it would be futile to try to stop them. We'll simply have to watch, be patient and wait for them to slip up.*

It was then that Professor Gomez mentioned, "We might consider contacting the mountain troopers stationed in Mérida." Professor Gomez continued, "I know Major Bezada, the base commander. I have often worked for the Army and Bezada's mountain troopers are experienced climbers who would lend a hand, if asked."

Considering the small force at his disposal, Jack concluded, "Assistance from the Venezuelan alpine troops seems to offer the best, perhaps the only, prospect for success."

This would call for a change in plan. Once the German force crossed the Río Chama into Mucuy, Professor Gomez would have to race to Mérida and return with Bezada and his men. Professor Gomez prayed with all his being that Bezada was at his base, but there was no way to find out now. They would have to wait and see.

Jack weighed the possibilities. He was ordered to thwart the German bid to recover the gold-platinum ore. This left him with wide latitude as to what to do with the recovered gold and platinum. He likely would have to leave it in Venezuela one way or the other; either in the mountains, or elsewhere, if the Germans managed to extract it. International law would not allow the Americans to take the gold and platinum in time of peace and there was no war on at the moment.

Jack wondered about Bezada and asked Professor Gomez why they should trust him with information about the Germans. Professor Gomez answered, "We haven't much choice, but I know the Major. He'll help us."

On the second day, Professor Gomez and Jack drove up country to link up with the *Motilone*, while Pat ferried Celine and the elder Dr. Ford to *Mucubaji*. From Mucubaji it was a short walk over the moraines to Apartaderos where they would set up a base and wait for the rest of the group.

Jack and Professor Gomez dropped their car at the plantation where two *Motilone* warriors waited for them. They walked up the coast to find a good vantage point to watch for the raiding party. The temperature was near forty degrees Celsius, and judging by the sweat running down their bodies, the humidity had to be close to 100 per cent.

They soon lost about as much sweat as they produced and Jack thought they were coming into equilibrium with the environment. He often joked that once you achieved equilibrium you wouldn't mind the high temperature. He had worked in so many hot, dirty, and inhospitable places that this one didn't bother him at all. It was all part of the job.

Night comes fast in the tropics, and soon it was nearly pitch black, with a blissful drop in temperature. With a half moon there was precious little light, which would make it difficult, and maybe impossible, to spot a submarine much less a raiding party. Intelligence predicted midnight and it was getting onto eleven PM when he caught the thin trailing wake of a periscope between one and two kilometers away. Some fifteen minutes later the sub broke the surface, coming up so fast it appeared like a rocket making Jack think the boat might be in trouble.

Then to his amazement, a second sub surfaced, and as he watched with his binoculars it pulled in closer to shore. He could see that all was well. Deck parties were releasing rubber rafts into the water and men were climbing down into the rafts. The raiding party was moving quickly and he tried to count them to get some idea of its size.

Without looking over to Professor Gomez and two Motilone warriors who lay beside him, Jack reviewed, "I count six men to a raft on average and eight rafts giving a total of around fifty men."

Professor Gomez watched as the figures disembarked on the shore and then advised, "Let them move off before doing anything. The Motilone will not lose them."

Jack murmured assent and watched the invasion force keeping his binoculars between blades of grass. "They paddle quickly as a group," he noted, "so they're probably well trained, and possibly an elite force."

Leho, one of the Motilone warriors whispered to Professor Gomez, as Jack continued to study the U-boats and rafts. Finally, Professor Gomez translated, "Leho counts about sixty Germans."

"How do your guys do it," he answered.

"They have lived in the bush all their lives. You'll see. They'll track the Germans long after they land."

The lead raft hit the beach first, with troopers spreading out quickly to each end of the beach, and to the dunes straight ahead. He counted seven men in the first boat, so there could be more like fifty-five or even sixty invaders in total. This was a sizable force and they definitely would be in need of help to deal with it. Major Bezada had better be on duty in Mérida. They were going to need him.

Eleven

German Agents Raid the Andes

August 1, 1939. The raiding party spread across the beach at precisely 11:45 PM, about fifteen minutes early. They obviously had good intelligence and realized the beach was deserted.

By their very movement, Jack surmised they were a special unit, most likely German marines or paratroopers, probably all volunteers. They would be hard to outwit and they were probably well armed and equipped for combat. How they would hide their weapons until they got deep into the Andes he had no idea. Still more importantly, they would have to bring a great quantity of explosives, and hide all of it as well. Jack noticed the submarines spent little time on the surface, probably no more than thirty minutes to land the force, submerging with speed. The land force was now on its own.

Without binoculars, the *Motilone* with them could only see the invaders as black dots. Through his binoculars, Jack could see the raiders carried rifles but he could not make out if they wore uniforms. They would have to get closer and most probably the force would move quickly inland, bivouacking during the day, traveling at night.

The *Motilone* motioned them to follow, as they wanted to get a closer look at the force. They left their position and marched quickly toward the beach.

About fifty minutes later they were close to the landing spot but the Germans had left and there was no trace of what had transpired about an hour ago. As the *Motilone* picked up the German trail, Jack noticed they were very good trackers, even in the faint light of a half moon they missed nothing. A slight imprint in the sand here, a single blade of bent grass there, provided clues as to which way the Germans had marched.

About two hours later the lead *Motilone* motioned for all to go down and soon faint voices were discernible to Jack, definitely German voices. The force had camped, most probably for the rest of the night. Now they could circle the camp and get an accurate count. Jack couldn't understand German and wished he had brought his father. *Too late to think of that now,* he thought.

He looked at Professor Gomez and crawled closer, whispering in his ear, "Keep talking low and to a minimum as our voices carry just like the German ones."

"The *Motilone* use only hand signals," whispered Professor Gomez. Jack wished he had said nothing.

Then Professor Gomez whispered to Jack, "One of the Germans mentioned Major Mueller. He must be the commander."

So, Gomez understands German, Jack thought. *What a wonderful surprise.*

Jack assumed the Germans would move with speed. He whispered again to Professor Gomez, "I heard Spanish being spoken in the camp, which might mean that Professor Jahn is with them."

After a couple of seconds, he added, "I'm also sure they landed out of uniform and are wearing field clothes. Apparently they'll head inland with a Spanish interpreter and pose, just as intelligence indicated, as advisors of one kind or another. The question is can they slip by any police or government officials they might encounter?"

The force was heavily armed with *Schmeisser* machine pistols and at one point Jack was close enough to see a silenced pistol, probably a *Mauser.* He saw lots of boxes and supposed that many were packed with demolitions or ammunition of one kind or another. With the amount of freight they were carrying, they would have to have transport, and supposedly, it would arrive in the early morning. They were only one kilometer or so from the dirt track, so it would be slow going to get all their gear to the road to rendezvous with whoever would pick them up.

* * * *

Jack slipped off to circle the camp making mental notes as to the number of soldiers and baggage. He watched his companion, one of the *Motilone* called Tiju. He was impressed by his ability to move silently and 'patrol' as the military types called it. *Tiju* could fade into the forest while keeping his weapon at the ready. Jack thought he could probably let loose with one dart after another and not miss a thing. He was at home in the bush in a way that few people are capable, and if you were looking for him, you would not see him until it was too late.

Jack was beginning to like these chaps, or at least this one. He thought they were every bit his equal. The two men continued to reconnoiter and then made their way back to Professor Gomez and his friend. They silently signaled it was time to pull back and wait. The Germans might send out roving patrols, and if they did, it would be relatively easy for the two groups to stumble upon one another. With the *Motilone* in the lead it would be possible to follow the Germans the next day.

The two *Motilone* tribesmen motioned to move off to the northeast, and when they were safely out of earshot, the lead tribesman suggested, with Professor Gomez translating, that they follow a path for about three kilometers and then hold up on high ground to wait for the Germans. He was sure they would take the Timotes Road, or an unused parallel dirt road, that had been built decades before for travel up country from the coast. Jack nodded assent and the four moved off to bivouac and get some sleep. They might need rest, if the Germans decided to move fast. At least it was cooler now with the temperature just below 30° C.

Once safely away from the German raiders, Jack discussed the reconnoitering he had accomplished with Professor Gomez. As far as he could determine these were experienced and well-trained troops. Very possibly they had experience in the Spanish Civil War. They were exceedingly well armed and presumably well equipped. The very fact that they carried so many heavy crates, most probably with enough explosives to carry out their gold extraction, did not bode well for his little group to stop them. This operation was beginning to turn into the most difficult of all 'projects' he had directed in the past. Jack wished he was in Turkey again. Comparatively, his Turkish operations were easy.

Soon after daybreak ten trucks appeared on the dirt track below their bivouac and Jack could see a number of figures scurrying out of the bush carrying crates of equipment. This was a well-organized rendezvous, and you had to hand it to them, it was very well planned. The Spanish speaking person appeared out of the lead truck and Jack fixed his glasses on him. In the dim early morning light he could see he was tall, blond and well built. He couldn't be sure but he did fit the description of Professor Jahn.

So, finally I've got a glimpse of Celine's old boyfriend, he thought. *Forget it, he told himself. This is work and you know what they say about mixing work and pleasure.*

But still it nagged him.

Moving closer, he and Professor Gomez watched from a hillside as the Germans moved their equipment to the coast road.

As they took note of the operation, Professor Gomez whispered to Jack, "The tall fellow is Heinrich Jahn. I'm sure of it. I cannot believe the Germans have invaded us. It's unbelievable."

Jack offered nothing but continued to study the entire group. The little talking he heard came from the helpers; the Germans used hand signals. Most probably they were German paratroopers, the best trained of all German military units. While they wouldn't be jumping from planes on this mission, there was little that they couldn't do. Their training was complete and they were expert at hand-to-hand combat and rescue missions of various kinds. They were said to be superior to British commandos and in the American army, as yet, there was no unit quite like them. He counted ten locals and at least forty-five or fifty Germans.

Their leader, presumably the Major they had overheard, stood next to the tall blond man with the latter giving all the orders, presumably in Spanish, although Jack and Professor Gomez were too far away to hear exactly. With minimum delay, the convoy started off on the Timotes road while Jack pondered their next move. With the slow crawl of the trucks, he figured that the load must be very heavy and most probably consisted of explosives and ammunition.

Professor Gomez predicted, "They'll need to hold up in Timotes and they must have a contact there."

Jack suggested they make their way back to the plantation, pick up the car, and follow them at a discrete distance. He wished he could radio his father but there was no way to do this as the radio was in the plane. Presumably his father and Celine were safe in Apartaderos and in the meantime had set up a base in the place described by Professor Gomez. Their only alternative now was to follow the Germans, but at least they were right on schedule. German punctuality certainly had its good side.

They took their time walking back to the plantation as they did not want to make contact with the convoy and it would be wise to let them push ahead on the Timotes road. Given the state of the road and the heavy load it would take most of the day to get there.

Jack advised Professor Gomez, "Tell the *Motilone* that we will contact them if we need help on the way out and thank them for me."

As Professor Gomez translated, they both looked at the *kukri* slung over his shoulder and smiled at him.

"They would like another demonstration," said Professor Gomez, but Jack replied, "It isn't over yet but tell them they may get one later on."

Noting the *Motilone* were satisfied with his retort, he continued, "I think these troopers will have a strong rear guard, so we'll have to follow slowly and watch our step. If discovered we'll have to pretend to be geologists with the Survey; well you don't have to pretend, but I do."

After pausing for a moment, Professor Gomez said, "I think we could pass for field scientists and luckily we have maps and hammers in the car."

Jack did some quick calculations and figured that if they left now, about three hours behind the Germans, they should catch up with the convoy around 5 PM. They would take it slow as he was sure the Germans would be watching their rear.

They turned to say good bye to the *Motilone* but they had vanished without a sound or trace. Jack looked at the ground and noticed they had been standing on rock and left no trace. Only Jack's boot prints were visible in the sand along with those of Professor Gomez.

"These guys are good," Jack noted admiringly. He looked at Professor Gomez who smiled that 'I know they are' kind of smile.

Professor Gomez added, "They've been at odds with a succession of governments, first Spanish and then Venezuelan, for centuries. They trust virtually no one and for good reason."

Thinking that Jack might like to know more, he added, "They are descendants of the Caracas Indians, who lived further east along the Caribbean Coast. The *Motilone* had to fight fiercely to overcome Spanish oppression. And fight they did for a century and a half, after which the Spanish established a tentative hegemony over them, more like an uneasy peace, broken from time to time when the *Motilone* rose up in rebellion."

Jack interjected, "What area do they control today?"

"One government after another learned to keep their distance so a large portion of the coast from *La Ceiba* south is almost totally controlled by the *Motilone*. The Germans were lucky to avoid contact with them for, if the main *Motilone* tribe had seen the landing, they might have attacked them. By now the two tribesmen who observed the landing will be on the way to report the landing party and the convoy."

Summing up the situation, Professor Gomez added, "While the *Motilone* might follow the Germans to Timotes, they'll not venture beyond that point, as this would mean eventual conflict with the State Police or the Army. But they'll surely be on the lookout for the return party and what they had collected for 'export.' The Germans will have their hands full on the coast."

Jack reasoned they might have to fight the *Motilone* as well as the Germans on the way out.

Jack thought, *Maybe it's possible to buy their assistance?*

He would have to discuss this with the professor later on. Buying their loyalty and assistance was a lot more to his liking than fighting them. He was starting to mellow with age, he felt, for in the old days, he would not have hesitated to try and find a ruse to outsmart the locals. Well, as they say, *Times change and so do people.*

*   *   *   *

Jack and Professor Gomez packed their gear in the car and drove off, turning left onto the dirt track that would take them to the main Bobures-Timotes road. They talked little, as Jack drove along the gravel road. Then Jack realized that, if they were stopped, it would be better to have Professor Gomez in the driver's seat to answer any questions in Spanish. They changed places and drove on. Jack decided, in case they got into deep trouble, it would be best to have his revolver at the ready, so he put it on the front seat under a shirt. He would rather have it in a shoulder holster, but it was too hot to wear a jacket, and without one he couldn't hide it.

They drove slowly and looked the landscape over very carefully. This would give them cover if they were stopped for questioning. To keep up the appearance of doing field research, Professor Gomez placed some maps on the front seat to use as a decoy if that eventuality occurred.

Jack remembered that he had left his extra ammunition in the trunk, and wished he had put it in the back seat in case he needed it in a hurry. His knives were also in the trunk and he should retrieve them as soon as they stopped somewhere. After two hours he asked Professor Gomez to pull over so he could relieve himself.

Funny thing about getting older, he told himself, is that you need to *drain the snake* more often and it is a definite inconvenience.

Jack noticed that Professor Gomez rarely had to relieve himself; he seemed to be in excellent shape just like his father. Both men were well into their sixties and the elder Dr. Ford had retired just three years ago. Retirement didn't stop him from doing research!

No sooner had he returned to the car, than a truck from the convoy appeared down the highway. The truck slowed and stopped ahead of them. A figure emerged from the passenger side and walked toward them. Jack could see it was the blond man and he was unarmed. He stopped short of the vehicle, blinked sharply and put his hand up touching his cap, saying, "Why Professor Gomez, I believe. What brings you out here?"

Gomez somewhat startled at first, recovered quickly, saying, "We're on a geological/botanical project with Professor Ford here from the University of Florida. He's interested in species growing on or near major fault lines and I'm showing him around."

Jahn studied their vehicle and looked Jack over. Jack took in Jahn's every move as he walked closer to the car. A near perfect specimen, Jahn was well built but without any distinguishing characteristics, outside of his blond hair and blue eyes. Jack could see why Celine might have become interested in him. Even though he had never been in the military, he exuded a kind of military presence. At least he looked the part.

"And you, Professor Jahn, I heard you left for Germany. What brings you back to Venezuela?"

Jahn was slightly shaken at Gomez's remark but with a shallow, still firm voice, replied, "I'm leading a mining advisory project for Geological Survey."

Jahn hoped his explanation would ring true with Gomez, but after exchanging a few minor bits and pieces of information, he realized that, if Gomez checked with the Survey, he would find the truth that no exchange existed. Would Gomez believe him?

Jahn studied Gomez and his passenger trying to decide what to do. He was tempted to signal the truck. In back under a tarp two paratroopers with machine pistols lay concealed awaiting orders. One word from him and they would destroy the truck and its occupants.

He decided to let 'sleeping dogs lie' and allow Gomez and his visitor to go about their business. It seemed they were stopping to collect specimens. This would occupy them long enough for him to rejoin the convoy outside of Timotes and leave them far behind.

Gomez and Jahn wished each other success in their ventures. Jahn walked back to his vehicle and drove off down the road the way he had come.

Once in the German vehicle, *Leutnant* Junghan asked, "Who're they and what're they doing here?"

Jahn replied, "They're botanists collecting specimens," and left it at that.

*   *   *   *

Jack breathed a sigh of relief, summarizing, "We're very lucky to have talked our way out of what most surely was a trap. Jahn was lying. I'm certain there were soldiers in the back of the truck, who almost certainly would've opened fire, if Jahn had requested it."

Jack had watched Jahn closely to make sure he stayed between them and the back of the truck. Professor Gomez was shaken slightly as Jack added, "If Jahn had moved away, I was prepared to open fire on the truck and kill him in the process."

Gomez realized, *this American is more than what his father made him out to be. The Motilone were right. He's a killer and a ruthless killer at that! Celine might be interested in him, even infatuated with him, but he'd have to tell her that he's unscrupulous, and like a caged animal, capable of almost anything. No wonder American Army Intelligence picked him for the job of stopping the Germans.*

Jack and Professor Gomez decided to halt for a time and carry on with their botanizing. Perhaps the Germans had stopped just up the road. They might even be watching them now as they spoke and planned the operation for the rest of the day. For the better part of an hour they went about the forest looking at plants and making notes. Finally, Jack offered, "I'm sure Jahn is watching us, or if not, he surely has detailed the task to one of his party."

"What do you suggest?"

"We'll give them plenty to look at, and report. After an hour or so of this foolishness, we'll continue slowly up the road following the rear guard of the convoy."

Jack silently congratulated himself on his diagnosis that the rear guard was highly trained. He remembered all the books he had read about Hannibal, which pointed to his success coming partly from speed, his flanking patrols, and above all his strong rear guard. The Gauls had found out, as had the Romans, that to attack his rear was to invite disaster, as his rear echelons held the hard core of his army.

This German force was equally professional, well trained, and its rear guard was hard core as well.

Jack realized he would have to watch out for Professor Jahn as he was a wily character. Had he acted on his own or had the commander, Major Mueller, sent him down the road to check the rear?

Jack wasn't sure, but from the way Jahn handled himself, he might prove to be a formidable adversary. However, his position between the car and the truck, whether deliberate or unconscious could have been a calculated risk or a mistake. Nevertheless, Jack decided to never assume anything with this fellow, as he seemed clever and devious, much more so than he had thought originally. And so was Major Mueller as he had no doubt assigned Jahn to check the rear of the column.

Even though they had been intercepted with ease Jack was sure they had managed to convince Jahn that they were on a botanical project. Surely, what Professor Gomez told Jahn sounded realistic enough, and if we were actually looking for changes in plant species across fault lines, where poisonous fluids could find their way to the surface, the collaboration of botanist and geologist was logical. Jahn had noticed sampling equipment with them and maps, so all looked realistic and plausible. Jahn seemed satisfied but then there was the question that Gomez might check with the authorities. This was the weak link that could bring the whole German operation down and Jack's great concern was that, when Jahn reported finding he and Gomez together, Mueller might think that Jahn should have raised the alarm and had them killed.

Anyway it didn't matter as they were free, and on the move, but they would have to be very careful. They followed the same routine of driving a short distance, and then checking the map and walking around looking at the vegetation. What Jack most feared was an ambush but there was no other choice. They had to continue on to Timotes and they expected to find the Germans either in the town or nearby.

* * * *

Jack and Professor Gomez finally arrived at the outskirts of Timotes around sundown and there was no sign of the convoy. They decided to drive into town to look for lodging, as Professor Gomez knew there was a pension right in the middle of town. Once they checked into the pension, they drove off looking for a place to have dinner and soon they noticed one of the convoy trucks parked near a restaurant. They drove on past the restaurant, and then pulled off the road about 200 meters away, hoping they could conceal the car and watch the restaurant to see where the truck went.

Soon, four men appeared near the truck and drove off to the southeast toward Apartaderos. So, the Germans were staying outside town, probably camped somewhere nearby. They followed the truck at a discrete distance, and eventually about 5 kilometers down the road, it turned off and headed north.

Professor Gomez watched for a time, then offered, "I'm familiar with the road and know where they'll camp."

The two men then drove back to Timotes, picked up some food at a local café, and went to bed. The morning would come early and they needed all the sleep they could get.

About 5 AM, Jack rose and wakened Professor Gomez, who rolled over for a few extra winks.

Finally, Jack roused him, saying in a loud voice, "We must move along quickly, take a different routine from yesterday, and if possible, get ahead of the Germans. It'd be best if we could get to Apartaderos first, find Dad, Celine and Pat and make plans to follow the convoy toward Mérida."

Responding to this, Professor Gomez rolled out of bed and dressed quickly.

Most probably, Professor Gomez was correct and the convoy would be heading for Mucuy and the *Coromoto* Drainage.

They drove out of Timotes, following the highway to Apartaderos, hoping the Germans would not be moving so early. As they neared the turnoff where they had seen the truck leave the road, all was quiet and peaceful, but as soon as they passed it, Jack had second thoughts. What if the convoy changed course and headed somewhere else?

He asked Professor Gomez about this, saying, "Where else could they go?

Professor Gomez replied, "That road is a dead end, and if the gold is up there, then von Humboldt did not find it. No, the gold is in or close to the *Coromoto*. It's closest to Mucuy. That is where the Germans are headed, and come to think of it, that is where Professor Jahn carried out some of his field research. He's most familiar with the area, and Jahn must think it ironic that after all his research, von Humboldt found the gold and platinum, and he missed it."

Jack thought long and hard about this and then Gomez added, "He's the logical choice for advisor to the German mission. However, if he leads them to the gold he'll be a traitor to his own country, and if government troops catch him, he'll hang for treason."

Considering all this, Jack tacitly agreed with Gomez. "You must be right," he said, and he felt much better about it as the thought crept in along with others.

But would Jahn swinging from a rope remove the competition for Celine? I have to stop this or I will miscalculate and miscalculations are always deadly.

They moved along, with all the speed they could muster from the old Dodge. About four hours later they stopped at the crest of a hill above Apartaderos. Jack got out of the truck and looked over the scene in the valley below. With houses stretched out along the Río Chama he could see the two hotels that Professor Gomez had told him about. Situated on the northern edge of town they were a likely stopping place for the Germans as they made their way up-country.

*   *   *   *

As small Andean towns go, Apartaderos was a small agricultural village, with no more than 200 inhabitants most of whom were potato farmers feeding the large and growing market in Caracas and Mérida. With a one-crop economy based on potatoes, the farmers were at the mercy of fluctuating prices, but they could do little more than deliver their potatoes to buyers from the cities, go-betweens or middlemen with transport and money.

Miguel and Julian, two local farmers working their fields above Apartaderos, were surprised to see two men and a girl walking toward town from *Mucubaji*. The girl, like one of the men, was younger, much younger it seemed. The other man was much older but still moved with a lively gait and had no trouble keeping up. They walked briskly. Obviously the men were from somewhere far away, as they were fair, gringos most likely. But the girl looked Spanish and had to be Venezuelan. Where had they come from? They could have walked up from Santo Domingo and over the divide, but that was not easy to do as the road had not been completed and only a dirt track existed between the two towns. Perhaps they had come from the *Los Frailes Mission* where the monks had given them shelter and food.

The two farmers wondered what they were doing in Apartaderos and watched with interest when the strangers turned in at Jose's place nearly in the center of the village. Jose would fill them in shortly. There were few secrets in a town the size of Apartaderos where Jose ran the local watering hole — the only one worth drinking at in town. They would find out what the visitors were up to when they stopped by Jose's Place for a drink but in the meantime they had work to do.

*   *   *   *

Jose looked up when Celine, Pat and the elder Dr. Ford walked into the bar. He remembered Celine; who could forget her? She was a beauty and he remembered she came from Catalonia originally and for a pure Spaniard — a Catalan — she was amazingly docile and polite. Normally the Spaniards, especially the women, were full of themselves and often quite arrogant and self-serving. She wasn't anything like this and he had always liked her. She visited Apartaderos often, in the company of her father, when they were doing geological research in the area. They seemed to come always in June during the rainy season, for some reason. This year they were a little late.

Celine walked up to Jose saying, "We are here to meet my father who is leading a geological/botanical expedition from America. This is Professor Ford and his assistant Pat from the U.S.. My father and Professor Ford's son will be here shortly and we'll need food and lodging."

Jose pointed to a table near the fireplace, "Please, take a seat and I'll see what we can prepare for you. This is not the usual tourist season, but I'm sure we can accommodate you. I'll have rooms prepared for you in the hotel."

As they seated themselves Celine noted a policeman seated at the bar. This might be the only police officer in the local area and perhaps it was the one officer who carried an unloaded gun and for good reason. Her father had mentioned that one police officer had shot himself in the foot trying to put down a disturbance. Hence the chief of police had taken all his ammunition but left him with the gun. The whole population got quite a laugh out of this but said nothing when he was around. As they ordered lunch she noted the officer got up and left without paying them any notice at all.

The trio waited through the night and the following day, wondering all the time when Jack and Professor Gomez would finally appear. About midday on the second day, while they were having lunch in the restaurant, Jack and Professor Gomez drove up to Jose's place. Jack wondered if this was the best place for them to stay as the convoy was due in soon and they were sure to stop here. Should they risk a second encounter with Professor Jahn? Obviously, Jose and half the town knew they were here and someone was sure to tell Jahn.

Professor Gomez obviously sensed what Jack was thinking and counseled "We've little choice *amigo*. The Germans most probably will stop here, but they daren't do anything as there is a police officer in this town and if they do anything to you here, it will be reported in Mérida and the police will investigate. This is the best cover for us, and if Jahn shows up, we'll tell him we're bound for *Mucubaji* and the Santo Domingo watershed. That should please him as we will be going in opposite directions."

Jack thought, *this stratagem might create problems, for, if we follow the German convoy and are discovered somewhere in the lower Río Chama valley, the game will be up. Anyway it appears we have little choice in the matter.*

*   *   *   *

Later that evening, the German convoy appeared coming in over the pass to *Aguila* Peak. At the head of the convoy, Major Mueller assessed the layout of the town. He could see the upper Río Chama Valley before him and the roadway leading toward Mérida. Situated on the broad lower reaches of an outwash fan, in the valley draining *Aguila* Peak and *Mifafi*, he suddenly remembered how his intelligence section had arrived at the code name *Black Eagle*. How perceptive of them to use a local name! Anyway perception was what they were good at, and that was the essence of the intelligence business, to be able to perceive the future outcome of an operation. He hoped their perception was all encompassing and that they hadn't overlooked anything.

Mueller stopped the lead vehicle and swept the town with his binoculars. "Nothing unusual; everything looks to be in order," he concluded, without looking at his passenger. He passed the binoculars to *Herr* Jahn and asked, "Your opinion *Herr* Professor."

As he waited for a reply, the Major remembered that originally he had been skeptical of taking Professor Jahn along. But when he looked at the size of the operation, and *Herr* Jahn's obvious expertise in geology, he knew it was the only way to go. And Jahn had proved to be very willing and able. He had a certain *forte* both in his professional field and with the men. Moreover, he had the qualities of a leader and showed good organizational sense. He would make a good officer.

After sweeping the town, Professor Jahn replied, "All is quiet. A few peasants working the fields, nothing more. Everything is normal. We can proceed."

Heinrich Jahn's parents had been *fellmonger's* dealing in sheepskins and hides, but this fellow was a cut above that. He had definite confidence in making split-second decisions, or maybe just bravado as Hans, his second-in-command thought, but he was pulling his own weight. He would remind the *Hauptmann* that killing Gomez and the American would have created more problems than it would have solved. In his opinion, Jahn had done the correct thing by getting information and not giving out much. Anyway German paratroopers did not kill civilians.

Mueller waved the convoy on and they drove closer to Apartaderos. Thinking about Professor Jahn, he thought, *I'll have to stop calling him professor. It doesn't fit the military profile.*

Mueller had to admit Jahn was providing all the information they needed and it was worth keeping him in the lead vehicle in case they ran into someone with questions. So far they had seen only local farmers who paid little attention to what appeared to be government vehicles moving along in a column. As they moved closer to the town, Mueller thought how backward and decrepit the hill country looked. Relative to Germany it was like driving through the Stone Age.

Looking over at *Herr* Jahn, Mueller asked, "Is there a place in town where we can get food and find a place for the men to camp?"

"Yes," Jahn answered, "at Jose's place in the center of town."

Mueller replied, "We'll have to exercise extreme caution here as one slip-up will give away the whole mission."

He gave the word for the lead truck to go into town and the remainder to stay outside, with one Spanish speaker per vehicle, in case someone with questions unexpectedly happened upon them. He hoped Jahn could secure lodging quickly as the men needed rest and they couldn't possibly drive down the Río Chama road in the dark. Vehicles moving at night might arouse suspicion, and they needed to move along at an orderly pace during daylight, to reach the trailhead at Mucuy about twenty kilometers away.

The lead vehicle drove up to Jose's place in town. As Jahn went in to see about rooms he was startled to see professors Gomez and Ford together with three other people having a meal by the fireplace. Celine's presence really rattled him, but he realized he couldn't back out.

Stiffening somewhat to attain composure, he stammered slightly, "How coincidental to meet you once again. Still botanizing Professor Gomez? I thought I left you along the coast road."

The encounter made him ill at ease and he could feel the sweat building up under his hat, droplets wetting his hair.

Professor Gomez leaned back in his chair, answered, "We've our group together now including Celine, my associates, and their assistant. We'll be heading toward Mount *Mucuñuque* in a day or so, and then down into the Santo Domingo River Valley ending up at *Los Frailes.*

Looking at his dad, Jack said, "My father is most interested in the therapeutic qualities of the *Espeletia,* the common *frailejón* used by the Indians to cure influenza and the common cold virus. He's interested in the taxonomic variations of it, as we have done research on it all over the tropical mountains, from Kenya to New Guinea. My interest is to study toxic fluids emanating from around the Boconó Fault, so we're lucky to be able to kill two birds with one stone, don't you think?"

Jahn nodded, smiled thinly, and then turned to Jose, saying, "My group needs a place to sleep. Is it possible to double up my crew in your three cabins out back? We'll be moving out tomorrow as we're on a government mission with Geological Survey."

Jose replied, "It'll take a little time to fix up the cabins for so many visitors but it can be done."

Herr Jahn answered, "It won't be necessary as we have our own bedrolls and some can sleep on the floor."

This seemed to satisfy Jose, who nodded to go ahead. Jahn tipped his hat to Celine and bid Dr. Ford and his little group goodbye.

*   *   *   *

Once outside, Jahn climbed into the lead vehicle and Mueller noticed a little sweat on his forehead.

"What is it?" he asked. "You look like you've seen a ghost."

"I just might have," he replied. "It was Dr. Ford and Gomez and they weren't alone."

Now Mueller was stiff in his seat.

"Who was in there?" he asked.

"Five of them, all having supper" replied Jahn.

"Professor Gomez, his daughter, Dr. Ford, his father, and an assistant. They say they're studying the *frailejón* and toxic fluids associated with the local fault systems. It's plausible, but there are too many coincidences. We keep running into them. It's almost as if they know what we're doing, but that's impossible isn't it?"

Mueller thought for a moment, and then replied, "Remember the report from the Embassy in Caracas, the one relayed to Intelligence and passed to me by the U-boat captain. The message said there were three Americans with Professor Gomez and his daughter, in the German Club, in Caracas, having dinner not longer than a week or so ago. Is this a coincidence?"

Turning away from Jahn, he looked at the restaurant, and asked, "Had they just coincidentally gone out for dinner and wound up in the German

Club, or were they really trying to deflect attention by showing up at a place where they would be noticed?"

Looking directly at Jahn, Mueller continued, "Maybe they did this with the purpose of posing as scientists enjoying a meal before setting out on a botanical expedition, or maybe they really are doing science?"

Heinrich sat rigidly in his seat, and while starting to sweat, said nothing.

"Was it a real expedition or a feint?"

Mueller has the habit of putting everything in military terms, Jahn thought, but he wondered if this was really a force out to stop them. Who could have sent them? The Americans? The British?

They are hardly a force, he thought

Mueller seemed to read his mind, saying "It's not likely the Americans are here on a military mission. America is not at war with Germany, not yet anyway. Our intelligence, the best in the world at the moment, has no information about American involvement. It must be just a coincidence, a minor report from Caracas, nothing more. After all, we have the men, the firepower and the munitions. My paratroopers are more than a match for the local police and the army such as it is. No, this is just happenstance, and somewhat unluckily for Drs. Ford and Professor Gomez should they discover the real plan. They are expendable!"

Heinrich stiffened somewhat at the thought that Celine might be killed but with pursed lips he looked at Mueller and shrugged. "If they're lying they'll pay for it."

The fatherland is everything, he thought.

Mueller leaned closer to Jahn, asked, "Did they say when they're leaving?"

"In a day or two, Major."

Mueller considered this for a moment, added, "Well then, we'll leave the rear guard to make sure they depart and then catch us at *Mucuy.* There should be no problem, Jahn. Try not to sweat so much."

Jahn was taken aback by his remark and resented it. Somehow meeting Ford and Gomez had a bad ring to it. He was sure they knew more than they let on, but how much? And how far would they go and what would they do? Major Mueller was right though, the best strategy was to make sure they departed in another direction.

After dinner, Jack, his Dad, Celine, her father and Pat retired to their rooms. They had a brief discussion in Jack's room and decided they had best start for *Mucubaji* on the following day. Since it was about 150 meters higher than Apartaderos, they'd have the high ground from which to watch the convoy, insuring it moved out down the Río Chama.

Jack said, "I think the Germans will watch us and they'll probably leave their rear guard to make sure we leave for Santo Domingo. I expect they'll follow us until we disappear over the divide."

Pat noted, "The float's well hidden along the shore of the lake so I doubt they'll find it." Anyway they decided to leave next morning.

* * * *

Major Mueller issued orders to rise early and organize the convoy so they could leave by 0800 hours for *Mucuy*. They might not make it in one day but he wanted to try. The rear guard of *Herr* Jahn, and led by *Hauptmann* Hans Pfeffer, his second-in-command, would see that Professor Ford's party left in the opposite direction. They were not to leave Apartaderos until that mission was accomplished. *Herr* Jahn remarked, that once in the Santo Domingo drainage, they would be out-of-touch with authorities and checking on the validity of the Geological Survey Assistance mission would be virtually impossible.

Herr Jahn started to feel better about their prospects. The only question was whether or not Dr. Ford and his party would actually leave. If they didn't leave, he knew Hans was ordered to deal with them by assassination, if necessary. They were German paratroopers and they didn't kill civilians. But if Dr. Ford was acting for a foreign power against Germany, he would follow the convoy and they would deal with him.

Hahn's paratroopers were well trained and it would not take much imagination to think about how they would carry out their orders. Heinrich watched Hans slowly pull his survival knife from its 'soundless' scabbard checking the blade. It was sharp, but as usual, this didn't stop him from using his stone to hone it down a little more. The scabbard intrigued Heinrich because normally, when you pull a knife out of a sheath a slight rubbing sound is heard. Yet, his knife makes no sound whatsoever.

In the bush, at night, with no wind, silence is deafening and the sound of a knife being pulled is enough to give you away to the trained ear. Heinrich had an eerie feeling, even from afar watching Dr. Ford, that he was such a person, one with a trained ear. He would hear it and most likely he would react to it. Heinrich flinched slightly as Hans suddenly whirled and threw the knife into the pine wall hitting a large knot directly in the center.

Heinrich had heard that in paratrooper training in Bavaria, Hans was judged the most accurate knife thrower amongst the officer cadets.

Obviously, Hans hadn't lost his touch with the lethal weapon, he thought. Heinrich hoped he wouldn't have to use it on Dr. Ford, for although he might be the enemy, he was a scientist not unlike himself.

*   *   *   *

Jack and his group rose at 7 AM and wandered into the dining hall for *desanyuno*. A little breakfast and coffee should set them up for the day. As the Germans also rose for breakfast and filtered into the room, Jose had a hard time trying to serve all of them. Some of the Germans had already eaten and Jack noticed they paid with *bolivars*. They were also very quiet and rarely spoke even to one another. As Jack paid up at the cash, he ran into *Herr* Jahn on the way out.

"Leaving today Dr. Ford," Jahn said.

"Yes," Jack replied. "We're collecting just above town and then planning to hike to Santo Domingo. And you?"

"Our itinerary is to drive through *Mucuchies* to Mérida in two days. We will be working in the *Mucujun* Valley after that."

Jack said "goodbye," and walked away, knowing they would be watched and that they would have to be very careful. He joined his father and Professor Gomez in his room and told them what Jahn had said. The best strategy was to leave at their leisure and walk toward *Mucubaji* keeping a close watch on their rear.

The Germans were not the only ones to watch the rear. Jack was expert at it and he wanted to be sure that he was right about his hunches. They left at 10 AM and walked up the path from Jose's toward the bedrock notch above the hotel. The path led through stands of pine affording thick cover, making it easy to watch the trail from dense patches of forest. It also provided cover to anyone trying to follow them.

These guys are professional, Jack thought. *They would not be easy to detect.*

About 200 meters from the notch a large boulder surrounded by pine with thick branches offered lots of cover.

Felix considered they might hide here, but Jack directed, "You, and the others, continue on along toward the divide. Take your time, and collect as many specimens as possible. I'll hide in the trees, with the boulder as cover, and watch the trail. If discovered, I'll say I'm collecting specimens as well."

The group continued on and very soon they were up in the notch.

Jack, comfortably situated in the trees, found he could peer over the boulder without being seen from the trail. He had only been in position for about ten minutes when he saw a pine branch move to the right of the trail. Then he saw one figure move out onto the trail and motion for three others to follow. The lead man was the short stocky man whom he judged was an officer; the other three were probably troopers and all appeared to be experienced bush travelers. They moved expertly through the underbrush keeping the trees between them and the notch.

However, they aren't looking to the flanks. They aren't that perfect, he thought.

Now Jack considered he could be in a perilous predicament, if they went all the way to the notch, and counted the figures below them on the other side. They would realize that one was missing. He watched praying that the disappearing figures in the notch would satisfy them that the Ford party was leaving for other parts. The four men continued along the fringe of the trail watching the departing figures. Then they stopped and looked around at their flanks. Something told Jack they were suspicious.

The figures then disappeared into the surrounding brush and he couldn't see them, which made him increasingly uneasy. He thought about abandoning his position and then realized that the best course was to remain still.

Suddenly two of the men appeared along the trail; one continued on up to the notch and the other went back along the trail whence he had come. The other two he couldn't see and he was sure they were making a sweep of the surrounding area. He started collecting some alpine wild flowers growing in the clear areas between the pines. He numbered a few sample bags, just in case the Germans showed up, and he took out his notebook.

He thought about unfurling his *kukri* and then decided to leave it in the pack. He fingered his revolver just to make sure he could grab it quickly, if the need arose. Then just below him and to the left he heard a twig snap. Responding to the noise he moved and a large bird, the *paraulata*, took flight. Watching the bird land in a nearby tree, Jack hoped it had not alerted the Germans, for if it had they would know exactly where he was hiding.

The Germans were close, and if discovered, he might have to fight. He unfurled his *kukri*, slipped his revolver from the holster, and waited. The sound of slight movement came closer and Jack's body went taut, and then relaxed, as he was ready to spring if need be. He saw a shadow, a thin wisp of an outline, moving slowly across the ground ahead of him, and then he heard a whistle, much like the local *paraulata* and it came from the trail.

The shadow stopped and then slowly moved away. One of the group had called the flanker in and Jack relaxed. He watched as the four grouped up near the clearing in the trail and then moved away toward Apartaderos. He was satisfied they would leave now for *Mucuy*, most likely satisfied that he and his father were what they said they were — botanists on an expedition.

Now the hunters became the hunted as Jack followed them along the path to Apartaderos. He dared not stay very close as they might be watching their rear again, but they appeared to be in a group and they walked fast toward the town. He got to within a half kilometer of Jose's place and saw that the column had left. The four men walked to their truck, and drove off down the road towards Mérida.

Jack walked up to the notch to join the rest of the group and filled them in on what had happened. They would follow but only after a few hours. He was sure they would find the Germans in *Mucuy*, preparing to negotiate the cloud forest, and venture up into the *Coromoto*. They lay down in the alpine meadow above Apartaderos and took in the serene vista before them.

Through his binoculars Jack could see the rear guard driving away to the south. The farmers were hard at work in the fields with their oxen. The wind was picking up and the blue sky of early morning was dissipating into cloud that would surely bring rain.

The 'one o'clock rain' will come early today, he thought. In the meantime a short rest is most welcome. The immediate threat is gone.

*   *   *   *

They walked slowly back into Apartaderos, picked up their car parked in back of Jose's place and drove toward San Rafael de Mucuchies where Professor Gomez said they could have a decent lunch. They needed to let the convoy move ahead, a long way ahead, so they could have maneuvering room. Along the way, Jack thought about the long and dangerous road they must follow.

What if someone else had found the gold and platinum, and all this was for naught? Assuming the Germans recovered the gold and platinum, how would he wrest it from them?

All this was like a fluid in his mind changing shape and form all the time. They were vastly outnumbered and he would have to rely on split-second decisions that could literally make or break the whole operation. He was especially mindful of Celine, and he did not want anything to happen to her, at least not on his account. So far she was pulling her own weight; she provided considerable input, and some of her comments had been very revealing. She was bright, she understood geology supremely well, and according to his father, Professor Gomez had trained her in the field since she was seven. It showed! She knew all about gold and she knew the Andes perfectly, from every drainage basin, to every topographic irregularity. She was invaluable, and of course, she spoke the language perfectly, another asset. But counting his assets and comparing them to the Germans, he realized he was still at a great disadvantage.

Professor Gomez suggested they split up when they got to the *Mucuy* turnoff on the Río Chama highway. He thought he should go to Mérida to find Major Bezada while Jack should reconnoiter the *Mucuy* trailhead. Jack agreed, but he thought the mountain troops should not come to the trailhead until he gave the word, because, if the Germans had left a rear guard, or listening post there, the presence of troops would give them away.

He told Professor Gomez, "We'll need the ten best troopers in the company and all should be well armed."

They drove to *San Rafael de Mucuchies* for lunch, and Jack thought the food splendid, just as the professor had predicted. Over lunch the five adventurers almost forgot about the mission. At this point, Jack suggested that Celine wait out the operation in Mérida, in comparative safety.

Celine disagreed saying, "I have been in the field with my father numerous times, in Colombia and Brazil, with bandits about. I can take care of myself as well as any man."

Jack was embarrassed, turning a strong shade of red, as he realized he had hit a nerve bringing a predictable response. She was a woman but she was also an equal. He would have to treat her as such.

The warmer mountain air at lower altitude almost made them drowsy. Jack thought that, in other circumstances, he might even have taken time off for a nap. However, when lunch was over, they drove out on to the highway and on down the Río Chama towards Mérida. They hoped all the Germans had left the highway for *Mucuy*, but they had no way of knowing exactly.

Professor Gomez mentioned a side road about three kilometers from the *Mucuy* turnoff where they could leave the main road and have a view overlooking *Mucuy*. With luck they might be able to count the vehicles at *Mucuy* and determine if they were all there. There were ten in all. If the rear guard was out on the main road, they would have a vehicle with them. Jack agreed this would be the best plan.

When they reached the side road, Professor Gomez turned off, and after a short distance, he stopped and said, "We can get out here and have a look."

Walking over to the edge of the terrace, Jack realized they had a superb view of *Mucuy*. Focusing his binoculars, he could see several vehicles in the small village, and after a minute or two he totaled nine trucks in all. One was missing. It was a good thing they had stopped otherwise they might have blundered into a roadblock and perhaps a fusillade of gunfire.

They would wait until the last vehicle appeared and then move on to Mérida to find Major Bezada. Professor Gomez hadn't been in Mérida for months and he had no way of knowing where Bezada might be. He could be out on patrol, but the weather had been so rainy that he imagined he would be at his base catching up on the usual backlog of paperwork. Like many modern day armies, the Venezuelan Army was mired down in a paper war. For every soldier who carried a gun, it seemed eight or ten were shuffling paper forms of one kind or another. Even the mountain troopers were subject to a deluge of paper from time to time. But if Major Bezada wasn't at his base it would be difficult to get any help at all.

They ended up spending the night on the terrace, as the truck didn't return until early the next morning. Apparently the German commander was taking no chances and maybe he fully expected the 'Ford Brigade' to come charging down the Río Chama highway. When they saw the truck pull into the center of the village, they drove back out onto the main road and headed down valley to the capital of Mérida State.

*   *   *   *

The headquarters of Commando 5 of the Venezuelan Army was situated at the junction of the *Mucujun* and Chama rivers. When Professor Gomez drove up to the main gate, he was relieved to see Bezada's horse tied to the hitching rack, along with the horses of his mountain troop.

Or at least he thought it was the entire troop. The guard asked their business and warily eyed the other four passengers in the car. He knew Professor Gomez and his daughter, but the other three *gringos* he had never seen before. He phoned the Major's office and was told to let them enter the post. They drove on up to the headquarters building and got out of the car. A sergeant showed them into the Major's outer office and they were told the major would be free momentarily. After a few minutes they were led into Major Bezada's office whereupon he rose to shake hands with Professor Gomez and Celine. Jack, his father and Pat were introduced and they all sat down.

Professor Gomez said, "Jack is the best person to explain the situation we're in," and Jack quickly summarized what had happened, with the professor translating.

Major Bezada's eyes widened when he heard of von Humboldt and the gold and other rare metals, and they widened still further when Jack said there was a German raiding party loose in the *Coromoto* Valley. The major immediately said he should radio headquarters, but Professor Gomez and Jack advised against this as they didn't know who else might know about the German operation.

It was entirely possible that higher ups in the government might have sanctioned it in the first place, as Venezuela was friendly with Hitler, and there were rumors of gold having left the country for Switzerland with the former Gomez (no relation to the professor) government. Major Bezada admitted this might be a possibility.

Jack proposed, "We follow the Germans up the *Coromoto*, reconnoiter their operation, and determine precisely what they're up to. If we manage to foil the German operation, then Bezada could arrest them. If not, we could follow the Germans out of the Andes and prevent them from escaping with the gold."

Professor Gomez offered, "If the gold-platinum lode is captured by Bezada, he'll come out a hero. His superiors will be forced to disavow any knowledge of the gold and the German operation."

"Yes," said Professor Gomez. "This looks to be the best plan."

The Major was interested in Jack's role in this and American involvement. Knowing the United States Government would disavow any knowledge of his operation, Jack replied, "I was hired by American Military Intelligence to intervene if the Germans try to remove the gold and platinum, and to use all means available to stop them. The American Government does not wish to steal the gold and platinum from Venezuela, but we also do not want to see it in the hands of the Germans, as it would be used for a sinister purpose."

Still, Jack knew he couldn't be seen meddling in South American affairs, as he was here 'unofficially.'

He smiled thinly, thinking, *Not even American Embassy officials know of my presence here.*

This seemed to satisfy the Major and he said he would select a dozen of his most capable men and lend assistance to them. He said it was normal for five to ten man patrols to move around in the mountains, either on maneuvers or on specific missions, and that their presence in *Mucuy* would not arouse suspicion.

The trip to Lake *Coromoto* would take at least two to three days, and the cloud forest was not a barrier they should attempt lightly, for there were terrific thunderstorms that occurred there, and with the dense foliage, poisonous snakes and tarantulas, they would find this a formidable obstacle.

"And so will the Germans," Jack added.

"Do you like tarantulas," the Major said.

"I know tarantulas," Jack replied. As a member of the family *Theraphosidae*, The Andean tarantula lives and burrows in soil and feeds at night on insects, small frogs, toads and mice. With a leg spread of twelve centimeters (five inches) these spiders have hairy bodies and legs, are dark colored, and have sluggish movements. While they can inflict painful bites, and have a fearsome appearance, they are harmless to humans.

"But I hate tarantulas as much as snakes," Jack added.

Professor Gomez replied, "You'll see both señor and soon!"

The Germans now had a twenty-four hour head start and Jack thought another 24 hours would give them a breather and allow the German mission to settle in. They didn't want to be 'hot on their heels' and Jack mentioned to the Major, "They have superb formations with a very alert rear guard. They'll employ the same tactics in the mountains, so your Venezuelan troopers will have to be very alert, and move cautiously up the *Coromoto.*"

They planned to move into *Mucuy* slowly on the following day and if all was clear, they would hike up into the cloud forest, and follow the Germans in to a point where they could gain altitude, and look down into the valley to see what they were up to. Jack prayed that the Germans would not do the same thing for two groups up high might collide with one another.

Jack and his group stayed with the commando unit that night dining with the Major in his quarters. After graduating from Central University in Caracas, Señor Bezada had joined the army. In his younger days he had enjoyed mountain climbing and loved the Andes, so when an opening appeared in the mountain troops, he had applied. From a subaltern in his younger days he slowly rose through the ranks to command the army unit in Mérida — *Commando 5.* With the army spread so thin he was pretty much the law in every direction for about 100 kilometers. The nearest commando unit was in Barinas on the eastern side of the Andes.

The following morning the group left by horseback from the military post. Major Bezada considered horses to be the best transport to approach *Mucuy,* and that was the way they always went into the mountains. They could leave their horses at *Mucuy* and there would be no vehicles should the Germans send out a team to reconnoiter their escape route. The farmer who took care of the horses could be trusted to keep silent and a few extra *bolivares* would seal his lips forever.

The *gringos* could be explained as visiting officials from the United States, but nevertheless their presence would raise some eyebrows especially since the Germans would have just passed through, going in the same general direction. But as we often say in the Deep South, m*añana mui amigo,* said the major, "We worry about it tomorrow."

* * * *

Mucuy was very quiet when the group rode in through the village, and on up through a magnificent stand of cedar, to the farm where they usually left their mounts. The farmer was surprised to see so many troopers and *gringo* visitors. He had farmed in *Mucuy* for twenty years and in all that time he had never seen so many foreigners and *gringos* all coming at almost the same time. Watching the farmer and the Major, Jack realized the alpine troopers must occasionally stop here, as the farmer seemed to know the Major really well.

Judging by his looks, the farmer was a man who had worked outside all his life, plowing fields with his team of oxen. He was all sinew, with not an extra ounce of fat on his lean frame. He looked sixty or so, but most likely he was in his forties. Hard physical work had a way of aging the body.

Doing excavations, whether for archaeology or agriculture takes its toll, Jack thought.

The Major explained they were on a government mission and the farmer seemed satisfied, although he shook his head with a certain amount of disbelief. Jack mentioned there were no vehicles. The farmer indicated the trucks had left two days before, apparently after the Germans marched into the *Coromoto* for what purpose he didn't know. The foreigners had a pre-arranged dropping place for their vehicles at the farm near the cloud forest boundary. The Germans also had a lot of equipment and they had hired about twenty of the villagers to help with foot transport through the cloud forest. They had paid them well in cash and the villagers had been only too eager to help.

The villagers were expected back in three to four days. Major Bezada thought they should intercept them and get the full story, but Jack wanted to bypass them, let them come down. They would reconnoiter the German camp by themselves. He didn't want to have one of the villagers, climb back up into the *Coromoto* to alert the Germans in the hopes of a reward. Group integrity and diligence was what counted now and they would need to keep their force together until they could figure out how to trap the Germans and stop the gold recovery operation.

Twelve
Jack Ford Steals the Gold

On the following day, the Ford group, together with twelve alpine troopers led by Major Bezada, moved on up the trail to Lago *Coromoto*. They were assisted by the German troop to some degree, as they had left an excellent trail in what was a very thick forest with enormous undergrowth of climbing figs and epiphytes. They moved with a point guard, flankers being all but impossible in the thick forest.

Despite the German trail making, the going was slow, and the point had to be relieved every 200 meters or so. After only a few hundred meters the column stopped when the second man in the formation was nearly bitten by a coral snake.

Jack realized that this would be a difficult passage and the presence of snakes gnawed at him; he hated snakes. He looked at Pat and predictably he was smiling, as he loved the little devils. One had always to check the cockpit of the plane as he often flew with them to Jack's horror. But the big threat was a possible discovery by German patrols or hired porters and he was sure the efficient Major had given orders to keep the rear secure.

Julio and Sergio, two of Major Bezada's troopers were the best point men, so Jack decided to spell them periodically, and to continue stopping every 100-meters or so, to the end of the first day. Placed side-by-side the two troopers were direct opposites in size with Julio short and thin and Sergio tall and well built. But in patrolling skill, both were senior sergeants with years of experience in the bush, tracking thieves and bandits. Listening intently, Jack could hear nothing, but he was sure the Germans were not far ahead. He decided to take Sergio, Julio and Professor Gomez with him to probe the trail and try to find the German camp. He wished he had the *Motilone* with him, as they would be at home in this forest, and they moved without making a sound.

The trail they followed was like an animal trail. The foliage was still underfoot, and it would be easy to step on a snare and find oneself dangling upside down from a *polylepis* tree. Here the trees were tall, well over twenty to twenty-five meters, but the Major said they would become stunted in the upper reaches of the forest where all species diminished. They took three or four calculated steps, then stopped and listened. Voices would carry far, even in this dense foliage, and Jack hoped the porters would be prone to talking amongst themselves. The Germans, of course, were trained to be silent.

They had gone about four kilometers when Jack heard the first voices and realized the force must be just ahead. He motioned to Julio and Sergio and Professor Gomez that they should return to their own group. There didn't appear to be a rear guard and the Germans had made less than six kilometers in two days. At this rate it would take them at least four or five days to break the timberline.

* * * *

Back at their bivouac, the group huddled over the maps and Professor Gomez said, "When we cross a small stream up ahead, we could veer to the north, leave the Germans to thrash on toward the *Coromoto*, and establish our own track toward a rock buttress about three kilometers away. Once at the buttress, we could negotiate the steep slopes and gain altitude quickly, putting ourselves above the Germans when they enter the *Coromoto*."

The route was untested, of course, but the advantage was that they would be in position to watch the German soldiers when they first entered the valley. The topography of the buttress was such that, if they wanted to enter the *Coromoto*, they could probably find a route down off the east side without being seen below.

Jack liked this plan and Major Bezada said his troop could handle the climbing with no problem. They moved off the path in case the Germans sent a patrol to check their rear, and set up a bivouac about 100-meters to the north. The night passed without incident. Even with a full moon, the forest was pitch-black. Occasionally the wind moved the tree canopy, but for the rest of the time it was silent. The next morning they waited until about 10 A.M. before moving out, and then Jack took the point about 20-meters ahead, followed by Sergio and Professor Gomez.

After two hours of slow going, Jack called a halt and advised, "Professor Gomez, and I'll move on ahead with Sergio to find the German force and/or the hired porters and the rest of the group should stay put."

He and Sergio moved out. They had not gone more than 200-meters when Jack heard someone coming and motioned for Sergio to alert the others. He and Professor Gomez slipped off the trail, hid under a magnificent large leafed tree, and listened intently. Jack noticed you could almost hide a medium size person under one leaf.

Soon three figures materialized on the trail not three meters away from them. They lay absolutely still as the three soldiers passed by. Jack hoped that Sergio had warned the others and that they had moved off the trail. He also hoped the three would not see any markings in the trail that would alert them to the presence of another party.

Jack heaved a sigh of relief when the three stopped at a fallen tree, deciding to light up, exchanging in the process some idle banter. So boredom on patrol was not limited to the American Army, he thought. The German Army had a bit of it too, and paratroopers to boot. Professor Gomez said nothing and the two men lay in their hideaway for the better part of thirty minutes. Obviously, the German patrol wanted the Major to think they had walked farther than they had. Shortly thereafter they started back up the trail to the *Coromoto* and passed once again within a few meters of Jack and his partner.

Once out of earshot Professor Gomez confirmed what Jack had suspected. "The Germans are moving slowly with their heavy loads, but the space is too confining and sooner or later either we or they will slip up and run into one another with terrible effect."

Jack replied, "It'd be good to find the stream you spotted on the map, veer off from the German trail, and beat them to the summit."

Professor Gomez nodded but said nothing.

Jack figured they would make another two kilometers today, maybe more, and with luck his group should make it to the stream by nightfall, or early tomorrow.

They rejoined the main group and waited a couple of hours to give the Germans time to push on ahead. In the meantime they ate a bit of jerky that Jack always carried with him. Major Bezada's men offered some dried and salted meat and fish; the meat had the taste of jerky and the fish something like kippered herring. As they opened their canned food Jack advised, "Take the meat out, close the cans, wrap the remainder tight and put the cans back in your packs. Smell carries, and if the Germans have an experienced bushwacker with them, he may detect us."

Later they moved out on the main trail and with Jack on point they moved on behind the Germans hoping that there would be no rear guard contact. By mid afternoon they came to the stream they were to follow to the north. The main group followed the stream while Sergio and Jack followed the German force to determine just how close they were to reaching the timberline. Jack cautioned his father and Professor Gomez not to leave any sign that they had left the main trail. They must move with great caution and not leave footprints or bent plant stalks.

About three hours later Jack and Sergio heard movement up ahead and they immediately left the trail for cover. Soon three figures appeared on the trail, the same as before checking the rear area. He had to hand it to the Germans. They were very careful and methodical. This patrol passed by them and disappeared out of sight. Now he had a problem with the Germans being between him and Sergio and the remainder of his group. He surmised his group was well along the stream by this point, so there should be no problem. They would wait and the patrol should show up within the hour; perhaps they would stop for a smoke and return in a short time.

After forty-five minutes, the patrol came along and passed close to their hiding place. After a few minutes Jack and Sergio moved out on the main path and beat a hasty retreat to the stream. Once there the two men moved off the path hopping on the many rocks in the streambed, so as not to leave a trail. Soon the vegetation enveloped them on both sides of the stream and they continued along it for about two hours or more until they caught sight of their main group.

Professor Gomez was in the lead and after another hour he called a halt. He thought it was about two kilometers to the rock buttress and with hard work they might make it by nightfall. Jack was for pressing on so that they could rest at the base of the escarpment and start off fresh in the morning. He recounted quickly how close they had come to being overrun with another German patrol. It had been very close.

It took a little longer than expected but with last light, they reached the escarpment and found a place to bivouac for the night. To Jack's relief no snakes had been encountered on the way in, but then they had gained enough altitude not to expect any. He was wary of the rocky terrain, as snakes loved rocks, and there might be no end of them just waiting for some unsuspecting person to fall asleep right on top of a den. Finding a spot next to Celine and her father, Jack spread out his blanket and pack, reminding himself that snakes generally were never found above 2000 meters. He knew they were well above 2500 meters so snakes couldn't be living up here. He balanced his environmental knowledge against the rock pile that looked like snake country and convinced himself altitude had killed them off. He stayed up for awhile thinking about this and then finally dozed off next to Celine.

Celine looked at Jack and noticed that even with all the hiking he looked clean. How could this be? She looked over at her father but he had nodded off as usual. What was it with men like these? With all the events of the last couple of days, they could fall asleep at an instant. She wondered if her father had gone over the edge. He was staking everything, including his position and reputation, on the word of a friend and his son.

There might be more to this than what Professor Ford had outlined to them. On the surface it seemed plausible enough. The Germans were certainly here and they were up to something, presumably just what Jack and his father had predicted. Professor Jahn was with the Germans and taking an active part in their operation.

Convincing herself that they were on the right track, Celine watched the last of the light drop away into total darkness. She pulled the blanket over her and tried to move her pack around to find the best position for her head. No matter how she shifted the pack something always stuck into her skin. Wrapping the blanket around under her head she drifted off to sleep.

*　　*　　*　　*

The next morning saw Major Bezada and two of his troopers up on the ledges at first light and soon they disappeared out of view. Jack started up after them with Pat. At first they could scramble the slopes but soon they needed to use ropes, and climbing was by belay only. They could not shout as voices carried and even here they were close enough to the Germans to be detected. They used hand signals and soon they were some 300-meters above the valley floor and the vegetation was thinning. Above them they could see stunted trees indicating they were close to the timberline at 3000-meters above the sea. Another four or five hours would put them above the timberline, and from there they would have to carry out careful reconnoitering, for at any time the Germans would break out of the forest, and they would have an unrestricted view of the heights above.

At the timberline in late afternoon, Jack decided to move around on the heights above during the night, as there was just enough moonlight to make out nearby forms. It would be dangerous, but even if the Germans had posted an advanced guard in the valley below they would not likely see them moving above. They filed out cautiously, the same three including Jack and his two mates. While they could not speak to each other, each person was part of a team. Jack wanted to see what the heights looked like and where they could hold up to observe the Germans without being detected. Soon they found what they were looking for. At about 3600 meters they found a large break in the rock that widened to a gully on the *Coromoto* side.

About twenty meters down the gully a narrow rock slit provided an unrestricted view of the entire *Coromoto* Valley. There was even a fresh water supply with a stream trickling down through the gully. It was perfect as an operational base and they reckoned that coming and going would be possible without being seen from the *Coromoto*. The bad side was that cooking was not possible and they would have to continue using dry rations, which they had counted on from the beginning. Jack thought they might be here for some time and he began to think of setting up a camp on the lee side of the buttress to rotate the group.

A few could keep watch on the Germans and the rest could enjoy a coffee and some hot food. He realized the prevailing northeasterly wind would likely not alert the Germans to their presence, but if the wind shifted to the northwest, they might be discovered. With enough food for about three weeks, Jack wondered how much food the Germans had brought with them. Too bad he had not inquired in *Mucuy*, but the farmer said they were well equipped. Presumably they didn't show their weapons so he probably was referring to food. Maybe they had more than a two to three week supply.

As a devilish grin spread across his face, he thought, *Maybe dad could slip in and have some wiener schnitzel with them.*,

They worked their way down to the main group and bivouacked for the night. The Germans would be up in a day or two, perhaps sooner. The way they operated he surmised they would have an advanced guard that would be in the valley by the next day. So it would be good to set up an observation post early the following day and establish a camp on the north side of the buttress immediately. This they did early the following day and as events transpired they beat the German advance guard by only a few hours.

Later the same day eight paratroopers moved through the bamboo at timberline and set up a camp at Lago *Coromoto*. Lying next to Professor Gomez, camouflaged with grass cover, the two men took stock of what was happening below. Jack looked at the sun to be sure he could use his binoculars without reflecting light that might alert the Germans to their presence.

Slowly he focused on the group, saying, "I can see the short stocky officer who had scouted near us a few days ago. With him are seven paratroopers who are busily preparing the camp. They don't appear to speak but use hand signals."

Handing the binoculars over to Professor Gomez Jack lay back in the grass thinking. The Professor took a broad sweep of the valley, slid lower in the grass to avoid being seen and handed the glasses to Jack. The two men looked at one another without saying anything but thinking over what they had just witnessed.

Finally Jack said, "I hope they don't send out flanking patrols because if they do we may have to move. Should they discover our observation post we'll be in for one hell of a fight. We must watch them carefully, all the time."

Jack continued his surveillance, observing the weaponry they carried. Those with machine pistols and side arms he judged to be officers and noncoms. The rest carried standard-issue German army rifles, carbines he thought. So, they will have one hell of a range, and he didn't want to get caught out in the open with them shooting at him.

Jack's mind drifted to the near future...what to do and when to move?

Should we wait for them to finish extracting the gold and then try to foil their recovery or should we whittle them down in place and stop them before they managed to recover it? The latter would take some doing as they were outnumbered. The former was more likely to bring success, but how long would it take to recover it all. Could the Germans mine all the gold and platinum in one operation or were they planning on several missions like this one?

In Venezuela, movement in and out from the coast was comparatively easy (with limited police and army patrols), so maybe the Germans did plan to return. He would soon find out and he would likely have to reconnoiter their camp sooner or later to see what progress they were making. It would be difficult to go in and out undetected, but it could be done.

As he continued his observations, Professor Gomez slid away and rejoined the rest of the group.

*   *   *   *

The next day around noon the main force appeared and spread out around the lake to take advantage of the few camping areas. The shore was dotted with large boulders, some as large as small rooms. Camping would be cramped with limited space for tents, but Jack noticed that the *Coromoto* River, draining out from the moraine at timberline, was covered with bamboo, which made for excellent concealment. He had already made up his mind that when it came time for peeking at the enemy he would do it alone through the bamboo. He might even wear the bamboo as he had done numerous times before as a kind of jacket, perfect camouflage to conceal him from the Germans. When he crouched down he would look like the local vegetation and he would be virtually undetectable at a distance of even a meter. Yes, the bamboo would do nicely.

After settling in for several days, the Americans and Venezuelans realized the Germans considered the region up valley of Lake *Coromoto* to be safe, as they did not bother to patrol it, although they were extracting gold and platinum from outcrops there.

As Jack and his dad watched the Germans, Jack said, "They're concentrating all their energy on extracting the precious metals. They're pretty sloppy with their security. Nearly everyone is working on the extraction."

"Yes," said the elder Dr. Ford, "It appears that some of the German force, at least, is expert with explosives. They're removing some of the ore with

149

straight shafts and chisels. On other parts of the outcrop they're using single sticks of dynamite of low yield so as not to make too much noise."

Steadying his binoculars to get a better view, Jack added, "Boulders of gold and platinum are covered with dynamite powder and mud, so the back pressure of the mud when the dynamite is ignited, splits the boulder."

At the same time two groups of German soldiers explored the placers, at the lower limit of the moraine. It appeared they were having considerable success extracting gold grains and nuggets so far as Jack could tell at a distance with his binoculars. They had to take great care in their surveillance to insure sunlight did not reflect off the binoculars and alert the Germans.

*   *   *   *

After several days, Jack decided he would have a closer look at the operation, and so he decided to slip off the rock buttress, and approach the German camp through the bamboo forest. He would move off the following day, lie up in the forest until dark, and then with sufficient camouflage reconnoiter the camp during the night to see what he could discover.

The next day he left by the same route they had entered the rock buttress and within three or four hours he was cautiously moving up the trail toward Lake *Coromoto*. He had to exercise extreme caution as the Germans probably had periodic patrols moving along the trail to insure no one found the way to their camp. Sensing that he was getting close to the lake, Jack moved off the trail and through the bamboo to the south. Soon he could see faint light filtering through the forest, the trees becoming shorter and shorter. The roar of the water issuing out of large boulders in the moraine masked all other sound; even birds could sing unheard by anyone near the creek.

I can easily approach undetected, he thought.

Jack decided to approach from the far side of the valley so he could watch the Germans just before nightfall. If they followed their usual schedule, they would work right up to dark, and quit around seven thirty. By six o'clock he was in position and he could watch the bedrock and placer crews at work busily removing material from the valley floor and preparing new charges to blast rock from the outcrops.

In just over a week they had removed an enormous amount of rock and sediment. With his glasses, he could see *Herr* Jahn inspecting the samples, discarding some of them, and directing the loading of sacks for storage near their camp. A group of six soldiers were seen loading sacks and leaving through the forest edge, presumably moving some of it into the lower valley. He would have to be very careful on his return trip not to run into this patrol; as if he did it would likely be impossible to escape. Reaching down to his holster he pulled his revolver thinking to check the cylinder but decided the clicking sound might carry. He had checked it earlier so he slid it back into the holster but felt for his two *pukkas* and his kukri insuring they were right where they were supposed to be, just in case he needed them in short order.

Just after 7 PM, the light faded fast, and the up valley group returned to the camp. They did not leave a guard and so just after nightfall, Jack, covered with tussock grass and *Espeletia* leaves, slowly made his way up the valley to have a look at the outcrops. Even with faint moonlight, he would not expose himself if he crawled around bedrock obstacles and moved very slowly.

About an hour later he was at the lower outcrop, and there in the faint light, he saw the first of the gold outcrops and close by an enormous vein of platinum. The Germans had left plentiful samples about and he quickly filled his pockets with abundant ore for his father and Professor Gomez to look at. From his own experience, he believed the gold to be from hypogene (deep) sources and most probably close to 99 % pure, with little silver content. The platinum he was less familiar with, but if it contained iridium in any quantity, its value was immeasurable.

Not believing his eyes, after examining the outcrop, Jack couldn't help remember tales of the *Domus Aurea* in ancient Rome, the *Golden House of Nero* renowned for its gold-lined walls, much like the *Coromoto*. Dismantled by the Flavian Dynasty after Nero's suicide in 68 A.D., Jack wondered if the same would happen here. Would the Germans extract all the gold and platinum and carry it off to fuel their war machine? But this was no time to daydream, he thought, for if he was discovered here, escape would be next to impossible.

After making his way slowly down valley he inspected two of the placers and was amazed at the size of the nuggets. He was sure he had seen one of the Germans holding a nugget about the size of a baseball, but he was unprepared for the sight of even larger nuggets in the second placer. This was truly a find of astronomical proportions.

Dad and Professor Gomez will love looking at this stuff, he thought.

After collecting samples from both placers he slipped back the way he had come, noting again that the rushing water overrode all sound. The rise of a slight wind covered any movements he might make on entering the forest and finding the trail.

Carefully he approached the main trail. He listened at the edge of the path for several minutes, to insure the path was free of patrols. He walked slowly along the path to the stream cutoff, and then being careful not to leave any sign, moved off the main trail and toward the rock buttress.

Climbing in the dark is about as hazardous an operation as can be imagined, but soon he joined his mates just after midnight. Exhausted, he curled up under a blanket, and quickly drifted off to sleep. The samples would have to wait until first light for inspection.

Thirteen

Ford Undone

The following morning Jack awoke to find Professor Gomez, his dad and Celine staring at him and at the samples they had removed from his bags.

Professor Gomez spoke first, saying, "I don't believe it. This is the purest material I have ever looked at. I think the gold is nearly 100 % pure. The platinum probably contains rhodium, osmium and iridium, although it will require precise laboratory tests to confirm the composition. It's priceless without any doubt. How extensive are the outcrops?"

"They are very extensive," said Jack. "And the only thing that will stop the Germans is the weight of material they will have to carry out. It looks to me like they are concentrating on the platinum and they already have a heavy load. From the sound of things down there, I think they will be winding up the operation soon and retreating with what they've mined. We'll need to watch them carefully."

After considering their situation, Jack advised, "We could split up, with some of our group reconnoitering the German camp, and the remainder staying here to watch the Germans and follow them out. If the Germans split up it may be possible to capture their rear guard and some of the gold and platinum they've mined. We can stay put for a while and follow them out, or if they leave a small group in the valley, we might try to capture them. I don't think they'll waste time when they pull out and they could be at the coast within a few days."

Professor Gomez thought this over and replied, "It's the only logical way. I speak Spanish and German and can interpret for Jack, so I'll go with him. When shall we leave for the German camp?"

"I think we should reconnoiter the camp tomorrow," said Jack, and then he lay back to consider what he had just said. A number of thoughts occupied his mind.

What if the Germans don't leave immediately? What if they have other plans or another route of escape? Where could they go from here and safely remove the gold-platinum load to Germany? They have the zeppelin but could they reach Venezuela with one? It might not be impossible and the load they are carrying will be heavy in a submarine.

He closed his eyes and nearly fell asleep until he realized there was much to plan and do before they could split the force up, and above all they had to continue watching the Germans without getting spotted from below.

He crawled out from his bedroll and the tent to find his father studying the German camp. "How goes it Dad?" he asked.

His father looked at him with a quizzical look, finally replying, "Do you really think you can take on this entire unit, steal all their precious cargo and defeat them."

Jack thought for a moment and weighed what his father had said. An astute observer, the elder Dr. Ford had probably concluded from watching the Germans that they were serious about their business and might likely succeed in their enterprise. Jack studied his father's face for what seemed like the longest time and finally replied, summing up the situation.

"They have numerical superiority and they've greater fire power. We've surprise on our side and a smaller force. We also have the plane, which they do not know about and we have greater mobility. If they split their force it might make it easy for us to capture a small group. Anything we can do to upset their timetable will be to our advantage. Everything is in place now and you can be sure they'll follow a schedule to meet their subs at the coast."

After reflecting for a moment, Jack added, "There's no other way out for them and they have first to negotiate the cloud forest and then get through the *Motilone*, not to mention the local police."

He thought through what he had just said and then realized there were many possibilities. The police likely wouldn't be a problem, and even if they did run into them, *Herr* Jahn would likely talk his way out of any trouble. The army was sparsely distributed, so much so that Major Bezada thought it improbable they would run into other army units. Only the *Motilone* and the cloud forest were major obstacles to a successful escape.

But Jack had learned that even well laid plans were subject to uncertainty. Random events connected with vehicle malfunction, chance encounters with local people, and unforeseeable natural factors, might intervene to thwart the German escape plan. Even the submarines might present a problem. If they were discovered in Maracaibo Lake which was barely thirty meters deep, there would be little in the way of hiding places for them.

He thought again about the submarines and decided he had to be right; they were the only means of escape. Most probably the German force would need two or three of them. The subs were taking quite a chance operating in shallow water and the distance to the coast had to be over 100-kilometers. Of course, the Germans might try to smuggle the cargo out, but heavy cargo might be inspected. No, he thought, *evacuation by submarine made sense.*

His father tensed and turned to Jack, "They're packing all their gear. I think they'll leave shortly and maybe even before tomorrow. What shall we do?"

Jack said, "Give me the binocs."

He swept the valley to take in the entire situation and soon realized that the Germans were concentrating all their heavy packs loaded with precious cargo near the big boulder close to the forest edge.

"The soldiers are lashing all the packs with heavy rope. Two small groups are still at work in the upper valley presumably working the vein ore and bundling up several sacks."

Jack continued sweeping the valley with his glasses but satisfied himself that the mining operation was coming to a conclusion.

But just as Jack was stashing his binoculars in his pack, there was a frightful explosion, much louder than all the previous ones. Pulling his glasses out of the pack, he trained them on a tremendous pile of rock that had been blown apart trying to make sense of the situation. All of a sudden he realized the sky was getting darker as a massive thunderstorm was about to break loose. Then he heard thunder. If anyone heard the blast, they would consider it came from the thunderhead.

"These German troopers are crafty," he said as his Dad looked on.

Jack walked over to Major Bezada who was packing his kit, said, "It's time to organize our group and split up."

"Do you think this is wise Señor?" asked the Major.

"It's the only way to counter their escape plans, Major. We've got to follow them out, and with some of our group near the coast, maybe they'll get careless when they withdraw. After all they don't think anyone is up here watching them and with the pile of rubble they just blew up they may leave some of the group to clean up the ore and bag it to follow later."

"Yes, you're right, but I think I should slip down ahead of the Germans in case there are any problems with the villagers. They must not give our presence away and I'm afraid the Germans might hire them to help carry the load to Apartaderos."

Jack had overlooked this aspect of the withdrawal, and answered, "As you wish Major. I'll stay with Professor Gomez, Celine, Dad, Pat and your troopers. Maybe you should take one or two troopers with you in case there are any problems. Stay in *Mucuy* and stay under cover until we come out. And when the Germans withdraw, send two of your men up the trail to alert us as we'll be watching our point with keen anticipation."

"Okay, Jack, and good hunting."

Soon the Major and three troopers were ready to leave. Jack bade them farewell, watching them make their way off the rock buttress quickly following the path off to the north and west that would take them back to the main trail. If they hurried they could be in *Mucuy* before nightfall and arrange to hide on one of the nearby farms where they could observe the German withdrawal. As soon as the major and his men disappeared, he motioned to Professor Gomez to join him at the observation post.

Professor Gomez, Jack and two of the troopers took turns watching the valley. They were certain the Germans would leave the valley the next day.

Curiously, the detail up valley appeared to continue working one particular outcrop. Perhaps they intended to stay another day or two to finish their work. Two tents were left standing the next morning as the main force prepared to move out.

Jack was delighted at the opportunity to take on part of the group and so he and Professor Gomez talked over the possibilities.

"We could follow the path down onto the main trail and then take the small group of Germans from below," Jack offered.

Watching Gomez and gauging his reaction, he continued, "Or we could work along the buttress to a higher position, sneak up on the Germans from above, and rush them. If we chose the first option we might run afoul of the main force, but the second option means exposing ourselves in open country."

While Professor Gomez thought it over, Jack offered, "The second option is the safe one. If we move at night, with a full moon, we will have enough light to make it safely into the upper valley and fall on the Germans at their camp near the lake. The light works both ways and there is a chance of discovery."

"Yes, I suppose it's better to attack from the upper valley."

Jack finally made up his mind to split up with part of the group remaining in the observation post. Perhaps they could catch the German party after sundown when they would least expect it.

Jack and his group watched as the sun went down to see if the Germans would put out a patrol but all seemed quiet in the camp. They estimated that there were ten men in the group and they did not appear to post sentries. They seemed to settle in for some food and then rest, most probably to depart the following day. Judging by the number of sacks they had carried down to the main camp they would leave with a heavy load. Soon the sun was down and with only moonlight available to show them the way, Jack, Professor Gomez and six of the troopers were off along the rock buttress heading nearly east to a point where they could easily descend into the valley. Pat and Felix stayed with Celine up on the ridge along with the remaining troopers.

Once at the wide gully leading down to the valley floor Jack warned them to keep the gully wall to the west between them and the German camp and to spread out as they descended. Stealth was what would see them through this operation. Slowly they worked their way through the gully and luckily no one turned out a rock despite the poor light.

Reaching the valley floor, they descended through the grass and *Espeletia,* to a point on a moraine ridge just above the German camp, where they could get a better view of the ground. Jack realized they had obvious topographic advantages they might use to get closer, most notably the large boulders around the camp. They were now about 150 meters from the Germans and Jack could see only one sentry. He was propped up on a boulder next to the tents.

Jack whispered to the others, "There's only one sentry and he seems to be dozing off."

Obviously, the Germans did not suspect anyone could be watching them, and so it would be easy to take the sentry down without alerting the rest of the camp.

Jack whispered, "I can take care of the sentry."

Looking the situation over, Professor Gomez replied, "Sergio is excellent with a knife. He can disable the sentry with little trouble. The rest of the group can take the tents."

So, Sergio slipped away keeping the ground cover between himself and the sentry. He worked his way slowly down the side of the canyon and came up on the sentry from behind. At the same time Jack, Professor Gomez and the troopers worked slowly down the middle of the valley. They were within thirty meters of the camp when the sentry disappeared off the top of the boulder.

Sergio signaled to attack. Jack and the troopers cut the tent lines, and Professor Gomez yelled in German to surrender immediately or be cut down. A German officer, disentangling himself from the collapsed tent, emerged firing a pistol and was quickly cut down by one of the troopers. The rest appeared dazed and disoriented and obviously they had been taken by surprise.

All nine remaining German troopers were quickly disarmed and tied up while Professor Gomez started untying several of the packsacks to look over the contents. It appeared that the Germans were trying to take the last of the platinum and they had a considerable quantity of it. Professor Gomez estimated that they had about 300 kilos of it, and maybe more. What concerned him the most was that the main force might come back to pick up the last sacks.

They had no way of knowing if Major Bezada and his men had managed to get to *Mucuy* ahead of the Germans. Even more worrisome were German intentions, which might be to return, or to wait in *Mucuy* for the rear guard. Looking at the still dazed German troopers, Jack wondered if they were really an elite group, but just then he saw that some of them wore uniforms with wings under their fatigues. They were German paratroopers, and most likely, he and his men were just plain lucky to have caught them in their tents asleep with only one guard. Would their luck hold?

Professor Gomez questioned the German soldiers but could find out very little about their plans.

Coming over to Jack, he reported, "They'll not talk despite the threat of turning them over to the police or the army. Perhaps they had approval for this mission from higher ups in the Venezuelan government, or perhaps they're prepared to die here to please the Führer."

Jack and Professor Gomez decided to post a guard and rest up for the night and leave the following day. They would have to descend slowly, exercising great caution, as the Germans might well be on the way back up to carry the last samples down to *Mucuy*.

Suddenly Jack felt weary, and one look at Professor Gomez told him that they had reached the limit of their endurance. That they had successfully countered part of the German escape bid, slowing them down, spoke well for their efforts. Jack estimated that with the new trail in place, it would take no more than a day, perhaps two, to reach *Mucuy* and the Germans were likely there now.

*   *   *   *

The next morning the group woke early and they started to pack. Jack planned to leave the gold-platinum bags hidden in the timberline underbrush until they could be retrieved later on. As he was carrying two bags away from camp, he suddenly realized the tussock grass was moving. He stopped dead in his tracks as two paratroopers with carbines stood up and motioned to him to drop the sacks. He put his hands up and turned around to see Professor Gomez and the Venezuelan troopers in a similar fix.

Soon the captured Germans were released and his force was subdued. Hans, the second- in-command of the German force smiled as he looked Jack, his troopers and Professor Gomez over. He said in German to Professor Gomez, "I would personally kill you were it not for orders from my commander to exercise extreme caution. Luckily Gomez was a Venezuelan citizen, as were the mountain troopers with him. Dr. Ford was another matter entirely. He was hardly on a botanical trip, and where were his father and assistant?"

Hans became irritated when Jack indicated they had gone to alert the authorities and they had a two-day head start.

Walking over to Jack, Hans asked once more, "Where are they? Where is your father, his assistant and the girl?

"I told you. They are off rounding up the police and alerting the government."

Jack hoped Hans didn't put the government people together with the Army. The Army was already alerted. He watched Hans try to figure out where they might be, craning his neck around looking at the higher cliffs, apparently thinking for the first time that they might have come from above.

Then Jack saw Han's pistol coming at him and all faded into blackness.

The Germans tied up Jack's limp body along with Professor Gomez and the troopers. They left them by the lake, with a warning that if they followed them, they would most certainly be killed. To insure they didn't escape and follow them out they took their boots and tied them securely together. It would take them sometime to loosen their bonds, to free themselves, and without boots they would find it slow going in the cloud forest. They might even find it impossible and slowly starve to death.

As Jack regained consciousness Hans bid him goodbye. With a wicked smile, he warned, "I should have killed you. Anyway I hope to see you again, Dr. Ford, and if I do, you'll die."

For good measure Hans took Jack's knives and revolver. The Germans were expert with ropes and knots and although Jack struggled with the ropes he had a raging headache, one that would not go away. It took him and his group over two hours to work free of the ropes.

*   *   *   *

Watching from the observation post the rest of the group felt pretty helpless as the Germans rounded up their raiding party. Pat had a rifle but he couldn't fire because the distance was too great. Despite sighting his rifle in on the coast, Pat realized he couldn't risk firing from their observation post. Normally a calm person, Pat became visibly aggravated as he watched the Germans tie up Jack and the rest.

Even the elder Dr. Ford, sensing Pat's rising emotion, summarized the situation, "There's little we can do."

With his voice trailing off, he picked up his binoculars and studied the situation unfolding in the valley below. After a few minutes, said, "It appears the Germans are preparing to pull out and they are leaving Jack and the rest of the group tied up in the camp."

"No shots were fired," said Professor Ford, as he scanned around with his binoculars. Then he stiffened, saying, "Jack is limp. But they've tied him up along with the others, including your father, Celine. I think they've beaten up Jack." The thought of this made the elder Professor Ford grimace. The more he thought about it the more he realized he was getting mad but at least Jack was tied up so they did not kill him.

I must get my feelings under control, he thought. *Emotion destroys all prospect of rationality. Jack is alive and we need to get down to him with speed to see to his recovery.*

As the Germans were pulling out, Pat organized the hill party to move down on the German camp as soon as it was safe to do so. With Celine and the remaining mountain troopers, Pat led the way off the rock buttress down into the *Coromoto* Valley. As they started their descent into the lower valley, Pat tried to convince himself that all was okay with Jack and Professor Gomez, and that he would find them both in one piece when he arrived at the German camp. They had to move with care as no telling if the Germans had booby-trapped the encampment.

*   *   *   *

Jack had been out cold when he was tied up so coming to he realized the bonds were tight, very tight indeed. He rolled over and looked at Professor Gomez who had been working on his bonds, loosening them somewhat. As Jack, with a horrid headache, started to work on the ropes holding his wrists, he heard, "Finally, I'm free or nearly so."

Rolling over he could see Professor Gomez standing up, untying the rope from his arms. Soon he was over Jack untying his hands, cursing all the time in Spanish.

At the camp and feeling pretty much outwitted by the Germans, Professor Gomez said, "The situation is pretty bleak. We may not be able to get out of this place without boots."

Jack looked glum but tried to put a brave face on their situation. "There are always alternatives, Professor. We'll get out."

"How?" said Professor Gomez.

"With the *Espeletia* leaves and *Polylepis* bark, Professor," Jack said.

"They're tough, elongated and flexible and can be tied around our feet. They won't be as good as boots but we'll manage. Let's get going and round up as many as we can find. We need to start manufacturing our footwear."

Professor Gomez, looking incredulous, started cropping the *Espeletia* leaves and *Polylepis* bark

It took some time to accomplish this, but soon the boot manufacturing process was underway, and within a short time the group had made great progress in producing boots of *Espeletia*. Reinforced with *Polylepis* bark, there was enough canvas from some of their jackets to make a nearly waterproof covering, producing a practical boot. The bark was rough enough so that it formed a tread, much like the sole of a mountain boot. A large sewing needle was recovered from one of the packs, along with thread, allowing them to stitch up the canvas making the boots nearly waterproof. They weren't perfect by any means but they would get them safely out to *Mucuy*.

Shortly thereafter the rest of the raiding party including Pat, the elder Professor Ford, Celine and the rest of the mountain troopers crept into camp. They were relieved to find that everyone survived the capture. Although Jack had been knocked out by the German officer, no one was severely injured.

Celine was elated to find Jack no worse for wear, although she thought his age was beginning to show. He had been outwitted by the Germans; not only outwitted but captured as well.

"Okay," Jack said. "We move out tomorrow as soon as possible."

Jack rested against a pack the Germans had left and realized how tired he was. Although his headache remained it was nothing like what he felt when he had first regained consciousness. Then he drifted off into blackness, as black as the cloud forest itself. During the night he dreamed that the gold-platinum shipment made it to the coast and that the Germans escaped with it, somewhere...and then his dream faded.

The dream had such an effect that he woke with a start around 5 AM. He couldn't get back to sleep. For an hour or more he was restless, and with his eyes closed, he continued to see the same images carrying sacks of gold and platinum to waiting submarines. He resolved then and there that this must never happen and he would do all in his power to stop it. But at the moment his powers were minimal and he even wondered if they would make it out to *Mucuy*? His troopers were tough. He had been caught in tight situations like this and made it out in one piece. Professor Gomez was strong for his years, and Jack could count on him, his daughter and his father. With daybreak they would start out.

After resting all night, and huddling under blankets left by the retreating Germans, they planned their descent to *Mucuy*. They hoped the Germans believed they were completely disabled and that they wouldn't send a force up to annihilate them. Nevertheless they moved with a point consisting of Jack and Sergio, with the rest of the group about 20-meters or so behind. Jack gave the order for no talking. They would use hand signals all the way down. If discovered the point force would lead the Germans off on a chase through the forest.

"This might prove difficult," exclaimed Jack, "as we have fewer weapons now."

Luis, one of Bezada's men, smiled and produced a knife, one of the long knives carried by the alpine troopers. He proceeded to cut some bamboo and to fashion some spears, adding, "Running at full speed you can kill with one of these."

"Fine," said Jack. "Only our opponents are well armed and you'd be cut down before getting to them."

"Perhaps," said Luis, "but a little farther along in the forest we can make spears out of *Polylepis* trees, and they are much different, as you can throw them with effect." We also have two Enfield rifles and ammunition.

"Okay, "Jack said. "We move out as soon as possible." He then lay back to wait.

*   *   *   *

An hour or so later with the sun rising slowly behind the Humboldt Massif, they gathered up their few belongings.

Jack said, "We must be careful as they may have planted a force to stop us, and there is the possibility of traps, such as snares and even pits with stakes in them. I'll take the point with Luis behind me and we'll move with as much speed as possible."

A short time later they set off through the bamboo. Jack was very careful to look at everything near or on the trail as there was no telling what the Germans had left to trap them. He was especially afraid of snares with the *Polylepis* trees but at this altitude there was only bamboo and he doubted that the Germans would have stopped to dig a pit and place stakes.

But one can never tell, he thought. *We just have to stay alert and look for anything different or unusual along the trail.*

They parted the bamboo and moved into the forest and stopped to let their eyes adjust to the dim light. Jack could see the path was well worn now which was good as any snares, or other obstacles would stand out and be relatively easy to spot, or so he hoped. They moved along with surprising speed and Professor Gomez was amazed at how well their improvised boots were holding up. They proved a bit slippery, but on the whole, not bad and with decent cushioning they actually made walking quite comfortable.

After moving along a kilometer or so Jack signaled a halt and asked Professor Gomez to call up one of the other troopers to take point. He cautioned the point to keep his eyes and ears on guard all the time.

His face taut, Jack said, "The point should stay ahead about 30-50 meters or so just in case, and no talking whatsoever."

They changed positions and moved out on down the trail deeper into the forest. Soon they encountered *Polylepis* trees and Jack signaled again for a halt. He warned the point to beware of snares and so they continued on. Another few hundred meters and Luis signaled for Jack to come forward. The point had spotted a snare tied to a large *Polylepis* tree. Miguel, the point man, had spotted the tree before he saw the snare and he had nearly stepped into it.

"These guys are good," said Jack, "Very good."

Professor Gomez and the elder Dr. Ford nodded in agreement. "If there's one snare, there could be more," said the elder Dr. Ford.

Jack relieved the point man and they released the snare and continued on down the trail. After making at least three kilometers, Jack motioned to stop as they were very close to the side trail near the rock buttress. They needed a rest, and above all, they needed water. Walking with their improvised boots was very tiring. They had to continually watch their footing on the clay-rich soil and as they descended the clay underfoot increased. Even a slight slope brought considerable sliding and some of the men had fallen several times.

After a short break they continued on down the trail keeping a close watch for more snares, or any other traps the Germans might have left for them. Finding none they made over six kilometers by sundown. Rather than risk running into another snare or even a German patrol, they decided to bivouac off the trail so that they had a good place to watch unobserved.

Moving away from the trail, Luis was ahead clearing the vines and epiphytes away, when suddenly he yelled and ran back towards the group. Jack grabbed him realizing he had been bitten by a *Mapanare* or most probably a *botrous* snake, the two most deadly species in the cloud forest. He forced him to the ground and quickly took one of the sharpened *Polylepis* spears to use as a knife. Realizing that Luis had a knife he dropped the spear and pulled the knife from its sheath, quickly cutting open the leg wound. It bled profusely. Jack knew he had only a minute or so to suck out the venom or Luis would die. He sucked and spit blood until he was sure he had it all.

Looking at Luis he imagined the man had seen the grim reaper as he was as white as a sheet and nearly immobilized.

"Don't worry Luis," he said, "I'm sure I got it all." Then he realized that Luis, looking at him with the wildest face, did not understand English.

He called Professor Gomez over, said, "Tell Luis all is okay and to rest now and for the remainder of the night."

He covered Luis with a blanket and told Professor Gomez, "Warn the others to check for snakes and make sure everything is secure."

*   *   *   *

The next morning Jack, his dad, Professor Gomez, Celine, and the troopers started off just after first light. They had little food, and thirst was becoming a real problem, as there was little potable water available on this section of trail. They moved cautiously. They were now close to the halfway point and today they had to make at least six or seven kilometers to put them close to *Mucuy*.

Jack thought, *if we get to within two kilometers, we could bivouac again, and send a team of two to reconnoiter the situation. We can't just break out of the forest without first reconnoitering the village.*

The forest being so dark, it was difficult to judge the time, and almost impossible to know when the day was coming to an end. The light just suddenly faded away and then total darkness enveloped all and everything. On this second day the group halted at a point where they judged they had come some twelve to fourteen kilometers. They thought they had about two hours before sundown and Jack decided that he and Sergio would push on ahead to see if they could make it to *Mucuy*.

Once darkness fell it would be impossible to continue on and, of course, they could not return until morning. The rest of the group looked like they could use some rest, so as usual they moved off the trail following a small stream to set up a bivouac where they could remain unobserved by anyone using the trail. Professor Gomez advised Sergio as to what Jack had in mind. Jack couldn't help but notice that, despite the fact that he and Sergio spoke two different languages, they communicated well with hand signals. Sergio understood perfectly what they had to do once they reached *Mucuy*.

Sergio and Jack moved off down the trail at a fast clip, or so Professor Gomez thought. He watched them fade off into the forest and soon he could see them no more. They moved fast for a time and then Jack held up his hand to slow down. They had gone only a kilometer or slightly more when he thought he heard voices. Maybe the village was closer than he thought? The vegetation seemed to be thinning and there was light off in the distance. They had better be very careful because, if the Germans discovered them so close to their camp, they would likely kill them. They needed weapons and above all they needed boots and food.

The voices coming to them were Spanish, not German, and Jack looked at Sergio noticing a smile erupting over his face. This seemed to be a good omen. Walking very slowly they came to the edge of the forest and could see down to *Mucuy*. There were a few people walking in the road but the vehicles were gone. They watched for perhaps twenty minutes, before Jack motioned to Sergio to go and have a look, and find out what had happened. Sergio gave

Jack his knife, and he slipped off into a field, walking straight toward the nearest house.

In a few minutes he returned and imitated a man behind the wheel of a truck, pointing to the bridge off in the distance, indicating that the Germans had left. Although the light was getting low, Jack decided to hurry back to where the group had bivouacked to bring them out. He made the trip of two kilometers in twenty-five minutes, found the group, and led them out. It was nearly 7 PM when they reached the forest edge. To be sure all was as it should be in the village, Professor Gomez and Sergio went ahead and returned with a rifle.

Professor Gomez reported, "The Germans left this morning for Apartaderos. Major Bezada and his troopers are safely billeted in a nearby farm and they have procured some additional weapons."

Jack summed up the situation, with Professor Gomez translating, "We've been very lucky so far, but we'll need weapons, including knives, rifles and revolvers. Can you get any here?" Professor Gomez handed the rifle to Jack along with some ammunition.

He told Sergio, "Take some men and see what you can round up for us." Jack added, "We'll pay for whatever the villagers can provide."

"Okay señor," said Sergio. He called two of the troopers over and they left walking down the main road of *Mucuy*. It didn't take Sergio long to report back that there were only two rifles in the village, and he already had one of them, an Enfield. He did, however, manage to round up a half dozen knives and some spare ammunition. Food was being prepared for them in the village and Sergio thought the villagers would find some boots for them. Whether or not the boots would fit exactly was another matter, but for now the main thing was to get some sleep.

Major Bezada had earlier warned the farmer holding all his horses that the Germans would arrive soon and that he should keep the horses for their group as they would be following the German force. The horses were safe in the farmer's barn and he was only too willing to help out. Jack decided to bed down for the night, and follow the Germans at first light, using the horses left behind by Major Bezada. The pieces were falling into place. Now it would be a race to Maracaibo.

Fourteen

The Race to Maracaibo

August 20, 1939. While the Germans retreated to Apartaderos, Jack and his group replaced their improvised footwear with boots bought from local inhabitants in *Mucuy*. They were not ideal by any means and most were old and well worn, but better in the long run than what they had worn on the way out through the cloud forest. They had food and horses now so they were mobile. Although a little short on weaponry, Jack was amazed at the quality of the knives, which were balanced so well they could be thrown. And the rifles were adequate, although they would have to be sighted in to be accurate. Ammunition was a problem as they had barely 150 rounds for three Enfield rifles.

They would follow the German force and wait for an opportune time to attack them. The tactical plan now was to watch and wait for the right moment to catch the Germans off guard. Presumably Pat could manage to get the float plane out of *Mucubaji,* with his father and Celine aboard, and he could ferry them to the coast once the Germans evacuated Apartaderos. Some of the troopers could follow with the second airlift.

Jack advised Professor Gomez, "We should move out to Mucuchies and try to get within observing distance of the German column. If we wear mountain ponchos we will appear to be local farmers on horseback."

After reflecting for a bit, Jack continued "I suppose the Germans are half way to Apartaderos by now, but with horses we should catch up to them by tomorrow. They'll have to stop in Apartaderos to pick up food and lodging. If they split up there, we might have a chance to take part of their cargo and perhaps recover our weapons. I don't think they'll waste any time getting to the coast."

"I agree," said Professor Gomez.

Jack kept working various options over in his mind, but there seemed to be no alternative. The Germans would try to make the coast in the shortest possible time and offload their cargo onto the submarines. Of this he was certain! He hadn't heard any news broadcasts in nearly a month, but war was surely imminent. For all he knew, it might have started already. And what would the U.S. position be? It would probably be a European conflict, but most likely U.S. Intelligence would want the gold-platinum shipment to Germany stopped dead in Venezuela.

He remembered his orders; *use all available means to prevent export of the gold-platinum lode to Germany, including deadly force if necessary.* He also remembered the part, *all reasonable funds to be expended to achieve a successful outcome.* This was the part he liked best, because as usual with funding agencies financing field work in archaeology, their parsimony was the subject of great irritation amongst his colleagues.

Researchers usually had to pay their own food and lodging as the granting institutes paid only air and vehicle transport. And of course the necessary field equipment including revolvers, rifles, telescopic sights, throwing knives and other necessary and assorted paraphernalia had to be purchased out-of-pocket. One could go broke trying to get ahead in the academic profession, but then that had always been his lot in life. And his father's as well.

Government contracts were the way-to-go, he thought.

Jack was no businessman and cost accounting was certainly not his strong point by any means. He always came out about even, but at least he came out alive. Suddenly, he realized he was starting to revel in the past, and this was no time for daydreaming, even if daydreamers changed reality while nighttime dreamers 'Woke to find it.'

Jack liked this quote from T.E. Lawrence, but the mission was all that mattered now, and if he didn't concentrate on it, he would slip up somewhere and this time he might not come out alive.

Some little voice deep in his subconscious told him that he and Hans would meet again and this time Hans would try to kill him. The last time up in the *Coromoto* had been very close and he was sure the next time would be the final test. One of them would likely die over this. So, it was best to try and find the right situation to reverse the odds but at the moment he did not have the slightest idea how to do this. At least they were moving and they had weapons. The Germans did not know they were close behind.

They rode to the Mérida-Apartaderos road, with part of the group leaving to retrieve their vehicle and an army truck at Mérida, with the others continuing along the main road to Apartaderos. At one of the small villages above *Mucuy* they stopped and asked about the German convoy.

One of the local farmers reported, "They passed yesterday afternoon, several trucks heading for Apartaderos, I think."

"They're all ahead of us," observed Professor Gomez, "and I think they may be in Apartaderos by now. Should we ride on and try to make the town by nightfall?"

Jack thought for only a second or two, then said, "The best idea is to get as close as possible before nightfall. With our woolen ponchos I doubt they'll think we're anything but local shepherds or *llaneros*, if they catch sight of us. Now, let's get on up the road and see what the Germans are up to. As before, they'll stay at Jose's place and it'll be easy for us to reconnoiter it and look for an opportunity to strike."

"*Si señor*," said Professor Gomez who, turning in the saddle, said to the mountain troopers, "*Allez, Apartaderos amigos.*"

They galloped off along the road.

As they rode, Jack thought, *Very soon we'll have to split up. If we're observed riding in a column, we'll look like cavalry and that might give us away.*

After about four or five kilometers he stopped the column, and explained to Professor Gomez, "It'd be best if we stretched out our column, with one or two soldiers riding about a few hundred meters apart."

He and Professor Gomez would take the lead, with the remainder of the group following along at irregular intervals. This way, if the Germans observed them they would likely not be alarmed at all.

At *Mucuchies*, Jack and his group stopped for coffee and food at the local café and found that the Germans had done the very same thing the day before. The Germans had paid for everything in *bolivares*, the café owner remembered, saying, "They spoke very little, and always in German, which I do not understand."

The café owner believed they were heading to Apartaderos on a government mission, but he couldn't provide any additional information.

With Jack and Professor Gomez in the lead, they approached Apartaderos from down valley following close to the Río Chama, hoping to avoid detection riding over the lower terraces. It would be hard to approach the town without being detected so they decided on the direct approach. With ponchos over their heads, and swaying forward in the saddle, they appeared to be *llaneros*, or farmers headed home. They hoped the Germans did not have patrols out for, if they did, they would surely stop them and then everything would unravel and the whole enterprise would likely come apart. They were now only two kilometers or so from the town and still no contact with the Germans, not a single sign of them anywhere.

Jack and Professor Pedro Gomez reached the broad outwash fan that draped over the catchment draining *Aguila* Peak and *Mifafi*. At this point Jack called a halt, took out his binoculars, and scanned the town in the waning light to see if he could detect any sign of the German force. He could only see some vehicles near the hotel, but he couldn't get an exact count.

Jack directed, "Pedro, ride on down valley, pick up the others, bring them here, and turn up valley along this small creek. Meet me about one kilometer up the valley. I think we'll bivouac there, watch the center of town, and see what's happening."

"Si *amigo*," said Professor Gomez, "I'll find the troop and meet you up valley as you say."

He rode off following the small creek down into the main valley.

Jack studied the situation, concluding that, either the Germans were satisfied there were no pursuers, or they were being very careless. He knew they were anything but careless, so they must be satisfied that pursuit was impossible. Still, it wouldn't do to act with haste, especially since they usually protected their perimeters and he was sure they would post a guard all the way round Jose's place. It would be best to wait until later and then reconnoiter the hotel and try to have a close look at the situation. Yes, he would wait for Professor Gomez and then make some plans.

About an hour later the sun went down, and soon thereafter Jack heard the horses' hooves, as the troop made their way up the creek bed to where he waited for them. They dismounted and he reported what he knew to Professor Gomez who interpreted for the troopers.

Jack advised, "It'd be best to rest while the opportunity affords itself," and Professor Gomez again translated this to the men.

They posted a guard and then found a suitable place to doze off. Jack told Professor Gomez to wake him around midnight and indicated what he had in mind.

"It'll be difficult to get close and what if they catch you," Professor Gomez said.

"I'll have to take the risk," concluded Jack, who added, "We have to know if they are all there and I only wish I could speak German well enough to hear what they have in mind."

Professor Gomez replied, "I'll go with you."

Jack replied, "No, it's too dangerous and all I need is a count. I am sure they'll pull out in the morning, and by then we'll have our vehicles, and can take the plane to the coast and wait for them there."

Professor Gomez, distraught at hearing this, thought he might never see Jack again. If the Germans caught him they would likely kill him.

*   *   *   *

Just after midnight Jack followed the creek toward the center of town, and after a distance of half a kilometer, he moved off to the north taking a nearly straight-line approach to Jose's place. There was a half moon and the light was good enough to provide silhouettes. He would have to be careful and avoid going over the top of topographical obstacles, as that would present an outline of his body to any observant German sentry. He moved with speed at first and then took to stopping every five minutes or so to listen for several seconds and sometimes a minute or two.

Years ago, when he worked in Bolivia and Peru, the Indians there always stopped when moving at night, to listen for the sounds of the forest. He had taken the instruction seriously and had followed their example on all his missions. Move silently and slowly, then stop and listen to the sounds of the night. There are always sounds, both natural and human, and the human ones might prove lethal. And now, as he closed in on Jose's place, he tried with all his being to listen intently and filter natural from human noise.

The birds were all asleep but there were still crickets and the wind in the few trees. Yes, he had a clear signal from nature. Now he concentrated on any extraneous sounds and soon he heard a murmur. It was language, idle chatter, and it came in the form of German. They were careless and they were talking about 100 meters upwind and the wind was carrying their conversation to him. He couldn't understand what they were talking about, but that didn't matter. The Germans were there and they had sentries out. It was instinct that caused him to deviate from the main route and detour up a small creek to the west of town, the same instinct that told him now to bypass this sentry post and come around to Jose's place from above.

The upper route would take time, but it was the safest approach, so he backtracked about 100-meters and headed almost due north toward the higher ground. He would have to constantly watch the light and the high ground, as a silhouette would be deadly. It took him the better part of an hour, but at the end of it he could see directly down on Jose's place. In the dim light he could make out at least four sentries working mainly in pairs and not moving at all.

They must feel very secure, he thought. He could see several vehicles and noticed there were still lights on in two buildings. There was nothing to be gained by staying here, so he decided to return the way he had come. He mentally mapped his escape route off the hill, toward the hummocky ground, and along a small creek. He would have to stop every three or four minutes to listen intently and find any observation posts they may have set up.

He was about to leave the hummocky ground when he saw one of the sentries practicing with his *pukka*. The other sentry left to go into the cabin leaving the lone man trying, without much success, to knock a bottle from the top of a fence. Back tracking toward the cabins, Jack unsheathed the knife Luis had given him and moved slowly keeping close to the ground, hoping the sentry would not turn around.

Jack remembered thinking about optical physics applied to stalking. The eye becomes accustomed to a scene and does not detect minute movement so that a well camouflaged stalker moving inches at a time could avoid detection. He hoped the physics applied here.

He dare not use his rifle, as one shot would bring the paratroopers into the courtyard.

Jack fingered Luis' knife that he had tested for heft and balance to throw. Stopping to insure the other sentries couldn't see him, he threw his knife butt first, taking the sentry down with a strong blow to the head. The man was out cold!

He checked the vehicles thinking he might blow one up but decided against it, as it would be hard to escape even with a distracting conflagration. In one vehicle though, he found his boots, his revolver, his old knives, and the professor's boots. Quickly tossing them into his pack, he checked to see if the revolver was loaded, stuck it into his belt and went over to the incapacitated trooper to retrieve his knife.

Now he had four knives!

There was no activity outside the cabins and after listening intently for a few seconds, he decided this would be a good time to leave.

Looking carefully around the wall of the cabin, he could see a second sentry looking down valley, across the tiled rooftops below. Cradling his rifle, the sentry lit a cigarette, and started to turn toward Jack's hiding place. Jack could hear him walking slowly toward his end of the building and he started to edge away. Then he realized his best defense would be an offense — a very lightning offense.

Jack drew his *kukri*, realizing that the sentry had destroyed his night vision by lighting a cigarette. He stepped out from the wall and with one throw butt first the sentry fell to the earth with a dull thud. The man was down but not quite out giving Jack just enough time to fell him with a fist to the head. Re-sheathing his knife and slipping it onto his belt, he dragged the young soldier over to the wall where he could hide him in the shadows. He was struck by his youthfulness, barely eighteen, he reckoned.

He would have to move carefully now, as there was another sentry about on the opposite side of the compound. Taking down two of them was a bit of luck; three might bring out 'Murphy's Law' and everything would become too complex. He was 'controlling events' he told himself and it would be better if he could keep it that way. Time to clear out!

After moving nearly a kilometer or so, he was careful to stay higher than the first sentry post he had discovered on the way in. At one of his listening posts he heard voices but this time they were not stationary and were headed directly at him. He found the side of a gully, and faded into the grass at the edge of it, just as he caught sight of the two sentries headed directly toward him.

He eased his knife from its sheath keeping the blade hidden beneath his jacket to avoid reflection in the dim light. He would have to remember to paint the blade black, as one of these days a reflection from it might cost him his life. The two soldiers stopped on the top of the gully about ten meters from him, presenting perfect silhouettes as targets. Jack watched them with amusement as they each lit cigarettes and chatted on about something of little importance.

Striking a match had destroyed their night vision. It seemed all these German sentries smoked too much!

If he had used his two throwing knives, he could take both of them out here and now, but that might raise the alarm and he did not need the place swarming with soldiers who were much better armed than he was. Jack remained perfectly motionless watching the two enjoy their nicotine break. Soon they butted their cigarettes, looked right over him, crossed to the next gully, and disappeared into the night. That had been close but he was confident there were no more Germans to worry about.

He gave them about five minutes to move along, and then he started off in the direction of the small creek to the southwest. About thirty minutes later he spotted Sergio just where he had left him and soon he was explaining what he had seen to Professor Gomez and the troopers. They were all awake now, except for Pat, Felix and Celine, and Jack was surprised to see it was nearly 5 AM. He said to Professor Gomez, "I need some sleep, if only for an hour or two. Wake me if anything happens or if anyone stirs near Jose's place."

Jack lay down and soon drifted off to sleep. The others watched him while Professor Gomez summarized what Jack had observed on his reconnoitering mission. They could expect some movement soon, they were certain.

*   *   *   *

About 7 AM vehicles started leaving Jose's place in good order, one after the other, and soon they were all moving along the Apartaderos-Timotes road, up and over *Aguila* Peak. Jack watched them with his binoculars and he could see the Major and *Herr* Jahn in the lead vehicle. They were following the same routine as on the way in and one could bet the rear guard was as strong as ever.

Now, it was time to move to *Mucubaji,* and hope that the float plane was in good working order, as they would need to move quickly to the coast. It would take the Germans two days to make the trip to the coast and it would be necessary for Pat to ferry three loads of troops there to stand any chance at all of defeating the Germans. If Professor Gomez could find the *Motilone*, maybe they would agree to help him stop the Germans. Just as the *Motilone* tried to stop von Humboldt, they would most certainly be interested in stopping the Germans, especially if they knew what cargo they were carrying.

As soon as the Germans had moved off about three kilometers, Jack said, "Get the men to mount up and let's head for the lake. We need to send the first load of people to the coast within the hour. I will keep six troopers with me, but Professor you must go with the first load and try to enlist the *Motilone* to help us. Promise them anything they want and tell them they'll be well paid. We'll need them. Dad will stay with me in case I need a translator."

At that point Celine interrupted, said, "I'll go with you as well. You may need Spanish translations."

"No," Jack said, "it's too dangerous."

She compressed her lips. "No, I'll go with you, and I can take care of myself."

Jack had learned not to argue with her, and he mounted quickly, leading the way along the creek to the main road. They rode up past Jose's place hoping the Germans hadn't left a 'listening post,' and much to their relief, found it was all clear. Continuing up over the water divide to *Mucubaji*, and approaching the lake, Jack could see the float plane nestled in along the shore. The plane, covered with canvas and branches, blended in perfectly with the rest of the shoreline. You couldn't see it until you got very close.

Pat was first off the horse, and with the others helping, cleared away all the branches so that he could pull the tarpaulin off the big float. The windscreen was nice and clean, just as he had left it. He quickly checked the engine oil, turned on the ignition and had someone crank over the propeller. The engine growled, sputtered slightly, and then roared to life. Pat was serious now and intent, staring at the instruments, and checking the oil pressure and fuel gauges.

All was as it should be and he signaled Jack to start loading. He handed Jack three of the Enfield rifles and a revolver that he had stashed under the seats along with some ammunition. In addition he pulled out two kabars and a survival knife he had picked up at an Army and Navy store in Chicago. He had thought they would come in handy and now he silently chided himself for not buying a few more.

Jack smiled, and said, "I don't know where you got these but I think I can put them to good use. Thanks Pat! I won't see you again until La Ceiba. We'll link up at the plantation. It is the safest place for a rendezvous. I don't think the Germans know about it. You'll have to leave the plane at the La Ceiba wharf."

Pat indicated that all was well, and as Jack watched, Professor Gomez and two of the troopers boarded the plane for the coast. It was still early enough to take off with the denser air, but Pat indicated he would have to taxi around the lake to create waves that would release some of the drag on his floats. Nevertheless, it would be touch and go with a load like this and Jack noticed a breeze coming from the north. As he watched, Pat taxied fast across the lake, raising some large waves. When he got to the far end of the lake with the lake surface as rough as possible, he gave the big float full throttle into the wind.

Pat barely lifted off on the north side of the lake, narrowly missing some boulders on the moraine there. After gaining some altitude, he flew down the Santo Domingo valley and very soon reached a point where he could fly north of *Aguila* Peak and out of range of the retreating German column.

*   *   *   *

Jack stood momentarily transfixed at the sight of the disappearing plane and then said to his father and Celine, "We'd better move and keep an eye on our friends. I wonder if they'll stop in Timotes as they did on the way in."

Jack bent over to pick up the knives that Pat had given him. One knife he slid on his belt and the other he put in the inside pocket of his jacket. He took the one at his side out of the sheath and threw it into a tree not more than a few meters away. He liked the way it handled. Throwing it would be easy. He imagined the second knife would handle the same way but he would test it later on after they caught up with the Germans.

They left the remainder of the troopers waiting for the plane to return, mounted up and rode down the valley to the small farm where they would wait for their car and truck coming up from Mérida. The car, a 1937 Dodge, had a powerful six-cylinder engine and very good traction, making it especially useful in the mountains.

Soon the vehicles from Mérida appeared, led by Major Bezada, and driven by some of the troopers. They split up with Jack, the elder Professor Ford, and Celine in the car and some of the mountain troopers in the truck. Luckily, the troopers had stopped to pick up some rifles, revolvers and some extra ammunition. The others would have to ride horses.

What a sight they made with the car out ahead, followed by the truck and troopers on horseback dressed pretty much as mountain ranch hands. Whereas before they had little in the way of arms, now they had fourteen additional rifles making a total of thirteen armed men in their group and four in the coastal group. Celine loaded a revolver and slipped it into her belt. Jack walked over to her, handed her a holster and said, "It's better to use the holster. Remember to not leave a round in the chamber, just in case."

She looked at him smiling, as if to say, 'I won't shoot myself.'

Things were certainly looking up as they drove up toward *Aguila* Peak on a strangely warm sunny day. Normally this time of year the weather was marginal, certainly with more rain than today, but mountain weather was always unpredictable. This day was brilliant and maybe that was a positive omen of good things to come.

In the late afternoon Jack reckoned they were close to the turn off near Timotes where the Germans had bivouacked on the way in. Would they do the same on the way out? With this on every mind, they kept a close watch on the road ahead. Jack thought it best to let the horsemen go first to see if the Germans had put out any sentries. The horsemen would not arouse suspicion, if the Germans intercepted them, but the car would likely bring gunfire, as the Germans would know they were being followed.

Two of the troopers led the group, with the rest holding back out of sight, and with the car in the rear. Soon the lead troopers appeared saying the entire German force had left the road to bivouac about five kilometers to the north. This was the time to slip past them and either hold-up at Timotes or head straight for the coast. Jack decided to move at a fast clip for the coast and rendezvous with Professor Gomez at the plantation. He hoped for some help from the *Motilone* as they were going to need it.

They drove on with the troopers following close behind. It was dangerous driving at night but they had little choice, so they stayed close together using the headlights of the car to light the way. Jack prayed that the Germans did not have sentries out near the main road for, if they did, they would certainly be interested in an automobile with several passengers, followed by a truck laden with supplies and ammunition, heading away to the coast. As they passed the side road there was no one to be seen and all appeared quiet. It was about sixty kilometers from Timotes to the coast, and at full throttle on the gravel it would take five or six hours to get there and somewhat longer for the horsemen.

Arriving at the coastal plantation about midnight, Jack finally realized he was exhausted. The troopers, too, looked worn out and he knew they needed some sleep to prepare for the next day. Professor Gomez reported that two plane loads of troopers had made it in to La Ceiba and that Pat and the plane were fine. Jack realized he would need the plane to contact Señor Sanchez and report on the German mission. With no means of contacting Sanchez from the mountains, or even from Bobures or La Ceiba, he imagined the American agent would be starved for information. Perhaps he had new intelligence on the subs.

Pat was up early in the morning after securing the plane at the float base. Professor Gomez had found his two *Motilone* friends, but after leaving him at the plantation, they had disappeared into the bush. They needed sleep above all, and then they needed a plan, as the Germans would arrive soon and they would have very little time to stop them from escaping with the shipment.

Fifteen
The Motilone

Early the next morning, Jack awoke first, and looked around the cabin to find Professor Gomez missing. He went to the window and looked outside. In front of the cabin Professor Gomez was sitting on a crate talking to three *Motilone* all decked out with face paint and carrying spears and blowguns.

All decked out in warpaint, thought Jack. *They must be planning something.*

Jack wondered how serious this was when Celine appeared at his shoulder.

"Amazing how my father gets along with these people. Most Venezuelans are afraid of them, but Papa works here all the time and they accept him. He's almost one of the tribe and probably they like him because he treats them as equals and of course he identifies all the stones they bring out of the forest. He has managed to survive all these years where others have disappeared after trying to cheat them or beat them into submission."

Jack took all this in and marveled at Professor Gomez's demeanor, which said that all was well with him and the men with him.

Soon the old man turned, walked into the cabin, and finding Jack by the window, said, "The Germans are on the coast road. Last night they engaged the *Motilone* in a fire fight. Three warriors were killed, one wounded. Four or five Germans were either killed or wounded and the *Motilone* won't be satisfied until they draw more German blood, but for now, they've retreated into the forest. They'll help us, but they don't know how to deal with the German firepower as they have machine guns, many more than the Venezuelan army."

Professor Gomez continued, "They want to know our plan and also they

179

want to know what the Germans are prepared to die for. The Motilone suspect the Germans are carrying something valuable such as gold. They do not know about the platinum and I am a little worried that if we don't tell them now they'll find out later. If they do find out they'll consider it a breach of trust."

"We should decide on a strategy now and stick to it," said Jack.

"If we're not truthful with them they might turn on us later and believe me they are formidable opponents. They're not afraid of death," said Professor Gomez.

Jack considered this and counseled, "We must make a plan and then consider the amount of information we'll give to the Motilone."

"But first, do the *Motilone* know exactly where the Germans are now? We need to know the German positions and offloading point before planning an attack."

Thinking for a moment, Jack looked at Professor Gomez, who added, "I suspect the *Motilone* do know but we won't know this until they return with the rest of the tribe."

"When will that be?" said Jack.

"Very soon, from what they've told me."

"I think we need to take stock of our weapons and ammunition, clean the weapons, and get our kit set for operations in the forest. Also we need fuel for the car and Pat will have to see to this as soon as possible."

Pat interjected, "I filled the extra petrol cans on the way in so there's ample fuel to operate along the coast. Also, I found a truck at the abandoned plantation down the road, checked it out, and found that it can be 'hot wired' and with fuel will run quite well. It isn't great but we can use it to ferry the troopers and the *Motilone*. So, we have three vehicles. You might want to ask Luis and Sergio to go and collect it."

"Yes," said Jack, "this is perfect. But first let's lay out the weapons and ammunition and then clean the rifles and revolvers."

"Okay," replied Pat, as he headed out the door to the car to round up the spare rifles.

The other troopers started taking their rifles apart, field stripping them to insure they were in proper working order. Jack spun the cylinder in his Ruger to insure it was empty, pulled the cylinder pin, and then removed the cylinder and looked down the bore. Yes, it was a little dirty, but it always paid to strip and clean weapons, if you wanted to count on them and avoid misfires. He pulled some oil and little felt patches out of his kit, assembled a small ramming rod, and started to clean the barrel and cylinder.

Jack oiled everything and wiped it clean. Putting the revolver together, he slid it into his holster. His knives, more lethal than the revolver when necessary, did not need much care, although the blades had to be treated with oil and one had to be careful to wipe them down. He spread all his blades out — the *kukri*, two kabars, two *pukkas* and the one the farmer had given to him. He picked up the double sheathed *pukkas*, drew one and threw it at a bottle which a split-second later exploded off a shelf. He sheathed his other knives, cleaned the blades, and then threw one of them into the wall. Everything was in order. All that remained was to implement a plan that he hoped would solve all their problems and prevent the Germans from escaping with the gold-platinum.

As he put his knives into his pack he caught Celine watching him with a most quizzical smile.

I'll bet you've done that hundreds of times?" as she stepped forward to have a closer look at the revolver.

"Thousands would be more like it," he answered, as he handed her the long-barreled 22. While she looked at it he took out his 44 that he had recovered in Apartaderos and started cleaning it.

Celine opened the cylinder on the 22, spun it to insure it was fully loaded, and then handed it to Jack, saying with a devilish smile, "You left one in the chamber. This is dangerous, remember?"

"Only when the enemy is nearby. You don't want a misfire on the first round,"

Jack replied, his wry smile unfolding across his face.

Celine decided she was beginning to like this adventurous rogue despite his devil-may-care attitude.

But I had best hide it lest father discovers my feelings.

She knew she was growing fond of Jack but she also knew that her fondness for him would cause more than ripples. It could wait.

"Do all archaeologists carry an assortment of knives and revolvers?"

"They do if they want to survive and survival is my main aim in life."

"Do you have any other aims?"

These questions were becoming heavily loaded, Jack felt, as he hesitated. For once he was lost for words to come up with the right answer. He could see Celine was enjoying her quips, prodding his inner feelings.

"Well that depends on time and circumstances. Right now I wish I could take some time off and relax. But circumstances dictate otherwise and I am sorry to have embroiled you in it. Events are controlling my every action and I wish it were otherwise."

He could sense Celine wanted a different answer but he couldn't think of anything that would make any difference. Without any reply she smiled and walked away.

Fouled up again. Why couldn't I come with something softer, nicer, something she might like, he thought. *I may not get another chance. Oh well, by tomorrow*

I might well take up permanent occupance here. If the Germans win out I may end up in the ground.

*   *   *   *

Celine had returned to her bunk lying there hot and uncomfortable looking at the thatched roof and wondering if the wretched heat would let up once the sun was down. The trip seemed to be coming to an end from a series of interminable encounters with the Germans trying to haul their precious metal cargo to the coast. Savoring the silence with everyone outside, she reflected upon the continuous snoring that had permeated the cabin all night. Her father and the elder Dr. Ford had created wave after wave of horrific thunder with the rise and fall of their snoring, crest after crest of each wave ending with a sputter of flagellating tissue in their throats. She was tired but too hot to sleep. Anyway they would get underway soon.

As she lay there she thought of Jack just outside the door, concentrating on him with an intensity that alarmed her. She conjured him up in her mind as if he were standing in front of her. The face that could please and threaten all at the same time, that engaging smile and speckled grey hair that flung itself at you out of his immense beard. She could see him clearly now and started to talk to him as if he were really there. Getting hold of herself she decided it was unwise to voice what was really going through her mind. She was becoming enamored with this man.

Celine was a quiet, insular girl not given to emotional displays of any kind. Most of her life had been spent, first within the confines of family and the Catholic Church, and later within the discipline of the Earth sciences. Science had taken over from family and church, instilling in her a methodical mode of thought, somewhat predictable and even more burdensome and constraining than God. She had learned to live within the discipline required of her scientific endeavors and she realized her earlier religious upbringing had prepared her well for her professional life. Some things in life were more demanding than God and family. Science was one of them.

While she was totally happy working with her father in the university, this adventure with Jack Ford was something new and very different taking her to a totally new level. When she thought about him even now that he was outside with her father, she smiled almost instantly and her body exuded a film of sweat, not from the heat and humidity of the room, but from the thought that Jack was so close.

Rising from her bunk wet with sweat she realized she needed fresh air. Pulling on her sandals she dropped softly to the floor and walked over to the window. Outside she could see Jack, the elder Dr. Ford and her father talking.

*　　*　　*　　*

Jack went over the escape route in his mind, concluding the Germans would be through Valera by this time, probably arriving north of La Ceiba in the next few hours. They couldn't offload their cargo there as it would attract attention, so they must have a disembarkation place in mind to the north or south. It would be logical to the north as this was closer to the straits leading out into the Caribbean. Professor Gomez watched Jack and knew he was thinking about the plan.

Finally he spoke up, "If you are thinking of La Ceiba, it is the loneliest stretch of beach on the lake. *Herr* Jahn would be well aware of it and will advise the Germans to offload their cargo there or close by, probably to the north."

Jack turned to Professor Gomez, nodded, and asked, "When do you think the *Motilone* will return?"

Professor Gomez replied, "I don't know exactly but I think they'll be along as soon as they know where the Germans are and how many we face. They are tough señor but they are afraid of the German machine guns."

"So am I," answered Jack, as he thought through the inventory of their meager arsenal and concluded they would have to find some additional weapons. Maybe the *Motilone* could help out with this problem, and even if they couldn't, their blowguns could come in very handy.

But where were the *Motilone*?

Jack counted fourteen rifles, which meant they had four unarmed troopers. The supply of ammunition was only a meager forty rounds per rifle. He had a revolver with about sixty rounds and six knives. It looked like the balance was with the *Motilone*. If they showed up and if they would help, it might be possible to stop the Germans.

*　　*　　*　　*

Celine stood on the porch listening to Jack and her father exchange ideas. Off in the distance the sky was darkening and lightning illuminated the horizon. Rain would drift in soon and hopefully bring reduced temperatures and some relief from the sweltering heat. Professor Gomez leaned against a fence post, thoroughly engrossed watching Jack clean his revolver. It seemed to Gomez that Jack cleaned his weapons all the time, no matter what.

Neither of them saw Celine on the porch.

A streak of lightning caught Professor Gomez's attention and he turned to study the approaching cloud. A loud crack of thunder that sounded closer than it actually was rattled a few cans on the porch railing.

Without showing any concern, Jack finished cleaning his revolver and turned to look at the approaching thunderstorm. "I love the noise, light and above all the rain. It should cool us all off."

Professor Gomez continued to study the cloud but then noticed Celine watching both of them from the porch. He wondered how long she had been there as he did not hear her come out of the cabin.

"Time to eat supper, Jack," Professor Gomez said. "By the time the storm passes we must be ready to move to the coast."

"It'll be dark soon," Celine added

Jack stood there, bare feet spread wide apart, illuminated in the fading light.

Frequent flickering lightning strikes make him look like some heroic figure out of an ancient Greek mythology, Celine thought.

Celine led the way and they entered the cabin to wait out the storm and cook up supper.

"My turn with the cuisine," Jack said, as the advancing front of the storm swept up the road to the cabin.

After a meal of corn fritters, melon and smoked fish, Jack walked out on the porch to find Celine and her father out looking at the stars. Despite the earlier storm, the sky was perfectly clear this night with not a cloud anywhere. The moon was nearly full and seemed to illuminate just about everything nearby. A full moon was not nearly so good for the German operation but it was useful for Jack.

Jack considered, "Everything hangs in the balance now with the *Motilone*. If they come in with us we might possibly stop the German evacuation and if they don't, we most probably will not be able to do anything barring the unexpected. I don't know what to do about the platinum, but maybe it'd be best to tell them that the Germans have a double load of gold and little silver. They may find the platinum anyway, and if they do, they'll know we're telling them the truth."

Professor Gomez gave a sigh of relief and dropped into a chair. Looking relieved, he said, "I'd hoped you would come to that conclusion."

As Professor Gomez gazed off into the distance he saw his two *Motilone* friends leave the forest running with that typical gait of theirs, one fellow more lopsided than the other, but both making considerable time.

He added, "They've probably run all the way from their village about twenty-five kilometers away."

The *Motilone* stopped at the porch and spoke to Professor Gomez with no apparent strain or loss of breath. It was almost as if they had just stepped out of a vehicle, although one of them was sweating a little. Both wore black and brown headbands, no shirt, shorts of a sort and sandals made from old tires, probably Michelins.

They carried their blowguns and an assortment of darts in a pouch along with bottles of different liquids that Jack figured consisted of several poisons for different targets. He noticed one of the *Motilone* dousing several darts with a black liquid, which Professor Gomez had said, was curare. All their bottles consisted of curare as they intended to fight to the death. Curiously, he remembered von Humboldt's description of native use of curare for hunting animals in his *Travels* and now he was witnessing its use by hunters intending to stalk human prey.

Jack was somewhat taken aback when Professor Gomez said, "Four more of the tribe were attacked and killed by the Germans and the entire German force is only ten kilometers away on the coast road, apparently heading for the beach area north of La Ceiba."

Looking at Jack with a deep curiosity written across his face, he added, "About fifty *Motilone* warriors are due here inside of an hour and they're all armed with blowguns."

As Jack thought this over, Professor Gomez continued, "They've captured a machine gun, two machine pistols, and some ammunition. They don't know how to use them, but they think you'll show them."

Jack smiled, said, "They apparently think of everything."

He couldn't wait to see them but then he thought about transport, and asked Professor Gomez, "How in the world will we get them all to the coast road?"

"They'll run. Ten kilometers is nothing to the *Motilone*. They could easily run all the way to Maracaibo City."

Jack looked at Celine who was absorbed in the preparations. She knelt on the floor bent over some boxes, meticulously counting some packets of food and ammunition. She turned to look as Jack walked in, her face calm as ever, but there was a new wariness this time. She turned and continued counting the packets fully cognizant of Jack behind her.

Jack went over to the sink, put his head under the faucet, and pumped water over his head. As he dried himself, he looked at Celine and realized she was about the most beautiful woman he had ever seen. Her blue eyes, the color of the Mediterranean, had the deepest blue hue possible She looked younger than her twenty-some years possibly because she had few worries with a position in the university and her father looking out for her. If they got out of this okay, he wondered if there was any future for the two of them. She seemed to like him, and she worried about him he knew, but beyond that he wasn't sure about the depth of her affection. She was reliant, and as dependable and knowledgeable as any man or woman he had ever known, and she was bright.

From her reticence he figured her father had warned her about him and for good reason, as he was little more than an adventurer, a hired mercenary.

Granted he had an academic job, a position in a respectable institution, but he never turned down a challenge. When there was contract money involved, whether or not from the museum, the government, or some collector of antiquities, he would take it. The thrill was part of it and the challenge begged his participation. He couldn't avoid it, and even though he was getting older, he reckoned, sooner or later it would kill him. No, such a man is not worth staking a life on, and this woman deserves more than an adventurous archaeologist and fortune hunter.

He was lulled out of his deeper thoughts when he heard Professor Gomez say, "The rest of the *Motilone* are here and what a sight they make mustering in the yard."

Jack looked out over the porch and was impressed with the mob before him. They were all decked out in paint and looked fearsome with their blowguns and headbands; some carried spears which from the tactical point of view was a new twist.

Professor Gomez came up to Jack, said, "The Motilone want another demonstration with the knife. They heard from my two friends about your ability and they want to see you ply your trade so to speak. This will be the glue that binds us together *amigo*, so be careful what you do, and above all don't miss anything with the blade."

"Can I move?" Jack said.

"What do you mean?" said Professor Gomez.

"I'm much better if I move," said Jack.

He jumped off the porch, and with the knife coming off his hip with speed, he put the blade into a tree not a foot away from one of the warriors who dropped his spear. Part of the group fell to the ground when they sensed a second knife might come their way. The rest were dumbstruck with amazement.

Professor Gomez grinned with this demonstration as he knew the *Motilone* were impressed. They surrounded Jack speaking excitedly and Jack smiled that malicious smile of his. Celine, holding a hand over her mouth, seemed frozen in time. She had only heard about the knife from her father, and truly Jack used it as an extension of his hand.

Jack handed the spear back to the *Motilone* who lost it and slapped the man on the back. At first he seemed upset but soon he regained his composure and joined the other tribesmen surrounding Jack. Yes, he had found the 'glue' to hold them together and he was sure they would do as he asked.

*   *   *   *

Jack outlined his plan after the Motilone explained where the Germans were on the coast. Runners would be coming in soon to explain precisely where the Germans encamped for the night. They had to wait. Jack explained that it would take sometime to offload the gold and that was the time to hit them. They would need to move to the beach area, reconnoiter the camp, and attack. The *Motilone* brought up the machine gun and machine pistols and ammunition.

Jack picked up the machine gun and realized it was a nine millimeter weapon. He estimated the *Motilone* had brought over 400 rounds of ammunition in belt and another 500 rounds in a cartridge case. The machine pistols were *Schmiesser's*. There were at least 10 cartridge clips for the pistols and he decided to take one himself giving the other one to his dad.

"And what do I do with this."

"Dad, just don't shoot yourself," Jack said, with a smile.

Then he thought better about it and wished he had given it to one of the mountain troopers.

While they waited for the *Motilone* runners to arrive, Jack outlined his plan to deal with the Germans. With Professor Gomez translating, Jack said, "I need a diversionary attack by you guys, to direct attention to a portion of the German perimeter.

With his peripheral vision he noticed Celine grimacing at mention of 'guys,' he corrected himself, saying "everyone."

But first I need to penetrate close to the German encampment and try to figure out when they will contact the submarine."

He was sure the subs would come up only after dark when there was no chance of detection. If the paratroopers put out patrols, it might be possible to intercept one, and use captured uniforms to get into the German camp.

"Tell them, they'll be paid, somehow, even if we don't capture the gold," Jack said.

It worried him that he couldn't contact Señor Sanchez as the HF radio in the plane was not working to peak perfection and did not have the range. Yet, he knew that somehow he must get a message to him, and quickly.

At this point Jack decided honesty was the best policy with regard to the German cargo and he counseled Professor Gomez, "Tell the *Motilone* that in addition to the gold, the Germans are escaping with platinum or *platina* (little silver), and little silver contains a metal called iridium."

Giving time for this to sink in, Jack added, "It's not so much the value of the platinum, but that the iridium will be used to make faster military aircraft to fight their enemy, people just like us. If we can stop them we might avert the coming war, which is bound to spill across much of the world."

As Professor Gomez translated his message, he sensed a certain apprehension among the warriors, their faces exhibiting a range of fear and suspicion, and most certainly of evil.

As he gazed at them he thought that the Germans would think the same of him and his little band of saboteurs. Evil is a moral concept, he thought, a calamitous, pernicious conduct that could only result in misfortune; it could only depend on your point of view. The *Motilone* spoke to Professor Gomez but looking at them, Jack could see defiance in their eyes–*they are with us*, he thought.

Professor Gomez replied, "They don't understand the iridium exactly, but they trust you, and they'll help. They grieve their dead and want only to kill Germans. They'll fight for the gold señor and they expect a split. You can have the *platina*."

Between their penetration of the camp and the *Motilone* attack it might be possible to escape with some of the German gold-platinum. The *Motilone* liked this idea because at least at night they had some chance of success. The big problem involved the submarines. If the Germans offloaded the gold-platinum to the U-boats how could they disable them?

Pat said he could build a mine or mines to disable the bow planes and ballast tanks, but the problem would be to get them in place to do the job. If they sunk the subs in Lake Maracaibo, the Venezuelans could recover the cargo at a later date and the Germans would be deprived of their precious cargo.

As Jack and his group were mulling this over, *Motilone* scouts arrived with news that the Germans had bivouacked at the beach about sixty kilometers north of where they had originally landed, some 15 kilometers up the coast road. They had encamped for the night, and it looked like all was stillness, with no one on or near the stretch of coast they occupied. There was a full moon and the *Motilone* were grouped up in the forest to the south of the German encampment. They could attack at any time but they had only five rifles; the rest would be done with blowguns and spears and of course they needed reinforcements.

Jack decided that this was as good a time as any to look over the German force and see what was tactically possible.

They loaded up the trucks and car and headed off for the coast. Because of their frequent problem with German patrols, Jack cautioned against a headlong drive to the coast. They would approach the coast road, turn north, and stop about 5 kilometers from the German camp in case they were actively patrolling the entire coast. With Professor Gomez translating, the *Motilone* said their warriors would be looking for the truck and car as it proceeded along the coast road, and that they should drive with the moonlight only.

There would be no traffic on the road at dusk. Jack marveled at their knowledge. How did they know he had a truck? They started off and drove with headlights until they made the coast road. Once headed in a northerly direction, they shut off the lights, and used only moonlight. There was plenty to see with moonlight and since the coast road was flat, or nearly so, there was no problem cruising along at 40 to 45 kilometers per hour.

*   *   *   *

After about a half-hour they spotted two figures waving at them from the middle of the road and they slowed down to a crawl. Sure enough two *Motilone* warriors came up to the vehicles and after some minor translating they learned the Germans were about six kilometers away. The *Motilone* camp was only a short distance away in the forest and they could drive there and hide the vehicles. Jack decided this was the best plan at the moment. After they parked the vehicles he could go with a select group and have a look at the camp.

If he was right the Germans might already be in contact with their evacuation force. He told his father and Professor Gomez that he might need some help getting into the camp. They both volunteered to help him with this subterfuge that might yield some positive result. He took Luis and Sergio with him, along with Professor Gomez and his father, and they drove off to a point about two kilometers away from the camp where the *Motilone* were sure they could park unnoticed and leave the vehicle.

Soon they were close to the German camp and Jack could see the perimeter. They were in scrub forest complete with semi-deciduous trees well concealed from the shore. The Germans had patrols out and they also had a radio mast erected over the camp, so they must be in touch with the submarines.

Major Mueller was efficient as usual, Jack thought.

As Jack watched, one patrol left the main body, and moved off beyond the perimeter of the camp starting to come their way. He cautioned his father and Professor Gomez to wait here, while he took Luis and Sergio to intercept them.

If they could capture this patrol, they might stand a chance of getting into the camp, create some chaos and even escape with some of the gold and platinum. Between their position and the German patrol there was a long gully that might be just what they needed to surprise them. They headed straight for it taking care not to present a silhouette by crossing over high ground. Soon they were in the gully and Jack, surprised at its width, was pleased to see much vegetation hanging over the side, affording many hiding places. He took some of the vines and draped them over his shoulders and the two troopers did the same.

Sergio actually looked like a bush. They knew the Germans would have to traverse the gully to get to the beach on the opposite side and they would want to insure that no one was there. Sergio took one side of the gully and Luis and Jack the other. They waited fading into the grass on the sides of the gully. Jack carefully unsheathed his *pukkas* thinking he might not be able to get close to the troopers and he might need it to disarm one or two of them.

Soon they heard the Germans talking which indicated confidence that no one was listening. Jack held both blades, one to throw butt first the other blade first. He chided himself again for not painting the blades black to avoid reflections that might give him away. Two of the Germans walked almost directly toward Jack and Luis, while the third stopped to light a cigarette. They had to be confident of no intruders to do this, and he heard the first soldier say something to the last man in the column which, judging by the tone of voice, had to be something like, "Put out the cigarette, you fool."

After lighting the cigarette, the third man fell behind his mates and temporarily lost his footing. They were now only meters away. The first two soldiers turned to look back in his direction and then Jack and Luis sprang on them. Luis knocked the first man cold with his rifle, while Jack hit the second with the blunt end of his knife. He dropped his rifle, stunned at the sudden attack, and then Jack hit him with his revolver. The third man stood transfixed for too long a time and Sergio, grabbing him from behind, knocked him out.

They stood in the moonlight looking at the three disabled paratroopers. Removing their uniforms, they gathered up their weapons and ammunition, and tied them up. When they came to they wouldn't be able to get out of the gully. Jack, Luis and Sergio left to find Professor Gomez and the elder Professor Ford. He would need one of them to wear the officer's uniform and get them into the camp. He prayed that the uniform would fit, the garrison watch complacent, and he hoped with all his will that there was no challenge/ password.

He thought about returning to the gully to interrogate the Germans to find out about a password and gave it up because of the time involved. They would need to penetrate the camp at precisely the time the *Motilone* attacked.

Once back at their rendezvous point, the elder Professor Ford and his son donned German uniforms. Dad was a little old to be a *leutnant* in the German paratroopers but that was the best they could do. Looking at the chevrons on his jacket Jack reckoned he was a sergeant. Oh well, an officer and a gentleman, and an enlisted man. With his father's command of German they might just pull this off and slip into the German camp.

Jack counted on the diversionary attack to distract the guard and hoped they could get into the camp without difficulty. They made a handsome pair and the *Motilone* joked that they hoped they didn't mistake them for real Germans otherwise they might end up with a dart in their backs. When this was translated, Felix grimaced. Jack smiled and the two set off toward the German camp.

The *Motilone* headed west planning to attack the German camp from the coast road. Major Bezada and his troopers planned to attack from the coastal dunes. They set the time of attack for precisely 9:00 PM and Professor Gomez went with them to translate. Celine did not want to leave her father but he insisted she stay with Pat back at the vehicles.

*   *   *   *

About forty minutes later, Jack and his dad crept up to the crest of a small dune and looked at the German camp barely fifty meters away. There was only one guard and he looked bored, his gaze fixed on the shore. There was little action in the camp and Jack was thinking the entire force must be asleep. Perhaps they were off schedule and couldn't contact the submarine? Anyway they were certainly not loading the cargo tonight. This was a good omen and it would give them time. He looked at his watch and whispered to his dad that they had less than ten minutes before the *Motilone* attacked. His dad murmured something about how foolish he felt, and then Jack remarked, "Stop talking and think about speaking only in German if we are challenged."

At precisely 7 P.M. the *Motilone* and Venezuelan troopers opened up on the west perimeter and Jack was not surprised that many of them got to within a few meters of the German sentries. Two of them went down in the fusillade of darts, which were followed by rifle fire directed at the tents. An improvised grenade exploded close to the aerial post, toppling it precariously on its side. The Germans, wearing various articles of clothing, spilled from their tents and organized a firing line that began systematic shooting in the direction of the attack.

The guard facing Jack and his father, distracted by the gunfire, hardly noticed the two 'Germans' walking into the compound. One soldier was working a field phone as Jack and his dad came up behind him. The elder Professor Ford was appalled when his son took him down with a well-placed knife throw at ten meters. They moved behind the German vehicles to give them cover. Jack found one vehicle with large crates that seemed to contain a cargo of gold-platinum. He jumped in the cab, couldn't find the keys, and motioned to his father to join him.

Jack cut the ignition wires, touched them together and the engine coughed into life. He backed the vehicle out, turned, and drove out toward the coast road. The entire road was clear. They drove along at a fast clip hoping the *Motilone* could distract the Germans for another few minutes. The firefight raged on and they were certainly doing a good job and probably taking one hell of a beating. Jack hoped they had the right cargo but there was time only to drive at speed to make their rendezvous point.

Now it was time to see if Pat had repaired the radio and managed to relay a message to Señor Sanchez. It looked like the Germans would escape with their precious cargo, or most of it at any rate, and there was little they could do about it.

PART III

The Exfiltration

Despite all his efforts Jack Ford made minor gains against the German invasion force but failed to stop the transfer of gold and platinum to the coast. Everything depends on the tactical plan in place and the timely arrival of the U-boats. Without transport the German force will have to abandon the mission, fade into the countryside and risk capture, or worse, imprisonment. The threat of imminent war looms over both forces, and once declared, British forces in the Caribbean will have authorization to shoot and sink. Time is as great an enemy to the Germans as Ford and his saboteurs. If only they can escape the coast and elude the British, they might have a chance to make it home to Germany. Everything for them and for the Allies hangs in the balance. It might go either way and luck will play a big roll in the outcome.

Sixteen
Radio Contact

31 August, 1939. At precisely 7:30 PM, *Kapitän* Walter Hahn, commander of U-501 and in overall command of *Aguila Negra*, ordered negative ballast and one-third turns on the screws of his U-boat. He had been on the bottom for hours, waiting for the onset of darkness, when he could surface and make radio contact with *Raven*. He brought the boat to periscope depth, raised the scope, and surveyed the surrounding lake surface, taking the entire picture into account in less than fifteen seconds.

After a minute or two, he caught sight of the periscope of U-231, which was due to surface with him. It was dangerous to have both boats on the surface at the same time, but "Time is of the essence" they had been told by Military Intelligence, "If spotted, dive, and leave the area immediately. *Aguila Negra* is expendable.

The boats are not," or at least that is the way his orders read. He didn't like the thought of leaving paratroopers stranded on the Maracaibo Coast, but 'orders are orders' the manual said.

All was quiet and deserted on the surface. He ordered the boat *auftauchen* (to surface), and imagined that U-231 was doing the same, but he would soon see. He watched his chief helmsman (*Obersteuermann*) work the controls and gently surface the boat. As the boat broke the surface, the main hatch was released, water poured into the control room, and two lookouts scrambled ahead of him to the conning tower. He climbed up after them followed by the deck gun crew. Since they were in shallow waters and might be attacked by small gunboats, it was wise to have the gun crew on standby. As Walter swept the surrounding lake surface with his binoculars, he noticed that U-231 was exactly opposite him no more than 200 meters distant.

He was at this time 30 years old, of moderate height with broad shoulders, straight jet-black hair and beard and a face weathered by time at sea. Praeger, his telegraphist (*Funkgefreiter*), followed up onto the conning tower and stood waiting for orders.

Without turning around, Walter ordered, "Message to *Sonne*. No contact with *Raven*. In position at extraction point. Will advise. *Humpback* out."

"Aye *Kapitän*." Praeger copied the message down on his board and scrambled down the ladder to the control room.

Walter straightened up to stretch his back and flipped the binocular cord over his neck, letting the glasses settle against his chest, satisfied that all was well in the still water of the lake. His new binoculars, made by Zeiss, were larger than the old marine binoculars he was used to, and therefore gathered more light, and the night image they produced was truly amazing. The image with light from a full moon was sharp and clear. Even without his glasses, he could see *Kapitänleutnant* Adolph Langsdorff, commander of U-231. When he was certain Adolph was looking he gave him an energetic wave. Dropping his glasses into the black case with a German eagle on the front flap, he considered the code name for his mission-*Aguila Negra. How fitting*, he thought.

The moonlight was bright and Walter knew that made them excellent targets from the shore. He yelled down the hatch to stand by the radio for a message from *Raven*, the code name for the land segment of *Aguila Negra*. It was now precisely 8 PM and they couldn't hold this position for long. They had carried out the same maneuver the night before without success and, if there was no response tonight, they would have to follow their orders which were explicit. They were to dive and leave Maracaibo immediately heading past Maracaibo City and the straits, link up with the *Sonne*, and sail to the Caribbean Sea where they would meet up with the Raider *Riesen* off Trinidad on September 1.

War was imminent and Walter remembered his secret orders given to him when he left Germany. The cargo he was to pick up in Venezuela was of prime importance to the security of the Reich. As commander of the recovery mission he was in charge and he was to use his discretion, but above all the two U-boats under his command were not expendable. He hoped with all his being that *Raven* was on time. He was precisely at the offloading point, and if everything had gone according to plan, Major Mueller and his group should be in position. The silence was deafening!

Walter looked around the conning tower. The two lookouts were at their posts, lads named Colman and 'Blondy,' methodically scanning the sky, their binoculars oscillating in concert with one another moving in wide arcs. Theirs was the job of alerting the crew of enemy activity, to insure the boat had time to dive before being attacked from the air or sea.

Diving into 25 meters of water hardly guaranteed safety much less survival, he thought. Looking over the side, he muttered to himself, *the only good thing is the silt-laden water, nearly opaque making it impossible to see deep into the water column.*

The cook has the easy job, Walter thought, *only to cope with the taste and whim of the boat's officers. The lookouts are sentinels with many tasks to call out positions of enemy vessels and aircraft. Every man aboard depends on them, from the deck gun crew to hands carrying equipment from one end of the boat to the other.*

The lookouts scarcely acknowledged his presence as he walked from one end of the conning tower (*Wintergarden)* to the other, so intent were they on scanning the sky and the horizon.

The night was becoming brighter with the rising moon, the silhouette of the shore sharper and doubtless, because we could see the coast more clearly, the throbbing of the engines increased in volume, until it seemed loud enough to awaken every native. Walter wished he could move in closer to shore but realized the depth would not allow it. He would have to wait and hope *Raven* arrived on time.

Walter's First Officer asked permission to enter the conning tower. "Come up, Wolfgang," Walter replied. As Wolfgang climbed up the bridge ladder, he could see concern in Walter's face but he also noted his *Kapitän* seemed pensive, almost as if he were reflecting on something. Looking about the still water of the lake, Wolfgang noted the lookouts were alert and scanning in every direction with their binoculars.

"What do you think Wolfgang? We still have no contact and we can't stay on the surface much longer. I have no idea if *Raven* is in position just inland from the dunes."

"Aye, *Kaleu,*" he replied before correcting himself, "Er, *Kapitän,* sorry."

"*Kaleu* fits just fine Wolfgang. Walter fits fine as well."

"How long have we served together Wolfgang?"

"Since '36, you've been the master. First *Kaleu (Kapitänleutnant),* now full *Kapitän.*"

"Aye, but at sea we are informal Wolfgang. You know that as well as I."

Wolfgang said nothing but looked off into the distance thinking of all the operations he had been on with Walter in the lead.

"We can't stay here forever Wolfgang. This shallow pond and that stinking jungle will likely end up with us on the bottom. You can't hear a thing out there, no wind, no people, no nothing not even rain. Where is *Raven?*"

Raven was a black ops (operation) mission, meaning no communication with base and the action report not attributable, that is, no one would be decorated as a result of it. *Humpback* was secret, and not black, meaning they could communicate with their base as the situation warranted.

*   *   *   *

At 8:15 PM the radio sputtered with a general call from *Raven* to *Humpback*, their assigned code name. *Humpback* acknowledged and they immediately changed channels in case they had been intercepted.

On channel B the message came in loud and clear, "*Raven* in position, ready to offload, and awaiting instructions. Engaged enemy in firefight ending one-half hour ago. Entry area now clear and secure, over."

"*Humpback* acknowledges. Recovery starting now."

Kapitän Hahn signaled his second-in-command who slid down the gangway into the control room and gave the order for shore parties to disembark.

U-boats had small, crowded spaces but these two had every non-essential piece of equipment removed for the mission, and that did not amount to much, as nearly every bit of space housed important instruments. Five spare sleeping quarters were fabricated into the boat, to take the extra men on-loaded from a German sub-tender off the coast of the Leeward Islands. His crew, reduced from forty-six to thirty-nine, was a bare minimum, almost a skeleton crew to add extra sleeping quarters. He would pick up the seven crewmen, now serving aboard the tender, when the mission was complete. The German Navy did not have a separate 'silent service' group, so his submariners would not feel out of place serving *Kapitän* Pirien aboard the *Sonne* while he operated in Lake Maracaibo to complete the mission. Yes, he thought, Germany had a small navy, but an efficient and well-trained one, nevertheless.

The paratroopers and crew had to 'hot bunk,' sleeping in shifts to use every inch of space since they had left the tender off the Caribbean Coast. Everything was cramped, but fortunately all the extra rations and weapons had been offloaded with the assault force. Now they would be loading a new and heavier cargo. Sailors quickly brought their rubber rafts up through the forward hatch, inflated them, and dropped them over the side in what seemed to be smooth slow motion. Within twenty minutes the shore party was on its way. *Kapitän* Hahn could see the same was happening on U-231.

Walter grabbed the microphone and ordered, "Praeger, radio *Sonne* before we dive, "Established contact with *Raven*. Extraction in progress."

As Praeger copied the message and prepared to open a channel, Walter gripped the control room rail, leaned slightly to one side and spoke to his officers. "I haven't much to say but you all know the score here. We're very vulnerable and I won't pretend we're safe. If we're discovered by naval or air units we'll have a difficult time eluding them in this shallow pond. But if you do as I order we'll make it out, you and I together."

Praeger was busy working the radio but took Walter's comments in stride as he tapped out a coded message on continuous wave. There was silence in the control room as Praeger waited for an acknowledgment. As he heard the three dashes that indicated message received, he slipped off his earphones and swung round in his chair to see various degrees of concern chiseled in the faces of his peers. He engaged the boat intercom, acknowledging, "Message sent."

We don't all love the Kapitän, he thought, *but he's the man to get us through this in one piece.*

The more Praeger thought about it the more he realized just how terrifying the Maracaibo Lake appeared. None of them would escape if they were discovered. There was no place to run and hide.

As the sailors paddled to shore, *Kapitän* Hahn ordered "lookouts below, engines stop, dive the boat." He followed with ease, sealing the main hatch, as the boat came to minimum periscope depth at fifteen meters, nearly half way to the bottom of the shallow lake. They were secure now, with the shore party on its way, *Raven* intact and ready to disembark, and right on schedule.

What was worrying was the report of a firefight. It must mean they had been intercepted by someone. But who? The police or the army?

Then Walter remembered the intelligence report mentioning a coastal tribe that might mean trouble as they were continually fighting the government. He remembered they carried blowguns, which gave him a chill and he raised the collar on his coat, as if it might deflect a dart. Somehow the steel skin of his U-boat seemed to provide a sanctuary and better protection against death by poison dart.

He wondered how Mueller and his men could stand to fight against such people. Walter thought this might have been why he chose a Navy career. He had an even deeper chill when he thought of the prospect that the blowgun people might return. If they killed any of his shore party, he would find it difficult to safely man the boat. The thought of losing his command to an ancient blowgun wielding tribe seemed ironic to him as the Führer was always calling up the ethics and bravado of the ancient German tribes to strengthen the fabric of 20th Century Germany. There would be a certain irony in being defeated by 20th Century stone-age natives. This disturbed him profoundly but he tried to forget it and concentrate on the business at hand.

With the periscope he followed the shore parties and could see they were making good headway toward the beach. Spread out in a wide arc, he could see figures on the beach, who had to be paratroopers securing the area. He could also see two or maybe three vehicles on the beach and other figures taking off cargo sacks for shipment to the subs. This would be a slow process as the rubber rafts could handle at best 100 kilos dead weight spread out in smaller sacks with two men rowing. The plan called for two out of the four man crews to stay on shore to help with offloading the cargo.

Depending on weight, nearly two-fifths of the cargo was to be stored on U-231, which was to set course straight for the sub-tender when the operation was terminated. U-501 was to rendezvous later with the sub-tender off the Maracaibo Straits where she would transfer the remaining cargo and paratroopers. She would then make for Trinidad and join a wolfpack forming up in the western Atlantic.

*   *   *   *

While his mind was drifting to the future, *Kapitän* Hahn was suddenly jerked back to the present by gun flashes on the beach. The landing party was under fire from the forest and at the worst possible moment. He saw one of the rubber rafts capsize and sink while the other three rafts managed to out distance the rounds fired at them. They would soon be over the boat.

He ordered *auftauchen notfall (surface the boat, emergency)*, and the U-boat came up at a steep angle looking like a rocket when it broke the *surface*. Quickly looking around the bridge, he realized all his officers were manning their stations with their usual efficiency and skill. *This'll be a very tricky operation*, he thought.

Kapitän Hahn ordered the deck gun crew to standby, and not to fire, unless fired upon. He also turned to his third-in-command, *Leutnant* Dietrich, "Klaus return with the shore party to the beach, apprize me of the situation as soon as you can, and determine if the disembarkation can continue."

As planned U-231 remained submerged, although her periscope was sweeping the lake surface, and no doubt her *Kapitän* was aware of the situation. When U-231's periscope came abreast of his conning tower, Walter gave the all clear signal to indicate he was diving. The shore party pushed off, *Kapitän* Hahn gave the dive order *tauchen (dive)*, sealed the hatch, and U-501 again came down to 15 meters.

*   *   *   *

On shore, the situation was serious but not unrecoverable. Major Mueller had lost three more men, two wounded and one killed in a second firefight. These *Motilone* were fierce fighters and even with patrols out they had penetrated between them and attacked his main force. On withdrawing, his patrols had come under fire, but the main problem was that they had sunk a raft and killed one of the shore party. The gold-platinum on the raft could be recovered, as the depth was only about three meters, but this would take time.

The *Motilone* and Venezuelan army troopers had slipped away again as they had about three hours ago, but even with patrols out they had managed to determine what the Germans were up to. Major Mueller calculated they had a force of between fifty and one hundred men mostly armed with blowguns. But they also had a machine gun, which unnerved him somewhat, as they were apparently learning how to use it, and if properly manipulated, they could wipe out a good portion of his force.

The shooting would sooner or later attract attention even in this deserted and desolate area. They had only about five hours to transfer maybe three more loads of cargo, two more than they anticipated. He began to think that maybe they would have to bury some of it and leave it for another time, but then his paratroopers were renowned for bringing back their quarry. On this mission they had buried their dead when usually they carried the bodies out. They might have to change the rules and leave some of the gold.

As he walked the perimeter giving orders to his men, the Major thought of all his past missions mostly on the Polish Frontier and in the Alps, but also along the Baltic Coast and in Africa. How he disliked the Tanganyika patrols. They reminded him of this tropical place, with its heat and humidity, and above all the snakes. They had been lucky on this mission, with only two men bitten by these infernal creatures, both surviving their ordeal. Just then one of his squad sergeants came out of the forest supporting a second man who looked dazed and walked with a limp. He turned and walked over to the two men.

The sergeant saluted, and reported, "I killed a boa constrictor that attacked one of my men. It was a good five meters in length."

The Major replied, "Well done!"

Then the Major thought, *Think about something like snakes and suddenly they appear.* He could do well enough without them.

Looking at the two soldiers, he fully appreciated the close call they had with the snake. He had seen one boa kill a mule, and the sight was not pleasing, then or now. The sooner they disembarked the better.

He was talking with the sergeant when he heard, "Major Mueller," and he turned to see a young navy *leutnant* coming his way.

"Lt. Dietrich, Sir. *Kapitän* Hahn sends his compliments and needs an instant appraisal of the situation. I'm to report back to him with the next cargo load with information about the mission. Can we continue offloading the cargo? More to the point, is the area secure?"

Major Mueller replied, "My patrols are chasing the *Motilone* back into the forest and my base perimeter is secure, at least for the moment. The *Motilone*, reinforced with Venezuelan troopers, are led by an American. They attacked part of my force in the mountains and followed us here. I have lost three men with four wounded, and one of my trucks was stolen complete with its cargo of around three hundred kilograms of gold and platinum. I have nine trucks left with about 5500 kilograms of cargo and fifty-four men including four wounded, although they are capable of helping with the cargo transfer."

After a few seconds, he added, "Provided we can move three more loads to the boats tonight, and finish up the following night, we should be right on schedule. Advise your *Kapitän* that, should he abandon the mission, I'll need time to bury the remaining cargo and transfer my men to the U-boats. And ask him to send an extra raft or two with the next shore party. My men can row out to the subs as well as navy ratings."

"Aye, aye, sir," said the *leutnant*. "I'll tell him."

He turned and ran to the shore where one of the rafts was waiting for him. As he surveyed the beach, he could see all was orderly and under control. Machine gun emplacements were at both sides of the offloading area and the trucks were well hidden and under guard in the forest edge close to the beach. Major Meuller was in complete control despite the *Motilone*.

Nearly at the shore, he stopped to look at one of the dead savages on the beach still clutching his blowgun. One of the paratroopers standing nearby said, "Awfully efficient weapon they have. They got poor old Schmidt here right in the head. Dead inside of a minute, he was. Trouble is, they don't present a target, and you could just as easily shoot a bush as hit one of these devils."

The *leutnant* took another look at the dead body and then waded out to the raft. Looking back at the beach as they rowed to the U-boat he was strangely reminded of Robinson Crusoe, a tale he had read as a child. This beach reminded him of Robinson's beach for some reason but he couldn't place it exactly. Robinson Crusoe was alone or thought he was alone on an island beach. They were most certainly not alone, although they were on a beach. He guessed it was the similarity of the beach and forest that brought the memory back, but he couldn't refine it to a greater degree. Perhaps it was all the tracks in the sand?

Then the *leutnant* fine-tuned his report as *Kapitän* Hahn was not one to waste words. He wanted a situation report and he knew his boss would react to it. *Kapitän* Hahn had not risen to flotilla leader by random chance. He was an excellent U- boat *Kapitän*, and in trial games with surface patrol boats, he always came out the winner, never once losing to surface craft attacking U-501. He knew the limits of his boat better than anyone and his crew was one of the best in the fleet. He had trained with U-231, and both boats had operated together, to hunt surface craft of all types in the Baltic and in the Icelandic and Norwegian seas.

Leutnant Dietrich knew the crew would follow his *Kapitän's* every order, as if their lives depended on it, and with the onset of war very close, their training would keep them alive. They knew it and *Kapitän* Hahn knew it.

Looking at the beach, the *leutnant* thought that the war had already started. It was now 2 A.M., on the 1st of September, 1939.

They couldn't know it, but the invasion of Poland was already underway, and there was less than forty-eight hours to go before the declaration of war.

Seventeen

Submarine Pickup: U-501 and U-231

With less than three hours to sunrise *Kapitän* Hahn watched the fourth load of cargo heading out to U-231. He would stay submerged carrying out surveillance of the surrounding area while the cargo was offloaded onto his sister boat. With time ticking away he knew they were behind schedule and only one more load to be transported before morning. Less than half the cargo would be transferred this night which meant they would have to work overtime the following night to complete the mission. From what *Leutnant Dietrich* had told him the beach was secure, the cargo was being reloaded into small bags for easy storage, and everything was nearly on schedule.

Kapitän Hahn was worried about the intervention of the *Motilone* and mention of American involvement. How had the Americans been alerted to this mission? With Americans on land could there be American submarines waiting for him to complete the operation and reenter the Caribbean. If they were there, they would not intervene, as they were not yet at war with Germany.

But then they had intervened on land, so anything was possible. The thought made him uneasy.

For the moment they were in position and the offloading was nearly on schedule. *Quit worrying,* he told himself. *The officers and men will sense it and I don't need jumpy and trigger-jittery — what did the Americans call it? 'Trigger happy'- seamen at this stage in the cruise.*

Walter realized they would have to start earlier on the following night. As he opened the ship's log and began to enter this comment, Lt. Dietrich climbed up into the control center, saluting as he topped the gangway.

"*Kapitän*, I've calculated the weight distribution to find U-231 will be nearly 600 kilograms too heavy if we load her share of the cargo. They simply brought too much down off the mountain. It's not the weight so much as to where to stow the cargo and troops."

"Redistribute the load, Klaus, anyway you can. We must take it all out."

Jawohl, Herr Kapitän.

"But now we are down to personal belongings."

"If necessary, jettison them, but leave no identification marks on them. Have the torpedo officer weight them down with anything he can find that we don't need. The men will understand and I'll speak to them later."

Klaus knew the gold and platinum were important to the Reich, but personal belongings were also important, and the crew would be disgruntled with the order to jettison personal gear.

A discontented crew is a dangerous component to factor into a mission like this, he thought.

Klaus only knew what he heard from *Kapitän* Hahn in confidence. *Kapitän* Hahn had been given his orders in the presence of General Bayer, Chief of C Section, Admiral Dönitz, Chief of the Navy, and Admiral Canaris, Chief of Naval Intelligence. Reichsführer Himmler had been present, he was told, but mentioned only that the operation would be a "total success."

So far they had been discovered, not only by a stone-age tribe, but also by the Americans, and they had lost some men, in addition to a truck loaded with precious cargo. Their success would not be "total" and he hoped Major Mueller could explain what happened. C-section did not expect anyone to make mistakes.

Anyway he would see to his calculations. He pulled out his slide rule, and laying it across the navigation strike table, started to compute again the weight they would have to drop to take on an extra load of gold-platinum. With a high weight per unit volume, the gold-platinum cargo would have to be spread across the mid-section of the boat. Stowing it, so as not to upset the boat's center of gravity, presented something of a problem. Rolling up his sleeves he started to run through all the numbers again checking all the weights.

On their next communication with U-231 Klaus knew he would have to confirm the weight already loaded. Somehow they had to find a way to move the cargo out into the Caribbean, transfer it to a sub-tender, and then return to pick up the remainder. But there was precious little time for this. To compensate for the sample weight it would be necessary to jettison at least 600 kilograms of cargo and he was sure he could not find it in personal belongings. They might have to jettison some of the torpedoes and store a portion of the cargo in the torpedo tubes. This seemed to be the only way out of their difficult situation, but then they would be defenseless. It would be the *Kapitän*'s decision. On top of this they would have to evacuate almost the whole of the landing force in U-501, which would strain the crew compartments to the limit.

Kapitän Hahn watched the last load leave the beach. He swept the surrounding lake surface with the periscope and satisfied himself that the area was clear. He focused again with the lens on his scope and boosted the magnification. The sailors were rowing and headed for U-231. He looked at his watch and noted that it was 0600 hours. It would be light soon, so they would have to bottom the boat and wait out the day, to begin transferring cargo after dark on the 1st. He would surface along with U-231, when the rafts were close by, and send a transmission by HF radio that all was proceeding according to plan. *Aguila Negra* was on time and *Raven* was underway and nearly terminated. The offloading operation should be completely terminated early on the third.

He gave the message to the telegraphist, who would encrypt it with his enigma machine, and send it while the boat was on the surface. He also ordered the signals officer to make light communication with U-231 and ask about weight limits once they were on the surface. How much more could he take?

Walter sent for Leutnant Dietrich and waited for him to climb up into the control room. Dietrich, who hailed from Koblenz, stood nearly six feet high and was built with massive shoulders which slowed him down moving from one compartment to another.

When he appeared, Hahn said, "Klaus, you'll have to go ashore again. I'll need precise information on numbers of sacks and weights for tomorrow night. Take the extra raft and three men to help with the transfer. We haven't a minute to lose. Klaus, take care of yourself, as the American element in this is ominous."

"*Jawohl Herr Kapitän.*"

"And Klaus, I shall not be able to bring the boat up at all during the day, so if anything goes awry use your own discretion. That is an order. Remember we have many friends in Venezuela, so you should be able to ride it out somehow."

Klaus nodded, and moved off to find the three seamen he would take with him. He would take Dirk who was near the upper limit of weight for a submariner, but would have little difficulty carrying any amount of cargo. He would need three strong lads like himself, as they would all have to pitch in, officers and men alike.

*   *   *   *

Sitting on the bottom waiting for the shore party to return with punctuated periscope sweeps of the surface stretched everyone's nerves to the limit. Finally, rafts were shoving off from shore heading out with another load. The rafts were near enough now so that *Kapitän* Hahn gave the order to surface the boat and U-501 came up quickly. U-231 was already trimmed off, near to the rafts, and taking on cargo. The signals officer was at station sending his message, the signal lamp shutters blinking out a bewildering series of dots and dashes, a kind of lantern Morse Code. Soon a reply came that U-231 was close to capacity with 2500 kilograms loaded. They would have to jettison gear, and maybe torpedoes, to take on much additional weight.

Kapitän Hahn told the signals officer to send a message telling U-231 to change plans, submerge, and head north to rendezvous with the sub-tender off the straits in the Caribbean Sea. She was to proceed at top speed which should put her in the open sea around twelve hours from now or around 5 P.M. If she offloaded her cargo with speed she should be back around late afternoon the following day, the 2nd. U-501 would remain on station here and await her return. The only alternative was to jettison torpedoes and this he could not bring himself to do. They would have to alter their plans.

Kapitän Hahn scribbled a message for the sub-tender and gave it to the radio officer for encryption. Changing plans in the middle of a mission was always dangerous as it made everything more complex, and complex missions break down. What was it the naval tactical manual said — - 'keep it simple or risk failure?

The fewer components in any mission, the less the chance of defeat.' He had just added an element that would reduce his personnel and firepower and one he had not counted on when they planned the mission.

Moreover, the mission was becoming too complex.

Could Mueller hold? Would U-231 return on time? Could they handle the increased load in U-501?

There might be more questions, but if there were, he couldn't think of them now. What he really needed was more time.

Soon it would be light and he would bottom the boat and tell the men to rest. They had to be careful about air consumption and quality. Thirteen hours was a long time to stay on the bottom, but they had done it before. He made a note to remember to ask his engineering officer to check on the oxygen and carbon dioxide levels and work out the maximum time he could stay submerged with increased personnel aboard. He was happy to have Klaus and three seamen off the boat, as this meant more air for the remaining crew.

At the attack desk in the control room, Walter looked over the charts, fixing a proposed course for the next few days.

Not too much variation in what's possible, he told himself. He could hear the resonating noise of ballast pump no. 2 in the forward hold and made a mental note to ask the chief of the boat about it. It sounded as if one of the valves was sticking and if so it would have to be dealt with. This silt-laden murky water had proved to be a curse. Already they had three times the normal problems with the ballast pumps, clogging of the valves and other malfunctions. The sooner they offloaded the gold and platinum and made for the open sea the better.

Walter was beginning to hate this place.

They couldn't risk surfacing until at least 7 P.M.. What worried Walter even more was that U-231 would not be due back until at least the afternoon of the second, which meant they might have to risk a late afternoon extraction of Mueller's force and they might be spotted from the air or from land. He would just have to wait and see, but unknown elements were cropping up all the time, and they were worrisome.

For some reason he kept remembering the naval tactical manual, and he decided that if he got out of this alive, he would reread it and maybe even rewrite it. There were always unknown elements that would complicate an operation, only it seemed he had more than his share of them.

Turning to his exec he said, "I don't like all these unknowns cropping up all the time. They are ominous." Wolfgang nodded, but said nothing.

U-231 completed cargo loading and signaled she would be getting underway. The sub-tender had radioed that a rendezvous should be possible about thirty nautical miles off the Venezuelan coast at position xy-231 on their classified grid system, a complicated location finding system used only by German submariners. They would be on station and the weather was fine with light wind, broken cloud, and little swell.

The tender radio message also mentioned there was little surface traffic in the Gulf of Venezuela and they could offload there in an emergency to shorten the water link between coastal Maracaibo and the tender. *Kapitän* Hahn thought he might have to risk this later on.

What really worried him at this point was the possibility of collision with underwater obstacles or wrecks in the Maracaibo Basin. Their bathymetric charts were excellent but there was always the possibility of unknown wreckage, either sunken vessels or debris from the oil drilling platforms that might present problems. They had made it in and Adolph was an excellent navigator.

He should make it out into the Caribbean Sea without difficulty, he told himself.

The twenty-four hour forecast was excellent for offloading cargo in the open sea. They expected little to no surface ship traffic. At least this part of the mission was looking fine. *Kapitän* Hahn watched as U-231 slipped beneath the lake surface and disappeared. He too would go down soon as sunup was closing in on them.

*   *   *   *

Lieutenant Domingo Mendoza, piloting a Heinkel He59 seaplane, was cruising at 1500 meters on a patrol from Maracaibo to Bubures at the southern edge of the lake. Twice a week Domingo and his observer flew a patrol around the margins of the lake, overnighting at Bobures on its southern edge. The following day they continued on to Lake Valencia, southwest of Caracas, and thence along the bulge of the Venezuelan Coast to Punta Cardón, north of the Gulf of Coro, and along the western margin of the Gulf of Venezuela.

This day, nothing had gone right after leaving Maracaibo. Twice he had to put down in the Maracaibo Lake to fix the fuel pump and it was still not working at full capacity. He normally flew at 1000 meters altitude to give him a better look at the ground but he feared he might have fuel pump trouble again and would need to glide far enough off the coast to land. Trying to stay just off the coast he flew through patchy cloud that covered much of the eastern side of the lake. As he neared the southwestern coast, he could see trucks out on the beach off the port side of the aircraft. His observer yelled over the radio, "Make a turn and let's go lower to have a look. I caught a glimpse of a shadow in the lake. It might be a barge, or it could be a sub. Very strange. Now I've lost it in cloud again."

Mendoza radioed he would dive and drop down to 800 meters, fearing if he went any lower he might well have difficulty landing if the engine went out. As he brought the seaplane around, he watched the altimeter tick off the loss of altitude. He and his observer had flown this coast many times, almost always without incident. While they had caught smugglers before they had never observed trucks on the beach along the coast. What was the long dark shadow his observer had seen? Maybe it was just that a shadow. There's nothing down there with the exception of pineapples, bananas, cocoanuts, boa constrictors and the Motilone.

The He59 was one of two planes that comprised the entire Venezuelan Air Force in 1939. It was a two-float twin engine bi-plane, designed principally for reconnaissance during the clandestine movement in Germany to rejuvenate the Luftwaffe in the early 1930's. Mendoza's plane had seen action in the Spanish Civil War with the *Legion Condor,* being eventually sold to Venezuela for coastal patrols. Powered by BMW 12 piston engines, she carried two 7.92 mm machine guns, one in the forward and another in the ventral positions. As he leveled off for a run over the vehicles on the beach, Mendoza remembered the two 100 kg bombs they normally carried had been left behind at base due to a malfunctioning bomb release switch. *No matter,* he thought, *If need be we'll use the machine guns.*

As he approached the vehicles he could see they were normal cargo trucks, all empty and apparently abandoned. There were a few bodies on the beach, a flagpole and sandbagged positions, possibly a machine gun, nothing more. As he approached some figures slipped into the forest and disappeared, probably Motilone. He couldn't see the black shadow his observer had reported as he flew over the trucks at 800 meters. "Now hang on Max, while I come in off the deck. I want a closer look at all that stuff on the beach."

He took the He59 right across the beach, noting the number of trucks and bodies, and trying to pinpoint the exact location relative to La Ceiba. He was sure there was a machine gun in the sandbagged position and headquarters would take a keen interest in it. Where would the Motilone get a machine gun? He would radio his base and alert them to the 'smuggling operation,' if that is what was going on here. The 'black shadow,' though, he would leave out of the report as they couldn't verify it for certain. It certainly wasn't a barge. His observer was of the opinion it might have been a submarine but Mendoza dismissed it. After all, who would be crazy enough to bring a submarine into Maracaibo? It was a shallow lake. Submarines couldn't enter and exit the straits. *No, this situation is best handled by the Army,* he thought. *If I land and those devils come out we might not get out of there. Better to head for Bobures.*

Eighteen

The Passage

September 1, 1939. *Kapitän* Adolph Langsdorff, brother of the Captain of the German pocket battleship *Graf Spee*, had spent nearly fifteen years in the German Navy, graduating from the Naval College in 1924, and slowly rising up through the ranks to command of one of the newly built class VIIC U-boats. U-231 was built specially to larger size and greater displacement than all other class III and VII boats.

As one of 56 operational submarines in the German Navy at the start of World War II, U-231 had been diverted to *Aguila Negra* from her original mission, which was to plan a major assault against the British fleet at Scapa Flow where the battleship *Royal Oak* and the aircraft carrier *Courageous* were moored in protected anchorage. *Aguila Negra* was deemed of greater importance to the Reich than the sinking of major enemy vessels, and of course, the war had not yet started.

U-231 was armed with the new magnetically fused torpedoes which in trial runs had proved somewhat unreliable. Intended to detonate under the keel of enemy vessels, they were designed to break the target in half, and thus send enemy warships to the bottom in record time. If it came to a conflict with British or American boats, *Kapitän* Langsdorff hoped his new torpedoes would outperform the older versions that had caused so many problems.

Adolph was generally happy with his boat, as was *Kapitän* Hahn. Built by Blohm and Voss in Hamburg, the type VIIC boats had surface displacements of 769 tons and submerged displacements of 871 tons, with a length of just over sixty-seven meters and a beam of six and a half meters. A two-shaft propulsion system of 2800 horsepower, with diesel engines and electric motors generating 560 kW, produced surface speeds up to seventeen knots and submerged speeds of eight knots.

With a crew of forty-four, four bow tubes and one stern tube of fifty-three cm diameter, fourteen torpedoes, one eighty-eight mm deck gun, and one thirty-seven mm and two twenty-mm anti-aircraft guns, U-501 was a formidable attack submarine far superior to boats in use by England and the United States. Only Langsdorff and Hahn, plus a number of other submarine officers, knew about the special paint developed at *Deutsche Werke* at Kiel, which gave an extra knot to submerged running; both U-501 and U-231 had hulls coated with this new paint giving them a slight edge in underwater speed.

Built on the River Elbe by *Deutsche* Shipyard at *Finkenwerder*, U-501 was larger than the VIIC boat, with an 1120 ton displacement and length of eighty meters. She was a prototype for the IXC boats being heavier and larger than U-231, and therefore taking longer to dive — an additional ten seconds. With two six cylinder diesels which produced 4400 horsepower and electric motors of 1000 horsepower, she could make eighteen knots on surface and up to nine knots submerged. Normally owing to her larger size, with a crew of forty-five and four watch officers, she carried two midshipmen and an engineering officer. On this cruise her crew had been cut to 39 to save space for the precious cargo and paratroopers.

Adolph turned these figures and classifications over in his mind as he set course for the Maracaibo Straits and the Gulf of Venezuela leading into the southern Caribbean.

Adolph ordered, *Skop auf!* He waited for the handles to come up, snapped them down and started a sweep for quick look around.

"Nothing unusual," he murmured. "Set course for the isthmus," he ordered.

If we're discovered we'll not make it into the open sea, he thought.

But no surface craft are visible which satisfied him. And we are safely on course for the straits with estimated time of arrival at just after dark. He gave the order for normal operations, turned the bridge over to his second-in-command, and put in for some much needed rest.

Lying down in his cabin, Adolph thought how far submariners had come from the first vessels imagined by Leonardo da Vinci, and later ones built by David Bushnell in the eighteenth century. Those early egg-shaped vessels were notoriously unstable and operated by a single crew member turning a propeller by hand. As he had a keen interest in naval history, Adolph had read all the manuals and many books on the "silent service."

He remembered Robert Fulton's *Nautilus* and its first underwater venture on the Seine River in the early nineteenth century. His design, with rudders for steering and compressed air to replenish the cabin air, was later used by the Confederate Navy to build submarines during the American Civil War.

We've advanced significantly since the early days, he thought.

As he lay in his bunk, he read a treatise by John Holland who built the first subs for the U.S. Navy at the turn of the century. With a dual gasoline-battery powered craft, Holland developed a system of water ballast for submerging and horizontal tilting rudders for diving that became the forerunners of the hydroplanes used on modern submarines including U-boats. Holland's *Argonaut* was the first submarine to navigate in the open ocean, and as he drifted off into a deep sleep, Adolph pictured the bridge and control room of this instrument of war that would be developed into the advanced design of the *"unterseeboot"*–the modern submarine. Then slowly his dream slipped off into oblivion.

*   *   *   *

About six o'clock Adolph woke from his deep but fitful sleep, looked at his watch, and realized he must have been very tired indeed. He had spent over eight hours in the sack. Just then his watch officer rang up to say they were within sight of the narrow straits leading into the Gulf of Venezuela and the Caribbean Sea.

It will be tricky maneuvering into the Caribbean if any surface craft are about, he thought.

Rising, he pulled on his boots and dressed quickly, stopping briefly to look in the mirror. He had slept but he still looked tired. He knew his nerves were taut and he wondered what lay in store for him once they got out into the Gulf. Telling himself he had to stop worrying, he walked briskly from his cabin into the control center where *Leutnant* Werner Ehrmann was bringing the periscope down after a sweep of the surface.

"Nothing to report, *Herr Kaleu*. Surface clear and we're within eight kilometers of the straits, directly on course to the open sea. We should be through the straits in an hour and at the sub-tender in two and half or so."

"Jawohl, Werner," Adolph responded, thinking, *we've been very lucky so far. I hope our luck will hold.*

The drilling platforms along the east coast of the lake, constructed originally in 1922, expanded in 1936, had been a problem for navigation, but luckily a German agent in Venezuela managed to secure a map of their exact location. The intelligence on the drilling platform positions was excellent, so much so that on the way in both U-boats were able to skirt the drilling rigs by charting a course down the center of the lake, which was also the deepest part. The bathymetric map showing the depth contours in the lake was also extremely accurate and Adolph wondered how naval intelligence managed to find the information.

Oh well, not to dwell on it, he thought. *They have their ways, it seems.*

"What's the course, Werner?"

"340 degrees true, *Kaleu*," Werner replied.

"Rig for silent routine, just in case," Adolph commanded, and the boat went to near emergency conditions, with almost all noise eliminated, to prevent prying subs in the Caribbean from learning their position and speed. A dropped hammer or loose piece of equipment clanging within the U-boat might be heard through the straits and out into the Caribbean by British or American submariners.

Adolph knew the crew hated 'silent routine,' as it left each man nearly 'frozen' in place, but it couldn't be helped. Silence was essential as they slipped out through the straits into the deeper water of the continental shelf.

U-231 had its escape route well laid out in advance, so all they could do now was wait and see what happened once they broke out into the expanse of the Caribbean Sea. The tender was on station and expecting them. They were on course, on time, and barring interception by a foreign warship or sub, anything was possible.

Once out into the Caribbean Sea, Adolph made a quick calculation that they would be over 100 fathoms of deep water; he maintained his depth of eighteen meters and made frequent sweeps of the surface to ensure that no ships might intercept his boat. Just over an hour later, he sighted the tender and surfaced his boat about 1500 meters from the disguised merchantman.

Once on the conning tower he could see the deck crew of the merchantman manning their machine guns and opening the hold to unfurl hoses and replenish his fuel. Cases of food were ready for offloading to his boat. *Kapitän* Pirien, commander of the *Sonne,* an armed merchantman, was a first-class officer, highly efficient, typical traits for which the surface navy was famous. Few verbal orders would be necessary as the merchantman prepared to transfer fuel and supplies to U-231, while she, in turn, transferred her cargo of gold and platinum to the tender. While the transfer proceeded, the crew made ready to return to rendezvous with U-501.

After looking the situation over, Adolph ordered, "Lookouts stay vigilant."

Picking up the mike, he ordered, "Leutnant Horst, man the deck gun."

The transfer would take two hours and a chance encounter with ships or aircraft was foremost on Adolph's mind. The thought of discovery and interception might give their operation away and they were dangerously close to the Venezuelan coast. Reminding himself of what he had thought earlier, that anything was possible and only the cover of darkness would protect them from discovery, he ordered his officers to proceed with speed and to maintain radio silence.

As Adolph watched, the tie-up proceeded as usual. Fueling hoses were linked up and the sub started taking on diesel fuel, while numerous crates of gold and platinum were off loaded and replaced with much needed supplies. Across on the tender, he could see the burly figure of *Kapitän* Pirien on deck, no doubt spurring the men on to greater speed. He too, would not want to get caught so close to the Venezuelan coast.

They had not expended any ammunition with the exception of small arms, which had been used to re-supply Mueller. They still had a full stack of torpedoes and ample ammunition for the eighty-eight, thirty-seven, and twenty mm guns, so it was mainly fuel and food to take on and gold and platinum to offload. As he watched, a steady stream of crates was being transferred by hydraulic lift from the forward hatch on his boat to the tender.

The British and French, despite much planning with their subflotillas, had nothing as well engineered as the German tenders, the latter sufficiently equipped with hydraulic lifts to transfer cargo and ample storage, vessels that could take on significant tonnage of cargo. Krupp had fulfilled every expectation of the Kriegsmarine when the initial order went through to build cargo-transferring equipment and storage containers.

They will be through offloading in record time, Adolph thought.

Just then his second-in-command yelled up the gangway that the offloading of cargo was fifty-percent complete. Looking at his watch, he realized it had taken only just over an hour to remove half the cargo of gold and platinum. Refueling was nearly complete and in another hour he would be able to get underway and return to the Maracaibo Lake.

Adolph knew time was running out as war was in the wind and it was imperative for the operation to wind down so they could escape into the open sea. If the British ever discovered the operation and bottled them up in the inland lake, they would have a hard time escaping into the Caribbean. Navigating the Maracaibo Straits was tricky and dangerous but fortunately they had only to find the main channel and follow it out into the Gulf. It was akin to navigating the Bosphorus from the Black Sea to the Sea of Marmara. It wasn't recommended procedure and neither the Bosphorus nor Maracaibo had ever been done by submarine.

Our penetration through the straits is a first, he thought.

The operation was a test for the new class VIIC and prototype of the IXC boats, but they had to escape as continued production of this new design demanded additional trial runs to test the new hulls for speed and depth. U-231 and 501 were the only two boats of their kind in existence.

They could easily reach 200-meter depth, and possibly 250, with their new strengthened steel. Calculations they made on their transatlantic voyage showed that submerged running, with the dual propulsion system and frictionless paint gave them in excess of eight knots, on average about eight and a half to nine knots, if they could escape underwater currents. With favorable stern currents they could often exceed ten or eleven knots, so they were faster and more maneuverable than British, French and American boats, which they would soon have to face in open combat. It was one thing to attack unarmed merchantmen, quite another to face other subs in underwater duels and come out intact. Without doubt they would soon face both surface and subsurface enemies in close combat.

After another hour the offloading was complete, lines were cast off the tender and *Kapitän* Langsdorff signaled the tender that he was making for the straits. The tender would head into the open sea and operate along a prearranged navigation triangular course until needed again when the two boats emerged from the inland lake.

Pirien signaled by light, 'Safe voyage,' as U-231 slipped her moorings and hove-to from the tender, steering a straight-line course of 190° true for the South American Coast.

U-231 made full speed on the surface, and when the straits were within 5 km or so, she dove to traverse the narrows undetected. As he slid down the gangway pulling the hatch cord behind him, Adolph remarked, "Venezuelan lax security is unbelievable. No foreign navy could get close to the German coastline and remain undetected as we've done all along."

Werner smiled, and turned to look at the planesmen, ordering, "Twenty degrees on the dive planes, level off at forty meters."

As the deck tilted underneath him, he steadied himself.

"Steady on course, *Kaleu*."

"Very well," replied Adolph.

Making full underwater speed, U-231 made way into the lake, and headed for a rendezvous with U-501, about 110 km to the south. Steering 170 degrees, Adolph reckoned that it would take 12 hours to make contact. Navigation reported a stern current giving them an extra knot; funny they had not detected this current on the way out?

Sensing a busy time ahead taking on more cargo and personnel, Adolph left his second-in-command at the helm, and retired giving orders to wake him if there were any developments.

*　　*　　*　　*

Sr. Sanchez entered the Hotel Royale in Maracaibo City, purchased a paper from the news vendor near the door and settled into a chair in the lobby. He had a few minutes before his scheduled rendezvous with Mr. Williams, attaché with the British Embassy in Caracas. It was never good to rush meetings like this and one never knew who might be following along to record the rendezvous. Enroute to the Rv it was best to pause, carry out some innocuous exercise, like reading a paper and take note of all around you. Anyone settling down near you could be a tail.

Only three people occupied the lobby, two men and a woman. He memorized their main physical features and color of clothes with his peripheral vision and kept on reading. He let another ten minutes pass and noted a free flow of bodies coming and going out of the lobby. The three people who were seated when he came in stayed in place. The couple didn't worry him at all as they were waiting for a vehicle. The lone man seemed engrossed in a cigar he was fondling, apparently trying to decide whether or not to light it. Finally, with five minutes to go before his scheduled meeting with the British agent, Sr. Sanchez rose from his seat, neatly folded his newspaper while taking a final imprint of the three, and left through the revolving doors at the entrance.

Entering the street he turned left and took the Boulevard Bolivar two blocks to a traffic signal where he crossed to the east side, stopping to look in a shop window. The reflection from the window gave him an imprint of the main street and he could see the image of anyone who might have followed him out of the hotel. The street was clear with the exception of a woman walking in the opposite direction and a dog looking for scraps.

No tails, he thought. *Excellent.*

He walked along another few blocks and turned onto Boulevard Santander which would take him to the Park of the Revolutionaries where he would meet the British agent. Mr. Williams was more than a mere letter carrier for the embassy. He spoke fluent Spanish, posed as economic attaché while in reality he worked for the British Admiralty, connected with British Intelligence. Sr. Sanchez did not know his rank but imagined he was a mid-grade officer, most probably with considerable command and intelligence experience. Despite the heat Mr. Williams always wore a white blazer, most probably to obscure a revolver. Like himself he would insure no one followed him to the drop point but they had to be careful as German agents were thought to be operational across Venezuela and UK Embassy staff the most likely targets for German agents to follow.

As a journalist and part of the Venezuelan National Radio Corporation, Sr. Sanchez had to be extremely careful about who he contacted. Using the powerful transmitting equipment available to him, ostensibly to contact other parts of the corporation, he leaked Intel to a US base in Florida using variable frequencies. With the war ratcheting up to a high level he would have to be diligent not to be compromised. Slipping away into the population would be easy for him but there was only the length and width of South America to hide out in, and if discovered, German agents would kill him.

The new Intel he had for Mr. Williams could not go by radio. Unlike previous reports, the priority on this one was simply too high to risk a compromise or leak.

Rounding a turn in the path, Sr. Sanchez noted the park was empty, the hour a bit too early for strollers and a little late for the normal bird watchers who often frequented the area. Seated next to a fountain where rushing water obscured conversation that could be overheard by someone carrying out surveillance, Sr. Sanchez could see the familiar form of Mr. Williams, slowly thumbing through a magazine. He put the magazine away as Sr. Sanchez sat down next to him. The two men had been through this ritual many times, using many venues, but they both liked the park as it gave a more or less unrestricted view in every direction. But this meeting was top priority and both men knew the present situation report regarding the German Mission would determine British operations over the next 24-48 hours. The War was hours old and already major clashes had occurred in Europe. The Caribbean would soon see its share of conflict as the Germans maneuvered to escape with their precious cargo.

After exchanging nuances about the weather, Sr. Sanchez recounted the brief report he had received from Professor Ford. "Our contact trailing the German recovery operation reports a firefight with the Germans near La Ceiba, less than 24 hours ago. He enlisted help from Venezuelan army elements and a local tribe who made marginal gains against the Germans and stole some of the ore, how much we do not know. The Germans suffered some losses but have regrouped and by now have managed to escape with the bulk of their force and most of the gold and platinum. The U-boats, two of them, are even now enroute to the straits and should rendezvous with a German tender sometime over the next 24 hours. Our contact will soon fly out over the Gulf to look for the tender and the U-boats. Only capable of reconnaissance, he will be in a position to observe and hopefully report. He's having problems with his radio so my reports are occasional at best. I will contact you through the usual channels as soon as I have something."

Mr. Williams smiled saying only he would be in touch regarding their next meeting. Rising quickly he strode off out of the park, most likely to a waiting car that would take him to a safe house where he could radio a report to naval elements out in the Caribbean. Sr. Sanchez did not know to whom he reported but then he did not need to know. He only knew he was to give Williams the full report holding nothing back. His report to his French contact was entirely different, the report doctored up quite a bit with some relevant information deleted. He intended to follow his orders, American citizenship his only goal, and the way the war was shaping up he might be in need of a safe haven once the war widened. No one knew just how wide the war zone might stretch but there was every possibility of a global conflict.

*   *   *   *

September 2, 1939. About three hours later, call of a sighting from the conning tower sent Adolph racing to the command center, where his exec reported hydrophones had picked up low speed surface screws about 2000 meters out on a heading of 235 degrees true. Raising the periscope he noticed first the clear sky and bright sunlight. Then he caught sight of a cargo ship moving at slow speed and likely headed for Maracaibo City.

Nothing to get alarmed about, he thought.

Wiping sweat from his forehead, he ordered, "Maintain depth and speed for the rendezvous."

The surface ship was no threat to them, and with the return trip proceeding as planned, he gave his exec leave to sleep while he took over the bridge. Drinking some coffee he let his mind wander a bit and reviewed recent events. He hoped U-501 had picked up more of the precious cargo and that everything had gone well, although he had no way of knowing what had transpired after he left some eighteen hours ago. In another five hours he would rendezvous with U-501.

Once at the rendezvous, it would be pointless to bottom his boat as the cargo would be mostly offloaded from the beach and stowed in U-501. His task, as outlined by *Kapitän* Hahn, would be to take on paratroopers from the coast for transport to the tender.

Just after 1800 hours he made contact with U-501 by using his active hydrophone to ping her. When a single return ping was picked up, Adolph gave the command to surface and soon after saw U-501 coming up. On shore he could see men scurrying about with many crates piled on the beach. So some cargo remained to be loaded, presumably onto his boat. His signalman relayed orders from U-501 to send shore parties and begin offloading cargo and personnel.

The first shore party to return reported a fierce battle between the Venezuelans led by Ford and the shore parties. Several paratroopers had been killed along with some of the Venezuelans and *Motilone*. The paratroopers had counterattacked with some success.

Mueller signaled Hahn, "Another attack imminent. May have to leave cargo on the beach. Have been overflown by a coastal force seaplane."

Mention of a seaplane gave Hahn real concern.

Both Langsdorff and Hahn were desperate to dive as every minute exposed them to new perils and surely the Venezuelans had reported the boats to their government. Soon there might be more aircraft looking for them and there was the prospect of a blockade at the straits, which would mean real trouble.

As the shore parties were heading back to the beach, fighting erupted from along the forest edge where the German pickets were firing into the forest. Adolph could hear a machine gun firing and surmised the paratroopers were repulsing another attack.

Walter yelled down the voice pipe to the diving officer, "Prepare for emergency dive." The situation on the boat was tense, every man coiled up for emergency operations.

The situation was deteriorating and it was time to cut their losses and run. U-231 signaled U-501 for orders and soon a reply came that Adolph was to send every available hand to shore to assist with the recovery of cargo. He gave the order and soon five rubber rafts with four men apiece were on the way in to shore.

The fighting raged on, but it appeared the German paratroopers were getting the upper hand. Soon the German sailors reached the beach without difficulty and they began moving boxes to the rubber rafts. After a time the paratroopers fell back to the water's edge and the rafts returned to pick them up. A final count showed they had lost one truck load of cargo along with ten killed and fifteen wounded, or nearly half the remaining force out of action. About 1 in 5 of the attacking soldiers had been killed in action along with an estimated 20 Venezuelans. They had anticipated a costly battle if discovered, and while command headquarters would not be happy about the losses and conflict, it couldn't be helped.

Tonight, the 2nd of September, 1939, would mark the pull out from Maracaibo and Adolph hoped they could make speed for the Caribbean. While running on the surface the night before he had made encrypted radio contact with headquarters and learned that *Raven* was expected to terminate immediately as war could be declared at any time. He communicated this to *Kapitän* Hahn by light signal. "Kreigsmarine orders *Raven* terminate immediately. War imminent!"

Working all through the night they desperately tried to complete the cargo transfer and extricate the paratroopers before dawn. By 0800 hours, two hours after sunup, Adolph received a signal to dive immediately, and follow U-501 to the straits and on to the tender. It was now the 3rd of September, war had been declared, and they had lost the cover of night. Not to chance discovery on the surface, they would have to make the straits underwater, which would take more time.

Nineteen

The Chase

Jack, Felix and Pat watched from the cover of the pines as the last of the German force pushed off out to the waiting U-boats. Jack stood there, his hands pushed deep into the pockets of his German Army uniform, a mask of discontent stretched over his face.

It isn't my fault, he thought. *I'm not in charge; my handlers in Washington are the real power.*

He was beginning to think he should have turned down the contract. *Perhaps the government should send Huston and Smith,* he thought.

Jack was junior to any subaltern in the army, yet he still felt responsible for his failure to stop the German recovery operation. He felt hot and angry and most of all he felt scared for the first time in his life. A wound on his arm had stopped bleeding, blood crusted across a flesh wound where hundreds of sand flies crawled on the blood soaked bandage. Looking at the wound made him a little dizzy and he realized just how dangerous the situation was becoming for him and his companions. And now another wound, a scar to join all the others was becoming infected. But the bullet he took was meant for his dad who was just not cut out for an operation like this.

Why did I bring him along? What was I thinking? This would be a cake walk of some kind. Some cake walk, he thought.

Turning from watching the German withdrawal, Jack looked out over the lake, studying the mirror-smooth surface with an intensity born of the despair of their situation. As the slight frown on his face deepened, accentuating the lines of his sunburned face, he realized the outcome of their struggle. He had the rugged looks of a middleweight fighter, which is what he had once been while working his way through college, surviving in the ring and sometimes winning a fight. But the last round of this fight he had lost. And he knew it.

Felix looked at his son and wondered about the orders he had received from Army Intelligence officers. Jack had been evasive when he explained the mission to him in Chicago saying only that he was to observe the German mission and use all means at his disposal to thwart efforts to escape with the cargo of precious metal.

Felix wondered if "all means at his disposal" meant starting a minor war with the Germans and a full scale firefight on foreign soil. As Felix thought over what had transpired he began to realize that perhaps they had gone over the brink attacking the Germans as they retreated from the Andes to the coast. Sure the Germans had mined gold and platinum in the Andes, both important strategic metals important for the war effort, and made good their escape to the coast. But Jack could have taken the easy way out and reported their activity to Army Intelligence. Certainly Washington would find a way to stop them. Wouldn't they? After all, the American Navy patrolled the Caribbean. If the Americans couldn't handle this they could surely report it to the British.

It's really a British problem, he told himself, *and here we are with a smoking gun.*

Felix straightened his German uniform, pulling the sleeves a little tighter but no matter how hard he tugged the uniform was at least two sizes too small for him.

Why in the world did I let Jack talk me into impersonating a German officer, he thought.

And then stealing a truck full of gold and platinum right from underneath the German troopers had unnerved Felix to no end. He remembered the sweat coursing down his back as Jack struggled with the ignition wires, crossing them several times to start the truck. The elation that followed when the engine sprang to life was almost indescribable. Perhaps it was the adrenalin rush that attracted his son to missions like this.

It must be so, he thought.

A silence grew among the three men. It was a silence the three didn't like and Jack tore it apart by flinging a stone into the sand. The impact seemed to bring the three back to the reality of their situation, a reality none of them could have foreseen and one which they had tried their best to change.

"We've survived several battles only to yield to a tougher, more organized force," Jack said to his partners, trying to keep anxiety out of his voice.

"We can't let them get away with the cargo. The awful consequences of the gold and platinum in German hands are too terrible to contemplate, too horrible to witness."

Jack stiffened his torso as if to stretch his back muscles and ran his fingers through his straight dark speckled hair.

The elder Dr. Ford, turning to his son, hesitated a second, then said, "It looks like they won."

He was surprised to hear, "Not yet, they haven't. They still have to clear the Venezuelan coast and the southern Caribbean."

His father was astounded when Jack added, "We'll fly off to Maracaibo, and alert Señor Sanchez, so he can contact headquarters."

"What we need now is a sub-killer; another sub would make life a lot easier."

As his words sank deeper into his brain, Jack relaxed his muscles, the deep grimace slowly fading from his face.

"That's about it," replied the elder Dr. Ford. He looked at his two partners with a puzzled expression and said, "Any other ideas?"

They looked at the battlefield. The mosaic of battle included a toppled radio mast over a log-reinforced command post at the forest edge, several dirt tracks lined with firing pits, hastily constructed through the dunes to the beach, and the bodies of several Germans and Venezuelans. The *Motilone* had carried off their dead and wounded. The Germans had evacuated their wounded to the U-boats, leaving their dead where they fell, bodies arranged in grotesque forms clinging to various weapons, limbs outstretched in various bizarre shapes.

Thinking like a professional soldier, Professor Jack Ford, knew he had lost the battle, at least for the time being. Despite this, he realized the Germans and their gold-platinum cargo, could only head out from the coast into the Maracaibo Straits, where they would be vulnerable in the shallow water-but only for a short time. Once they maneuvered out of the Straits there was little to stop them escaping into the Gulf of Venezuela. If he could find a way to stop them transferring their cargo in the Caribbean Sea, he might still thwart the German mission. He had to find the transfer point and alert Army Intelligence. He couldn't stop them but the British could if they had warships patrolling off the coast.

"The only weak link in the German plan," Jack offered, "is the transfer point at sea. If we can catch them off the coast and radio our intelligence contacts we may prevent their recovery mission."

His two companions remained silent scrutinizing the German withdrawal.

As Jack watched the scene unfolding before him, the U-boats maneuvered closer to shore where they could pick up the rest of the German force rowing toward them. With his binoculars he could see the sailors and paratroopers unloading the last of their cargo onto the U-boats and then the rubber rafts were hauled onto the dark sleek crafts. It was then that Jack remembered his dream on the mountain: An implicit, clear message of failure with the Germans escaping into the vastness of the Caribbean Sea.

Good God, he thought, *what a dream that was, right out of King Lear, a strange vision of the future with German fighter aircraft out maneuvering British and French planes.* Somehow he couldn't let this happen, he couldn't fail.

Turning to Pat and his father, Jack pointed north toward the Caribbean, "They'll offload the ore onto a merchantman or sub-tender and we have to find it. If we can identify the ship and radio its position, we still have a chance to intercept and stop them. They'll have to transfer the cargo. The U-boats can't haul that cargo all the way to Germany."

Jack's father, agreed. "Finding the merchantman is our only chance. The subs will be out in the Caribbean in about twelve to fourteen hours. They'll likely transfer their cargo and be underway soon thereafter. All we have for our efforts is one truck full of gold-platinum and a few dead bodies."

Jack thought for a moment and then stooped to draw an outline of the lake in the sand. "I know, but at least now we know the recovery plan and with some luck we can still stop them."

He stuck a twig in the area just north of the Maracaibo Straits, the only possible escape route.

Turning to Pat, "We need the float plane to find the sub-tender, but we have to hurry. We also need to alert Señor Sanchez in Maracaibo City so he can radio Army Intelligence in Washington. I know the sub-tender is out there just beyond the Maracaibo Straits. It has to be there."

The three men shouldered their weapons, turned, wound their way down off the high dune, and walked briskly toward the figures spread out on the beach.

The *Motilone*, who had fought so fiercely with their stone-age weapons, had disappeared carrying off their dead. Professor Gomez and his daughter Celine, and their Venezuelan colleagues, were inspecting some of the gold-platinum samples captured from the Germans.

Jack looked at Celine for what seemed like the longest time. As he watched, Celine examine the samples, her thin, elongated fingers neatly cradling the larger chunks of gold and platinum.

Looking up at Jack, she smiled, saying, "It's unbelievable! The Germans mined an incredible amount of gold and platinum, much more than we imagined."

Professor Gomez handed a sample to Jack and his father, saying, "It's just as in the Andes, the highest grade ore I've ever seen anywhere...very soft gold and 99.9% pure. The platinum is also high grade and it likely contains a lot of iridium. Von Humboldt, the genius that he was, was also smart to keep this a secret. The ore itself is worth a fortune. When Heinrich stumbled onto the location of the gold-platinum lode he must have been torn between keeping it quiet and alerting the German military. Had he kept quiet about the precious metals he could have returned to the Andes at some point and made a fortune. "

The serious look on Jack's face underscored the gravity of the situation, for if the Germans made off with the gold and platinum they would have two very important assets. The gold would swell their war chest and the iridium in the platinum would give them a strategic metal.

Finally, Jack turned to Pat, "We've got to find the offloading point and it has to be somewhere just off the coast. Let's fire up the bird and go hunting."

Pausing for a few seconds, he added, "Dad, we'll drop you, Professor Gomez and Celine at Maracaibo float base. You wait there and plot the probable exit course for the tender and subs once the offloading is complete."

The elder Professor Ford unfolded a small map from his pocket. "They can't have more than three or four possible routes into the Atlantic from here, and they'll need, either a rendezvous with a surface raider, or a stop over to take on food and fuel somewhere, possibly at one of the islands, or along the Venezuelan coast. After what just transpired here I doubt they'll chance landing in Venezuela."

Pat pulled up in one of the captured trucks and they drove south along the coast road to La Ceiba where the floatplane was waiting all gassed up and ready for the sky. Jack started to mentally calculate the logistics. It is just over an hour to Maracaibo Float Base and maybe two or three hours before they could begin the search.

The subs were already over an hour out. Jack knew they would have to search a wide area for the tender and there could be many boats to check on before deciding on the right one. It would likely fly a Spanish or Portuguese flag, and from what he knew about raiders or armed merchantmen, it might be a big one, at least a two-stacker. They would have to wait and see. The main problem now would be to get to Maracaibo, refuel and search the Gulf before nightfall. He saw Pat looking at the sky and knew he was wondering about time to carry out the search. They might have four to five hours to search the Gulf before running out of light to navigate safely to back to Maracaibo.

The quintet raced for La Ceiba, raising a cloud of dust along the coast road, arriving within the hour. Jack was surprised to see four *Motilone* at the wharf. Considering they had fought a pitched battle with German paratroopers no more than four hours ago they somehow had managed to find their way to La Ceiba some thirty kilometers away.

Working time and distance out in his head, Jack said, "These guys are good. I couldn't do it, not eight to nine kilometers an hour, and not after a pitched battle."

Professor Gomez's reply startled him: "They think you could and that's why they're here."

A deep smile erupting across his face, he added, "You've earned their respect and that is unusual for a gringo. They want to go with you in the plane."

It took some time to explain to the *Motilone* that the plane could only hold five and even then the gas consumption was so great it reduced the cruising speed and area of search by maybe fifteen percent. Jack promised to return to get them, if it looked like a land battle might shape up, but otherwise he promised to return and pay them for their trouble and support.

Looking rather dejected the warriors watched as Pat fired up the twin engine aircraft, and went through his pre-flight check list. Pat motioned that all was okay giving the thumbs-up sign, and his four passengers climbed into the plane.

Pat taxied offshore testing the wind, wishing for more waves. With his heavy load he would have difficulty taking off across the glass-like, calm lake surface. He gave the beast full throttle and maximum flap on the ailerons. The floats on the big twin sunk deeper into the water responding to maximum thrust, and they raced forward over the surface, slowly breaking the suction and lifting off after a long run of at least a kilometer.

"She's heavy alright and way over acceptable gross weight," Pat said to no one in particular.

Pat turned to Jack, "Thank God for the minor sea breezes. We needed them to lift off."

Jack looked at the lake below becoming smaller as they gained altitude. He didn't have the heart to tell Pat that he took a sizable number of gold and platinum samples with him from the captured truck. No doubt the weight of the samples equaled that of an extra passenger. He wouldn't mention that little item until they got to Maracaibo City where he could safely stash the samples with his father, Professor Gomez, and Celine.

As the big twin thundered over the lake, Jack wondered where the U-boats might be. The water, laden with silt, was so dark it was impossible to see into it to any depth. This didn't stop him from looking in anticipation of seeing two dark sleek shapes that would be the U-boats heading north toward the Gulf of Venezuela and the Caribbean Sea. But finding the subs would be sheer luck.

Within an hour the Maracaibo float base came up on their port side and Pat began his approach to set down just outside the landing buoys. He flared the overloaded plane at the last moment, and settled gently into the water.

They taxied up to the wharf and Jack jumped out into the warm, humid tropical air. He wondered why he bothered to wear an undershirt. Habit, he thought. He always wore one even in the hottest places on earth, and soon he would be dripping with sweat and salt. Reminding himself to take a salt pill soon, he tied up the plane. As he stretched on the wharf, he felt hunger gnawing at him and realized they hadn't eaten since the morning.

"I'm beginning to feel famished. We should pick up some food at the hotel and take some with us in the plane." Jack could see from the look on his father's face that he had said the right thing.

Pat refueled the plane while Jack went up to the hotel with his father, Professor Gomez and Celine. On the way he turned to his father, "No doubt Sanchez knows where we are and will contact us directly. Fill him in on recent events will you, when he shows up."

"You mean tell him we, I mean you, failed and the Germans made off with the cargo?"

Jack said nothing but gave him that *don't taunt me* look.

Felix rubbed his lips which made him appear to be chewing gum, gave Jack a sharp salute and continued toward the hotel.

In any case, Jack thought, *it's imperative to notify American Army Intelligence as to the German recovery plan and the present situation.*

Jack left them at the hotel after a quick meal and took a taxi back to the wharf where Pat was going through his pre-flight checks and getting ready to take off. He ordered the taxi driver to stop above the wharf, paid the man with a hefty tip and grabbed his pack with food for Pat. After getting out of the cab, he stood for a minute or two looking at the plane and the broad expanse of Lake Maracaibo.

A beautiful place, he thought, *but with the discovery of oil in 1922 and expanded oil recovery starting in 1936, it's beginning to bear the scars of the industrial world.*

If all Edens of this world contain minerals or oil, they're doomed, he said to himself. He had seen it in many places world-wide, and as an archaeologist he was well aware of greed. He was a bit greedy himself.

As he approached the wharf Jack could see Pat working on the engine, cursing his rotten luck of having to clean a plug in this wretched heat.

"What have we here? Engine trouble again."

"What took you so long? I could have used another set of fingers."

Not wanting to agitate Pat, Jack turned to an assessment of the problem at hand, relating, "Somewhere out in the great lake two U-boats are steering a course for the straits and within four or five hours they'll likely be on the surface traveling at top speed for the open sea."

Pat looked at Jack and stopped tightening the plug. "Aye, Jack, the situation is futile. Even if we find the tender or merchantman, what can we do to stop the transfer of the precious U-boat cargo?"

Jack leaned up against the engine housing but said nothing.

Pat continued, "The float plane isn't armed, but the tender likely carries antiaircraft weapons."

Pat waited for a response and finally Jack opened up, "The IXC U-boat carries a full array of antiaircraft weapons, most probably including cannon. We might even get shot down if we venture too close."

"Jaysus, Jack, this is my new plane. I love America but this whole thing is a British war."

Pat continued tightening the plug as Jack watched, thinking, *Very soon Pat's loyalty would undergo the supreme test.*

Twenty
Sub-Tender Rendezvous

Following a course of 345 degrees true the two U-boats cruised at a top speed of just over seven knots. There was little in the way of current in the lake to speed up or slow down the boats, and the heavy load made for slower going in their race for the straits. *Kapitän* Hahn considered that with the infrequent surface craft traffic, they might surface once they were away from shore and increase speed for the straits. Just after 0900 hours, he swept the surface with his periscope, and recorded that he could see the periscope of U-231 doing the same about 500 meters astern.

Judging a surface run too dangerous, he decided to remain submerged and continue at maximum speed on a direct course for the straits. The lake was calm so he lowered the scope to avoid detection. He gave U-231 double pings, the prearranged signal to run submerged, and both boats headed almost due north to take in the deeper part of the lake south of the isthmus.

Kapitän Hahn, thinking over his options focused on the reality of their situation. *What a pity we can't run on surface. It would cut the time in half.*

After ten hours and the onset of darkness, the lights of Maracaibo City came into view, there still being no surface traffic and no aircraft. *Kapitän* Hahn considered the prospects of surfacing and steaming right through the straits but decided against it. Transiting the Maracaibo Straits was not at all like running the gauntlet at Gibraltar where British vigilance and security made it difficult to slip undetected into the Mediterranean. But it was difficult, and with barely thirty meters depth, they were nearly aground when running at periscope depth.

With a garrison near Maracaibo City, on the western shore, they might attract attention, even with a waning moon. No, Walter thought, *this they couldn't chance.*

Telephone communication was impossible here, but maybe the Americans or the Venezuelan Army had radio communication with their base, and if they did the shore garrison here might be alerted.

What a sorry prospect for us if we are attacked by shore batteries, he thought.

His hydrophone operator reported, "I can hear U-231 behind us; all else quiet."

Walter acknowledged the report, looking about at the officers in the control center, imagining that Adolph must be doing the same thing.

What a bit of luck that Adolph had been chosen to command U-231 and accompany Walter on this cruise. They had both entered the navy in the same year, graduating from the navy academy at Kiel in 1928. Even though Walter was mission commander they had similar experience, and had been given command of the first class VIIC and IXC boats, much to the envy of their fellow officers, some of whom had been eyeing the new vessels, hoping to command them. There were many senior officers, with distinguished records even from the first war, who wanted command of the new boats, craft known to be superior to the older class VII and III boats. Even the hydrophone equipment aboard was new, and superior to the older boats, and much superior to the British and French subs using asdic. The Americans would soon develop their own sound navigation and ranging equipment-sonar but for the moment the German Navy was in the lead.

U-501, fitted out with the first radar-radio detection and ranging equipment, had the edge over other boats, as it could detect surface shipping within nearly 10 km. Operating on a sector scan, the radar beam was directed along an arc of 25° so it was highly directional. Originally developed in 1932 by Robert Watson-Watt and Sir Henry Tizard in England, it was presently undergoing considerable modification in Germany and in America. It was top secret in the German Navy and only five U-boats were fitted out with this new and important gear. Together with hydrophones it made stealthy attack from surface and subsurface craft well-nigh impossible.

Class B torpedoes in both boats, the latest in magnetic design and superior to earlier versions, proved greatly superior to the impact detonation fish fired by older boats. He and Adolph were two of a kind. They thought alike and he knew he could count on Adolph in any situation. He was an excellent commander, with a first-rate boat and an excellent crew.

After Walter had successfully evaded surface picket ships outside of Scapa Flow, barely two months ago, the crew knew he was the *Kapitän* to serve with. He had the magic that kept them alive. And it was no coincidence that his sister ship U-231, also with him at Scapa Flow, had been chosen to accompany him on this mission.

The *Kriegsmarine* took notice of the after-action reports which showed they had penetrated the picket ships and got to within torpedo range of two large battleships and the aircraft carrier *Ark Royal*. Had they been at war with Britain, sinking the three ships would have been a certainty, and what a prize the Kriegsmarine would have had for itself and its chief, Admiral Dönitz. Even Hitler was impressed and everyone in the German Navy knew that Hitler considered the navy a force only third in rank behind the Luftwaffe and Wehrmacht.

*　　*　　*　　*

Turning recent events over and over in his mind, Jack concluded that the U-boats would offload all their heavy cargo, and most of their personnel onto the tender, and the tender would then make for the open Caribbean and the Atlantic.

Again, he wondered, *would a German raider venture into the Caribbean to link up with the tender?*

While he couldn't dismiss this possibility, it was more likely probable that the tender would try to rendezvous with a raider somewhere in the Atlantic. The subs and tender obviously had the range to make the trip to Venezuela from Germany, but then so did the raider.

First, they had to find the tender, report its position, and see how events unfolded. As he had told himself many times before, anything was possible in a situation like this.

He couldn't know that Germany, England and France were already at war. Two days before, Germany had invaded Poland.

Pat taxied out into the channel, advanced the throttle, and headed into the wind. Taking off toward the northeast, they circled low over the lake in a futile effort to find the black shark-like shapes that outlined the U-boats beneath the surface. They saw only murky lake water and nothing that would give away the position of the subs. Pat slowly advanced the throttle and turned the ailerons, changing direction, as the plane rose to cruising altitude at 1000 meters.

He mentioned to Jack, "We should stay low for awhile to save fuel; once out over the straits we can go higher to look over ship traffic from a distance."

"Whatever you say, Pat."

After crisscrossing the area beyond the straits, they moved off to the east over somewhat deeper water, and soon spotted a large merchantman heading toward the coast. It flew a Danish ensign, and as they got nearer, Jack could see it was big, with two funnels, and a large section amidships that could easily conceal antiaircraft guns. The rear cowling was bulky and could hide either cargo or four-inch guns. It was making reasonable speed for a merchantman, as they estimated from the bow waves, in excess of 12 knots.

Pat made a sharp turn and started a descent that would take them across the stern of the ship. They flew to the northwest bringing the port side of the plane across the stern of the vessel, but except for a few crew members with binoculars giving them a quick look, they noticed nothing unusual about the ship.

Jack noted, "It could well be headed for Maracaibo City with a cargo of textiles or other manufactured goods."

After studying the ship, Jack added, "It looks very trim, well painted and maintained even for a Danish vessel. For a merchantman it's making very good speed."

They came around the bow of the ship and took a look at the bridge where Jack could see the bridge crew using binoculars to look them over as they passed. If this was the tender, the crew would be alerted to the fact that a float plane was taking an unusual interest in them. Jack looked at Pat, "Of all ships we've seen, this is the most likely contact for the U-boats. Despite the Danish ensign, I think she's German and too well powered for a normal merchantman."

Thinking for a moment, Pat replied, "I agree. I think this is the rendezvous vessel for the U-boats."

They circled off to the north and headed west, to give the impression they were flying away from Maracaibo. Once losing sight of the merchantman, they headed southeast to Maracaibo City and the float base.

Looking over at Jack in the right seat, Pat asked, "Should we radio her position to Sanchez. He'll need to contact Washington."

"No," Jack replied, "They might intercept our message, and we want them to think we aren't interested in their location. The U-boats will link up with them sometime during the night and with luck we might intercept them early tomorrow morning. Let's get back to base."

"Roger boss. We'll be running on fumes soon."

Pat trimmed the throttle and adjusted the elevators to lose altitude. Checking the compass he noted a slight drift and adjusted his heading, five degrees to port.

Looking at his watch he estimated, "About fifty minutes to touch down."

Jack nodded but said nothing as he continued to study the charts on his lap.

*   *   *   *

Approaching the straits of Maracaibo (Plate Three), Walter took a quick sweep of the surface. As his navigation officer waited in anticipation, he reported, "Only lights of Maracaibo City. Practically no lights at all where the garrison fortress is located. All is quiet. *Skop runter!*"

Reversing his cap, Walter noted the relieved look on his shipmates. "Looks like an uneventful passage."

Walter gave the prearranged ping to U-231 following about one kilometer astern, and headed almost due north toward the sub-tender that anxiously awaited a transfer of cargo, so it could leave for the eastern Caribbean and the long voyage home.

About three hours later the sub-tender came into view. Walter pinged U-231 to signal he was surfacing. He broke water at a high angle because he had to blow all his ballast fast to bring the boat up quickly with its heavy load. At the top of the ladder he waited for the hiss of compressed air that signaled the boat was above water. Walter unscrewed the hatch and scrambled up onto the conning tower as water rushed out through the superstructure.

Soon, both boats were tied up at the tender about forty kilometers from the Venezuelan coast and offloading began in earnest. It was the middle of the night and there was every chance they could be discovered by surface ships or aircraft. Worse yet, they might be intercepted by submarines, which would compromise the mission. Walter was jarred by a sudden thought, *if the Americans have alerted the British, it could bring a British response.*

Surely the British had surface warships in the Caribbean and they might send them to investigate.

*   *   *   *

A small British flotilla, consisting of a cruiser, three destroyers and two submarines, was deployed carrying out war games near the island of Trinidad in the eastern Caribbean. At 1800 hours on August 31, the Flag Officer of HMS *Lion*, a battle cruiser launched in 1910, signaled his escort that he had "black" orders for the two subs operating as opposing forces. When the lead sub, HMS *Thrasher* came abreast of the *Lion*, she made light communication 'surface immediately' toward the periscope. Within minutes *Thrasher,* and her sister ship *Upright,* came to the surface. The captain signaled his lead destroyer escort that he needed to see the two sub captains on his flagship and the destroyer sent out a motor cutter to bring the two officers to the flagship.

Plate Three. The southern Caribbean Sea from the Maracaibo
Straits to Trinidad showing the rendezvous area of the sub-
tender, positions of U-501 and U-231 and the major engagement
positions of attacking British submarines and surface craft. Map
source — "The CIA, World Factbook," public domain.

Within a half-hour the two sub captains were on the bridge of *Lion* and
Admiral Prescott, flotilla commander, indicated they should follow him to
his cabin. Once there the Admiral opened his safe and removed the latest
command orders from the Admiralty. The dispatch had been decoded, sealed
and stamped *Top Secret*.

Breaking the seal, the Admiral read off the report, "Both subs are on
'black status,' meaning you are authorized to use your own initiative and

maintain radio silence. You are further ordered to leave the coast of Trinidad, make with all speed to the Venezuelan Coast off Maracaibo. There you will rendezvous with a destroyer and frigate steaming toward the Venezuelan Coast from St. Vincent. The destroyer *HMS Plymouth* and the frigate *HMS Titan* are 1.5 days out. Remember no radio traffic as the Germans are as adept at intersecting signals as we are. Also our intelligence is sketchy at best, based almost entirely on American contacts. It could be totally erroneous.

Captain Retchford, commander of *Thrasher*, read the orders with certain disbelief. He knew the situation in Europe was tense and that war was imminent, but the last thing he expected was to be diverted to the western Caribbean. Britain had over 100 subs operational in the home fleet. He couldn't imagine why they would sail to Venezuela when they would be needed at home. But judging by the serious demeanor on the Flag Officer's face it wouldn't do to ask.

The *Lion* and her escort were to proceed with haste to England; *Thrasher* and *Upright* to intercept a German merchantman suspected to be operating off the Gulf of Venezuela in concert with two U-boats. The mention of U-boats sent a shiver down Captain Retchford's spine. The worst possible scenario for submariners was the possibility of conflict beneath the surface. Once submerged, submarines did not have radio contact with one another, and while they could use their active asdic to ping each other, this was detectable by enemy subs, and not advisable. There was always the possibility they might collide with one another, because once submerged they were essentially blind; following only acoustical echoes they picked up on the hydrophones.

Assuming that the bathymetry or underwater topography was accurately known he was sure they could operate effectively, but he would have to check with his navigation officer. Both officers saluted.

Admiral Prescott wished them *Godspeed* as they left his bridge and hurried along the passageway toward the deck and the motor cutter waiting for them. Neither of them spoke but both new this would be far from the usual peacetime war games they were used to. This would be the "real thing" and U-boats on their first mission would present the ultimate test of their training.

Twenty-One
Submarine Duel

The huge hydraulic crane was working cargo from U-501, while U-231 took on some of the remaining diesel fuel and food. The sailors worked hard to transfer all the cargo but it took time as there was an enormous load and others had to care for some of the wounded who would surely die of their injuries before getting home to Germany.

Climbing down from the *wintergarden* (conning tower), *Kapitän* Hahn walked over the gangway between his boat and the tender and told *Kapitän* Pirien, "Put in at Willemstad on Curaçao, if possible, and transfer the wounded to hospital."

He was tempted to mention he might put in there on the way out of the Caribbean, and then thought better of it. There was always the possibility the tender would be intercepted by British warships, and the last thing he needed at this point was leaked intelligence information. The Dutch would not find a U-boat in the harbor amusing. About 0700 hours, on September 4, all the cargo was stowed aboard the tender and the last of the wounded were being transferred through the forward hatch of U-501. Walter returned to his boat, climbed up the bridge rails to the conning tower and looked forward and aft, estimating the work yet to be accomplished.

"We need to speed things up," he said to his first officer. "We're juicy targets for any British warship."

It was now first light and the trio of U-boats and tender were stationary targets, very inviting if war had been declared, and British boats were anywhere about. On the conning tower, it looked to Walter as if they might make it out without any complications and none too soon. Nevertheless, they were now two hours over their anticipated time of transferring cargo and personnel to the tender. This made him a little uneasy as he and his lookouts scanned the surrounding sea surface. Low-lying cloud gave some protection and cut visibility, but he thought, *this is not a good situation.*

*   *   *   *

About three kilometers from the moored tender and U-boats, the T class British submarine *Thrasher* picked up slow cavitation from the tender as it started its engines. Captain Iain Retchford raised his periscope, taking range and direction to plot a solution after ascertaining that the screws came from a merchantman tied up to two subs. He could clearly see the offloading process and he did not want to waste any time intercepting the enemy. Unbeknownst to the Germans, war was now over twenty-four hours old, and he had permission to attack enemy shipping wherever he might find it. While the merchantman was flying a Danish ensign, the U-boats were clearly German, their conning towers marked with the German cross. Almost unbelievably both boats were dead in the water, a sight often wished for, but rarely witnessed among submariners. He hoped his sister boat, *Upright,* had picked up the cavitation but he had no way of knowing for sure.

T-class British subs were built from 1937 on with surface and submerged displacements of 1090 and 1575 tons, and length of just over eighty meters. Like the VIIC class U-boats, they had two shaft propulsion, with 2500 horsepower diesel engines and 1450 hp (1081 kw) electric motors, giving surface and submerged speeds of fifteen and seven knots respectively.

With a crew of sixty-five, the T-class boats carried eleven fifty-three centimeter torpedoes with six internal and two external bow tubes and three external stern tubes along with a four-inch deck gun and one twenty-millimeter anti-aircraft gun. Larger than the VIIC class boats, the T-class boats did not have the new magnetic torpedoes. Having similar speeds to the German boats, they were somewhat less maneuverable.

Captain Retchford decided on the direct approach. He had surprise working for him and his tactical situation was excellent with the U-boats moored to a tender. Suddenly his asdic officer signaled the U-boats had started engines. He gave the order to surface after deciding to attack. With his conning tower awash he prepared to fire a spread of two torpedoes dead ahead on headings of 210 and 215 degrees true. Despite the low light and cloud cover he could see a perfect silhouette of one U-boat directly ahead and he intended to sink it with a direct hit at close range.

Knowing this would alert the tender and the other U-boat, Iain hoped *Upright* would circle the moored craft, and attack from the opposite direction.

"Running time on the fish?" he asked.

"Running time is short, around forty seconds," his navigator reported.

Iain ordered, "Engines to stop, open outer doors, prepare to fire tubes one and three."

After a pause of ten seconds, he ordered, "Fire tubes one and three," and momentarily there came a shudder, the boat reeling as the torpedoes left the tubes.

At the same time he saw *Upright* break the surface and steer off to the west in a wide arc that told him she was after the boat on the opposite side of the tender. While his attack officer was counting off seconds to impact, he ordered his gun crew to man the forward deck gun. At this moment the U-boat started firing at Thrasher, scoring a direct hit on the conning tower, knocking out all communications, and starting a fire. Some of the command center personnel were injured in the blast and one of the lookouts was thrown into the sea.

With blood dripping down his neck, Captain Retchford ordered, "Reverse engines." When there was no response he went below to take stock of the situation. The sub was taking water and listing a few degrees to starboard. While he looked about him there was a terrific explosion and he surmised the U-boat had taken a direct hit.

Thrasher was taking water but listening to the tempo of the pumps he reckoned the boat could stay afloat despite the damage. Picking up the intercom he ordered, "Hands stay on station. Bilge report flooding. Engines to slow reverse."

As he put the intercom down he felt the soft touch of a medic bandage being put against his neck and recognized the face of his no.3 who was applying it. Slumping into a chair he felt dizzy and then realized shock was setting in as he lost consciousness.

*   *   *   *

Jack contacted Señor Sanchez after landing at Maracaibo City and reported what they had found off the coast. Sanchez told them to confirm the offloading, if possible at first light and report to him by radio, in code, and on an alternate frequency rarely used by aircraft.

They would use the code words 'dolphin' for submarine, 'tuna' for tender. They were not to mention the cargo by name and above all they were not to pay undue attention to the tender. After a few hours' sleep, Jack and Pat taxied down to the wharf, and Pat started his pre-flight check all over again. The plane had been refueled the night before, so they were in the air just as first light appeared over the Mérida Andes off to the east.

As they roared along the lake surface, Jack mentioned how quickly they leapt into the air.

Pat replied, "Much easier without so many passengers and your damn samples."

Jack just smiled, and thought, *it's impossible to fool Pat. He's on to all my usual tricks.*

Flying almost due north, they passed the Maracaibo Straits and flew out over the Gulf of Venezuela. Jack had no knowledge of the lake currents, but assuming the subs were traveling most of the distance underwater, they should have rendezvoused with the tender sometime in the middle of the night. They must still be offloading their cargo and it would be great if they could catch them at it.

They flew at 1500 meters to allow maximum coverage and they headed for the most likely rendezvous area west of Aruba. They tried the HF radio but could not raise their headquarters at Maracaibo. Pat reckoned they were not high enough, saying, "I wish I had brought the better radio. I have a 200 watt transmitter back at home. Too late for that now."

Jack barely nodded at this information. Running all possibilities through his mind he hoped they were on the right track.

With the main shipping channel south of Aruba, the tender would have maximum security and safety to the west or northwest of the island. An hour and a half later they passed about forty kilometers off the western coast of Aruba and started their search.

Twenty minutes later, after crisscrossing a relatively calm sea, they spotted the tender and the two subs tied up to her. They knew they had been seen from the surface, so they stayed a respectable distance away, flying off to the north where they could make a turn and fly down west of the tender.

Jack looked at Pat, said, "So they made it out!"

After a few seconds, he continued, "If our Intelligence people are on the ball, they'll have alerted the British, and...," his sentence trailing off as he watched, almost with disbelief, the scene unfolding beneath them.

Suddenly, the early morning was lit by flashes from machine guns and heavy cannon, followed by a brilliant explosion that sent flames erupting into the sky. They circled closer to the tender to see the U-boat on the northern side slowly list and begin to slip beneath the surface. A sub off to the north was firing at the tender and a second sub was circling the tender to the west.

As they watched, the tender got underway and moved off to the east. One of the attacking subs was on fire, and the U-boat tied up to the port side of the tender was sinking fast, presumably hit by torpedo. The U-boat looked to be doomed as they could see men hurling themselves into the sea. She was sinking stern first. The bigger of the two U-boats, cast off her moorings and dived appearing to have escaped with a second sub, presumably a British boat, chasing it.

There were sailors in the water and a third vessel, a submarine, was approaching from the north, presumably a British vessel. Judging by the debris in the water, it looked like there had been a horrific battle, and while the Germans had taken some hits, the merchantman where the U-boats had likely transferred their cargo, was escaping.

Gaining altitude Pat was able to raise Sr. Sanchez on the radio, passing an abbreviated message of what they had just witnessed. Getting three mike pings indicating message received, Pat yelled over the roar of the engine to Jack that they had to return to base to refuel or they too would end up in the drink.

Bringing the float plane back to 195 degrees they overflew the battle site and headed for Maracaibo to report to Señor Sanchez and pick up the rest of their group. Professor Gomez and the elder Dr. Ford would no doubt have plotted all the escape routes by this time.

Soon the wharf at Maracaibo Harbor came into view. Pat overflew the landing area to make sure it was okay and then flared the float in for a perfect landing. They taxied up to the wharf and tied up.

Once back in the hotel, the elder Dr. Ford remarked, "I think they'll have to head for Aruba or Curaçao. Willemstad harbor on Curaçao is the best bet."

Looking over the maps, Jack concluded, "I agree. They've got wounded who need attention. I'll bet the tender puts in there, looks after the wounded, picks up fresh supplies and then heads for a rendezvous with a U-boat."

The others agreed. "So let's head for Willemstad. Can we do it, Pat?"

"No problem, boss," was the reply. "But first I have to gas her up," he said.

Two hours later they were airborne for Willemstad. Señor Sanchez was on the radio to Washington with the news that they would try to intercept the merchantman. If she was in Willemstad harbor it would depend on events as to what they could do. Events were controlling everything now; they most definitely were not making events on their own.

*   *   *   *

Frank Knox was ushered into the Oval Office by FDR's aide and looked at the President without speaking. Taking a seat while the aide left and closed the door, the *Sec Nav* remarked first about the general intelligence structure, saying, "Chief, we've got to put Donovan on to 'mix and mash.' Our various Intel gathering units have to be combined into one cohesive organization. It takes too long to get any worthwhile information in place, analyze it and act on it. For example, Sanchez's Intel on Professor Ford and the status of the German Recovery Mission took days to get to New York. Army Intelligence in Florida sat on it for hours and then finally sent it to the Washington office which did the same. Donovan will have to 'crack the whip.' Now that Donovan has beefed up his operation in NY next to Intrepid's base maybe he will take a strip out of the British playbook and search the army for top officers to take on Intel roles. We cannot continue to operate disfunctionally like this and we need people to move, so to speak, and act with speed."

FDR listened intently and decided his competitive strategy amongst departments, at least in this instance, would have to change. He would order Donovan and Hoover to quit jostling for position and start sharing **all** information.

"I understand, Frank, and trust me. I'll make it plain to both Donovan and Hoover that intel must be shared and acted upon. I'll direct Mr. Hoover to insure all military grade intel goes directly to Donovan. I also want Navy and Army intelligence amalgamated into the OSS. You can keep your strategic boys in house but all espionage people will report to Donovan. By the way, an executive order will go out tomorrow — The OSS will form up directly. We're going to need it."

"Now, fill me in on Venezuela. What's happened?"

"It's not terrific Chief. We had not heard from Professor Ford for some weeks but then he was operating in the black and we did not expect any report. Sporadic messages started coming in four days ago. Sanchez, our man in Maracaibo, got a message out that Ford and his group had tried to stop the Germans offloading gold and platinum onto U-boats in Maracaibo Lake. Apparently they linked up with some natives and the Venzuelan Army and were partly successful in capturing some of the cargo. The bad news is that the Germans managed to escape."

Frank paused, thinking FDR wanted to interject.

"Christ, the army. We may get some 'heavy weather' from the Venezuelan Government over this."

"I don't think so, Chief. Ford knows he's on his own. No 'official assets' were in place on this one. We're in the clear."

"Let's hope so. The last thing we need is a problem down south. Did Ford come out of this okay?"

"I believe so, from what Donovan told me. A recent communiqué from Sanchez indicates Ford is trailing the tender through the Caribbean. Sanchez also indicates he's alerted the British and a task force is heading to the Gulf to engage the Germans."

Frank could see concern in FDR's face. The whole worldwide political situation was spiraling out of control and there was little one could do about it. Soon the U.S. would become embroiled in it.

"Let's hope the Brits are successful. Maybe one of your Lend Lease destroyers will sink a U-boat."

"I think they're all in the North Atlantic protecting shipping but I understand the Brits have dispatched a sizable force to deal with the German Mission."

"Good, Frank, keep me up-to-date."

"Aye, Chief, will do."

With that the *Sec Nav* departed for Norfolk. Two new boats had finished sea trials and he wanted to give their skippers their mission orders directly. The east coast defenses were thin and pretty soon they would be directly threatened by U-boats. They had to reverse the situation, else the Germans land in Philadelphia.

The thought of Germans landing on the East Coast gave him a shudder. As he walked out of the White House toward his car and driver waiting for him in the parking garage he wondered what motivated people like Professor Ford.

Was it patriotism, adventure or simply the thrill of it all, he thought. *I'll probably never find out but this time around Ford might lose. If I had to place a bet on this one, I would put my money on the Germans. If they get out of the Caribbean with the platinum, the British will take a pounding, one that may well spell complete domination of the continent.*

Nearing his car his thoughts shifted to Norfolk and the subs. *Germany is ahead of us in this game.*

*   *   *   *

On the conning tower of U-501, *Kapitän* Hahn responded to fire coming from U-231 by ordering lines cast off the tender. As he yelled the order to his deck crew he noticed they were already making way to leave the tender. Taking a last look around the conning tower, he yelled, *"Tauchen Notfall! — - Emergency Dive!."*

While the lookouts raced below, he took stock of the situation as the forward hatch party secured the port. After insuring the forward hatch was secure he slid down the rails pulling the lanyard hard, securing the hatch, all in one motion.

With U-501's engines barely engaged, he ordered, "Full turns on screws! Maximum deflection on bow planes!"

Watching the hydroplanesmen rig for depth, he felt the boat pitch forward.

Walter knew the attack had come from the surface and he had no intention of staying there.

Max, Chief of the boat, ordered, "Crew forward to speed the dive," and all but a skeleton crew raced through the 'knee knockers' or compartments for the bow of the boat, which was normal in a situation like this.

Kapitän Hahn's last observation of the surface, before sliding down the conning tower rails, was of the tender firing to the north either at a surface ship or at a sub. He surmised it was a sub but it was safest to dive and seek cover in the depths below. He hoped *Kapitän* Pirien could find some way to escape whatever calamity had come his way, but he had no way of knowing what that calamity was.

His worst fears for U-231 came when the hydrophone operator reported "Explosion off the starboard quarter."

He imagined U-231 had taken a torpedo. As they sank beneath the surface, the hydrophone operator reported, "Twin screws overhead on surface, coming round the tender, heading directly for us."

Kapitän Hahn ordered, "Ninety degree turn to port. Plot course away from the closing vessel. Helm, steer 130 degrees, maximum turns on the screws."

The Krupp-built diesels performed as usual giving a maximum nine knots.

The hydrophone operator reported, "Closing screws are from *Unterseeboot*. She's submerging but going off on heading of 070 degrees."

Kapitän Hahn felt himself relax a little. He ordered, "Speed to one-third, silent routine."

For the first time he felt sweat running down his back and realized his shirt was soaking wet.

They had escaped, but only barely, and the enemy sub was out there looking for them. The hydrophone operator reported the sub was turning to follow them and then *Kapitän* Hahn knew he was locked in what all submariners fear more than surface attack, a life-and-death struggle with another boat.

Most likely this was a British S or T class boat and while there weren't too many of them, they were considered very efficient and well armed.

They don't have the magnetic torpedoes which gives me an edge, he thought, *maybe the one crucial factor that will get us out of this.*

Presumably, the British had found his two boats and the tender. As he considered the implications of this, two things stood out in his mind. One was that the Americans were involved and they must have alerted British Intelligence, who for once, acted upon it. Second, war had to have been declared, as they wouldn't have attacked without a declaration of war.

How did I miss that? he thought. *If Adolph knew, he probably went to a watery grave with it.*

After about fifteen minutes of eluding the enemy, Walter surmised they could bottom the boat in about 100 meters of water and this they did settling into the mud on the continental shelf off the Venezuelan coast a little east of Maracaibo. They rigged for silence and waited.

After about forty-five minutes the hydrophone operator reported, "Twin screws coming close off our port beam at about six to eight knots."

Walter knew this was the enemy submarine running at about twenty-meters depth on a heading of 230 degrees and apparently searching for him.

He let the screws pass overhead until they had a distance of around 2000-meters and then ordered, "Blow ballast, one-half turns, steer 230 degrees, all silent."

The hydrophone echo was clear on the screen as Walter peered over the shoulder of his hydrophone operator. *Kapitän* Hahn thought for a moment of the North Atlantic, where numerous thermoclines and changes in water temperature produced a screen packed with false echoes. The warm waters of the Caribbean did not produce these effects making underwater detection rather easy. This target was about as clear as they get, and the British sub did not know he was rising, just behind. Soon their hydrophones would pick him up, but not too soon he hoped.

"She's a clear target, *Herr Kapitän*," the hydrophone operator reported while trying to boost the signal.

With the boat rising, he came up to twenty-five meters depth and looked at his hydrophone operator who reported, "No change in direction."

Walter ordered, "Up five meters; two fish ready to fire on trajectory — 230 degrees."

The hydrophone operator reported, "Course change of target to 250 degrees."

Walter ordered, "Helm, 20 degrees starboard," and waited a minute even though it seemed much longer. Then he ordered, "Change target to 250" and he counted the seconds waiting to give the firing officer time to adjust the azimuth. Then he ordered, "Torpedoes *los!*"

With a running time of four minutes, they waited anxiously counting off the seconds until impact. His magnetic torpedoes would hone in on the steel hull of the enemy sub and explode just under it. If they were duds, he was in trouble, as their screws would sooner or later alert the enemy that he was in the neighborhood and firing deadly fish at them.

As the hydrophone operator reported, "*Unterseeboot* turning 90 degrees," Walter realized the British had detected the incoming fish and were trying to elude them. One fish kept on a straight path, but the other followed the turning sub and four minutes and twelve seconds later, a terrific explosion nearly knocked the earphones off the hydrophone operator in U-501. To a submariner the death of fellow members of the silent service is a terrible event, as it would seem to precede their own imminent demise.

The crew of U-501, including its *Kapitän*, did not cheer the news that the pursuing sub had been torpedoed. *Kapitän* Hahn ordered the boat to periscope depth and what he saw confirmed what the hydrophone operator had reported. Flotsam and bodies littered the surface of the sea, and yes there were survivors. Probably the boat had been near to the surface to get some of the crew off and into life jackets and rafts. He could see two or maybe three rafts and many floating sailors.

Glück auf! (Good luck!), he thought, as he ordered a course back toward the last reported position of the tender.

U-501 came round to an easterly heading searching for the tender.

Twenty-Two
Pursuit to Curaçao

About four hours had elapsed since the attack on the tender and *Kapitän* Hahn ordered a circular course to return to look over the battle site. Thinking events over, he was sure U-231 had sunk, but the tender might have managed to escape. Everything hinged on the other submarine. *Could they have radioed for help?* He weighed his options but knew he could only know the full story by returning to the site of the engagement.

Looking at his chief of the boat, he ordered, "Ahead two thirds, silent routine."

He looked at the faces of his officers and knew what they felt. Detection by other submarines, their worst fear.

About two hours later navigation reported they were within range of the battle site. Walter ordered the periscope up and the sight unfolding about 1500 meters away sent a chill up his spine. Two British ships-a frigate and destroyer- were picking up survivors from U-231, and one was fixing a towline to the stricken British sub. He had the range and could sink both vessels with well-spaced torpedoes from his bow tubes. If he fired on the British ships he would without doubt kill some of his own men.

"Where is the tender?" he asked his second-in-command, as he brought the periscope down. "Did it sink or escape?"

He looked at the three officers in the control center, who were as startled as he, when the periscope thudded into the long sheath-like cradle that held it in place ready for the next observation.

"There's no sign of the tender," he reported, as he looked over at the attack table.

"Plot a probable course for the tender in an easterly direction, Klaus."

Klaus and his assistant pulled out the map scrolls for the southern Caribbean and started to plot probable escape routes around Curaçao, computing azimuths and speed.

He ordered a slow turn to the north to look at the other side of the British warships and slowly the helm responded. They moved at minimum speed with slow turns on the screws to avoid detection on the surface. Surely the British had asdic and almost certainly they would be listening for visitors. If they caught him out here they might well destroy him.

Once on the opposite side of the British ships it was apparent the tender was nowhere to be seen. Had it been sunk? Walter counted the men still in the water and those crowding the gunwales of the ships that he could make out as German sailors. There didn't seem to be enough bodies to account for the tender, so maybe they escaped into the open sea heading for the Atlantic, or for friendly ports where they could hide.

Walter decided to abandon the idea of attacking the two warships even though they presented him with inviting targets. It was more important to find the tender and escort it into the Atlantic for its rendezvous with the German armed merchantman *Riesen*. He ordered a course along the South American coastline, about fifty kilometers from shore, with the hope that he might catch up with the tender. U-501 slipped away from the warships, dropped to 50 meters depth, and set a course of 110 degrees true.

The cramped quarters on U-501 were a cause of some concern to Walter, as the paratroopers on board were not used to life on a boat, and most of them were suffering from inactivity. His crew were putting up with cramped quarters better than he expected and "hot bunking" had not proved much of a problem, either with the paratroopers, or his own crew. Full utilization of all bunks meant that there were always twenty-six men asleep or trying to sleep at all times, which provided more room in the passageways. Also, the air was getting close very fast with extra lungs pumping carbon dioxide into the submarine. Human movement was kept to a minimum to avoid over exertion and to preserve oxygen. They would have to run submerged for another while before they could surface after dark and radio for orders.

The minutes ticked slowly away and soon *Kapitän* Hahn reckoned they had sufficient darkness to risk running on the surface.

He gave the order, *"Auftauchen"* (to surface), and with ballast blown, the boat rose quickly; at eighteen meters he ordered, "Level the boat, *auf periskop."*

As he swept the surface, he could see a calm sea and a starlit night, with no surface craft.

Once on the surface, lookouts scrambled to the conning tower. Walter and his exec swept the sea surface with their binoculars finding it empty and quiet. In fact, the coastal current, normally strong along the Venezuelan coast, was hardly a problem for U-501 as it picked up speed and went to full cruising power. Navigation computed speed at seventeen knots, one full knot better than usual, and fast enough to put considerable distance between them and the British warships.

"Good to feel the wind again, eh Wolfgang?"

"Jawohl Walter, very good indeed!"

The British warships were a cause of some concern still, as intelligence debriefing was sure to lead to the conclusion that the gold and platinum load was on the tender for the most part, and the British were likely to come after it in hot pursuit. But where was the tender? Walter kept turning this question over and over in his mind.

Turning to his exec, perplexed, he asked, "Where would *Kapitän* Pirien have headed, in what direction and with what objective in mind."

Wolfgang answered, "One of the islands, Aruba or Curaçao, most probably."

"Maybe he put in at Willemstad, as I advised," Walter uttered.

His exec nodded, but said nothing as he kept looking over the charts.

Kapitän Pirien's original orders were to rendezvous with the *Riesen*, transfer his cargo, and take on fuel and supplies for transfer to other boats in the Atlantic, but the situation had changed, with the loss of U-231 and the ensuing battle. If he suffered battle damage he might have been lucky to limp away in the ensuing melee and escape along the coast. He might even have been tempted to put into port near Maracaibo City, but it would require a huge leap of faith that the Venezuelans did not know about the battle along the shores of Maracaibo.

No, Pirien was a competent commander, and Walter knew he was bringing his engines to full power when the British boat had come round his bow. He felt sure that the tender had escaped into the night and the British sub that chased U-501 had not had time to go after it. Pirien would have had some six to eight hours or more to make good his escape toward the Atlantic.

Walter ordered his navigation officer to plot a course for the open Atlantic, with a stop off at Willemstad on Curaçao, to see if the tender had tied up there. Running on the surface they could make Willemstad just before dawn the following day, so Walter ordered two-hour shifts on the conning tower for officers and lookouts. If intercepted they would dive and not risk a surface battle.

About ten P.M., U-501 radioed its position to Kriegsmarine Headquarters in Germany, and requested information about the tender. The radio crackled with encrypted information, and after the radioman decoded the message, the news that the tender had escaped and established contact with Kreigsmarine lifted the spirits of everyone on the conning tower. Its last reported position was northwest of the island of Curaçao, heading generally easterly toward Willemstad and the island channels north of the Venezuelan Coast. Pirien would likely heave-to at Willemstad before venturing forth into the southeastern Caribbean.

Everything depended on finding the tender and so U-501 continued on an easterly heading toward the Curaçao coast. Because it was the prototype of its class, built two years ahead of time, U-501 carried primitive radar. Holding its own in trial runs it was one of the first boats fitted with the newly developed radio-detection equipment with a range of 6 to 8000 meters. Tonight it would prove its worth as they cruised along the Venezuelan coast because with it they could pick up both surface coastal and ocean going vessels of any displacement. More importantly, it let them run on the surface where they could make maximum speed and recharge their batteries.

About 5 A.M. the hydrophone operator reported, "Surface screws, extreme range — about 8000 meters, closing fast at over twenty knots."

"Radar, do you have them on the screen?" As Walter waited for a reply he considered his tactical situation. Not good to get caught on the surface by a fast moving warship. Just then, the radar operator reported, "Two vessels, not one, steaming directly at us."

That report decided the issue. Walter ordered, "Lookouts below, prepare to dive."

Looking about the conning tower to insure all crew were below, he slid down the hatchway, pulling the latch cord behind him.

As a sailor tightened the hatch, Walter directed, "Change course to 075 degrees, come to periscope depth."

After a few minutes, he ordered, "Slow to five knots." Intending to take up position on the port side of what most likely were the incoming British warships, he wanted the best possible firing location. If the approaching warships were British he would engage them. As Walter thought over the tactical situation, his hydrophone operator reported, "Second set of screws, same direction."

The radar is working better than the hydrophones. Sector scanning with the new radar equipment seems to work well. We picked them up on radar first, Kapitän Hahn thought, as he looked around the control room. Everyone was at their post doing their job. And the new top secret radar was functioning properly and proving a major advantage along with the new hydrophone equipment. Improvements were being made every few weeks, and he fully expected to have even better surface and underwater detection gear when he returned to Germany.

U-501 came about and waited for the pursuing vessels to show themselves.

It was now getting onto 0600 hours and the first light of dawn would soon illuminate the surface. Waves of two meters would help to hide the scope making it relatively easy to attack. He brought the boat to fifteen meters, raised the scope and discovered it was a frigate. It was not alone; there were two of them heading directly toward Curaçao. The second ship was a destroyer escort. Both ships were steering a straight course, without any attempt to zig zag, which meant they did not consider the possibility of an enemy sub lurking nearby. With both ships heading 095 degrees, at a speed of twenty knots, he would need to set up the attack to fire at a range of 3000 meters, or closer if possible. U-501 was positioned nearly due north of the approaching warships.

The attack crew was working out the trajectories, the firing solution a spread of two torpedoes on the frigate at a range of 2200 meters.

Azimuthal heading due south, 180 degrees true. Walter swung the scope around to insure there were no other vessels lurking about and took a final reading on the two warships noting a five degree spread between the frigate and the destroyer.

"*Skop tauchen*, silent routine," he ordered.

"What's the running time on the fish?" Walter asked, as he wiped sweat from his face.

What to do about the destroyer. She'll certainly come after us once the frigate is hit, he thought.

"Set up the destroyer. Second spread of fish from tubes two and four."

"Running time for the first set of fish is four minutes, fifteen seconds," answered the torpedo officer. "We fire in four minutes."

Walter looked across at the navigation display and noted the five degree differential between the two sets of fish. He ordered, "Flood tubes one and three, outer doors open."

The torpedo officer set depth of the fish at two meters, which meant they would strike just below the water line. They would run close to the surface, but with a choppy sea, it was likely they would not be spotted until it was too late. The destroyer was a problem as it was steaming astern and to starboard of the frigate.

Walter decided on a second spread of two torpedoes to take out the destroyer.

"Spread of two fish on the destroyer, five degrees astern of the frigate, range 2400 meters. Set up firing solution."

He could feel sweat working its way down his back, his shirt sticking to skin as the attack table crew feverishly worked out the final firing solution. The clock ticked away. His line of sight was fixed on the TDC (Torpedo Directional Computer) that linked the periscope, gyro compass and torpedo circuits, which ultimately determined the accurateness of the data fed into it and the outcome.

If the fish hit the frigate, the destroyer would likely swerve and look for the sub with depth charges. The rules were firm on this in both navies, and Walter knew the destroyer would not stop to pick up survivors, as that would leave them dead in the water and open to attack.

But then, Walter thought, *you never know what will happen in the heat of battle.*

The attack officer reported, "Plot destroyer, two fish, ready to fire 195 degrees azimuth, range 2300 meters."

Four minutes later the first two torpedoes were fired. As the big boat shuddered with the release of the fish, Walter ordered, "Starboard five, maintain revolutions."

They would have to reposition the boat to hit the destroyer and this would take some twenty to twenty-five seconds. He could increase revolutions to speed up the change in position but the enemy asdic might pick up the cavitation and give their position away.

"What chance do we stand?" Klaus demanded.

"It'll be close, Klaus, very close."

Walter seemed almost electric now. Klaus could see his eyes blazing, as he watched the compass needle swing, bringing the boat into firing position for the second set of fish. For the first time, he could see Walter's shirt soaked with sweat, not from fear but from the tense tactical situation. Firing at this distance, at two formidable targets, posed quite a risk. If they missed, the warships would hunt them down like dogs on scent of a fox or coon. There would be twice the number of depth charges and the two warships would take up listening stations trying to pinpoint their every move.

Klaus could feel moisture building up in his armpits, spreading in a wide arc across his back, giving that awful stench that comes with toil and labor or just plain fear. He considered the entire control room crew could generate a gallon of sweat.

Klaus watched the trim as the diving officer struggled to maintain a level depth, the depth indicator and inclinometer fluctuating slightly.

"Steady the trim," Klaus ordered, as he watched Walter reach for the 'arm switch' to ready the next spread of torpedoes.

The seconds ticked by, each one seemingly minutes or hours. Klaus looked around the control room, the officers there seemingly frozen in place, blurred somewhat as space and time became distorted. Space seemed compressed, even warped, to Klaus as the control room closed in on him, with time slowed down. The second hand on the clock moved with deliberate slowness and he was sure it might never get to firing time.

A clanking noise beyond the watertight doors startled Klaus as he realized someone had dropped a tool. Before Walter could react, Klaus grabbed the interboat telephone and softly ordered, "Maintain silent routine."

He turned to watch his *Kapitän* raise and drop his hand while ordering the second set of fish to fire. Space and time were back in synchronous orbit. Time would speed up now as they counted off the seconds to impact.

Walter watched the gyrocompass until the boat reached 195 degrees true, and then ordered, "Fire two and four."

The seconds ticked by and after three minutes, Walter ordered, *Skop auf!*

He turned his hat sideways to give him an unrestricted view and ran the scope 360 degrees. Fear clawed at his belly. The sight that emerged as he shouldered the periscope sent his pulse racing.

The frigate was turning hard to starboard with the destroyer bearing down on him, less than 2000 meters distant.

He ordered, "*Skop runter*, emergency dive 200 meters, *Tauchen! Tauchen!*"

Allowing a good two minutes for the destroyer to overtop him, he ordered a change in course to 230 degrees true, in an effort to scoot underneath the attacking ship and escape the depth charges that were soon to land all about him.

About a minute later the first great shocks shook his boat as the *wasserbombs* exploded. Judging they were shooting too shallow, Walter ordered, "Depth 225 meters, minimum turns on screws, enough to maintain trim, continue on 230."

The hydrophone operator reported a circular course for the destroyer.

She'll be coming back, Walter thought, *and soon the frigate will join in.* Leaning against the attack table, he looked at the palms of his hands and realized he was sweating almost uncontrollably. He sensed the temperature in the boat was rising.

Funny, he thought, *I hadn't noticed the cabin temperature before.* No time to worry about it now. *Concentrate on the circling warships,* he told himself.

To make things worse, the frigate was heading their way and would presumably join its sister-ship hunting for the sub. At a speed of barely four knots, they slowly slipped off the attack trajectory of the oncoming warships. The British would be listening intently for any sound that would give away the U-boat's position.

Walter ordered, "Silent routine, maintain course and speed for five minutes, then cut engines and maintain depth."

Slowly the U-boat came to a dead stop at 225 meters. Knowing the bottom was only thirty or thirty-five meters below the boat, Walter considered settling onto the bottom, but decided to wait and see what developed. At this depth the pressure was so great that some seams were bound to leak and even worse the boat might start flooding. He would have to watch the trim. The slightest change in their center of gravity would alter the trim and change the inclination, a dangerous situation that might send them to the bottom at a precarious angle. He thought about ordering no movement among the crew but realized they were experienced enough to know what to do. He would have to wait it out and see what developed.

As with all new naval equipment, British asdic was the first of its kind, and had been pressed into service until new improvements could be made. Similar to American sonar, also in experimental development, the equipment was subject to false echoes and the turbulent effect of the screws on the frigate and destroyer produced all types of echoes on the asdic screen that did not exist. To Walter's relief the frigate and destroyer started firing depth charges off to the north, apparently chasing echoes produced by the cavitation of surface screws.

While depth charges were exploding three kilometers to the north, Walter gave the order to start engines and move off to the southeast on a heading of 140 degrees. After a few minutes the hydrophone operator reported, "High speed screws heading in our direction," which meant the frigate or destroyer had detected his movement and they were closing to renew the attack.

Walter thought, *what do Americans call a 'head on collision?'*

Ah yes, *playing chicken* with surface ships was easy. Knowing when to break off was the hard part. He could see consternation and fear in the faces of his officers. They had nearly slipped away into the vastness of the Caribbean only to be attacked again. He tried to put on a smile, but knew they would have to slip under the approaching two warships throwing depth charges, most probably with more accurate depth estimation this time.

Walter gave the order, "Come up to sixty meters rapidly, maintain speed and direction, one third turns on the screws." He hoped a rapid change in depth would go undetected on the surface, allow him to slip out from under the attacking vessels, and dive to great depth, perhaps bottoming the boat.

Following their training and experience the frigate and destroyer captains ordered depth charges set at 150 meters, while U-501 was riding just under their keels. The noise on the hydrophones was deafening to the operators as the two ships passed overhead loosening a barrage of TNT that sunk way beneath the U-boat before exploding.

Between the depth charges and the fast-turning screws of the frigates, the submariners could hardly stand the suspense, expecting at any moment to be blown to bits. As the screws were directly overhead, Walter gave the order for an alternate course and increase in depth. The U-boat turned slowly and then increased its turning rate as the screws went to full eight knots. It took nearly three minutes to execute the turn and to drop to 160 meters. The estimated water depth here was 180 meters and Walter ordered a slow drop to the bottom where he intended to wait out his pursuers.

Soon it would be dark but this would not benefit the German submariners who would have to wait for the warships to depart the scene before attempting to slip away. They could pick up the screws of two ships circling far and wide overhead, presumably the frigate and destroyer searching the underwater area for some sign of the U-boat.

Finally, after an hour or so, the noise disappeared from the hydrophones and the operator gave the all clear signal to the bridge.

Kapitän Hahn ordered, "Negative ballast, silent routine, depth fifty meters, one-third turns on the screws."

His face showed his concern. He intended to take no chances, as the warships could be dead in the water waiting for him to show himself.

The hydrophone operator reported, "All silent, *Herr Kapitän*."

"Periscope depth."

As he worked the situation over in his mind, Walter remembered the story of U-13, off Scapa Flow in World War I, blowing its ballast after losing hydrophone contact with surface vessels searching for it, only to find a destroyer bearing down with depth charges at the ready. An emergency dive took it out of harm's way, but only with seconds to spare. He did not want this to happen to U-501. A quick sweep of the surface with the periscope showed an empty and calm sea; no frigate or destroyer, only a serene seascape bathed in rising moonlight. He ordered the boat to the surface.

His orders were to assist the tender and he set course for Willemstad. The lookouts were told to keep a sharp eye out to the east, as the frigate and destroyer were likely under orders to find the tender. Most probably they were headed for Willemstad and just ahead of U-501. They had a slight assist from the coastal current and navigation reported they were making seventeen knots. Traveling behind the British warships, he judged they would be off the Curaçao coast around four A.M., just behind the British ships. They were off silent routine now and the boat, flooded with surface air, provided a welcome relief to the sailors and paratroopers still on board. They also had a chance to recharge their batteries that had run dangerously low during the undersea encounters of the past 48 hours.

At about 3:30 AM, radar reported, "Contact ahead at 095 degrees, one echo at the limit of their radar equipment, or around 8-9 kilometers distance."

Also, the hydrophone operator reported an echo on the same bearing and with the same range.

At least radar and the hydrophone are synchronous, Kapitän Hahn thought, as he pondered his next move. They would close on the target and hope it slowed because at its present speed it could easily outdistance the U-boat. A few minutes later, the hydrophone operator reported, "Echo closer now, range seven kilometers."

U-501 continued on course at maximum speed even though the screws would announce their position and speed to the British ship. So far only one echo was detected which indicated only one ship. Had the other warship disappeared?

Navigation reported distance to target of five kilometers, which meant the surface ship had slowed for some reason either to reduce fuel consumption or to wait for a target. Could they be waiting for the tender? Maybe they were waiting for U-501, or for the other ship, which they still had not detected. At four kilometers, U-501 cut its speed to one third to avoid asdic detection. Approaching partially submerged with its conning tower awash, Walter hoped to catch the frigate or destroyer abeam, offering an inviting target. It was now close to five A.M., and still dark, but with enough moonlight to show the outline of the warship as they approached.

Navigation continued to show the echo dead ahead but still they could not make out the silhouette to confirm the identity of the ship. If they sunk a friendly ship, there would be consequences to reckon with at Kriegsmarine Headquarters, and if the frigate or destroyer discovered their presence they might never hear from headquarters again. If the warship was holding a lateral course toward Willemstad as they were, they would have to maneuver abeam of her to get a decent shot. Shooting directly at the short axis of a surface ship was risky, although with the new magnetic torpedoes it might work. The echo was moving at around twelve knots now, or just over one-third speed.

Kapitän Hahn decided to risk a stern shot with a spread of two torpedoes.

He ordered, "Flood tubes one and four, outer doors open, make depth of the fish four meters. Torpedo station, stand by!"

Navigation gave the same bearing — 095 degrees and distance of 2000 meters. They were closing fast now and at any minute he should be able to identify the silhouette and fire at her.

Just as this thought entered his mind, the silhouette came into shape before him, and through his binoculars he could make out the outline of a Hercules class destroyer, a type II.

Most probably, this is one of the two ships that previously engaged us, he thought.

Heavier armed than a frigate, this was a formidable target. As he gave instructions to prepare to fire tubes one and four, he double-checked the bearing with navigation and the range with the hydrophone operator and radarman.

After a few seconds he ordered, "Torpedoes *los!*"

Running time on the fish would be just over four minutes. He ordered depth set at twenty meters and course altered to 040, at one-third speed. U-501 dove and swerved off to the northeast as the fish sped to their target. *Kapitän* Hahn waited for the boat to steady at twenty meters depth and on the new course of 040.

He then ordered, "Periskop depth," and then shortly, *"Auf-skop!* (scope up)" for a surface sweep. Twenty seconds remained before impact.

Walter could see the destroyer had not detected the attack and that the torpedoes were right on the mark. A few seconds later and the hydrophone operator reported, "Terrific explosion, contact" and a flash of red light lit up the night sky dwarfing the moonlit sea. The ship was dead in the water with its screws permanently out of action. Her bow started to lift out of the water and it seemed flooding of the stern was in progress.

The Hercules-class destroyer appeared disabled and he could easily sink it now, but the rules of the old German Navy were to give sailors a chance to abandon ship and save themselves. He thanked his lucky stars that no political officers had been assigned to this mission otherwise they would be clamoring for a "kill" now and he would have to deal with them somehow. The political watchdogs had been termed nonessential personnel when the mission was in the planning stages, much to the disgust of the protocol department. This would be his decision to make and his only. He would give the British sailors a chance to get off their ship before sinking it. The pumps would take over he was sure, which would give it time, and intelligence on the Hercules was that it was fitted with the latest in watertight doors, so it might remain afloat for an indefinite period.

Torn between the need to find the tender with speed, and the urgency of the situation, Walter realized he had serious problems to deal with and they might be fatal. If the frigate returned, he might have to bottom the boat again. He swept the surface a full 360 degrees, but there was only the listing destroyer to be seen, with boats being lowered from her forward and after decks. A fire was burning off the stern deck, no doubt the result of some hydraulic or diesel fuel explosion ignited upon impact.

Walter was tempted to bring the boat to the surface but considered it too risky as the gun turrets on the destroyer were still intact, and likely armed and ready, and the second ship, the frigate had to be nearby somewhere. He continued to scan the surface and just as these thoughts entered his mind, he saw the frigate steaming at him in the early morning light. It was now six A.M., and with sunrise coming, the sea was taking on an iridescent glow that seemed to get brighter every minute. He knew the frigate would not slow or stop to aid the listing destroyer, as that would expose her beam to the enemy. She would aggressively search for the U-boat and even now the disabled destroyer was probably relaying what information was available on the attack and probable position of the enemy boat.

The closing frigate was an Apollo class vessel armed with torpedoes, four-inch guns fore and aft, and antiaircraft guns amidships. As Walter relayed this information, the attack table crew noted she carried the latest in underwater detection gear. She might also have newly fitted radar and while he thought all this over, he ordered, "Depth 100 meters, silent routine, change course to 090."

The second warship must have been lying in wait for the tender off Willemstad and luckily he had found the picket ship that was lying off port waiting to assist in boarding and taking the tender. It was just luck that he had put the picket ship out of action and brought the frigate out to assist.

Good old Pirien, he thought. *Sonne must be in port.*

Now the tender had a chance to escape into the open sea. He had to put some distance between the frigate and himself before he could dare surface and contact the tender. He hoped Pirien would size up the situation intelligently, and manage to slip out-of-port while the frigate was engaged, but he had no way of knowing what had happened at Willemstad.

As he headed off on a course of 090, the hydrophone operator reported the closing frigate was moving off to the northeast apparently chasing false echoes. With luck they might give the frigate the slip. He ordered lower revolutions on the screws to reduce cavitation and generate less noise, thus giving them the edge in this dangerous maneuver.

After twenty minutes the frigate was growing more distant and the hydrophone operator reported, "We're five kilometers northwest of the enemy."

It was light now and they would have to run submerged at half speed to escape the searching ship.

Twenty-Three
Willemstad

Flying to Willemstad, Jack ran the possible German escape route over in his mind.

Jack considered, "They'll take the southern passage south of Cayo Grande, and north of Margarita, to reach the open Atlantic between Tobago and Grenada. They must take this route to have deep water in which to maneuver. And there may be other U-boats assisting them."

The elder Professor Ford asked, "Are you sure one of the U-boats escaped?"

"Without a doubt. It was the big one too, much bigger than the one that got torpedoed," replied Jack. "It could be carrying part of the gold-platinum load."

"And what about the tender?"

"It escaped, somehow, with all its guns firing. The attacking boats missed it."

As he thought it over, Jack realized the U-boat would screen the tender. Even if the tender put in at Willemstad, the U-boat would not be far away.

We'll get lucky at Willemstad, he hoped.

He could feel it somehow. The Germans would be there, but what then? There will be troops on the tender and the main problem will be to find a way to cope with them.

Flying at 1500 meters, Jack ran the whole scenario from start to finish over in his mind. *Alexander von Humboldt had explored the high Andes over a century before and found a magnificent gold-platinum ore body in the Coromoto Valley. Von Humboldt probably decided to keep the Andean gold-platinum find secret since announcement of his silver find in Mexico had resulted in so much human depravity. Perhaps his royal permit forbade him to make a profit on mining ventures in Venezuela, or maybe he was disgusted with fraudulent assessments of his silver find in Mexico. He never mentioned the Coromoto find in the "Travels."*

Von Humboldt was a mining engineer par excellence, and judging by the quality of the gold-platinum samples, he must have known he had made a rare find. The stories about von Humboldt nearly exhausting his family fortune trying to finance his own scientific explorations in South America might be related to the Venezuelan gold. Also von Humboldt's report of mines in Russia carried out on commission from the Czar established his position as a prime authority on precious metals. What labyrinth had all von Humboldt's information passed through to come to the attention of German Intelligence?

The link involved Professor Jahn. Perhaps he had discovered the missing information in von Humboldt's journals. Herr Jahn knew the lay of the land and he had advised the Germans on all technical aspects of extracting the ore. Herr Jahn was a crafty one and quite capable of taking care of himself.

Had the Venezuelan Government given consent to Germany to extract the gold-platinum ore? This was a possibility. The Germans had done a brilliant job of mining the ore, offloading it onto waiting U-boats, and transferring it to a waiting merchantman, which presumably now was making speed to escape into the Atlantic. Possibly the merchantman had been damaged in the exchange with the submarines which must have been British. Maybe other British ships were ordered into the area.

Felix broke Jack's reverie, saying, "Señor Sanchez said help is presumably on the way. Army Intelligence in Washington must be aware of the situation and so are the British judging from what you observed."

Jack looked out across the Caribbean, said nothing in return, but remembered the antenna he had seen above Señor Sanchez's headquarters. It was a large rotating array of HF transmitting equipment; no doubt he could talk to Washington, with a signal registering nine by ten, something they couldn't do with the radio in the aircraft, despite the innovations Pat had rigged up.

His thoughts drifted away as the lush, green island of Curaçao grew larger through the glass canopy.

As they approached Willemstad, Jack strained his eyes to see the harbor, and as they got closer he could make out the tender tied up alongside the wharf. She was a fast ship to make the trip from off Aruba to Curaçao in less than three hours. They could only land off shore and tie up to the float base, to await whatever was going to happen. Now almost anything was possible.

At this point, Jack thought, *we'll have to get lucky. Events dictated by the*

Germans will control us. Better to be patient and see how everything unfolds once we are on shore.

Jack knew one thing for certain. Offshore the U-boat would be waiting, so whatever was going to happen would happen fast. The U-boat would not wait long.

*   *   *   *

Finding the tender tied up at the Willemstad wharf and taking on fuel and supplies, Jack and his group decided to watch from a nearby restaurant. Hoping to come up with some information that would be of use in stopping the tender in its planned escape, they watched the big ship. They did not have long to wait, as very soon after their arrival an officer and two sailors came down the gangway, and left the ship heading for the interior of the city.

Jack recognized the officer as Hans, and he, his dad, and Pat decided to follow them to see where they were heading. Professor Gomez and Celine went off to the harbor master's office to see what information they could dig up on the tender.

The German trio climbed up into the center of the city and after about ten minutes entered a shop that overlooked the wharf and the main market district. An antenna on top of the building looked to be used for very high frequency transmissions similar to Señor Sanchez's array and Jack decided they were probably using this building to contact their headquarters or for some other communication.

The route down to the ship passed an alleyway that they might use to intercept the three German soldiers. Jack reasoned that he and Pat could intercept them at gunpoint, incapacitate them and steal their uniforms. He was about the same build as Hans, and with a little verve and bluff, he might find a way to board the tender and investigate her cargo. They found the alley and waited.

Sure enough, in a short time, Hans and the two sailors appeared in the street above and walked directly toward the alley. Jack and Pat jumped out, surprised the trio, and forced them into the alley. Backing them against a wall, Jack thought that for once they were controlling events.

Hans muttered, "We thought we lost you" and then winced as Jack told him to get out of his uniform. Hans, his hands free, threw off his coat and rushed Jack managing to push him back against his father. With a side kick Hans knocked the revolver out of Jack's hand, the metallic thud as it hit the cobbled passageway reverberating along the wall of the alleyway. Hans rushed Jack swinging two wild punches, which Jack sidestepped, causing him to lose his balance.

"I've not been totally honest with you Professor Ford," Hans sneered. "I did some bare knuckle boxing in Munich before I joined the marines."

Jack stepped back, regained his composure and realized he would have to neutralize Hans. He moved toward the revolver thinking at all costs Hans would try to retrieve it. Pat and the elder Dr. Ford had their hands full training their weapons on the other two soldiers. Jack had lost the element of surprise and now it had come down to Hans against him and it could go either way. Crouching with his left pulled back, Jack hoped Hans did not remember he was left handed. Guarding with his right, Jack felt fear run down his spine at the way Hans took on a professional stance. He knew how to box and he appeared to know how to move. Hans rushed in with a punch that went wild and Jack felt Han's kidneys fold. Hans cried out with an agony that told Jack he would shortly be coming in for more.

Winding up for another assault, Hans came in swinging with both arms, one punch going wild, the other landing on Jack's rib cage. Recovering, Jack landed one on Han's jaw, cutting flesh which bled and another on his lower rib cage. Sensing he was getting the upper edge on Hans, Jack added, "As a student, I did a few stints hauling cargo in tall ships in the Caribbean with a real salty crew in tow. Tough going, with classes in barroom brawls and boot kicking, proved to be the best training ground. I came out top of the class."

His eyebrows arched high, Felix recoiled hearing this thinking *what a braggart.* "Get on with it, man. I can't stand here forever."

Hans was dripping blood now, his breathing labored, every breath taking longer. *Mon ami,* you are not the bare knuckle demon you claim to be," and with that Jack took him down with a punch to the mid section that winded him and a left cross he never saw coming. Hans folded up on the cobble pavement. Jack retrieved his revolver and motioned for Hans to get out of his uniform.

"Why did you have to hit him hard enough to bleed?"

"What?" Jack looked with disbelief at his father.

"He nearly took us out."

"I know but now there are blood stains on his uniform."

"Well, take a shirt off one of the other marines. I'll use it."

Looking at Pat, Jack said, "Tie up the other two and leave them here. I only need the rest of Han's uniform."

"And his boots."

He smiled as he rolled Hans over and proceeded to take his boots off.

Hans stirred from his beating as Jack pulled him up by his shirt, "Slip out of your boots and make sure you don't have a knife in there, or I'll shoot you here and now."

After tying up the three Germans, Jack put on Han's uniform finding that it fit perfectly. Moving close to Pat, Jack ordered, "If they try to escape shoot the three of them, and wait for me near the wharf. If they behave themselves, leave them here and they'll eventually free themselves."

As he fastened his belt, Jack said, "I don't intend to be long but if I'm discovered, I'll go overboard and you can pick me up out in the channel."

Pat nodded that he understood.

The elder Professor Ford stood transfixed at hearing Jack say he would jump off the ship.

"Don't worry, dad, I'll only go overboard in an emergency."

Felix raised both eyebrows upon hearing this but said nothing.

Straightening his uniform, Jack picked up Han's revolver, looked it over carefully to see that it was a standard issue Luger, and then slid it in his holster. He had to remember to keep this weapon as a souvenir as they were scarce in the U.S.

*   *   *   *

Jack looked carefully up and down the side alley and then walked briskly toward the wharf. He would need all his nerve to walk up the gangway past the sentries on duty there. If there was a challenge and password he would be caught. He remembered to put the uniform on exactly as Hans had worn it. Keeping the brim of his hat down low put a shadow across his brow hiding the upper part of his face, all of which gave him better eyesight in the strong sunlight. Imitating Han's gait as he walked up to the gangway, and past the sentries on duty there, he realized he would have to fight if they stopped him. The two sailors saluted as he went past.

Continuing apace, he smiled sardonically. *So the bluff worked*, he thought. Luckily the sailors were not so familiar with the paratroopers on board.

The deck was deserted in the afternoon heat as he headed directly for the forward hold.

Finding the deck cover loose he pulled himself over the side, dropped directly down onto dozens of wooden crates neatly stacked from the floor of the hold to the rim. In the corner crates were double stacked, two to a column. Climbing upon the lower crate he used a piece of angle iron to force open the lid on the top crate. Peering inside he found sacks of gold and platinum similar to what they had managed to steal from the Germans on the Maracaibo Coast.

Satisfied that the bulk of the precious metal shipment was aboard the tender he pulled himself back out of the hold, unfurled the canvas, and found himself staring into the working end of a Luger and one of the paratroop officers. He was unceremoniously pushed along the deck and ordered to climb up to the bridge where *Kapitän* Pirien looked him over.

With a scowl, his voice rising an octave, Pirien bellowed, "The U-boat skipper warned me about you. He said you were behind every move to recover the gold. Well, it seems you are our prisoner now and you may well spend the rest of the war in Germany. Tie him up and put him back in the hold."

"Jawohl, Herr Kapitän", replied the officer. As he was escorted back along the passageway Jack thought quickly about all possible options. He had none! The sentries were alert and armed. The officer behind him was just waiting for an excuse to shoot him, and behind the officer were two other paratroopers. He couldn't overpower them all.

They reached the hold, pulled back the cover, and motioned for Jack to climb in. They climbed down after him and told him to sit on one of the crates. They tied his arms first, then his feet, and told him to lie on his side. Once there they tied his arms down to his feet and left him with a warning not to try to escape as a guard would be posted to shoot him if he managed to get out of the hold.

As he lay there in the dark he remembered earlier experiences he had had with incarceration like this. When being tied up, it is a good idea to stretch your frame as much as possible, as later on when you relax the bonds become slightly loose. It is rather the same for a cat or dog, for when leashed, they have the ability to contract their neck muscles, eventually slipping out of their bonds. Strangely, he was reminded of his dog who always managed to slip out of his leash.

This is no time to reminisce about the past, he thought. *Time to concentrate on getting out of here.*

It is good also to work the fingers around to continually pick at the knots with the effect of further loosening them. This he did for several hours. He sensed it was getting dark and he could hear continual movement on deck and the whine of deck cranes that were loading supplies into the hold amidships. There was no light now, but he could feel the bonds becoming somewhat looser than before, and he could move around now.

He rolled into a corner and sat up which tired him and strained his arms. He remembered seeing a steel strap on this side of the hold when he broke into the crate and he tried to find it. When he failed at this he continued to pick at the knots and found his bonds loosening still more. Eventually he pulled one of the strands completely through and managed to get a grip on the next loop. Slowly he managed to loosen it up and shortly after he found he had released his wrists from his feet. Now he could work at his feet with his hands in front of him.

Soon he managed to free his feet and stand up which was a welcome relief.

Walking about in the dark proved disadvantageous as he bumped into things and he was afraid of making noise, which might bring the guard. He found the strap that he was looking for earlier and decided to try and rub his wrists across it to cut the rope. Wedging the strap under a crate so it could not move took all his strength but allowed him to continue to rub rope against steel. It wasn't perfect but with continued rubbing he could feel the rope parting. This took quite a while, but eventually the rope snapped and he was free, but unarmed. Finding a shovel at the end of the hold, he decided that if it came down to a fight he would use it to effect.

He would have to overpower the guard to escape the hold, so he pulled himself up to the rim of the hold and took a look under the tarp. Lounging against the bulkhead a sailor had carelessly left his rifle leaning against the hold. There was only one man on guard duty and he was not very alert. Jack judged the time to be about four A.M..

Jack realized he would have to disarm the guard and find someway to disable the ship if he was to stop the cargo transfer which surely would take place soon, most probably at first light or even before. He judged the distance to the rifle to be about the same for him as for the guard. If the guard yelled all would be lost. Just then the guard turned and walked away toward the gunwales, with his back to Jack.

This is it, Jack thought. As he rolled out of the hatch, Jack stumbled slightly and ran to the guard who was now turning around to see what had caused the noise. He caught him with a blow to the stomach, which winded him and he doubled over. Jack then hit him with the shovel and the sailor slumped to the deck. Dragging him to the hold, he lowered him down amongst the gold crates, tied him up, and gagged him. Taking his revolver he searched his pockets for extra ammunition. Finding only a bandoleer with ten rounds in it, he thrust this into his pocket, and slipped the weapon into his waistband.

Jack smiled. He knew he was now controlling events for a change, which was a lot better than having events control him. He wondered where Pat and his dad were and decided they would be waiting for him to make his move. He couldn't worry about them now, but he desperately wanted to find a way to disable the ship.

The four-inch gun on the stern of the ship would have to have a magazine to store ammunition nearby. He crawled out of the forward hatch and worked his way along the lower deck, which was still deserted. As he made his way amidships he could hear voices coming his way. Fading into the superstructure he found he could fit between two girders which hid his entire frame. He stood perfectly still as two sailors walked right past him toward the forward gangway. As soon as they disappeared, he breathed a sigh of relief, slipped out and continued aft to find the ammunition locker.

Coming along to the afterdeck Jack noticed they had posted a guard. Just as with the guard outside the forward hold, this man was sleepy, and anything but alert. Finding a belaying pin loose with some rope he unfurled the rope and hurled the pin across to the starboard side of the ship. The guard walked toward the noise and challenged it. Jack came up behind him and put him out with the shovel.

"Whoever said there was such a thing as a fair fight," he muttered to himself. Dragging the limp body aft, he put him under a tarp near the afterdeck hold. Luckily the guard had the keys, which he used to open the magazine, and inside he found a well-stocked supply of rounds for the stern battery.

Looking out through the magazine door he could see the deck was still deserted but he knew it wouldn't stay that way for long. The sun would be up soon and he judged the ship would be underway shortly thereafter. He needed to find a detonator and detonation cord, or failing that some kind of delayed fuse that could be improvised to ignite an explosion. He found some thin rope that could serve as a fuse but he would need to soak it in sodium nitrate to create the desired effect.

After searching the magazine he couldn't find any way to manufacture a fuse, but he remembered seeing a petrol can near the after deck gangway. He moved along the deck, retrieved the can, and dragged it back to the magazine. Slowly he soaked the rope in petrol making sure it was in a coil so he could drag it after him, ignite it at the last moment, and then dive overboard. He wanted the ship to get underway so he could blow the magazine over deeper water.

Standing near the magazine door he marveled at his good luck while staring at his det cord, thinking, *It should work.*

He didn't have long to wait. As he watched through the magazine door sailors were filing out on deck and preparing to take in the lines. The diesels started humming and the ship vibrated from the slow start up. Soon they would find the two sailors he had disabled and then they would find him.

Jack slipped the Luger out from his waistband, shifted it to his right hand and stretched his left hand to free up his fingers. His hands were still numb from the ropes and soon he would need to use the handgun. He fingered the matchbox he would use to ignite his improvised fuse, satisfied the numbness was fading with increased blood flow.

The ship slowly backed out into the main channel. She turned toward the harbor entrance, leading out first south and then east, making course toward Bonaire. He waited ten, then fifteen minutes and the ship picked up speed.

He couldn't wait much longer without being detected. They were well out of the harbor and proceeding in an easterly direction when he decided to make his move.

At first light, Jack had noticed a life raft tied to the superstructure outside the magazine. He used his knife to free it and decided to jump overboard with it once the fuse was lit. The two sailors who had hauled in lines from davits on the stern went forward, so with a deserted afterdeck, this was the time to act. Slowly he edged the magazine door open and with all his strength he hurled the raft across the deck to the port rail. Hauling the fuse out of the magazine, he lit it, and watched the trail of smoke heading for the magazine. Just as it approached the door he flung himself and the raft over the side.

A deafening roar sent flames leaping skyward from the stern battery. He could feel the effect of the blast as he hauled himself into the life raft. The tender was still underway but she had lost speed and a major fire was burning on the afterdeck. He could see figures racing around on the upper decks. Some were carrying hoses, others had rifles and some were firing at him, but with no effect, as the distance was too great.

*   *   *   *

When Jack failed to return to the wharf, Pat, the elder Professor Ford, Professor Gomez and Celine stayed up all night, fearing for his safety and imagining the worst. There was no way to storm the tender, so they just had to wait it out. When the tender hauled in its lines and made for the open channel, they raced for the floatplane planning to follow. Professor Gomez and Celine waited on the wharf to save weight in the plane.

Taxing along the channel, they lifted off and soon came up on the stern of the tender, about eight kilometers off shore. While Pat was making up his mind about what to do, the tender's stern exploded, and he saw a figure in the water with a life raft. Circling, Pat soon realized the figure in the water had to be Jack, so he dropped down to the surface, flared for a landing and headed directly for the raft. Coming around, he throttled over to where he could see Jack in the raft. Jack grabbed onto the float and hauled himself up into the cabin.

The elder Professor Ford grimaced at the sight of his son, soaked to the skin, and slightly the worse for wear after escaping from the tender.

"Your narrow escapes never fail to amaze me," he said with a wry smile.

As they watched, the tender was moving slowly eastward with a fire still burning on the afterdeck. The tender, heading on 090 degrees true, was listing slightly and running at reduced speed.

"Better lift off Pat. No telling where the U-boat is and if they spot us they will surely sink us.

"Aye boss."

"What!" Felix, taken by surprise was aghast, looking out the float window wondering if a torpedo was heading directly at them.

Pat hit the throttle and big float responded, racing ahead and slowly lifting out of the water. Gaining altitude, Pat made a slow turn and headed for Willemstad.

Twenty-Four

Beginning of the End

U-501 lay off Willemstad watching for some sign of the tender when suddenly the hydrophone operator reported, "Surface screws heading out of port at about ten knots."

Coming up to periscope depth and scanning the surface, *Kapitän* Hahn sighted the tender heading out to sea, increasing speed slightly, to about fourteen knots.

The tender was clearly heading for the open Caribbean, and with its heavy cargo, it appeared her top speed was well below the normal eighteen knots. He must have all the gold and platinum on board. There were no other ships in pursuit, so Walter gave the order to follow the tender, giving Pirien time to leave the coast of South America before making contact. He set a course of 090 degrees and the hydrophone operator tracked the surface vessel.

Suddenly the hydrophone operator reported, "Surface explosion, *Herr Kapitän*, in direction of the tender." *Kapitän* Hahn ordered, "*Periskop* depth *Notfall!* (Periscope depth emergency), and once at periscope depth, he ordered, "*skop auf*" (scope up).

He swept the surface not believing the scene unfolding before him. The tender was hit, apparently by an explosion, and about two kilometers astern a float plane was picking up someone out of the water.

"The American? Could it possibly be the American," he uttered to the bridge crew.

It certainly looked like the float plane that *Kapitän* Pirien had described. Walter wished the float plane had greater displacement as he would love to torpedo it. He considered surfacing to attack the float but decided against it as this would give his position away and the frigate might be near. Adding all this up quickly, he concluded Dutch naval forces might take exception to a boat in their coastal waters. A surface attack was out of the question.

As he watched, the plane started to taxi and slowly lifted off, warily circled the tender and flew off in the general direction of Willemstad. Everything was coming apart with the evacuation, he thought. Now the tender was partly disabled and somewhere behind him a British frigate was searching for both of them. It couldn't get much worse than this!

After an hour with no pursuit *Kapitän* Hahn ordered the tanks blown and U-501 rose to the surface coming up astern of the tender about 500 meters away. The tender slowed and *Kapitän* Hahn brought the U-boat close to the port side of the surface ship. Hailing *Kapitän* Pirien, with a megaphone, he said, "I want to offload some personnel and take on fresh provisions."

Pirien replied, "Understood."

Walter ordered the hydrophone operator and radarman, "Stay alert and on watch for surface vessels."

As the U- boat nudged closer to the tender, he could see *Kapitän* Pirien on the bridge, and his crew making ready to tie up to the U-boat. He sent his exec below to bring up the six paratroopers still aboard and to break the forward hatch to take in provisions.

Kapitän Pirien confirmed, "Professor Ford managed to sneak on board. After capture, he escaped, and later managed to sabotage the stern battery, causing a horrific explosion. I'm taking some water, but the pumps are holding, at least for the moment. I think I can make eleven to twelve knots, and provided the plates hold, I can make the scheduled rendezvous with Riesen."

Things are looking better, Walter thought. As usual, everything depended on the pumps.

It took about an hour to on-load fresh fruit, vegetables and some beef. *Kapitän* Hahn signaled the tender that he was ready to cast off and that he would follow her to insure they made the Leeward Islands, which would put them about 150 kilometers from their rendezvous point with *Riesen*. At that juncture they should have no problem contacting the Raider and U-501 would set course for a rendezvous with two U-boats off Trinidad.

It'll be good to bring this episode to an end, Walter thought. *And I'm sure Pirien would agree. The British frigate is the big question.*

He put the thought out of his mind, enjoying the sea wind, hoping for a quick termination to their present situation.

Running on the surface for a few hours or so would allow them to recharge batteries and maintain higher speed. They were now about forty kilometers east of Willemstad and fifty kilometers from the Curaçao Coast. They continued on an easterly heading of 090, at just over twelve knots.

Kapitän Hahn slid down the conning tower gangway leaving his second-in-command on watch with the lookouts. Ordering the deck gun secured, he checked with navigation about routes through the Leeward Islands and running time to get there. Just as he thought everything was in order the hydrophone operator reported, "High speed screws, 8000 meters and closing; one set of screws only."

Walter chided himself for thinking of the frigate.

Think about something and it appears, he thought

He signaled the tender, "Enemy vessel closing on us. We're diving and will engage."

The klaxon sounded, lookouts scrambled below, and his first officer slid down the gangway pulling the hatch cord behind him, tightening the hatch.

U-501 was beneath the surface in a record twenty-nine seconds. As he entered the control room he saw his exec tightening the hatch, and heard the hydrophone operator report, "High speed screws closing fast, 8000 meters; one set of screws only."

So it was starting once again, Walter thought, as he waited for the scope to come up.

Kapitän Hahn ordered, *"Periskop* depth eighteen meters; new course 250 degrees, or intercept for the approaching vessel."

"It must be the frigate, and hopefully without an escort," he said to Klaus.

Walter ordered "silent routine," and when the scope came up he reversed his naval hat, grabbed the periscope arms, and swept the sea surface trying to take in the entire picture as quickly as possible.

The "surface print," as submariners refer to it, is the position of a target or targets in relation to course and speed. A competent officer would sweep the 360° surface and memorize the print in less than thirty seconds.

"One frigate," he called out. "Double stack, four inch guns fore and aft, anti-aircraft amidships, no tubes."

Same as before and most likely the same ship we tangled with no more than twenty-four hours ago, Walter thought. Continuing to assess the tactical situation, he called, "She's steering 085 degrees true, running at twenty knots."

He ordered, "Attack crew, plot a solution."

The tender was now ahead of him by about six kilometers and staying steady on 090 degrees at twelve knots. He would have to buy time for the tender and certainly he would have to attack the frigate to give the tender a chance to get away. The frigate was now 6000 meters away and coming almost directly at him.

Geradeaus (direct ahead), he heard the hydrophone operator report.

To bring the boat abeam of the frigate, he ordered, "Change course to 290 degrees."

He hoped the frigate would not change course.

The frigate was not zigzagging which meant her captain was not suspicious of U-boats in the vicinity.

Walter ordered, *"Skop runter* (scope down), plot set on the attack table for an intercept in about five minutes."

If the frigate held its course he would fire three fish at her from the northwest and hopefully sink her. If he missed, the frigate might spend considerable time searching for him, which would give the tender the chance it needed to elude pursuit and make rendezvous with the surface raider.

Taking up a position about one and a half kilometers to the north of the oncoming vessel, *Kapitän* Hahn maneuvered to secure the best firing position.

His attack officer confirmed, "Our best position is at 2500 meters, adjust for strong coastal current, and fire a spread of three fish from the bow tubes."

Walter ordered, "Torpedo depth three meters," hoping not to leave a telltale stream of bubbles. Running time on the fish would be three minutes, twenty seconds.

Pausing for a few seconds, he added, "Open outer doors on 1, 2 and 4."

Walter ordered, *"Skop auf"* for another look.

Reducing speed to three knots, to generate less noise, he took new bearings on the target, and ordered, *"Skop runter"* (scope down).

There was little sense in leaving the scope up for long. He worried about the calm surface, which would make it easy to spot his scope and he knew the deck watch on the frigate would be vigilant, scanning the surface looking for him.

After two minutes he ordered, *"Skop auf"* (scope up). After confirming the direction and speed of the target, he gave the shooting order. With five seconds between firings, he ordered, *"Torpedoes los!"* and the scope came down.

Walter knew the crew in the torpedo room would be racing to ready a new set of torpedoes for the tubes; it was difficult moving the giant fish even with their new block and tackle and redesigned racks. The suspense on the bridge was apparent, electric even, as each crew member studied his equipment knowing one wrong move could spell disaster.

They waited intensely. The hydrophone operator reported, "I'm losing contact with the tender."

Ten seconds later, he reported, "The frigate could probably track her but she's out of range."

A minute and a half later the hydrophone operator confirmed, "Hit on the frigate, one fish, I think."

Two fish had either missed or misfired; one had hit amidships. *Kapitän* Hahn swept the surface to ensure no other enemy vessels were about and then described the situation on the frigate. The torpedo had hit amidships and she was taking on water. Her batteries were still presumably serviceable, but as she was limping along at five to six knots, she made an inviting target.

The frigate put her stern to the U-boat which meant she knew the position of U-501. Firing at her stern would be difficult at best but he couldn't risk surfacing the boat to destroy her with the deck gun.

Deciding to risk a shot at the stern of the frigate, he ordered, "Arm two fish with two meter depth; fire ten seconds apart from bow tubes one and four."

Ordering helm, "Come round to 170 degrees," he waited for the opportune time to fire. The forward torpedo room signaled all ready.

Kapitän Hahn ordered the scope up for one final sweep, noted the frigate had picked up speed, and was turning to run on him. With her speed up to twelve knots he had waited too long to fire.

Walter ordered, "Make depth 40 meters," and he grew tense, as he knew the frigate would pass over his boat.

The hydrophone echo was deafening as the frigate approached, and Walter could see fear etched on the faces of his officers. They were staring at him, with frozen faces that said he was "mad" to run shallow under this warship that was trying to destroy them. He too was scared, more scared than he could remember, and he was sweating suddenly as he realized he was trying to squeeze the sheathed scope handle. He couldn't remember ever doing that no matter how dangerous the situation. But he couldn't lose his nerve now!

The entire crew might be ready to "foul their pants", but they would do what they were trained to do and follow his orders!

They're a U-boat crew, he told himself, *they'll do what they're ordered to do.*

The frigate fired too deep with most of its pattern of depth charges, but the last few came shallow and once over the U-boat they changed to seventy-five meters depth. One charge shook the boat, partially disabling a hydroplane and bursting the number three ballast pump. These were not life threatening, but damage nonetheless, and it would make emergency diving more difficult.

He had underestimated this frigate captain, he knew, and he would have to use all his skill and experience to escape. Apparently, the frigate had at the last minute detected his shallow depth, right under their keel, and they had compensated for it nearly killing them in the process.

Yes, this frigate captain was no beginner; he would hunt and try to kill us, Walter thought.

Once the frigate passed over Walter ordered, "Helm, hard to starboard, new course 350 degrees."

Pausing for a second, he added "Make depth 150 meters," thinking to gain some maneuvering room.

The frigate would circle and search for him, he knew, and in the process waste precious time allowing the tender to escape.

Walter ordered, "Cut revolutions to one-third; rig for silent routine."

He would wait and see what developed.

Moving off to the north he waited for the hydrophone operator to determine the whereabouts of the frigate. She was still actively circling the area but apparently she was chasing false echoes. He cut his revolutions to one-fifth barely giving him maneuvering room at just about two knots. If the frigate took up the chase he would have to surface and shoot it out with her, but he hoped that in her present condition, with burst plates and taking on water, she would seek a safe haven to refit and repair. She would barely be able to keep up with the tender, much less overtake her.

The hydrophone operator reported, "Frigate moving off slowly to the east on a zigzag course."

Presumably she was trying to make Trinidad. She would not overtake the tender.

With nightfall U-501 surfaced to recharge her batteries and effect repairs to the ballast pump and hydroplanes. She cruised along at ten knots and made contact with Kriegsmarine Headquarters. *Kapitän* Hahn was startled to learn that the tender had apparently sunk somewhere northwest of Margarita Island. The exact location unknown, but apparently Pirien had scuttled her near one of the islands east of Curaçao.

It crossed Walter's mind that Kriegsmarine Headquarters might have fabricated this information to mislead the enemy but then he remembered coded messages from his enigma machine were considered unbreakable. Encrypted messages could only be read by someone using an identical machine to decode them. His new orders were to effect repairs to his vessel and rendezvous with Wolfpack Heinrich, operating between Trinidad and Grenada, hunting for tanker traffic.

Perhaps he and the frigate would meet again somewhere in the eastern Caribbean?

Twenty-Five
The End

Flying to Willemstad, Jack said very little, but his thoughts were full of *"what ifs."* He was sure he had fatally damaged the tender, but what if the bulkheads held and the pumps were strong enough to keep her afloat? Would she make it out of the Caribbean? Maybe Army Intelligence would be able to track her, he thought. Would she try to make Germany on her own? Most probably she would attempt to rendezvous with an armed merchantman or a German raider.

And what of the U-boat? Her captain was a wily one, escaping from the British sub attack and then sinking the *Upright* following an undersea duel. Her sister ship U-231, now on the bottom of the Caribbean, had completed offloading her gold and platinum onto the tender when the engagement began. The *Thrasher*, barely surviving the encounter with U-231 had been towed from the battle site; she would survive to fight another day, but she would need extensive repairs, first at Trinidad, and later in the U.K. before returning to active patrol. Her Captain, Iain Retchford, and most of the crew had survived the engagement, and were *en route* to Barbados aboard a British merchantman.

Taking stock of the situation and the outcome, Jack turned to his father and Pat, "All in all, we did pretty well, don't you think."

The elder Professor Ford with a wry smile on his face, said "We? You mean you. Pat flew the plane and tied up a few paratroopers, and I held the revolver, trying to remember which way to throw the safety to fire it. Luckily we all survived."

Thinking for a few seconds, he added "I can see the excitement in this that draws you into it. Like mountain climbing and chess there is a certain challenge."

Pat chimed in with, "You missed the periscope, Jack."

"What?" After a momentary pause, "What periscope?"

"That U-boat was guarding the tender and he had us in his sights," said Pat. "Didn't you wonder why I lifted off so fast?"

"You mean the U-boat would have torpedoed us?" said the elder Professor Ford.

"Exactly," said Pat. "He could set one of his fish for less than one meter and he would have taken us out. Quite a lot of explosive for a small plane, but then he would have put two and two together, and figured out that Jack had somehow managed to blow up the tender."

Jack said, "Yes, it would have taken only two or three minutes to calculate a solution, fire the torpedo, and sink us. Not with great effect perhaps, but at least we would not be around to cause the Third Reich any trouble."

"It's lucky for us that you were on the ball Pat," said Jack. "We have to get to Willemstad, and then on to Maracaibo City to see Señor Sanchez and find out what happened to the tender. If she escaped into the eastern Caribbean, she will be guarded by U-boats, and most likely escape into the Atlantic. If she makes it to Germany it'll be a sorry day for our side."

Thinking finally about Celine, Jack knew she would be waiting at the Willemstad wharf. Soon they could see Willemstad growing larger through the windscreen. Pat made a direct approach, there being little wind and swell to contend with. They taxied up to the wharf to tie up and Jack spotted Celine running toward the jetty where they would disembark.

As he jumped from the plane to the floating dock, she grabbed him and hugged him, saying "I heard the explosion and thought you might have been killed."

Taken aback that Celine was overjoyed to see him, Jack said, with that sardonic smile of his, "Me, get killed? It never occurred to me."

Turning slightly, Celine saw her father looking at her with disbelief in his eyes, saying nothing. His looks gave his thoughts away.

Celine then said, "Mother cared for you the same way, Papa. Now I know why."

Professor Gomez thought back into the far reaches of his memory and remembered his wife Matilde. How closely Celine resembled her, both in looks and temperament. She was a beautiful woman, just like her daughter, and while he could never explain it, she was drawn to him and of necessity to field geology. That is what he did and his passion for the field was something she could never dampen. It was always there, and she put up with it, even though she did not understand much of it.

Celine took to geology even at an early age, and while she resembled her mother in looks and temperament, she had her father's passion for reconstructing the past. Yes, she had done well professionally and now she was drawn to this American adventurer, this professor, or whatever he was. Professor Gomez looked over at the elder Professor Ford, the two exchanged glances, and then Jack's dad walked over to his friend, "They make a great team, don't you think?"

"You approve?"

"Only if you do," said the elder Professor Ford.

Professor Gomez thought for a second or so, "Well I warned her, but she's a grown woman, so she must make up her own mind."

The elder Professor Ford said, "She might get him to settle down into a teaching career much as you and I did."

"Do you believe this," said Professor Gomez.

"No, but I can hope," said the elder Professor Ford. "I don't know what drives my son. He has a passion for archaeology, and he's very good at his profession, just as we are with geology and natural history. He's an excellent teacher and well respected at his museum. But he's adventurous with a Xenophon-like attitude. Obviously Celine has some hold over him, as he pays attention to her, and this he has never done with other women, not that there have been many," he added, trying not to blush.

Thinking about the last few days, the elder Professor Ford added, "Jack seems to have luck on his side, just as Xenophon did all those many centuries ago."

The two fathers watched their offspring. They gave the appearance of belonging together. Professor Gomez thought again of his younger years with Matilde. *Yes, there are many similarities,* he thought. Celine would have to work out her relationship with this man on her own; after all it was her future and it was bound to have happened sooner or later.

After a dinner at the local hotel, they split up for a much needed rest. Looking in the mirror, Jack realized he had added some mileage over the last few days. He looked worn and tired and he noticed he had cut his wrists when freeing himself in the hold on the tender. He had also cut his shoulder somehow, apparently from his dive into the sea, or perhaps from climbing into the float plane, but he couldn't remember exactly where or how.

He really didn't care because at least he had survived to see Celine again; she was a dream to him, a reason to give up his adventurous lifestyle.

He should start to take his future seriously now, he thought.

After all he was getting older and the challenges were such that only a younger man should attempt them. *It was a 'law,'* he told himself; *quit while ahead and still alive.* But then, he thought, *the war was six days old and there would likely be many opportunities in the days ahead.*

He would have to think this one over carefully. Celine wasn't the type to wait, even for Jack Ford.

* * * *

The next morning after filling the plane with aviation fuel, they took off for Maracaibo City. After landing they met with Señor Sanchez at the Grand Hotel. He reported that the tender had not been located despite a surface and air search; its last reported position was east of the Bonaire Basin, and presumably it was headed for a rendezvous either with U-boats or with a German raider.

Jack noted, "She was underway and presumably holding her own with her pumps keeping her afloat. If the pumps failed, she might have sunk or become a derelict ship motionless in the sea. They had to find her before she linked up with her contacts or capsized in open water."

Señor Sanchez bade them goodbye and left with a man waiting in the lobby. When they entered Jack had wondered about the tall man in the lobby, but then forgot about him. Presumably he was a bodyguard.

* * * *

Retiring to their rooms, Jack considered his options. He could just leave Venezuela and return to Chicago with his dad. Or, he could ask Celine to come with him. He would ask her tomorrow and most importantly he would ask her father if he approved.

Much had changed in the English world even in the last decade or two, but in the Spanish world little had changed in familial relationships in the last half millennium. He would ask Professor Gomez and hope for the best. Celine would come; he knew somehow that she would say yes. And Cedric would find her a position especially since they had recovered samples of von Humboldt's gold and platinum.

As he drifted off to sleep he thought *of Heinrich Jahn and the U-boat captain. He didn't know the captain's name but his many close encounters with this man told him he was dangerous. He was a professional just like Professor Jahn. And what of Major Bezada? What would he do with the truckload of gold? Would he pay off the Motilone with it? They deserved it*, he thought! He couldn't remember exactly, but he knew there were several sacks of platinum on the stolen truck. He hoped the Major would take the advice of Professor Gomez and bury it somewhere, anywhere along the coast, so it couldn't be retrieved and find its way to Germany.

Back on the Maracaibo coast, Major Bezada uncovered the stolen truck covered with branches and leaves as camouflage. They had done a good job of hiding the truck. Even the *Motilone* did not know its whereabouts. There was a considerable amount of gold in the truck along with a few bags of platinum. He had decided how he would split up the spoils as soon as Jack Ford flew out of La Ceiba. He would turn part of the gold over to the *Motilone* for their services, with the remainder to the Army Chief of Staff in Caracas.

The platinum he would bury along the La Ceiba coast road for retrieval at a later date. He couldn't be sure which way his government would turn as events unfolded. South American governments in general were friendly to, and supportive of Germany, but from what Professor Gomez had told him, platinum was a special, rare, and strategic metal of great importance to any military power. To give it to Germany might have dangerous consequences.

Bezada remembered Jack saying that depriving the Germans of the platinum would have serious consequences in the forthcoming conflict that promised to be largely an air war. Lacking iridium, the German aircraft industry would find it impossible to give the Messerschmitt the extra velocity it needed to out fly the Spitfire. So much hinged on the platinum. Yes, he and Sergio would keep the location a secret until such time when they could lead the Americans to it. There was just too much German influence in Venezuela for his liking.

If Professor Gomez was right, and the platinum had large quantities of iridium in it, the Germans would be back. They needed it as a strategic metal for their fighter aircraft and they were out to avenge their treatment in the aftermath of World War I. They would be back and perhaps with a larger force. Then there was blackness and he faded off into a long sleep.

*   *   *   *

At precisely the same time Professor Jahn and *Kapitän* Pirien were busily engaged setting up an HF radio transmitter on the north shore of Margarita Island. They contacted Kriegsmarine Headquarters with an encrypted message saying that they had lost the tender. The entire crew had escaped to Margarita and they were waiting for pickup either by submarine or surface vessel. They had managed to salvage several samples of gold and platinum, although the vast bulk of the cargo was in forty meters of water near a coral reef at an unfrequented location. *Kapitän* Pirien had seen to settling the tender in with considerable skill; he had scuttled it in exactly the right depth of water where it would be difficult to find, but easy to recover its cargo. Most importantly, he had sent off the wrong coordinates in case his message was intercepted. Only his navigation officer and Professor Jahn knew the exact location of the sunken tender.

Kapitän Pirien and his crew awaited orders. Shortly they were told to standby for pickup by U-57 within a matter of hours.

Kapitän Pirien, looking dejected, said to Professor Jahn, "Where did American Intelligence find Professor Ford. If there are many more like him, the war is lost."

"He and his father make quite the team. They had me fooled most of the time. Just bad luck, I guess."

Professor Jahn looked out at the blue sea and wondered if they could ever recover the gold and platinum, and even if they recovered it, whether he could return to his country. No, he would have to face the future in Germany whatever happened.

*   *   *   *

Brigadier (Wild Bill) Donovan looked at the door to the Oval Office and wondered what was holding up his meeting with the President. He was fifteen minutes overdue and FDR was as punctual as Big Ben. Something urgent must be in the offing to hold up their meeting. He knew the President was in the midst of ongoing discussions with America's allies and with ambassadors of all major powers. The situation was changing by the hour as the British Expeditionary Force had landed in Belgium to take up position with the French. As he thought all of this over he suddenly felt a tap on his shoulder and realized the President's aide, Col. Ryan, was at his side.

"The President will see you now, sir."

Wild Bill rose and followed the Colonel into the office. The Colonel closed the door as Donovan strode over to his usual chair noting the Chief looked tired if not downright worn out.

"Give me some good news for a change, Bill, something positive."

Leaning forward in his chair, Donovan summarized the Venezuelan situation, "The German Mission to recover the gold suffered some setbacks due to Ford and his group but they appear to have escaped with much of the metal they mined in the Andes. A British task force engaged the Germans in the Gulf of Venezuela sinking one U-boat. The tender and another U-boat escaped but put in at Willemstad on Curacao. Apparently Ford managed to board the vessel, set off an explosive device, disabling the vessel as it attempted to leave port. Ultimately, the tender, loaded with gold and platinum sank off the coast of S. America. We don't know the exact location but we are continually monitoring the situation and will find it. Professor Ford was the man for the job as I knew from the start."

FDR leaned forward over his desk, elbows firmly planted on a pile of papers, taking in every word.

"By God, finally something positive. Why don't you enlist Ford in your group? Offer him a commission, anything."

"Well, Chief, I could but I think he's a complex character, part scientist and part adventurer. He did well in officer training at Columbia but dropped out near the end. He had a lot of trouble with superiors, failed to salute and didn't quite fit in to the military fabric. I might be 'Wild Bill' but he's definitely a wild man, clever, and totally unpredictable as I am sure the Germans are aware. I don't think he'll take a commission but I'll ask. I am sure he'll work for us as requested and certainly if the Germans return to salvage the wrecked tender we may need his services in the near future."

"Ok, Bill, use your discretion as you see fit. But I'd like to meet him when you can arrange it. The least I can do is thank him for his efforts."

As he rose to leave, Bill answered, "Will do Chief. As soon as possible."

Epilogue

December, 1939. The gold icons that started me on my trek to Venezuela, following the footsteps of von Humboldt as he explored the high Andes, stare into space as if they embody the spirit of the great naturalist himself. It is cold here in Chicago in the midst of winter, with northerly winds off Lake Michigan, and frequent storms caused by the clash of polar and tropical air masses. The weather in some ways mimics the clash of German paratroopers and my little force of saboteurs, who upset the Nazi plan to recover Humboldt's gold-platinum find.

For some months Celine has helped me to access records and documents related to the spectacular gold-platinum find in Venezuela, but the original information is in Germany with German Intelligence. Strangely, the conquistadors and later ore geologists had missed the gold-platinum ore that von Humboldt stumbled upon in one of the most inaccessible areas of the Andes. Just as the Conquistadores had missed the source of the Incan gold, the German military would have missed Von Humboldt's gold/platinum find had it not been for Jahn finding the old records and samples.

Cedric rewarded Celine with a position in the museum, and we are engaged, intending to marry in the next few months. Celine has asked me if the Germans will return to recover the sunken tender, perhaps try to forge an alliance with Venezuela and/or repeat the insertion they tried just prior to the war. The simple answer is most probably they will. In Europe, the British Expeditionary Force is allied with the French Army in trying to stem the Nazi tide rolling across the countryside. U-boats are out attacking convoys traversing the North Atlantic and the Luftwaffe is attacking England with deadly efficiency.

My father's calculation of the value of the retrieved gold is just over twenty million dollars, a tremendous sum of money. The exact weight of the platinum is unknown, but estimated to be in the range of 1000 kilograms, or just over

2200 lbs. It is not so much the monetary value of the iridium in the platinum, but rather its use as a strategic metal. Its dollar value would be in excess of ten million dollars, but its strategic value would be inestimable were the Germans able to return and salvage it.

Taking stock of the situation after conferring with Dad, Celine and Professor Gomez, the final report filed with Army Intelligence in Washington pointed out that, if the Germans came back to recover the sunken ore, they would be favored by knowing the exact location of the tender and the proximity of rather friendly allies in South America. Perhaps that is why the Germans are not torpedoing Venezuelan oil tankers, and while they have naval vessels in the Atlantic, they are leaving the Caribbean alone. My assessment is that they will return to the Venezuelan Coast and soon. Reports from Europe say that over 100 new U-boats are undergoing sea trials and will be operational very soon. Hitler is preoccupied with fighting in Europe, but before long he will come to need the platinum for his aircraft industry. How else can they make the Messerschmitt the equal of the Spitfire?

Oh well, Army Intelligence grinds along like any bureaucracy, and it is growing into a large organization, what with the European conflict, and fears we might get hauled into it. Even though I am too old for military service, it is possible to imagine that Mr. Huston and Mr. Smith will call again if German Intelligence tries to recover the ore. There are rumors of U-boats operating off the eastern coast of South America, so why not in the southern Caribbean?

In the meantime the quiet life with Celine is a comfort following our adventures in South America. Dad approves of our engagement, as does Professor Gomez. Teaching looks more attractive now than in previous years. Perhaps it's the tranquil atmosphere in the museum, but the funny thing is that it went unnoticed for many years.

Still the fate of Professor Jahn remains a mystery. Intelligence contacts in Washington say they know nothing of his whereabouts, or whether or not he survived when the tender sank. No doubt the U-boat captain survived, and is presently looking through the lethal end of a periscope. And the tender, whose captain managed to elude two British submarines, nearly pulling off an escape into the Atlantic lies somewhere in the southern Caribbean between Trinidad and Bonaire. The tender captain must be in command of another ship. He's a most efficient officer even if he did threaten to kill me.

If German Intelligence comes back for the ore, they will send the same trio of operators: the U-boat captain, the tender captain and Jahn. They nearly pulled it off the first time, and yes, they'll come back, either to Venezuela for more ore, or to recover the wrecked tender and its cargo. As coming events unfold, the Germans will develop an urgent need for iridium.

God help us if they succeed.

Apologia

The story of von Humboldt's gold was spontaneously conceived while I was engaged in glacial geological field work in the Mérida Andes during the summer of 1998. The book was pieced together following a review of historical records during 1998 and 1999, with the text undergoing several editions over the next several years.

I have taken considerable liberties with chronological information, including the timing of von Humboldt's fictional trip to the Venezuelan Andes in 1804. During this period, he could have traveled to the Andes, but there is no record of him having done so, despite gaps in his logs. For the purpose of continuity and to keep the story consistent, it seemed best to set the precious metal find in the year 1804. Thus, the gold-platinum discovery occurs just prior to his departure from Cuba for the United States.

Later in the story I had to call into service two U-boats not yet constructed in 1939; however, cloaking them in the mystery of "secret" seemed the best way to undertake the mission to Lake Maracaibo. German raiders and armed merchantmen were not on the high seas in 1939, but nevertheless I invented *Riesen* as a plausible contact in the Atlantic and *Sonne* as the likely name for the sub-tender supporting the U-boats. The modern 'Sonne' is a drilling ship used routinely to recover drill core from the deep sea beds of the world.

Radar was not fitted to U-boats until later in the war, but seemed a necessity for this mission fraught with submarine-destroyer engagements. German submariners referred to torpedoes as 'eels' but in the text I used 'fish,' as a term North American readers would be more familiar with from military fiction. Outside of historical figures in the text, any similarity between persons living or dead and the fictional characters described in the text is purely accidental and unintended.

Acknowledgments

I am indebted to several individuals who helped shape the final form of this book. My wife, Linda Mahaney, provided criticism and editorial assistance needed to maintain momentum during those periods when I felt I had ventured into *terra incognita* from which there was no escape. Over the years, Brian Reynolds, Petty Officer RCN (retired), provided numerous books on naval tactics and strategy that finally found a fruitful outlet. He helped immeasurably to maintain authenticity in naval nomenclature and description as used in the book.

Tom Lewis, formerly with the Royal Navy submarine service, helped with technical advice and put me in touch with members of the former Kriegsmarine in Germany, namely Frank Schachtner in Frankfurt, who in turn, established a link with Ernst Gerhardt, former commander of U210. Ernst helped to guide me through the labyrinth of submariner terminology as it was used in the Kreigsmarine.

Several colleagues at York University, Toronto, where I teach, helped in various ways. Helmar Drost coached me on the nuances and use of German and put up with many requests for adequate translations of German into English. John Unrau critically edited an early draft of the entire volume providing invaluable criticism. Hazel O'Laughlin-Vidal fixed all my formatting problems with the manuscript.

My Estonian colleague and friend, Volli Kalm, provided valuable information on Professor von Baer and the Museum of Natural History in Tartu. Larry Gowland and Beatrice Boyer read the entire manuscript and provided many helpful comments about style and substance, which saved me from several misjudgments. Kris Hart read drafts of Part I offering critical comment.

Pat Julig, my flight instructor, who once let me fly his Cessna, and who will disavow any connection with the archaeology, as it is portrayed in this book, guided me through the aeronautical passages with considerable skill.

Craig Hanyan strove to keep the story line, thin as it might be, as historically accurate as possible. Sergio Foghin streamlined my Spanish interpretations and provided important information on the Venezuelan coast.

Mike Milner, economic geologist *par excellence* and U-boat historian, coached me on the intricacies of mining gold and "little silver"-platinum. Douglas Montgomery, former radarman in the U.S. Navy and naval archivist, provided useful information on submarines in World War II.

Rudolf Harmsen and Michael Boyer edited several chapters with an "eye" to checking biological interpretations. Floristic names are from personal experience and V.Vareschi, *1970, Flora de los Paramos de Venezuela*, University de los Andes, Mérida, Venezuela.

John Dawson prepared the plates.

The chronology and notes of Alexander von Humboldt's explorations in the New World in his *Personal Narrative of a Journey to the Equinoctial Regions of the New Continent*, 1995, Penguin Books, London, 311 pp. provided a major primary source for the novel. I also liberally used von Humboldt's ideas and concepts as sketched out in *Cosmos, a Sketch of a Physical Description of the Universe*, 1850, 5 vols., Harper and Bros., N.Y.,

For technical information on U-boats and encryption code I relied on:

Blair, Clay,1996, *Hitler's U-Boat War, The Hunters 1939-1942*, Random House, N.Y., 809 p.
Blair, Clay, 1998, *Hitler's U-Boat War, The Hunted, 1942-1945*, Random House, N.Y. 909 p.
Kahn, David, 1998, *Seizing the Enigma*, Barnes & Noble, N.Y., 336 p.

To all these individuals, and to several colleagues and friends, who read portions of the early text and offered criticism and advice I am profoundly grateful. I hasten to add that any miscalculations or errors belong solely to me.